D0206034

Heart of Ice

"Fiercely entertaining, fascinating . . . Olsen offers a unique background view into the very real world of crime . . . and that makes his novels ring true and accurate."
—*Dark Scribe*

A Cold Dark Place

"A great thriller that grabs you by the throat and takes you into the dark, scary places of the heart and soul."
—**Kay Hooper**

"You'll sleep with the lights on after reading Gregg Olsen's dark, atmospheric, page-turning suspense . . . if you can sleep at all."
—**Allison Brennan**

"A stunning thriller—a brutally dark story with a compelling, intricate plot."
—**Alex Kava**

"This stunning thriller is the love child of Thomas Harris and Laura Lippman, with all the thrills and the sheer glued-to-the-page artistry of both."
—**Ken Bruen**

"Olsen keeps the tension taut and pages turning."
—*Publishers Weekly*

JUST TRY TO STOP ME

A WATERMAN AND STARK THRILLER

GREGG OLSEN

PINNACLE BOOKS

Kensington Publishing Corp.

www.kensingtonbooks.com

PINNACLE BOOKS are published by

Kensington Publishing Corp.
119 West 40th Street
New York, NY 10018

All Kensington titles, imprints, and distributed lines are available at special quantity discounts for bulk purchases for sales promotions, premiums, fund-raising, educational, or institutional use. Special book excerpts or customized printings can also be created to fit specific needs. For details, write or phone the office of the Kensington special sales manager: Kensington Publishing Corp., 119 West 40th Street, New York, NY 10018, attn: Special Sales Department; phone 1-800-221-2647.

ISBN-13: 978-0-7860-2998-3
ISBN-10: 0-7860-2998-6

First printing: December 2016

10 9 8 7 6 5 4 3 2

Printed in the United States of America

First electronic edition: December 2016

ISBN-13: 978-0-7860-2997-6
ISBN-10: 0-7860-2997-8

For Doris Lobe

PROLOGUE

Janie Thomas looked at the laptop she'd been ordered to transport to her second-floor office at the Washington Corrections Center for Women in Gig Harbor, Washington. It was against prison policy to bring any electronic devices inside the secure facility, but Janie *was* the prison superintendent. When she reached the checkpoint, she told her favorite officer, Derrick Scott, that she was running late.

"Rough morning," Janie said, an exaggerated look of displeasure on her face. She rolled her eyes. "Have a call with the governor's office in five minutes."

"He's never on time," the officer said. "Not with a meeting or getting a budget approved. But if you ask me, a crying baby in the middle of the night is at the tippy top of the 'rough morning' scale. I didn't sleep a wink last night."

"Tell me about it," Janie said, going through the detector. "I haven't forgotten those days. You'll get through them."

The African American man grinned, showing dazzling white teeth, as he passed Janie's briefcase over the counter instead of opening it to review its contents or send it through the scanner. She was in a hurry. Besides, the superintendent was always so nice, asking about the kids, sharing photos of her family.

Later the corrections officer would say that the briefcase weighed more than usual and he probably should have opened it, but she was, after all, the boss.

"She runs the prison," he later said to the FBI agent looking into her case. "What was she going to smuggle in? A set of keys? A file?"

A half hour later that same morning, Brenda Nevins was in Janie's office, purportedly to take on a special work assignment to help other inmates with life skills. Other inmates saw a huge irony in that reasoning, but didn't say a word. Speaking up against Brenda meant getting cut in the shower with a shank made of a mascara wand and the sharpened edge of a Pringles' can top.

Or poisoned at lunch with meds ripped off from the infirmary.

Or, worst of all, cut off from visitation with family.

"I run this place," Brenda had said when a new girl— a meth head from Black Diamond with more body tattoos then brains—stupidly challenged her. "You keep that in mind if you piss me off."

In her office the day she disappeared, Janie Thomas opened the laptop for the benefit of the woman who had told her to bring it into the institution.

Brenda smiled. "Nice. *Very nice.* Does it have video capabilities?" she asked as the pair moved from Janie's office to the records room—the only location in the Washington Corrections Center for Women that did not have the prying eyes of security cameras.

They stood face-to-face, a worktable separating them. Brenda had done her hair in the way she knew Janie liked—down, with slight curls that brushed past her shoulders.

The two of them were there to plot the escape.

Janie's *and* hers.

"It's an Apple," Janie said, caressing the silver case of the laptop. "The best. My husband helped me set everything up."

Brenda noticed a flicker of emotion coming over Janie's face at the mention of her husband, Erwin. She moved her mouth into a slight frown, a mirror of Janie's, albeit without the slight lowering of the chin. Quivering was too much. Not needed.

"Don't be sad, Janie," she said in a voice dripping with a practiced honey-sweetness. "I know this is hard. But your life belongs to you, and you have to live it as you were meant to. No more dreaming. No more wondering, baby girl. We are on the verge of our time. We have to take it together. We have no choice in the matter."

A tear rolled, but Janie didn't say a word.

"You know what we are?" Brenda asked. "You know what brought us together?"

Janie bit down on her lower lip. "We're soul mates," she said.

Brenda relaxed her frown, and her eyes brightened.

"Don't ever doubt that," she said. "Don't *ever*. I know that God or some higher power—whatever She is—has brought us together. That's right. The world will be all over us. You know that. They'll be watching and hunting and trying to stop us from doing what we must do."

"I guess so," Janie said, a tinge of fear clearly evident in her voice.

Brenda reached across the table and grabbed Janie by the shoulders.

"Get a grip," she said, her tone still compassionate, but a bit more forceful. "This moment will not only set us free but will define the future for so many others. The world will be watching, and we'll need to tell them the reasons behind everything we're doing."

"To help them, right?" Janie asked.

It was more than a question, almost an affirmation.

Brenda gave her head a slight nod.

"Yes," she answered. "It isn't about just *us*. Just you and me. I wish both of us could have come from other circumstances. Backgrounds free of the torment that sent us here . . . me to be a zoo animal, you to be my zookeeper. But life isn't fair. I get that. Life is what we make it. We're the example of living with authenticity."

Brenda watched Janie as a cat watches the family goldfish that twirls in the waters of its bowl.

Like the betta fish on Janie's desk.

"And we'll help people, right?" Janie repeated.

Exasperation was in order. Maybe a little bit of the takeaway.

Brenda threw up her hands. "God, are you even listening?" she asked as she let out a sigh. It was the kind of nonverbal punctuation with which she was particularly skilled. She was good with words. Good with presenting her concepts, no matter how outlandish. Repulsive even.

She could sell peed-on snow to an Eskimo.

"Really?" Brenda asked, drawing back as though she had been disgusted by Janie's words. "Really? This isn't about *us*. This is about the world. That's why we need to get our act together and get out of here. I didn't do any of those things they pinned on me. None of them."

Janie stayed quiet. Brenda was a lot of things, but Janie was all but certain that being a liar was not among the litany of attributes to which others might ascribe to her.

"Are you with me, baby?" Brenda asked. "Are you about to let go of the past and be what God wants us to be? She's calling for us. She wants us to be together, and yes, my love, She wants us to help others."

Brenda was all about empowerment.

"She loves us, doesn't She?" Janie asked. Before Brenda, Janie never used the feminine personal pronoun for God. It felt funny when she did it, but also emboldening.

"More like adores," Brenda said.

Janie let her body relax.

It felt so good to be loved for who she was.

"I'll be ready tonight," Janie said. "I'll send for you."

BOOK ONE
KARA

CHAPTER ONE

Homicide investigator Kendall Stark didn't know it, but she wouldn't be in need of a second tuxedo mocha that morning as she arrived in her offices at the Kitsap County Sheriff's Office in Port Orchard.

The email link that was about to be forwarded to her would provide enough of a jolt.

The new public- and media-relations specialist, Daphne Brown, cornered the detective and spoke with a kind of breathless excitement that tempered everything that came out of her mouth.

East Port Orchard Elementary wants you to talk about stranger danger safety! Tonight!

We are out of creamer in the break room! Where do we keep it? I need some!

We have a serial killer on the loose!

Do you like my hair this way?

Kendall said good morning and waited for whatever urgent missive only-one-speed Daphne had.

"We've already heard from all the morning shows," Daphne said. "I'm so excited. They want you on."

Kendall shook her head. "I'm not doing it," Kendall said. "I'm not doing any of it. I've learned my lesson."

Daphne pulled at one of her curls, and it bounced back into position. "You don't even know what it's about," she said. "How can you say that?"

"Its not a *what*, Daphne. It's a *who,* and I know that the *who* is Brenda Nevins."

The younger woman's eyes widened, but before she could speak, Kendall preempted her.

"There's nothing you can do," Kendall said. "I'm not required to go on camera. *You* are. You can do it."

Daphne dialed down her pushy enthusiasm. She'd been to a conference in Seattle the week before and had learned new techniques to influence what she considered a "resistant personality type."

Daphne fiddled with her department-issued smartphone.

"You better watch the link I'm about to send you."

"Why?" Kendall asked.

Daphne glanced up, a satisfied look on her face.

"Watch it," she said. "Then call me so I can work my PR magic."

Kendall didn't acknowledge Daphne's boast. She had no plan whatsoever of encouraging Ms. Brown to do anything, let alone work any kind of self-professed public relations hocus-pocus. She was so sick of Brenda Nevins that she couldn't imagine enduring one more minute of thinking about her. Brenda was on the front page. Brenda was the top-of-the-hour news. Brenda had even been featured on the front page of *USA Today*. She was a murderous prison escapee, and that made her a problem for the special agents of the FBI, not the investigators from the local Kitsap County Sheriff's Office. Not for Kendall.

After extricating herself from Daphne, Kendall made her way to her office and, against her better judgment, powered up her laptop and immediately went to her message inbox.

There it was, an email from Daphne Brown. No message. Just a link to a YouTube clip. Kendall clicked on the link and waited for the advertisement for a trip to Greece on a luxury liner reached the ten-second mark so she could X it out.

The video was entitled: *How My Story Began, Part One.*

Kendall could feel her heart rate accelerate a little as the clip worked its way from start to finish. Feeling a little sweat collect at the nape of her neck, she pushed her chair away from her desk and dialed Birdy Waterman's number at the medical examiner's office.

"Hi, Kendall," Birdy said. "What's up?"

"Are you in your office?"

"Yes," Birdy said. "Gloves about to go on."

"Can you come over here?"

Birdy hesitated. "I'm about to start an autopsy on a crash victim from yesterday."

Kendall pushed. "But you haven't started, have you?"

"No, but . . . what's this about, Kendall?"

Kendall looked at the YouTube video queued up on her screen.

"Put the corpse back in the chiller and get over here," she said. "Brenda Nevins has posted a video blog. You need to see it."

"Video blog? What is she, fourteen?" Birdy said.

"This is no joke," Kendall said. "Come over as soon as you can."

"Send me the link," Birdy said.

Kendall moved her mouse to copy the link, but thought better of it.

"We need to watch this together," she said.

"You're making it sound like a premiere of some show, Kendall."

Birdy was right.

"I think it is," Kendall said.

The image was high-definition clear and left no room for doubt. Brenda Nevins had not ever been a person who could lay low. She took the microphone, looking at the camera.

"The light is on, so I guess you can see me. Or you can see me when I post this. I'm not stupid enough to do this live. It pissed me off to lose the chance to be on TV to tell the world my true story. The morons in the legal system really screwed me on that one. I don't like to be screwed with. I'm the one who does the screwing. Right, Janie?"

She turned and tilted the camera to Janie Thomas, who was bound and gagged on a chair. Silver duct tape cocooned her forearms to the armrest. Her feet were out of view. The gag appeared to be black fabric, some clothing item.

"Looks like underwear," Birdy said. "Wonder whose?"

Kendall didn't answer. Her eyes were bonded to images on her computer's screen. In particular, Janie's terrified eyes riveted the detective. Though farther back in the shot, there was no mistaking the pleading coming from them, an urgent message that was stronger than words.

Help me.

Brenda let the camera linger on Janie, then on herself. She wore full makeup and a teardrop necklace that Erwin had reported Janie was wearing to work the day she went missing from the prison. The teardrop, an amethyst, nestled between Brenda's breasts.

Brenda was nothing if not consistent. She was always one to make sure people's eyes landed right there, Kendall thought.

Brenda resumed talking. "Janie, you know your baby doesn't like it when you don't answer her. Makes me annoyed. When I get annoyed, I need to do something to liven things up. You know, to break the tension."

For the first time, Birdy noticed a curl of smoke in the frame. She tapped her finger on the screen.

"She's going to burn her," she said.

"It's one of her favorite things to do," Kendall said, sliding back into her chair. "She almost did it to her child."

"Who does that?" Birdy asked.

The answer, of course, both women knew, was a sociopath like Brenda. Maybe no one had seen someone so profoundly evil in the annals of crime. Kendall had. She'd been in the cage with the predator when she interviewed her on the Darcy Moreau murder case. She'd seen the charm and pretense of being human play out, the sickening game of those who have no other purpose in life but to win others over and destroy them.

Brenda tugged at the chain around her neck, the amethyst rising and sinking, swinging back and forth like a hypnotist's watch.

"I know I shouldn't smoke," Brenda said. "It's a nasty habit that I picked up in county jail and carried over to prison. Not much else to do in that hellhole." She looked at Janie over her shoulder. "No offense."

Then back at the camera, those gorgeous but lifeless eyes, sucking in every viewer who'd ever look at the video. "Smoking really scares me. I do not want to be one of those women whose mouth is a sagging sphincter that wicks out lipstick and is an instant sign that she's getting old."

Brenda reached in the direction of the curling smoke. Her fingertips now held a cigarette. She took a deep drag and then, seemingly absentmindedly, examined the filter before exhaling a sliver of smoke.

"Plus I have to constantly reapply lipstick, and in prison—not that that's a problem at the moment—decent cosmetics are hard to come by," she said. "I let a hideous creature from Preston fondle my breasts in the shower as payment for a tube of L'Oreal that came into the institution in someone's rectum. Gag me. The things one has to do to look halfway decent."

Brenda let out a laugh.

Kendall shot a look at Birdy.

"She thinks she's a star," she said.

"A Kardashian, maybe," Birdy said, her eyes still on the video.

Kendall was caught off guard. Birdy was more Kerouac than Kardashian. "You watch that crap?"

"No," Birdy answered. "But Elan's girlfriend Amber does. She's over a lot."

The exchange between the forensic pathologist and the detective was that kind of forced break in the tension that people engage in when watching a horror movie.

The popcorn is stale.

Have to go to the bathroom.

I just remembered I left the water running.

"Suddenly," Brenda said, getting up and walking over to a now squirming Janie, "I'm hungry. Do you like Indian food, Janie? I love curry. Don't get me started on tandoori chicken. Love. Love. Love tandoori. Surprisingly, there was a fantastic Indian place in the Tri-Cities that I used to go to with my boyfriend. It had the best tandoori in the Northwest. Better than Seattle. Honestly. So, so good. Well, Janie, do you like Indian food?"

Tears rolled down the superintendent's face.

"When I was a girl," Brenda went on, "we held dandelion blossoms to our chins, and if it reflected gold on your skin it meant that you liked butter. Did you ever do that?"

Janie didn't answer. She couldn't, of course, even if she had wanted to. The black panties used to keep her quiet were tied so tightly that the corners of her mouth appeared to have dripped blood.

Brenda swiveled around to face the camera. Her eyes met the camera's lens with the perfection of a newscaster.

"Did any of you?" she asked.

She held her stare and then turned back to Janie.

"I want to make sure you are seeing this, but it's hard to manage the camera, the shot, the script, *and* the talent. I have newfound respect for TV producers and camera crews. What they do is not as easy as it looks."

Brenda took one more drag on the cigarette, making sure the camera captured the glow of its amber tip.

"Let's see if you like Indian food," she said, her voice completely devoid of irony. As the cigarette's red-hot end moved toward Janie's forehead, a terrified Janie turned away, her cries muffled in the lingerie that silenced her.

"Don't fight me," Brenda said, in words that were splinter-cold. "You know you can't win. You're weak. I'm stronger. You're smart. I'm smarter."

She grabbed Janie by the hair with her free hand and yanked so hard that it looked as though the captive woman's neck might snap.

"She's a monster," Kendall said.

Birdy didn't say anything. There wasn't anything to say.

"Let's see if you like Indian food!" Brenda yelled.

And then while tears streamed and Janie struggled, Brenda pressed the lighted tip of her cigarette into the center of Janie's forehead.

"Don't squirm, stupid bitch! Once I moved when the crappy stylist my mother took me to cut my hair. I ended up with bangs that made me look like a trailer park kid!"

Through the struggle, Janie's muffled scream was captured.

"A monster," Birdy said.

"Pull yourself together, Janie! You like Indian food! You do!" Brenda said, laughing as if she'd pulled off some practical joke.

Kendall knew it was a pretend laugh. All of Brenda's

emotions about others were as bogus as her breasts. She was incapable of recognizing the pain of others because to her, others were only objects. Things to be used. Things to get her whatever it was that she wanted.

To serve her needs.

Brenda turned to the camera and whispered. The whisper was fake too. She spoke loud enough for Janie to hear every word.

"Everyone who is watching this already knows that Janie didn't get her Indian dinner out. You already know that she's dead."

Brenda looked down at the cigarette she'd ground into Janie's forehead. It was still smoldering. She took another puff, breathing in the burning tobacco and the incinerated flesh of the woman who'd helped her escape from prison. She made a face and extinguished it.

"Did you find my mark on Janie, Dr. Waterman? Sorry about your little boy, Detective Stark. Kids love cookies. I was a cookie monster when I was a little girl."

Kendall looked at Birdy, gauging her reaction to being named. The reference to Cody and the incident at school was spine chilling. It made her skin crawl. If anything on the video was a shock to her, it was the fact that the two of them had been named.

Birdy stared at Kendall.

"She was too badly burned for me to observe the cigarette burn," she said.

In silence, they watched the clip to its end.

"God, I hope this goes viral," Brenda said.

The screen went black and another advertisement for a cruise popped into view.

"She got her wish, Birdy," Kendall said, ignoring the

ad and wondering why the advertising tool on YouTube thought she was in her 60s. "More than 500,000 views and climbing." She refreshed her laptop screen. "Five thousand more since we started watching."

Birdy looked at Kendall. Her expression was grim. "This is going to encourage her, Kendall. She's a narcissist who lives for this kind of attention. She craves it like we crave our morning coffee."

Kendall picked up her lukewarm tuxedo mocha. "Right. She's going to do something big."

"Unless we stop her," Birdy said. "She has to be stopped."

CHAPTER TWO

Jonas Casey was an alpha male who ate nails for breakfast and probably bungee-jumped off the Space Needle. The FBI special agent was in his early forties, with a slim waist, thick brown hair, and hooded eyes that barely betrayed what he was thinking. As good as Kendall was about reading people, Jonas Casey was a blank slate.

Until he spoke, of course.

"Look, we're treating this as a kidnapping case," he said, when he appeared in Kendall's office. "Jurisdiction, ours."

"No ransom," she said. "No kidnapping."

"Come on, Detective. Let's apply a little common sense here, all right? There's very little to suggest that Janie Thomas went with Brenda Nevins willingly. And before you chime in, yes, there is the video. Yes, they took Thomas's car. Yes, they might have had a history of some kind of an affair, but we really don't know the depths of it. Too early in the investigation."

Kendall felt her throat tighten. She studied his face,

looking for a shred of humanity in his puffed-up "I'm FBI" countenance.

"We have three dead people. Would you agree that we have a murder investigation at work here? Along with a missing person? And somewhere on that list is the kidnapping case."

"Agreed," he said. "You have your murders. We don't do murder. But we do own kidnapping, and we're not going away until we find Brenda Nevins. You agree that we're pretty good at finding people?"

"Yes," she answered. "You never found Jimmy Hoffa."

He ignored her jab.

"And we have more tools and technology at our disposal? Wouldn't you agree that's the case, Detective?"

"I've never said it wasn't. The point I'm trying to make is that this is Kitsap County's case and we're leading it."

The special agent shook a Tic Tac into his hand and then popped it into his mouth. "You're right and wrong at the same time. We're leading the task force and, yes, the homicides are yours."

After SA Casey left to talk with the sheriff, Kendall called Birdy to vent.

"The man is an ass," she said.

"What man?"

"SA Casey."

"Don't know him, but not surprised. Those FBI guys can be that way," Birdy said.

"He's a total glory seeker, coming into our county to tell us that we don't know what we're doing and that he's here to save the day."

"Sounds about right, Kendall. I know the type. You

just have to play along. They bore easily and from what I can tell, they spend most of their time looking at their pension portfolio and counting the days until they can get out of the bureau. No one likes it there."

Janie Thomas's photograph stared from its place on the corner of Kendall Stark's desk. Like all too many, it was a part of a file that waited for the wheels of justice to turn.

It showed Janie when she first took the position of running the prison. She wore a navy-blue pantsuit and a powder-blue blouse. Her smile was a wide grin, the kind that appeared authentic instead of practiced for the camera. Looking at the picture reminded Kendall of the memorial service held a week after Janie's body was recovered. If there had been a more confused, sadder service, the homicide detective could not quite think of one. Janie's family—her husband, her son, and her two sisters from Spokane—sat in the front row facing the minister as he talked about the power of love and how Janie cared about every single person in the room.

Of course he'd say that. Yet it wasn't a completely true statement. Funerals are rife with exaggerations and lies.

Behind Erwin was the woman he'd been seeing behind his dead wife's back.

Janie's son, Joe, looked down at his phone the entire time. Kendall figured it was a distraction that he needed in order to get through the ordeal. The two sisters offered up the kind of body language—turned away, stiff in the way they perched on the pews—that indicated that they blamed Erwin for pushing Janie away and into the arms of a monster. Kendall studied the row of those closest to Janie Thomas and concluded that the death of the prison superintendent didn't bring the grieving family together; it merely exacerbated the problems they'd all been dealing with.

It was a cop-out to consider Janie Thomas a complete victim. After all, she *chose* to be with Brenda. No one forced her to drop everything and everyone in her world to find solace, excitement, and even love. No one deserved such a fate as Janie's, but there were probably only a small handful of people at that church service who didn't allow it to cross their minds.

What was she thinking? Why would she throw everything away for the attention of a sociopath like Brenda Nevins?

Kendall had an answer. She'd seen it time and again in cases she'd worked on at the county and had certainly read about in the annals of the FBI's famed Behavioral Science Unit. Brenda was a predator and a very good one. The greatest skill a predator possessed was the ability to find the weaknesses of his or her targets. Brenda had clearly seen something in Janie that she could use to get inside the prison superintendent's head, turn her into what she needed, and then, in the ultimate act of betrayal, end her life when she was no longer useful.

CHAPTER THREE

Brenda Nevins looked into the tiny lens of the laptop's camera. She tilted her head in the light, trying to find the most flattering position. For her, it was all about finding the right angle. A little lift of her head and a very slight tilt made her look a few pounds lighter. She wasn't fat, of course. *God no.* She had the best body a good diet, prison exercise, and a skillful surgeon could create.

She fiddled with the top of her blouse, opening an extra button to show Dr. Fournier's handiwork. She thought back to the day she'd transformed herself with the insurance money. She'd picked Dr. Fournier out of dozens of well-known cosmetic surgeons. He was based in Orange County, California, but that wasn't a problem. Not only did she have the money, Brenda liked the idea of achieving physical perfection with the help of a man who'd likely worked on film stars. His assistant, Merle, led her into his overly chilled white marble and stainless-steel consultation office. A *Twin Peaks* TV show poster hung in a prominent location by the door. The art was meant to be sardonic, but Brenda saw it as further proof that her breasts were about to be placed into some very capable hands. He probably worked on one of those television stars. She couldn't remember any of their names, but they were famous.

That's all that mattered.

Dr. Fournier was in his fifties, though he was using all the tricks at his disposal to hang on to a younger appearance. He had a waxy-smooth complexion and eyes that indicated a recent lift. He wore his hair longish for a man of his age. Worse, a slight kink along the lower run of his wavy hair indicated he wore it in a small ponytail. Though thankfully not on the day they'd met. No matter what she said to him, his facial expressions vacillated somewhere along the spectrum between surprised and slightly astonished.

"I want all eyes on me," she said.

"You don't need larger breasts for that," the doctor said. "You're near perfection now."

Near had been the operative word. Near wouldn't do it. Not even close. She'd done everything she could to get out of the almost grave-deep rut she'd been in. She'd done the unthinkable. And she was glad to have done it.

"I like to improve myself," she said. "Near perfection indicates there's room for improvement."

"All right. Did my assistant Lee help you with the sizers?"

"Yes, she did." Brenda thumbed through the doctor's "boob book" and pointed to one of the many success stories, a twenty-eight-year-old from La Jolla named Sherin. "I've decided anything less than a D cup would be disappointing."

The doctor made a slight face, though it was hard to discern what response he was trying to convey.

"Are you sure?" he asked. "It could impact your lifestyle. Are you a runner, for example?"

"No," she said. "Not a runner. I move slow enough to make sure that I'm not a blur. I want to be seen."

Thinking back and somewhat caught up in the memory, there was more irony than the *Twin Peaks* poster, from that encounter with Dr. Fournier. She was *now* a runner. And while Brenda Nevins craved the spotlight, she did not want to be found.

She checked her makeup, pushed RECORD, and started talking.

"Hi everyone. It's me. Brenda Nevins. God, do I even need to introduce myself? You know me by sight, don't you? And if you don't, well then I guess you'll find out why someone has directed you here. So, here goes. I'll be video blogging from time to time and checking my stats for viewing to make sure that I'm keeping your interest. I mean, why wouldn't you be captivated by me and how I'm getting along after poor Janie's death? Janie was like a bottle opener for a twist top. Useful—no girl wants to break a nail opening a beer—but ultimately if you can snag a man you don't need to open anything on your own. Except maybe . . ." she gave the camera a come-hither smile, sure that she had her viewer hooked in that sexy train-wreck way she'd imagined her show. "You know what I mean."

Her eyes wandered over the screen as she tried to maintain a kind of newscasters' approach, facing the camera and yet not being completely zombie eyed. She wanted to look alert and sexy.

"Okay, guys," she carried on, "today I want to talk about Janie Thomas. Remember her from the last video? She's dead now—and I know I might get some haters after me, but honestly, I did the world a favor. Janie was a complete loser. A total bore. She was all over me because I gave her some attention. If you're thinking about sex, then that was part of it. But really, not that much. Janie liked me because of how I made her feel. I listened to her pathetic backstory. It was blah, blah, blah. *Poor me. Sad me. Lonely me.* Man, was that girl messed up. And, yeah, she was in charge of me and the other inmates. Honestly, I don't get our country half the time. They have someone like Janie bossing around someone like me. Really? *Really?* Who can get the job done? *Me.* Who can be ruthless to move the needle in the direction that makes sense? *Me.* Not her. Not her at all. Oh God, all she could do was whine about her childhood, her husband, and her son. She couldn't wring one ounce of joy from her pathetic existence. Her husband didn't pay any attention to her. And yes, Erwin Thomas, if you are watching—and I know you will watch—Janie knew all about you and that woman that you've been seeing. I wonder if Sandra Sullivan's husband knows about you too."

She paused as though she'd spoken out of turn and was embarrassed.

"Oops, my bad," she said. "I guess he knows *now.* I told Janie to tell him, but she was too weak. I can't imagine just sitting back and letting something *just* happen to you. Pretending to be passive and unaware is fine as a strategy until you dig in and plan your attack. Janie never got the memo on that. She just kept hoping things would get better. Hoping is for losers.

I've known that since I was twelve. Hoping is what you do when you have no power to do anything at all."

Brenda stopped to think. Janie was gone. Her husband had been trashed. Now, son Joe was about to feel the betrayal of a mother who'd been sucked into a deadly game—a game that she'd lost.

"How she agonized over filling out Joe's college entrance papers, including his essay. What was it? Oh yes, now I remember. 'Living Authentically When Others Pull the Strings.' Just wow. Really. How anyone with the flimsiest B average could write something so close to the bone would be beyond me. Janie was so worried that you'd get found out, Joe. She thought she was helping you and, if you ask me, you were lazy enough to let her do the heavy lifting. She did that for you. For your father. And what did she have for herself? Nothing, that's what. You'd think that a kindred spirit like me would have been what she'd been looking for all her life. You think she found me? That's a big laugh. *I* found *her*."

Brenda tilted her head back and rolled her shoulders to release some tension. She returned her gaze to the lens.

"In some ways I miss her," she said. "A little. I really do. She could rub out the soreness in my neck better than my last lover. Janie tried so hard. She wanted to please me. God, she tried. Kind of funny when I think about it. As if I'd ever care about her. And, get this, the irony of the whole thing was that she thought she was in charge of me. That out of the mess she'd made of her life, having the keys to the cellblock made her think she was in control. I pulled the strings. I did. I always have.

"That's all for now. More later. I promise. Probably should have a name for my show here, don't you think? I'll think on that. You too. Use the comments feature below. And if you know something nasty about someone, please post it here."

Like a seasoned YouTuber, Brenda pointed a lacquered nail downward to indicate the Comments field. A pause to make her point, and then she turned away from the camera. The screen went to a checkerboard block of other Internet distractions.

CHAPTER FOUR

Kendall Stark didn't expect anything from Jonas Casey, so when he showed up in her office with a couple of lattes she was caught off guard.

"Peace offering," he said.

She thanked him and took the coffee drink.

"I guess it would be wrong of me to refuse the olive, or rather, coffee branch," she said.

He smiled and slid into the visitor's chair across from her. A framed photo of Cody and Steven taken on their front porch faced him from the credenza, but the FBI agent didn't comment on her family.

"Look, we both know that Janie Thomas is a kidnapping case," he said.

Kendall pulled the green stopper from the plastic lid and took a sip. Caffeine, she hoped, would kill the throbbing headache that started about the time Brenda Nevins came into her life.

"We don't," she said. "Not really. As for what we really know is that—at least initially—Janie went with Brenda willingly."

"Yes. Agreed. Initially." He took a drink. "But that's not how things ended, wouldn't you agree?"

She couldn't argue with that. Janie didn't expect to die, though she might have been willing to die for her lover's freedom. But it didn't happen like that.

"Is the coffee the peace offering?" Kendall asked. "Or is there something else?"

He gave her his incredibly disarming smile.

"Right. Something else. Something I want you to think about."

He was probably playing her the same way he played other women who couldn't deny that he was handsome and magnetic. Still a jerk. But his looks and charisma somehow mitigated his true personality.

"What's that?" Kendall asked.

"We traced—and I'm using that word very loosely— the upload on Brenda Nevins's YouTube channel."

Kendall could feel her heart rate quicken. She'd been hoping for someone to tell her where Brenda was, how far she'd gone, and, more important, what it would take to catch her.

"Go on," she said.

"Like I said, loosely. Our guys in the lab—and that's no slam, this time it is a couple of guys—determined that Brenda Nevins uploaded her video in Iceland of all places. That didn't seem right."

"No," Kendall said. "How could she get to Iceland? She doesn't have a passport."

"She couldn't, of course. We checked to be sure. Dug a little deeper into the code and determined that it had bounced from Qatar to Spain and then over to Iceland. We checked again, and Brazil was added to the mix. You get the idea?"

"I'm not a computer expert," Kendall said. "But yes, I get that someone is helping her do what she's doing. And that someone knows a thing or two about untraceable IP addresses, servers, and the like."

The FBI agent had cut himself shaving that day, and a piece of tissue clung to a spot just above his Adam's apple.

Kendall fought the urge to pick at it.

"That's right," he said. "And by the way, I'm not an expert either. I only act like I know what I'm talking about so I can get what I need to get and then find what I need to find."

She liked him for admitting that. He didn't have to.

"So where does this leave you," she said, quickly amending her words, "leave us?"

"You've dug into the Nevins case as much as anyone," he said. "You probably have a feel for who might be able to help her with something as sophisticated as to upload files in a way that could not easily be traced. Not even by the FBI."

"No," she answered. "There isn't *anyone*. The people who knew her before prison are scared of her. None of them want a thing to do with her. I bet most of them sleep with a gun under their pillows."

"That fearful of her?"

Kendall set down her coffee. "No," she said, "that hopeful."

He cocked a brow. "Hopeful?"

"Yeah," Kendall said, "hopeful that they'd be able to shoot her in the head if she came for a visit. Believe me, there's no welcome-home celebration from anyone who ever knew her before she became famous for killing."

"You've talked to some of her," he let the word hang in the air, while he thought of the best way to rephrase it, "let's call them, mentors."

"Just one," Kendall said. "Jerry Connors is a non-player here. He's an older, male version of Brenda Nevins. Backed into a corner, warehoused, and still looking for the wrong kind of attention."

"She managed somehow," he said.

"She's pretty smart," Kendall said. "I have to call our IT guy here at the county once a month. I'm notorious here for screwing up my password and needing a reset. Ten letters, two special characters, numerals. And, right, don't ever write it down. It's getting ridiculous. But Brenda's wired differently. Maybe she could figure it out."

"It's pretty sophisticated stuff," SA Casey said. "And I'm about like you. Give me the days when my dog's name and last four of my Social were good enough."

Kendall laughed. "Tell me about it. Those were the days."

When he got up to leave, Kendall wanted to ask him how tall he was. He must have been at least six-four, but that was a question that would imply interest, and she didn't have any in him. Besides, she was married and very much in love with her husband, Steven.

"I don't think any of us should underestimate her intelligence," she said.

He gave her a look.

"We never underestimate at the bureau," he said.

"Of course not," she said. "I'm just thinking that she's the kind of brilliant person that knows how to use people in ways that the rest of us can't really fathom.

Janie gave up everything, literally *everything*, because Brenda got her to that point. She found a way to get someone to do what she needed done."

SA Casey lingered in the doorway. "She wanted to make those videos," he said.

His head was three inches from the top of the door-frame. He was definitely taller than six-four.

"And more importantly, she wanted to keep making them," she said. "She wanted the world to see all that she could do. How beautiful she is. How clever. How talented. She sees no distinction between fame and infamy."

The FBI special agent took in every word. Kendall Stark might have been a detective for a small county in the middle of nowhere, but her assessment on Brenda Nevins was close to the briefing he'd been given when he got the case. "Grandiose narcissist" was the label given to the woman who'd seduced and then murdered a prison superintendent.

Among a deadly list of her victims that included a TV producer, a bar owner, and a student teacher, were her husband, and her baby.

"She needed someone to help her make those videos," he said.

Kendall stood to walk the special agent out of the convoluted hallways of the Kitsap County Sheriff's Office—though it was clear he'd had no problem navigating his way to her office with that so-called coffee branch.

"Right," she said, still thinking. "Someone who knew the ins and outs of media, computers, services, and video."

"Someone," SA Casey said as they made their way down the hallway, passing the evidence room and records offices, "she could dispose of when the time was right."

He was right. Brenda's helpers had the shelf life of lettuce.

"Brenda Nevins sees everyone as an object," Kendall said. "No one is a person when she lays her eyes on them. All exist as merely something to be used by her."

"Whoever is helping her doesn't know that," the agent said.

"And when they finally figure it out," Kendall added, "I'll bet it will be too late."

CHAPTER FIVE

As a thunderstorm pounded the airspace over Port Orchard, Erwin and Joe Thomas sat in the lobby of the Kitsap County Sheriff's Office. Hanging above the receptionist's desk and console was a shiny steel image of salmon swirling around as though they were in the constant motion of the freedom of a river. There was a bit of irony there, of course. The fish-shaped figures were fashioned in a circle, chasing each other, going nowhere.

Janie Thomas's husband and son were in the same steely limbo.

A rumble of thunder pulsed through the lobby, and the receptionist looked up from the magazine she was reading.

"We don't get many storms like these," she said. "Almost scary."

The visitors and Kendall Stark looked over at her.

"Yeah," Joe said, "I had a kid down the hall from my dorm room that had his bass cranked up so loud that the first time I heard it I thought it was a thunderstorm. Pretty dumb, huh?"

"Not so dumb," Kendall said. "I had a boyfriend that played the bass so loud that I'm lucky I can hear anything anyone says."

The mood had been fraught with tension. The small talk was an opportunity to break the ice. Joe and his dad were there, she knew, because of the video blog Brenda had released.

Kendall extended her hand to Erwin, but he declined to greet her with a handshake. Joe, whom Kendall decided favored his mother with his coloring—hair and eyes—reached out.

"Detective, we saw the thing on YouTube," Joe said.

"I should have called you," Kendall said.

"You should have," Erwin said, standing with his arms wrapped around his chest in a defensive pose.

Erwin looked at his son. "He wants to know about her."

Kendall looked at Joe and offered a quick, sympathetic nod. She turned her attention to Erwin.

"Let's talk, okay?" She asked. "Follow me."

The aftermath of murder is never predictable. How people behave when the unimaginable transpires is a source of endless pondering and discussion among those who deal with it every day. Sometimes people act as though they'll never recover, that the death of the loved one is that line in the sand that will forever mark the rest of their days. Other times, relief seems to rear up, and the one closest to the victim starts planning a garage sale for the deceased's effects before a single word of a eulogy is a puff of vapor in front of a church service.

Erwin was bitter about his wife's betrayal, and Kendall understood why he felt that way. Her plan to just disappear with Brenda Nevins and give up everything he thought they'd shared had to have been a terrible shock. If the video blog Brenda had made about a potential affair with Sandra Sullivan had been true, then he'd have had to live with his part in what might have pushed Janie to do what she did. Their son, on the other hand, was an innocent. He'd loved his mother, and the fact that she walked away from him forever brought the kind of hurt that no child, no matter the age, could just pass off.

She led them to her office. No one wanted water or coffee. It wasn't going to be that kind of a visit.

"Look, Detective, I want to say one thing flat out. Brenda Nevins is a goddamn liar. That's what she is. I didn't have an affair with anyone."

Before Kendall could answer, Joe spoke.

"Get a grip, Dad," he said. "This isn't about you. No one cares about what you did or didn't do with Sandy."

Erwin kept his eyes on the detective. "I didn't do anything with her but talk."

"Whatever," Joe said. "I don't care. No one cares. We're here because we're sick of the press. We're sick of nobody telling us what's going on. No one even called us to tell us what was on YouTube. I got a text from a girl I used to date."

Kendall felt sorry for Janie's family.

"I'm sorry about that, Joe," she said. "I really am. I should have notified you the minute I knew of the existence of the recording. I don't have any great excuse, but I want you to know that it will never happen again."

"That's fine," Erwin said, eyeing his agitated son. "Things happen very fast, Detective. We're all still reeling from everything. Did you know that there were thirty-six media people on our front lawn this morning?"

Kendall didn't. "Are they on your property? You can tell them they are trespassing."

"I did," Erwin said. "They aren't leaving."

"They'll go away in time. They always do." she said. "In the meantime, if you have any problems—if *any* of the media harasses you—we can send a deputy out to make them comply."

Joe started to tear up, but he turned away so Kendall couldn't see. His father put his hand on the young man's shoulder.

"I'm sorry, son," Erwin said.

"It isn't your fault, Dad. "I just . . ."

Kendall's heart went out to the young man. He was fighting for composure in the way that young men do. No one can see them cry. No one can observe any trace of a weakness. Young men retreat into their own armor when they face disappointment, hurt, and the deepest kind of tragedy.

"We're committed to finding Brenda Nevins and bringing her to justice," Kendall said.

Erwin spoke up. "We know. I told Joe that."

Joe turned to look his father in the eye. "Dad, you didn't even love Mom. You got rid of all her stuff. You're hanging out with Sandy all the time now."

"Sandy and I are friends," Erwin said, pulling back a little.

"I don't want to argue about that anymore," Joe said. "I don't believe you, and you can say whatever you want, but if you had taken better care of Mom none of this would have happened."

Kendall tried to defuse the building resentment.

"No one could have predicted what happened," she said. "We've gone over everything. The FBI has too. There's no electronic bread crumb to follow that would lead anyone to believe something was happening between the two of them."

"Electronic," Erwin repeated. "Why did you use that word?"

"That's how we do things," Kendall said. "We look through data records—computer and phone, for example. There is nothing there."

Erwin shrugged. "That's because Brenda Nevins didn't have a phone or email."

Kendall couldn't disagree. "Yes, that's probably part of it."

"All right, no electronic trail, but what about other evidence? I mean, I think my mom was tricked," Joe dried his eye on his shirtsleeve. "She might have been coerced, you know. There's no real proof that she was really into that sick chick."

This was difficult. *Very.* Janie Thomas was dead. No matter what Erwin said, he had, in fact, moved on. Joe, however, was in limbo. He didn't want to rewrite everything that he'd believed was true. That his mom and dad loved each other. That the smiling pictures of the family that he'd rescued from the trash where his father had discarded them were proof of something.

It was only the remnant, the veneer of a lie.

"We don't know everything about what happened before Ms. Thomas and Brenda Nevins left the institution."

"But it's possible that Mom didn't go willingly, right?" Joe asked.

Janie's son wanted some glimmer of hope that his mother was someone that he knew.

"I'm sorry," she said, "but it doesn't appear that way at all. We have no evidence of coercion."

The younger man couldn't believe it. He didn't want to rewrite all that he'd thought about his mother.

"It looked like my mom was totally coerced in that video," he said, his voice rising a little. "It didn't look like she wanted to be there. I don't know how you can say what you're saying. She wasn't like that. My mom was a good person. Everyone on the Internet and on TV is making fun of her, calling her names, deciding that she was a worthless, stupid piece of garbage, but that isn't who she is at all."

Present tense had slipped into his words. Joe Thomas hadn't accepted his mother's death.

"She was manipulated, Joe," Kendall said. "She might have gone willingly with Brenda—and I believe she did—but once Brenda got what she wanted, your mom was no longer of value to her."

"She was of value to me," Joe said.

"To me too," Erwin added.

Joe's composure once again started to crumble. "What kind of person just uses someone like they are nothing? Like they are trash? Disposable?"

"She's a monster," Erwin added.

Kendall took in their words. It was a hard question to answer. Janie's husband was correct to a degree. There were very few people in the world who behaved the way Brenda Nevins did. In reality, that kind of evil was rare. It only seemed like there was a legion of them in the Pacific Northwest. It owed more to bad luck and a plethora of crime writers in the vicinity than to the gloom of the long winters. Indeed, there had been so many serial killers like Gary Ridgway and narcissists like Diane Downs who killed to such a degree they'd become legendary. Book worthy. Film worthy. Brenda Nevins was clearly headed in that direction. She might, Kendall thought, be the most notorious of them all.

"Look," she said, focusing her eyes first on Erwin, then Joe, "we're all doing what we can to apprehend her and bring her to justice. I'm on it. The FBI is on it. No one is going to stop looking for her."

CHAPTER SIX

Snuggled in her robe after a long, hot shower, Amber Turner wrapped a fluffy white towel around her head and flung herself on her bed to answer Elan's call. Calls were rare. Texting was the preferred mode of communication between the two of them.

"Hey you," she said.

"What are you doing?" Elan asked.

"If you really want to know," she said, shifting her weight on the bed and unfurling the towel, releasing her long red hair. "I just got out of the shower."

"I can picture that," he said.

"I'm sure you can," she said back, putting him on speaker as she worked a wide-toothed comb down the length of sectioned hair.

"Want to hang out today?" he asked.

Amber continued with her hair, first with her fingertips as she parted safe passage sections for the comb. She loved her hair. It made her stand out in a crowd. She'd only colored it once, a dreadful burgundy that she regretted when it made her hair look the color of a strawberry popsicle.

"So not a good color for you," her friend Kelly had said in what was surely the understatement of the year. She thanked God it was only a temporary color and that after three weeks of washing her hair nightly it had returned to the beautiful and natural ginger tones that made the green of her eyes all the more lovely.

"I guess so," she said to Elan. "I have cheer at two, and that'll last two hours."

"I could come and hang out at the track while you practice."

She smiled. "Sounds good to me," she said.

"Bye, Amber."

"Later, Elan."

Kelly had texted while she was talking to Elan.

Kelly: You want to do something after cheer?
Amber: Elan and I are going to do something.
Kelly: OMG! Elan and you. What's going on?
Amber: Nothing. Not really. I guess I like him. He's cute.
Kelly: Yeah. Quiet. But cute.
Amber: Not so quiet but definitely cute.
Kelly: See you at school.
Amber: K.

Amber slid to the edge of her bed and looked around, her hair ready for the dryer. Her room needed a makeover. Her mom still treated her like a little kid, with white wicker furniture and white eyelet edged curtains. She'd asked a million times if she could do something to change things, up. Even paint. But her mom always deflected her requests by passing them off to her stepfather, Karl. He couldn't care less about Amber. Everything was about Bryn, the new baby.

Bryn this. Bryn that. Whatever they said, Amber had an answer. Never aloud, though. Always just inside her head, where remarks went unchallenged and, most important, unpunished.

"We need to save up for private school for Bryn."

I didn't get to go to private school.

"Thank God Bryn got some melanin in her skin. She won't burn like her big sister."

I don't feel like a big sister. I wear sunblock, and it isn't like being a ginger is a skin disorder.

"We might need to move you downstairs so Bryn can be closer to us."

I'm not moving.

"Bryn is the cutest baby ever."

She is cute. Maybe not the cutest ever.

Amber finished getting dressed, grabbed her pom-poms and made a beeline for the door. Her mom, Sue, called over to her from the kitchen where Princess Bryn was being served something that smelled pretty good. Sue had been making homemade baby food, which she had never done for her eldest daughter.

"Hey! You need to eat, Amber!"

Amber looked over at her mom. Bryn had a big smile on her face, and Amber couldn't help but return a smile of her own. She hated that she did. As much as things had changed since Bryn's arrival, she couldn't blame it all on the baby. Her mom was in her early forties and, as far as Amber could see, had no business getting pregnant again. Seventeen years apart didn't make for great sibling relationships. In fact, it made for exactly what had transpired.

A house divided.

"I'm on cheer, Mom," she said, on the move again. "We don't eat. We all have eating disorders. Bye!"

Sue made a face, a kind of exasperated expression that was the counterpart of an eye roll, without rolling the eyes, that is.

"Not funny!" she said.

The door shut, and Amber got into her car.

CHAPTER SEVEN

The image was dark. So dark that it would be doubtful just how much enhancement any decent tech lab could manage. The woman's voice sputtered a few times, dipping in and out of what could be heard and what someone might imagine.

"It's me. Janie Thomas. I'm the superintendent of the Washington Corrections Center for Women, in Gig Harbor, Washington. I know that what I'm about to say will find little sympathy among some—if anyone sees or hears my message. I made a terrible mistake. Don't even know how things went so wrong. Brenda Nevins has me. She's made me do some terrible things. Really the worst things that a human can do to another, I did it. I'm so very, very sorry. I thought she loved me. I still think she might. But I also know there's something tremendously wrong with her. She's not normal. She's not like other people. She has an on-and-off switch that she alone controls. I really thought that I could help her and by the same token, she could help me. I was wrong. I have blood on my hands. I've done things that I would never have thought possible, things for which I will need to atone for the rest of my life. I'm sorry, Erwin. I'm sorry, Joe. God knows that what I've done has hurt you both. Forgive me. Erwin, I forgive you for the affair with Sandy. I wasn't there. I know that now."

Again, some movement of the device and another short pause.

"She's in the shower. She'll be out in a minute. I don't know where we are. She drugged me. I swear she did. Wherever we are, we have no cell service. Not at all. I'm recording this with the hope that I'll find a way to upload when we move locations again. Tonight, I think. She's coming now. She's crazy. She's dangerous. I love her."

In the background, Brenda's voice is heard.

"What in the hell are you doing now, Janie? God, I can't leave you alone for a second, can I?"

"I wasn't doing anything, Brenda."

"Give me that."

"What?"

"Give it to me!"

"Brenda, I don't know what you're talking about!"

"You ungrateful bitch, you've been calling someone, haven't you? Give me the phone."

"You're hurting me."

"Ask if I care, you idiot."

"I love you, Brenda."

"You don't know what love is, you stupid bitch. You make me sick. You've betrayed me, and I want to know who you've called."

"I didn't call anyone!"

Brenda's face appeared on the black screen of the video, filling it with her beautiful, but menacing eyes.

She blinked. She looked away, presumably in the direction of Janie Thomas.

"Made a video, huh? Aren't you the clever one, Janie? I never knew you had any aptitude for multimedia. I think I'll watch your little video to see what you've said."

"I was just playing around, Brenda, honest," Janie said. "Don't bother."

A long pause.

Brenda pointed the camera over to Janie, who appeared to be cowering on the bed. The bedspread was a solid blue without the benefit of a pattern to provide any clues as to where the taping had taken place. The framing of the shot was so tight that even the headboard had been cropped out.

"I'll decide just what you were doing," Brenda said, "and I'll also decide what I'm going to do about it."

The video went black.

CHAPTER EIGHT

Brad Nevins's wizened face looked like it had been carved out of limestone. It was craggy, pale. He wore a Seahawks sweatshirt and Levi's frayed along the edges by the heels of his shoes. His frame was angular and limp at the same time. It was as though all the life had been sucked out of him.

From the window he watched Kendall as she parked on the street in front of the house in the Tri-Cities where he and his late wife Elise had raised their son Joe, who had been their pride and joy. He wasn't like the other boys on the block. He was a homebody. A helper. He loved going out to the small ranch where the family kept some cattle and a few horses. When he was five and got his first pair of cowboy boots, he didn't take them off for a week. Slept in them even.

"You Stark?" he called over to her.

"That's me," Kendall said, pressing the button on her key fob to lock the car and then feeling a little silly for doing so.

Brenda's former father-in-law's neighborhood could not have been more tranquil. Every house was well

maintained. Every bush trimmed with a delicate preci-
sion. It was had to believe, Kendall thought, as she
walked up to meet Brad, that evil seeps its way so easily into a place like that. But it could. It did.

The evil was Brenda Holloway Nevins.

"Nice place," she said.

Brad smiled. "Kind of have to keep things nice
around here. The neighbors set a high bar, and you're
banned from the block party if you don't keep things
just so."

"You're kidding, right?" she asked.

"I wish," he said. "But yes, I guess a little."

Brad led Kendall inside. Fresh track marks cut into
the pile of the tawny brown carpet, indicating that
Brad Nevins likely did a last-minute vacuum run over
it before she arrived.

"Made some coffee if you'd like a cup," he said.
"Don't have any fancy teas if that's what you'd pre-
fer."

She smiled at the gesture. "Coffee's fine."

"Right back," he said, returning a beat later with a
couple of Seahawks mugs. He set one on the table in
front of her.

"You need to use the bathroom?" he asked. "Long
drive and all."

"No," she said. "I'm fine."

Brad sipped his coffee and waited as Kendall settled
in. "I wish I could say I'm glad you're here," he said,
"because the truth is I don't get much company. At
least not any company I really want to keep."

"The media?" she asked.

Brad set down his coffee mug. "Them too. But it's
mostly the cars with the looky-loos that drive by, point-

ing out where Joe lived, where he and Kara were last seen alive. Things had quieted down since, you know, everything happened. It's been a lot of years."

"Seven years isn't a long time when something like what happened to you and your family occurs," Kendall said, wondering if he knew that a story like Brenda's had the potential to last beyond his lifetime in the way that other serial killers' had.

Brad didn't disagree. "I guess you've dealt with this a lot in your job," he said. "Or, no offense, maybe you think you have. But I'll tell you one thing I know for sure—and I go to a support group, and I'm kind of an expert—someone like Brenda doesn't come along very often. Someone as conniving, cold, and evil as her is a freak of nature, and God doesn't make many of them."

Brad Nevins got it. He was right. Brenda was in a league of her own.

"And now she's back," Kendall said, easing him toward the conversation she'd come to have.

"Right. Like the resurgence of the plague."

A plague. That was an apt description, she thought.

"You think they'll catch her?" he asked, hope rising slightly in his voice.

She noted how he'd said, "they'll" instead of "you'll" when he phrased the question.

Kendall turned off her phone and set it inside her purse. "She can't hide forever," she said.

Brad allowed a slight smile to crease his jawline. "You don't know Brenda. She can do whatever she wants. She always has."

*   *   *

For the next hour and a half, Kendall Stark and Brad Nevins talked about everything that had happened to his son and granddaughter. How the sum of Brenda's reign of terror had ended up killing his wife, too.

"I tell people it was the breast cancer that took her," he told her, "but I know that she could have survived it if she'd had more to live for. Brenda took away everything. I'm not saying my wife didn't love me, but you are at that point in your life to know that the love she felt for her son and granddaughter was of a different measure. Brought more joy. And, really, a lot more hurt."

Kendall understood. Losing her own parents had been devastating. She cried a thousand tears over the loss and the sense of being left alone. Yet, deep down, she knew she'd lost them in the natural order of things. Parents die before their children. At least that's the way it is supposed to go.

Kendall had read the files and news accounts of Brad's son's and granddaughter's murders. What he and his wife went through was beyond horrific. She'd devoured every word of the trial. She'd scoured the Internet for all she could find. She felt she had to know the details of those crimes for a better understanding of how Brenda operated.

To know her better was to find her. At least Kendall hoped so.

"I'm sure you've laid in bed and thought about this over and over," she said. "Tell me about her."

"There probably isn't enough time in the world to tell you what makes her tick, if that's what you're after," he said.

"I am," Kendall answered. "I want to know. What

do you remember about her metamorphosis from daughter-in-law to killer?"

He'd finished his coffee and got up from his chair. He didn't really need another cup. He needed to think. After disappearing into the kitchen, he returned, a peculiar look on his face.

"That's just the thing, Detective Stark," he said, looking right at her with those sad eyes of his. "I don't think there was any metamorphosis—*your word*—I think there was always ugliness behind everything she did."

"Talk to me. Tell me what you remember about her. We don't need to revisit the crimes that killed your son and granddaughter. There has been plenty written about all of that. I've read it."

"There's about to be more," he said.

The remark puzzled her.

"I don't follow."

"A book," he answered. "Someone is working on a book. Movie people have called too. But I don't want a damn thing to do with them. They couldn't get it right if they tried. No one would believe it."

"Believe what?" she asked.

"The things she did."

"I need an example, Mr. Nevins," Kendall said. "I want to stop her. I want to understand just who she is and what is underneath her skin, what it is that drives her and, more than anything, how to stop her."

"Tall order," he said. "Skyscraper tall."

"Tell me about her."

He sat back down in his chair. "Want to know the first time I met her?"

"That's a start," she said.

CHAPTER NINE

Brenda Holloway was sixteen when Joe Nevins first brought her home to meet his parents. He'd begged them ahead of time not to call him "Little Joe" as they had since the day they brought him home from the hospital.

"It's embarrassing," he said. "I'm *not* little."

That was true. He *wasn't*. At seventeen, he was a six-footer, packing on muscle to a frame that needed very little padding. He had somewhat chiseled features like his father's, but his dark, dark hair was thick and wavy. Just like his mother's. Joe had been an achiever. He'd been on the debate team, was student body president, and was at the top of his class academically. He was also an athlete, having finished in the top five at the all-state track meet in two events—long jump and pole vault. His thighs bulged with muscle and he'd worked hard the summer he brought Brenda over to build up his chest through a weight-lifting regimen at a local gym.

"I don't think he would have taken steroids without a major push from that one," Brad Nevins said to Kendall Stark as they sat in the living room of the family home.

"That one" was Brenda, of course.

Joe was an only child, the answer to his mother's dreams after a pair of miscarriages early into the Nevins marriage. The couple waited an excruciatingly long five years before they tried to conceive again.

"My wife had a lot of depression about losing those two babies. It bothered me, too. Really it did. But not like her. After the second one, she took a job at the Merry-Go-Round, a children's clothing store downtown. It was like she had to have the hurt flung at her over and over. I don't know, like a person who'd had gastric bypass surgery goes to work at the Cheesecake Factory or maybe an ice cream store? Just seeing what you can't have over and over was like a strange punishment she put on herself. I told her we should try one more time to have a baby of our own, but honestly, I wasn't really sure it was a good idea."

"But it worked, right? That was Joe?" Kendall asked.

"Right," Brad said. "Thankfully there were no more miscarriages. Just a beautiful little boy."

Once Joe came home from the hospital, Brad said the boy stayed in their bedroom in a crib until he was almost two. His wife knew that babying a boy wasn't a good idea, but she couldn't help herself.

"'He's my miracle,' my wife said, over and over, as she rocked him to sleep. 'We waited so long for him and now that he's here, nothing will ever hurt him.'"

Those words were almost a curse, Kendall thought.

* * *

The day Brenda showed up for the first time was the beginning of the end of the Nevins family's hard-fought happiness, though it would take some time for her to do what she wanted to do.

"Don't judge me," Brad told Kendall, "because what I have to tell you has the tendency to not go over too well, you know, with women."

"Trust me," Kendall said, "I've heard everything from everyone."

"Fine," he said, still sizing her up. "I'll tell you exactly how it went down, and at the end of what I have to say, you'll wonder why it was that we didn't try to cut that relationship off at the knees. I have an answer for that. But first, the story."

CHAPTER TEN

It was the middle of summer, and eastern Washington was on full blast, preheat. It had been six days straight of egg-frying-on-the-asphalt weather. In fact, a couple of kids made the news by actually frying two eggs on the hood of a cop car parked outside the precinct. *That hot*.

But not as hot as Brenda.

She wore a cropped top and cutoffs that she'd made from Levi 501s. Her hair was different then, a coppery color with blond streaks. On anyone else, it would have looked ridiculous, but not on Brenda. She somehow managed to find a way to attract attention and still appear as if she wasn't even trying.

Both parents noticed that their son behaved differently around this new girlfriend. Different than he had been around others. He'd always been a gentleman when it came to how he treated girls. With Brenda, he was even more attentive. Almost too much. She was only sixteen, but it was clear she'd mastered the art of getting a man to do whatever she wanted him to do.

"Joey won't take me to a concert at the Gorge that I

want to go to," she said as she sucked Pepsi through a straw.

"Don't have the dough right now," he said.

"Dan says he wants to take me."

"Then go with him," Joe said.

"But, baby, I want to go with you. It would be zero fun without you."

"I don't have the money."

"You have a birthday coming up," she said, looking over at Elise Nevins.

A little startled, Elise answered. "Yes, you do. I think tickets to the show would be a great gift, don't you?"

Joe stared at his feet. "Pretty expensive, Mom."

"You only turn eighteen once," Brenda persisted.

A few minutes later, Brenda and Brad were alone in the living room. Mother and son were in the kitchen. Brenda sat in the sofa directly across from the recliner where Brad took his place.

"So hot out there," she said.

"A scorcher," he said.

"I thought you guys had air-conditioning," Brenda said.

"We do."

"Feels hot in here."

"Set at a constant seventy-four," Brad answered. "Could be cooler, but we don't want the power company to get every last dime we have."

She sipped her Pepsi and moved her legs under her on the sofa. In doing so, she allowed a flash of her vagina to show. She wore no underwear. The fabric that held her cutoffs together was like a twist of yarn.

"That's better," she said. "More comfortable now."

Her eyes locked on his.

You did that on purpose, Brad thought.

"You think she flashed you intentionally?" Kendall asked.

"No women does so unintentionally," Brad said. "I'm not saying that a woman wearing sexy clothes is an open invitation for some guy to stare at her. Say something to her. But, Detective, you have to know what I mean. There was something about the way she moved her legs, splitting them slightly apart and holding that pose just long enough to make sure I got a good look. It wasn't anything I'd never seen before. I've had my share. But here's the real deal, she was showing me what she had—not because she wanted me to get all jacked about her hotness—but because she wanted me to see what my son was getting."

Kendall was unsure how to respond to that. She'd never pegged Brenda's former father-in-law as a narcissist, but here he was making it all about him.

"How do you know that?" she asked.

"Because of what she did next."

Kendall narrowed her gaze. "Which was?"

"She told me."

"What did she say?"

"I'll never forget it."

After dinner, after Elise had given an early birthday check to Joe, Brad found himself alone with Brenda in the kitchen cleaning up while mother and son sat in the living room talking.

"I saw the way you looked at me," Brenda said. Her voice was low, only loud enough for Brad to hear.

Brad bristled. "I don't know what you're talking about."

"You want my pussy," she said. "Well, you can't have it. It's for your son. If you look at me that way one more time, I'll tell him. I swear that I will. I won't be victimized by a lecherous old man."

Brad tried to keep his cool. It wasn't easy.

"You've got it all wrong, and you're really pissing me off," he said.

She looked at him like he was nothing.

"You get pissed off when you don't get what you want, right? I get that. Boy, do I. My dad's like that too. But I will tell you one thing for sure. I will never let anyone stop me from what I want. I want your Joe, and if you judge me, push me, tell me anything I don't want to hear, I'll make sure you never see him again."

Brad could feel his face warm, but he didn't want to make a scene.

"Where is this coming from? What happened to you to make you such a paranoid mess?"

Brenda's eyes sparkled. She loved the confrontation. It was like having sex in a public place. She had to be quiet. She didn't want anyone but Brad to hear.

"I saw the way you looked at me," she said one more time.

"I didn't look," he said.

"Right now you're thinking about my pussy," she said.

She's nuts.

"I'm not."

Joe appeared in the kitchen.

"What are you two talking about? Looks intense."
He smiled, his disarming Joe-smile.

Brenda wrapped her arms around her boyfriend.
"Your dad was just telling me that he hopes we have
fun at the concert."

"It'll be awesome," Joe said, smiling happily.
"Thanks, Dad. Thanks, Mom. I'm going to take Bren
home now."

"So nice to finally meet you, Brenda," Elise said.

"Yeah, real nice," Brad said.

For the next hour Brad Nevins seethed. He drank a
couple of beers and let the TV flicker some sports coverage in his face, though he really didn't—*couldn't*—
pay attention and would have been at a loss to tell
anyone the sport he was watching, let alone the score.

"Joey," he said, when his son returned, "I need to
talk to you about Brenda."

"Dad," Joe said, "let's not."

"We need to."

Joe pushed back. "No, we don't."

"You're getting into something here that's not quite
right. I'm not sure how to say it."

"Look, Dad, I know what you did. She told me. It's
OK. I understand. I'm not mad at you."

"At me? What for?"

"You know. For taking a look. She's beautiful. It
happens all the time. Whenever we go out, some guy
comes up to her, comes on to her. Tries to get a peek.
She's hot. But I don't care. She's mine."

Brad was dumbfounded. His son was mesmerized by the girl. To fight him would only push him closer to her. Even so, he just couldn't let it go.

"I never took a look," he said. "She practically did the splits in front of me with no panties on."

Joe gave his dad a look.

"Don't go there. She's not like that. She's classy."

"Detective," Brad Nevins said to Kendall Stark, "there was nothing classy about Brenda. She took an incident and twisted it around to serve whatever it was she was after. The concert tickets, I guess. I think that's why she did that. She knew I didn't want to pay for those tickets. I wanted something more practical for his birthday. College money. Elise, on the other hand, just wanted to make our boy happy."

"Moms do that," Kendall said.

Brad looked over at a family portrait on a side table. "Of course they do," he said. "But I'll tell you one thing, and I want you to make a note of this in your notebook. Dads don't hit on their son's girlfriends. They don't. *I* don't."

Kendall fished for a notebook, though she didn't really need one.

"She did it to you, is that what you're saying?" she asked.

He took off his glasses and looked at Kendall. "Yeah," he said. "And I know what you're thinking. You don't think a girl that young could be that manipulative and, honestly, that scary kind of devious? Well I know of one who can. And she's the reason you're sitting right here, right now."

They talked some more about those early days with Brenda hanging around, trying to keep her extra-sharp claws embedded deeply in Joe's back. It was a rocky relationship. By the time Joe had graduated from high school and was college bound, he'd sworn off Brenda for the last time.

"Elise coached me on this. Told me not to drag the girl through the mud because by then I hated the sight of her. Told me that 'love is strange' and we'd best be careful in case she came back into his life."

"Right," Kendall said, "which she did."

"Yeah. Boy, did she ever. Joey was finishing up his degree at the University of Washington when he came home and said not only had they gotten back together, they were going to get married."

"That was a shock, wasn't it?" Kendall asked.

"Damn straight. Completely. We didn't even know they were seeing each other. I guess it's because he knew that I couldn't stand her. From the very beginning, from that very first day, I understood she was going to be a major problem. I just didn't know how big."

"He was in love with her," Kendall said.

He exhaled. "Even better. She said she was pregnant."

"But she wasn't," Kendall said. "Was she?"

"No. I don't think so. After the rush-to-the-church wedding—which we paid for because her family wouldn't have a thing to do with her—she miscarried the so-called baby. Said it happened at home. Didn't even see a doctor. Who does that? Elise was crushed by the loss of her grandbaby. It reopened all the old wounds from losing our two before Joe. I think Brenda played on that. Worked my wife real hard."

Brad offered to make a sandwich for Kendall. She declined, saying it was too much trouble, but she'd be glad to buy him lunch if there was a place nearby.

"Hello Deli is pretty good," he said. "And if we're lucky, Chelsea will be working."

Kendall didn't need a last name to know who Chelsea was.

CHAPTER ELEVEN

The hospital had a lovely view of the river. Elise, Brad, and new father Joe whispered among themselves while Brenda slumbered. A nurse came in and told them that the baby was fine. They'd be able to see her in the preemie care room down the hall in a few minutes.

"Has Mom woken up yet?" the nurse asked.

"Nope. Out like a light," Joe said.

"All right. Let her rest. I'll be back to check on her in a few. Why don't you go down and see your precious newborn?"

Joe and Brad went. Elise stayed behind to keep Brenda company.

Right after the Nevins men disappeared down the corridor, Brenda's eyes fluttered. She looked over at Elise, who was sitting next to her in a rocker.

"Good morning, Momma," Elise said.

Brenda wriggled a little and pushed the button to adjust her bed.

"Childbirth is not," she said. "Let me repeat, *NOT* anything that any woman should ever want to do. It's absolutely horrific. Ugh. So gross. And painful too."

"Kara is beautiful," Elise said. "So tiny, but so beautiful."

"I hope so," Brenda said. "I don't want an ugly baby. No one does. They say all they want is a healthy baby, but that's just what people say when they end up with an ugly little creature." She looked around. "Where's Joe?"

"He and Brad are down seeing your daughter. Are you feeling up to seeing her too? I can get the nurse to help us."

"No. But I would like to see the nurse," she said, pressing the call button.

A beat later, the nurse returned.

"I'll bet you want to see your baby, honey."

"No, I actually don't. I want someone to get my bag. I brought cocoa butter for my stomach. I don't want stretch marks."

When Elise and Brad drove home from the hospital, there was a kind of uneasiness in the air. The baby was beautiful and she was going to be fine—probably released in a couple of days.

"There's something wrong with her," Elise said.

"She's little, honey. She'll grow."

Elise shook her head. "Not Kara. I'm talking about Brenda. There's something really wrong with that girl. All she cared about was her stretch marks and making sure she'd have a perfect beach body when she got out of the hospital. She didn't care one bit about her baby. I'm not exaggerating. You saw it too."

"Yeah, Elise, I did," Brad said.

"She didn't even want to hold Kara. It was almost like I had to force the baby into her arms."

"She might be scared about being a new mom. It's a big change."

"Don't defend her. You and I both know something is up with her. She's cold like. She doesn't want to share the attention with her own baby. It's like Kara is competition for her or something."

"Not everyone is a great mom out of the box. Not everyone is like you, Elise."

She smiled at her husband's compliment. "Thanks for that, but I'm worried."

"Don't be worried. Brenda will adjust. All will be well."

Brad Nevins rested his hands on the table. He stayed silent for a long time. Kendall could see that he was re-living something painful, something so dark that he needed to process. He was a kind, thoughtful man.

"You know what?" he asked.

"What's that, Mr. Nevins?"

"Kara didn't have a chance. Not from the day she was born. Her mother could stand before a mirror holding that baby and only see herself. It's like Kara was never going to be anything other then a means to an end, and we didn't see it. We really blew it."

"You couldn't have known," Kendall said, knowing the futility of such words.

"Elise knew. She told me, and I didn't listen. I should have. I really should have. I had seen Brenda pull all kinds of crap from nearly the first day I met her and somehow, like a cat having kittens, I thought that having a baby would refocus her. You know, get her off the Brenda Train and have her see that the world wasn't all about her, all the time."

CHAPTER TWELVE

Birdy Waterman loathed the idea of looking over another medical examiner's report to ferret out some mistake in the autopsy. While protocol for all such examinations was clear and incontrovertible, examiners brought variables of their own to each forensic examination they'd conduct. Some were better record keepers. Some were more adept at seeing what was right in front of them. Some allowed the distractions of their busy, overworked days to get the better of them.

Birdy sat at her pristine new desk and fanned out the pages printed from the brand-new scanner/printer. There was no doubt what had happened to Joe and Kara Nevins. Kara had been suffocated before the fire and Joe had been drugged with a lethal combination of pills and booze. He'd been alive when the blast occurred. None of that was in dispute. Neither was the reason for the father's and baby's deaths.

Birdy looked up and surveyed her new office. It felt empty. Devoid of any personal touches. Bright white walls and gleaming ribbons of stainless-steel counters outside her interior window. Almost soulless.

Like Brenda Nevins, she thought. *Empty just like her.*

She dialed Kendall's number.

"Your day going any better than mine?" she asked.

"Depends on how bad your day is, Birdy."

"About a six," she said.

"Not good," Kendall said. "How come?"

"I don't know, Kendall. I was looking through the autopsy reports on Joe and Kara Nevins. I can't for the life of me see anything that will help us understand Brenda any better."

"Nothing?"

"No," Birdy said. "How about you?"

"Beyond the fact that she was a conniver who used sex to get what she wanted, no."

"Sounds like my sister," Birdy said.

Kendall laughed. "You don't mean that."

Birdy hesitated, pretending to weigh what Kendall had said. "No. Not really. I guess I didn't mean that."

"How are things with her?" Kendall asked. "With your mom?"

"Not good. Not good with either one of them. I'm going to have to go up there again any day now. It won't be long."

"I'm sorry, Birdy," Kendall said. "I know it doesn't help to have someone tell you that they know what you're going through, but I do. I really do."

"I know. Thank you. I'll get through it. Everyone does," Birdy said, before she changed the subject to something less painful. "Have you caught up with Brenda's mother yet?"

"I've driven by a half dozen times. No sign of her.

I'm going to make one more attempt, then I'm heading home."

"That sounds good."

"Hey, Birdy," Kendall said, before ending the call, "how do you like your new office?"

"Hate it," Birdy said. "Really don't like it. At all."

"But it's state of the art. You've always told me that the county had the crappiest lab equipment that you've ever seen."

"I did, and it does," Birdy said with an audible sigh. "I just feel out of sorts here. It'll pass. I know it will."

CHAPTER THIRTEEN

Brenda Nevins appeared on the screen. She'd adjusted her hair and makeup, possibly because there'd been some unkind remarks about her appearance in the comments section of her last YouTube posting. It was also possible that she'd flitted about the Internet and seen examples of other video blogs—especially those with young women suggesting makeup tips—and thought she could up her game.

"Hi all," she started. "Me again! So much has been happening that I wanted to come back on here and talk about some of the things that people have been saying about me. I want to set the record straight because I know how words hurt. I want to talk about my baby, Kara. Some people are saying mean things about what happened. I just want everyone to know that while I can take responsibility for what I've done in life, I will not have that one hanging on me. Do you know what it's like going to prison and being known as a baby killer? You probably don't. *I do.* It was awful. It was particularly awful because that's not me. I mean, not intentionally me. What happened with Kara was an accident. It really was. I loved that kidlet. I really did. I didn't know she was going to be home. I thought she was at day care," she said as she glanced at her computer screen and lost her train of thought. She'd obviously learned to talk directly to the pinprick of light that was the camera on her laptop, but couldn't help but look at herself.

She stopped recording. When she started up again, her mascara had been reapplied.

"Day care," she said. "That's where I expected my husband to take her. I thought if she were there, she'd be safe. Really I did. I know some people don't quite get that. I've seen the comments online and they are extremely evil. Nasty. I really blame Joe. If he'd done what he was supposed to do, Kara and I would be safe. People would have understood that I'd done what I had to do to save myself and my child."

She stopped and pointed to her eyes. "I don't know if you can see this because no one is helping me shoot this video, but I have a tear coming down right now. People say I don't have feelings, but they are haters and don't want to understand. They want to judge. That bitch Kendall Stark and her pal Birdy Waterman are at the top of the list of judgers. None of what happened to Janie would have happened if they didn't pounce on me for things I didn't do. I was pushed. I needed out. I needed to tell the world that I was innocent and that people should just back the hell off."

She produced a tissue and mopped her eyes. She'd thought of everything.

"Kara was everything to me," Brenda said. "They had it all wrong at the trial. They didn't put on any of the witnesses that could have helped me. My lawyer was a moron. I fell for his idiotic strategy. I fell for him. God, help me. I was stupid and desperate enough to let another man manipulate me. I've been used and abused, but no more. Never, ever again. I'm not going to be the girl who just sits back and pretends to be enjoying whatever some moron is doing to me. Not anymore. From now on, I'm the doer. I'm the one with the control. I'm the one controlling the shots. Baby killer? Don't push me. Don't even try. You'll regret the day you ever hurt me because my hate for the world is the armor that protects me. I'm bulletproof. You'll see."

CHAPTER FOURTEEN

Birdy watched from the sofa where she was reading the front page of the *Port Orchard Independent*. It was the usual—someone complaining that not enough was being done to repair a downtown restaurant that had burned and remained an eyesore, a listing of some potential names for the mayor's spot, and a human-interest story about a llama rancher from Olalla. Elan was down the hall in front of the mirror fiddling with his hair.

"She must be special," she called out, looking up from the paper.

The teenager cocked his head and grinned.

"What do you mean?" he asked.

Birdy smiled back. "Elan, you've been spending more and more time getting ready to go out the door."

He stepped out into the hallway, all white teeth and dark wavy hair. Elan wore a light blue T-shirt with some kind of a graphic design, though it was too abstract for Birdy if she'd been asked to describe it later. Which she hoped she never would. Around his neck was a silver chain that he always wore, but it sparkled more and Birdy wondered if he'd actually polished it. He had on dark dyed jeans. On his feet were black boots that made him look even taller than his 5-10 frame. With his mane of dark hair and his dark eyes, he was undeniably a good-looking kid.

Although, when she thought of it, Birdy could see that the boy had ebbed into a young man in the months since he came to live with her. They were a family, though their connection was fragile at first. The awkwardness of their relationship had dissipated following the disclosure that she was his sister, not his aunt as he'd always believed.

She'd always be Aunt Birdy, however, which made her very, very happy.

"Yes, so yeah, I'm kind of seeing someone," he said. "It isn't a big deal. You've met her already."

Birdy folded the thin, little newspaper and set it on the coffee table as Elan stuffed his hands deep into his pockets and slumped into the chair across from her.

"I have?" she asked, a little surprised. "News to me. Where? When?"

Elan scraped his fingers through his hair again.

He must really like her, she thought.

"That time when you dropped off my lunch, which by the way still ranks as one of the most embarrassing moments ever visited upon a nephew/brother. Like ever."

Every now and then Elan would tease her like that. He'd called her Aunt/Sister Birdy a time or two, though mostly Aunt Birdy, thankfully so, the preferred name he offered when speaking to others about her. She didn't mind. It had been a lot for Birdy, her sister, and Elan to deal with. The woman at the center of the long deception, Birdy's mother, Natalie, had remained inflexible about rectifying that discrepancy on the family tree.

He was her grandson and that was that.

"I thought we agreed to get over that lunch thing," she said, smiling.

Elan fiddled with his phone. "Yeah. Sorry. But really, it isn't just me. Most kids would rather starve than have their mom or aunt or sister come to school with a Tupperware lunch container."

The Tupperware was a total mistake. No doubt about that. Nothing said dork like Tupperware.

"You're avoiding the question," she said. "Who's the girl?"

"Amber Turner," he said, looking right into Birdy's eyes for a flash of recognition.

"I'm sorry? Who?"

Elan sighed. "Aunt Birdy, Amber's the girl that's one level above me, popularity-wise, but we've really been having a good time hanging out. She's the one that you thought had the cool hair."

A flash of recognition came to her.

"The one with the long, red hair?"

He smiled. "Yes, that one!"

"She seemed nice. Pretty too."

Elan made a disgusted face. It was exaggerated and meant to poke at something Birdy had told him one time when they walked down to the café at Whiskey Gulch and talked about life, girls, life and girls.

"As my aunt told me, *pretty* doesn't matter," he said. "Smart does. She's smart too."

Just then Birdy knew she could not love that boy any more if he'd been her own son. He teased her. He listened to her. That meant everything to Birdy.

"She's picking me up tonight," he said. "Going to hang out at the bowling alley. She's not only smart and pretty, Amber has a car, too."

"That makes her a total catch," Birdy said.

Elan grinned. "That's just what I thought."

"Bring her in to say hello," Birdy said.

Elan shoved his phone into his pocket. "We're not serious, Aunt Birdy. We're just hanging out."

"Sure, but you took more time on your hair just now than I do before speaking at a forensics convention."

Twenty minutes later, Birdy was in the kitchen fiddling with the ancient electric oven that had long threatened to give up the ghost and finally had. She surveyed the element to see if she could make do with it for another week. It had been hit or miss on its thermostat settings so much so that she'd relegated all of her cooking to the microwave. And that work-around had brought more than one disaster at mealtime. The broccoli casserole was a complete failure, though Elan insisted that no matter how she cooked it—microwave or conventional oven—it would have been an epic fail.

"No one likes broccoli," he told her. "At least no one I know does."

"I do," she'd answered back. "Do I count?"

"Yeah, I guess."

She heard Amber's car pull up, and Elan called out good-bye.

"Don't be late," Birdy said. "If you are you'll have to eat broccoli casserole every night for a week."

"That's cruel and unusual punishment, and you know it," Elan said as the front door slammed shut.

Birdy considered bowling cruel and unusual punishment, but it was better than hanging around the mall or even worse, on some remote Kitsap beach doing what teenagers do.

Alone and thinking of bowling, the forensic pathologist's thoughts rolled back to a decades-old murder that occurred at the Hi-Joy Bowling Alley at the base of Mile Hill in Port Orchard. It was one of the cold cases she'd added to a file box she called the Bone Box—cases that others had deemed unsolvable. She didn't feel that way. She was certain that a cold case was only a cold case until someone turned up the heat. She kept the Bone Box in her home office.

The victim in the Hi-Joy murder case was a thirty-one-year-old janitor named Jimmy Smith. It was a brutal crime—occurring long ago. Before Birdy was even born. Yet it resonated with her when she first took her job with Kitsap County. It had been the kind of messy case that brings the victim into the autopsy suite piece by piece. Literally. Jimmy had been killed with a hatchet.

Birdy studied those old crime-scene photos, the imagery of the brutality rendered in gorgeous black and white. She saw the force with which the assailant had struck the victim. She could see he'd been right-handed. That he was taller than the victim. That whoever had killed Jimmy had done so in a rage.

At first authorities suspected a robbery gone wrong—but the till was full and Jimmy's wallet hadn't been taken from his jeans pocket. It had long been suspected that the crime scene had been tampered with and that the man behind the murder was the chief of police. The evidence left at the scene was circumstantial at best—a shoe print matched the size of the chief's. Later his wife told investigators that he'd come home with bloody clothes.

It was the way things were handled at the time. The facts about the chief that had emerged over time were troubling. He'd been the only one to secure the evidence, elements of which swiftly went missing. And later, adding credence to the rumors of his potential involvement, he was convicted some years later of sexual assault and sent to prison.

Birdy wondered about two things as she gave up on the dying and possibly dangerous oven. She wondered why it was that her personal frame of reference for every little thing seemed to tie into murder? It was a bowling alley, a place of smelly shoes, rock and roll, and over-foamed beers. That's what most people thought. Not her. A park on a sunny day? That's where a girl had been raped. A shopping center she passed by occasionally in Tacoma? That's where a little boy went missing before a K-9 team found his body in a culvert two miles from the scene.

She couldn't answer exactly why it was that she often thought in those terms. Occupational hazard maybe? Sometimes she tossed it all off as something vague, that the tendency to imprint on things in a dark way was just how she was wired. Somehow she always could see the undertones of the grim under the sparkling veneer of pretty.

And the other question that weighed on her mind just then? Exactly what time did the appliance store open the next morning?

CHAPTER FIFTEEN

Hello Deli was one of those restaurants that prided itself on its use of fresh ingredients. Enormous posters of fruits and vegetables misted with water adorned the walls. Brad Nevins and Kendall Stark sat under an image of an eggplant that had to be at least five feet in length.

"I hear the eggplant is good," Brad said with a smile.

"Really? They have eggplant here?" Kendall smiled back.

A young man named Terry brought them water and ran through the daily specials with the enthusiasm of an undertaker.

"I'll let you chew on that for a minute," he said.

Kendall settled on a soup and salad combination, and Brad decided a meatball sub would hit the spot.

"Chelsea Hyatt owns this place?" Kendall asked.

"Yeah. Though it's not Hyatt anymore. She's had a few husbands. No. 3, I think. Last name is Morgan."

"She and Brenda knew each other quite well," Kendall said.

"Yep. Thick as thieves, those two. Probably accurate in every way."

"Grew up together?" Kendall asked.

"Nope. Supposedly met after Joey and Brenda got married. Brenda was working at the front desk at the Allstate office on 3rd and Chelsea was some kind of an aspiring agent—though she had a clerical job too."

Terry came back, and they ordered.

"Anything to drink?" he asked.

"Water's fine," Kendall said.

"I'll take a beer. Mac and Jack's if you have it on tap."

"We do. Twenty-two ounce or sixteen?"

"Sixteener."

As they waited for their food, Kendall caught a glimpse of Chelsea. She was a ketchup-colored red-head with cat-eye glasses and distressed jeans. It was either the look of a hipster or the look of a woman who raided her aunt's closet.

"Chelsea never testified at trial, did she?" Kendall asked.

Brad shook his head. "Nope. She disappeared right after the murders. Went to St. Croix or some paradise like that. Laid low. Came back here long after the dust settled."

"They really wanted to find her," Kendall said.

"Yeah, they did," Brad said. "But they didn't. And I guess they didn't need her after all. Got a conviction. That's all that mattered."

The food came. The soup looked good. It was a broccoli cheese concoction with freshly made sour-dough croutons for crunch. The salad, however, was a sad affair. All limp iceberg lettuce and carrot shavings. The meatball sub was the superior choice, but not the kind of thing Kendall would eat while conducting an interview about a criminal case. Sauce on the front of her blouse would evoke blood spatter.

And that wouldn't be good at all.

"She didn't do any media, did she?"

He picked at his food. "Chelsea said she had nothing to tell, but I think she was scared about what she knew."

Kendall set down her fork. Good-bye Deli would be a better name for the restaurant.

"How come you think that?" she said.

"She sent us a sympathy card right after Joe and Kara's funeral. She added a note to the standard 'thinking of you at this difficult time' imprint. It said something along the lines of 'I'm personally sorry for your loss.'"

"Personally?"

"Yeah," Brad said, while chomping on his sub. "Weird, huh?"

"Very."

"Elise ran into her after she came back to town. It was here. She opened up this place. Elise said that Chelsea told her that she didn't mean anything by using the word 'personally' and that she'd used it just to emphasize that she was sorry for the pain we were going through."

Interesting.

"Did you know her?" Kendall asked.

"She was in Joey's class. We'd run into her over the years at school events, but no, for someone who was 'personally' sorry, she sure didn't have much of a connection to us."

Kendall finished her soup, which was ten times better than the salad, and got up.

"I'm going to see if she'll talk to me," she said.

"Good luck," he said. "She's pretty buttoned up. Hasn't said a word about Brenda that I know about. Never been in the papers. Or TV. Radio silence, that one."

Chelsea Morgan indeed was a hipster. She had not raided her aunt's closet. As she leaned over the computer behind the counter, a feather tattoo on her shoulder caught the light.

Definitely a hipster's move.

"Chelsea?" Kendall asked.

Chelsea turned around. "Is everything all right with your meal?"

"Oh yes," Kendall said, knowing that there was no point in saying that the salad was terrible. "I wanted to talk to you about something else."

Chelsea looked at the detective warily and logged off the computer. "What can I help you with?" she asked.

Kendall told her who she was and that she was in town to find out more about Brenda Nevins.

Chelsea looked away. "I knew her a long time ago."

"I know," Kendall said. "But you might know something about her that will help us find her."

"No," Chelsea said. "I really wouldn't be able to help."

Kendall persisted. "Why is that?"

"Because I don't want to get involved," Chelsea said, her eyelids fluttering. "I don't want her after me. She's on the run now, and I don't want to give her any reason to make a pit stop in my corner of the world."

"Have you heard from her?" Kendall asked.

"Absolutely not," Chelsea said. "I wouldn't expect to hear from her. She and I are not friends."

"I know you saw her in prison, Chelsea."

Chelsea's face fell. She looked away at Terry, who was taking an order from a couple across the restaurant. Her eyes scraped the rest of Hello Deli and landed on Brad Nevins. She broke her gaze and looked back at Kendall.

"Look," she said, "I can't have this conversation here."

"Where can you talk? When?"

"I can meet you at River Front Park. There are some benches by the wading pool. I'll see you there in an hour."

"All right," Kendall said. "I'll be there."

Kendall returned to the table where Brad Nevins was waiting.

"She's going to meet me," she said. "I'll stop by your place after. Now, how do I get to River Front Park?"

CHAPTER SIXTEEN

The wading pool at River Front Park was bone dry. A sign posted nearby touted that the empty pool was a "sign of progress" and that soon it would be "better than ever." Kendall Stark sat on a bench and watched a man and his black Lab play Frisbee on the browned-out lawn that rolled from the parking lot to the river's edge. She fished her phone out of her purse and texted Steven that she wouldn't be home until late that night.

> Don't wait up. I promised Cody some Cheetos today. Can you give him some? Love you!

She added a heart emoji because she couldn't stop herself from doing so. She'd become obsessed with emojis. It was a habit she knew she had to break. ☺

Chelsea Morgan parked next to Kendall's white SUV. She climbed out of her Jeep and walked across the lot to the bench where Kendall waited.

"I don't want to be involved," Chelsea said.

Kendall looked up. "Then why are you here?"

"Because I can feel the heat being turned up," Chelsea said, sliding into the bench next to Kendall. "I know that she's out there somewhere, and I know that if she's not caught more people will die. And I can't have that . . ." she said, her voice fading into the breeze.

"On you?"

"Something along those lines," she said, her jaw tightening and her fingers nervously playing with her car keys. "I don't think that I had anything to do with what happened."

Kendall watched the Labrador pull the Frisbee from the air, and then turned to face Chelsea. She studied her face. It was lined. Tired. Marked with anguish. She was afraid, that was so evident. She'd felt ambushed in her restaurant, and there was nothing Kendall could do about that. She was on a mission, and Chelsea might have something she needed.

"When those words come out of your mouth it sounds as though you are trying to convince yourself of something," Kendall said.

"Maybe I am," Chelsea said.

Over the next hour, Chelsea talked about her former best friend Brenda Holloway Nevins. She started at the beginning—though it wasn't as early as Kendall had thought. While they went to the same high school, they weren't friends.

"She couldn't be bothered with someone like me," Chelsea said.

"I wasn't an A-lister." She laughed a little. "I mean, I have come a long way, but back then, not so much. Brenda was a climber. She was looking for people she could use to get what she wanted."

"Sounds like you didn't like her at all," Kendall said.

Chelsea looked away, her face reddening. "I didn't. Not at all. But here's the truth. I was kind of starstruck by her. She was so perfect. So beautiful. There was a coldness to her, but it didn't detract from how pretty she was. Sometimes photos look cold, but people still look and admire. You know?"

"Yes, I do," Kendall said. "And sometimes aloofness draws people closer."

Chelsea folded her arms around her chest.

"Right. Right," she said. "The fact that she was unapproachable only made kids want to get closer to her, like they'd cuddled up with a tiger or something and could brag about it. She'd flick away anyone like a bug on her arm. If you didn't interest her in a way she could exploit, she didn't have the time of day for you. Not a second."

"How did Joe fit in to all of this?" Kendall asked.

Chelsea took out a cigarette. Her fingers trembled as she held the lighter to it.

"He was everything she wanted," she said, exhaling. "At the time. He was good-looking. Had an awesome body—especially when she got him to juice up a little—and was smart. Ambitious. She thought that he could lead her out of town and into some fantasy she'd concocted for herself. He was a nice guy, no doubt. But really, he was never going to be her ticket out of here."

"You said you weren't friends in high school," Kendall said. "How'd you reconnect?"

Silence hung in the air. "That's the bad part," Chelsea

said. "That's the part where I feel kind of responsible for what happened."

Chelsea looked over at the river. She glanced around the parking lot. It was as though she wanted to make sure no one was there to hear what she had to say.

That no one being Brenda, of course.

"Why, Chelsea?" Kendall asked. "What was it?"

Chelsea inhaled deeply and tapped her cigarette on the edge of the bench. Ash floated to the pavement.

"The insurance company," she spat out. "That's where I worked. Where we worked. It gave her ideas. I gave her ideas."

Brenda was alone in the employee break room when Chelsea brought in a brown-bag lunch and sat down at the table across from her. Brenda was reading a copy of *Vogue* and picking at the congealed contents of the bottom of her Cup O' Noodles.

"Sad-sack lunches," Brenda said.

"We make a great pair," Chelsea said.

"We really should go out for lunch sometime," Brenda said, getting up and tossing the Styrofoam cup into a trash receptacle with gummed-up hinges.

"I'm on a budget," Chelsea said.

Brenda made a face. "Me too, unfortunately."

"You've got a husband, don't you?" Chelsea asked, though of course she knew the answer.

"I do," Brenda said. "Joe's working things out with his business. *Still*. It'll be a long time before we get anywhere, finances-wise. I just don't know how long it'll take."

"I'll never get anywhere," Chelsea said.

"I know," Brenda said, looking Chelsea over like she was meat in the "Manager's Choice" section of the cooler in the grocery store.

The remark and the look were callous. Ice cold. But Chelsea barely winced. It was if Brenda had given her a double dose of reality. By slamming her, Brenda was offering a great kindness. At least, that's how it felt whenever Brenda put her down. It was true, she was never getting out of there. Not ever.

"The only way I'll ever get a ticket out of town is if I'm the beneficiary on some millionaire's life insurance," Chelsea said, letting her words dangle in the popcorn-scented air of the employee break room.

"Good luck with that, Chelsea," Brenda said.

Chelsea went over to the coffee pot and poured some of the overboiled brew into a cup.

"Thanks for reminding me," she said.

Brenda scraped her nails on a bug bite that was giving her grief. Blood oozed and she watched it bead up, then roll to the tabletop.

"You don't need to be a millionaire to have a lot of money on your head," Brenda said. "Do you?"

Chelsea sat back down. She handed Brenda a white paper coffee filter.

"Blot the blood with this," she said. "And no you don't. You just have to be the beneficiary of someone who's purchased a large policy."

"Like your husband?" Brenda asked.

The wheels were turning.

Brenda soaked up the blood droplet. "Look," she said, unfolding the filter to reveal a kind of inkblot.

"I made a bloody heart," Brenda said.

Chelsea leaned over. It was gross, for sure. But it was a bright red heart made of blood.

"Cool," she said.

Chelsea grew quiet, and Kendall turned toward her on the park bench. Brenda's former coworker and friend refused to look into the detective's eyes. She sat facing the river.

"Something happened after that encounter, didn't it?" Kendall asked.

Chelsea stayed mute.

Kendall pushed a little more. "Don't you want to stop her?"

Still quiet.

"Think of Kara and Joe," the detective said. 'Think of the three latest victims. She's killed five people, Chelsea. Do you want that number to keep growing?"

"She killed six, Detective."

Kendall repeated the number. "Six?"

"Yeah," Chelsea said. "We had a temp working for us at Allstate. Her name was Addie Lane. She was twenty-three. She'd come from Manpower to work on a new filing project that none of us wanted to do."

"What happened to her?" Kendall asked.

Chelsea swallowed hard. "Brenda happened to her."

Chelsea needed to be more direct.

"I don't follow you, Chelsea," Kendall said.

"I don't want to get into trouble. I've been running from this for all of my adult life, and I thought I could just sweep it under the rug. Forget about it. Never even think about it. But I can't do that. I haven't been able to do that. I see Addie's face in my mind's eye every now and then."

Kendall caught her gaze just then. Terror and regret poured from Chelsea's eyes. She reached over and put her arm around the sobbing woman's shoulders, touching her dream-catcher tattoo.

This next question was a tough one to ask anyone. Chelsea was vulnerable. She was scared. What she was telling Kendall would never have been disclosed if Brad hadn't taken her to her deli that day.

"Did you help her?" Kendall asked.

Chelsea bristled, which brought Kendall immediate relief. She liked her and felt sorry for her. Secrets can be an enormous burden. She knew that first hand.

"No," she said. "I didn't know what happened to her until after Addie missed work. I swear I didn't know a damn thing about what Brenda was up to. I would have stopped her if I had."

Kendall believed her. "I'm sure you would have, Chelsea. Tell me what happened. Talk to me. I will help you any way that I can."

Chelsea swiveled over to face Kendall. Her eyes were wet, but she wasn't crying.

"After Addie died," she said, "a bunch of us went to her service. It wasn't like we knew her that well, but Brenda insisted it was the right thing to do. She said that we were her 'office family' and we needed to show support. I had no idea what was going to happen there. Really I didn't."

CHAPTER SEVENTEEN

The service was in a small Methodist church in Tonasket, an apple-growing town not far from the Tri-Cities. Since Addie Lane was young and single, most of the mourners were high school friends and a few older couples who'd known her family when she was growing up. Pictures of the dead girl hung on the memory board posted by the door showed her as a darling little blonde with big blue eyes and pink cheeks.

"A cherub without wings," said one elderly woman standing by the photos.

"She has those wings now," said a man with a sad smile.

Brenda introduced herself and Chelsea, telling the family friends that they were close friends from work.

"She was only a temp," Brenda said, "but we'll never forget her."

Chelsea didn't like the sound of that. Brenda had put emphasis on "temp," like it was some kind of twisted in-joke between the two of them.

After the minister gave a brief eulogy, family members and friends were invited to the front of the church by the altar to share a memory of the young woman gone too soon.

Though Addie's brother, Devon, could barely speak through his grief, his effort was valiant. He talked about his sister and how proud they'd been of her when she was the runner-up for Miss Apple Valley as a senior in high school. He talked about how they used to sneak away from their house to swim in the creek that ran through their family's property. Addie had a pet raccoon named Bandit that she'd raised with a doll's bottle when its mother got hit by a car.

"My sister was the nicest person you ever met. It was a real tragedy what happened to her. A real sad shame," he said.

Brenda got up and made her way to the front of the church. Her eyes were puffy from tears.

"I just want you all to know that we thought of Addie like a sister. She was our kid sister. We all loved her at the company. She was part of our family. She looked like a cherub without wings in those baby pictures by the door. Now she has wings. She has the most beautiful wings ever."

Chelsea lit another cigarette. The light had started to fade, and the river was turning to gunmetal gray. The man with the dog and the Frisbee packed up his SUV and drove away. It was just the two of them along the river then. Not even a gull or crow hovered by the trashcan to disturb them.

"What happened to Addie? How did she die?" Kendall asked.

Chelsea exhaled, and the breeze caught her smoke, pushing it at Kendall.

"Sorry," she said, fanning it away.

"How?" Kendall repeated.

"Car accident. Her brakes failed and she went through the guardrail."

"What makes you think Brenda had anything to do with that? Did she tell you? Did she confess?"

Chelsea leaned back and shook her head. "Brenda was never going to confess. She led me to believe that she cut the brake lines or something like that, but she never directly said so."

"How did she lead you to believe that? That's a pretty big thing for someone to hint at, right?"

"Yes, Detective, it is. She didn't say so. She left a book on automotive repair on her desk the week before Addie's accident. It might even have been the day before. I asked her about it. She said she was having brake problems, and she was going to try to fix her car on her own—to save money. There were a couple things wrong with that."

"Such as?" Kendall asked.

Chelsea shrugged her dream-catcher shoulder. "Well, for one, she was hooking up with a mechanic behind her husband's back, and she was all about trading sex for favors. One time I admired a handbag she had and she told me that some old guy gave it to her because she let him feel her up in the parking lot at the mall."

"Sounds like she was a prostitute," Kendall said.

"Something along those lines. I doubt she took money for what she did. She more or less bartered for things. I really think that if she was having brake problems she'd have given that mechanic of hers a hand job and called it even."

"You don't like her much, do you?" Kendall asked, giving Chelsea a little break from the story she was unwinding.

"I used to," Chelsea said. "I mean, I *adored* her. I thought she was the most amazing person that I'd ever met in my entire life. Sometimes I still think that. She was unencumbered by conscience, and that made it easy for her to really cut loose and live."

Hearing someone admiring another person for not having a conscience was a first for Kendall. She couldn't help but wonder if Chelsea thought Ted Bundy was the epitome of self-direction and self-centered prowess.

Except for the killing part, maybe.

"You said a couple of things tipped you off that she might have been behind Addie's death."

"Right. Later, after Addie died, and the police ruled it was an accident caused by a mechanical failure on her car, I mentioned to Brenda that I thought it was ironic that she'd been researching how to repair faulty brakes just before the crash."

"So you were suspicious, Chelsea? That's why you asked her?"

Chelsea didn't agree with that at all.

"No," she said. "Not at all. I mean, it was possible that I was a little suspicious, you know, subconsciously, I guess. It was her response that made me wonder. She told me she thought it was ironic that she was researching brake-line repairs the day after Addie died— a week before the ruling came down from the police."

"But it wasn't after the accident, was it?"

Chelsea shook her head. "No. I know it was before. I know she was trying to get me to believe it was after, but I remembered that it was Thai food day in the office. A Thursday. I remember the pad thai container on her desk right next to the book. Addie's crash was on a Friday. We were all off on Monday for the holiday. We found out on the Tuesday when we came back. By the following Monday, we'd learned the cause."

Chelsea hesitated over her cigarette pack, but thought better of lighting up another.

"There's something that's really been bothering me," she said.

"I can tell," Kendall said, reaching over to press on Chelsea's hand. "You're shaking."

Chelsea braced herself a little. She pulled back and wrapped her arms around her torso to stem the shudders that undulated through her body. One wave. Another. All the memories that she'd never given voice to had stirred something physical inside.

"I feel sick," she said. "Really, I think I'm going to throw up."

"Get up. Let's walk a little. You'll feel better," Kendall said, standing first and holding out her hand.

Chelsea stood and they walked toward the river's edge.

"I think I gave her the idea to kill Addie and to kill her husband and daughter. I think I did." She bent over and coughed, but didn't vomit. It was as though she wanted to purge her body of all that she'd been talking about, all that she'd held inside for so long.

"You didn't," Kendall said.

Chelsea held her ground. "I did," she said, looking

up at Kendall. "I told her about how insurance companies don't really investigate accidents. It didn't matter how much money was on the line. If the cops say it was an accident—and murder and arson are considered accidents—then they'll just pay up. It costs too much money to do a full-on investigation if the cops don't call it a homicide."

"But she didn't collect on Addie's death."

Chelsea looked Kendall in the eye. "She did," she said. "At least I think she did. She drove up in a new Miata three weeks later. She didn't have that kind of money. None of us did. She told me that an aunt had left her some cash, but she'd never mentioned any rich aunt before."

"You would have known if she'd collected. You worked for the insurance company and you processed claims, right?"

"Yes, of course," Chelsea said. "But that's just the thing. Maybe it's different now, but back then there was no cross-referencing between insurance companies. No automatic reporting to the authorities."

This was a lot to take in. The idea that Brenda was a serial killer was nothing new, yet it had long been believed by the authorities that her first kills had been her husband and daughter.

"You're suspicious," Kendall said, "but you don't know, and you shouldn't put it on yourself, Chelsea."

"One time when Brenda was routing the mail in the office I saw a letter from one of our company's competitors addressed to Addie. Brenda picked it out of the stack and said something about how Addie was trying to get a job there and she'd take care of it. She said it was Addie's dream job. That's so wrong. Insurance is no one's dream job."

"Did you see what was in the letter?" Kendall asked.

Chelsea gulped. "Yeah, I did. It was an application form."

CHAPTER EIGHTEEN

Elan sat on the nearly deserted bleachers overlooking South Kitsap High School's athletic field. He'd just completed four miles on the South Kitsap track, trying to keep his head on the run, instead of on Amber Turner. It was no easy task.

There was something very special about her. She was a little beyond his reach. Maybe a lot.

He didn't have the kind of confidence that some of the guys had. He'd never really had a serious girlfriend. Never really had a girlfriend at all. The last time he took a girl anywhere was on the reservation, when he squired his dumpy cousin, Millie-Ann, to a school dance. It was a mercy date for Millie-Ann, but it felt a little that way for him too. Maybe a practice run for when he had the nerve to ask out a girl.

It wasn't that he hadn't wanted to get a girlfriend; he just hadn't been able to summon up the nerve. He'd been unsure about how his Native American heritage would play in a small, almost completely white, town like Port Orchard. He wondered if the fact that he'd been living with his Aunt Birdy would keep him out of the hunt for a girl—who wants to hang out with some guy whose aunt cuts up dead people all day?

Amber Turner didn't seem to mind any of that in the least. She'd gone through all her school years in South Kitsap. She seemed bored with the same old, same old. She wanted to know what it was like living on the reservation (*not great, but not terrible either*), how it was living with a forensic pathologist (*she's nice, but a little bit of a control freak*) and if he'd been to any of his aunt's autopsies (*God, no*).

It was as though he'd been plucked from obscurity; from the anonymity of no longer being the new kid at a very big high school, to a guy with a girlfriend.

"Want to hang out at my place?" he asked when Amber found him on the bleachers. "My aunt's out running errands or something."

She smiled. "Sure. I'll drive."

"That's good, because I don't have a car."

"How'd you get here?" she asked.

"I ran," he said.

When he saw his aunt pull up in her familiar Prius, Elan jumped up and went outside to help her unload groceries.

"Amber's here," he said.

Birdy stooped to pick up one of her reusable shopping bags from the backseat. She shifted it into Elan's outstretched arms.

"Really?" she said, with mock seriousness. "Should I leave?"

Elan scooped up a second bag of groceries. "You're kidding, right?" he asked.

She shut the car door with her hip. "Yes. Kidding, Elan. And really, I'm not so sure it's a good idea to be alone with a girl."

"Nothing's happening."

"Well if it does . . ."

"We're not having this conversation," he said. "You know I'm not a virgin, Aunt Birdy."

Birdy looked right at him. "I didn't need to know that, Elan."

"Well, I don't care," he said. "I just didn't want you to think I was some loser and that I didn't know what I was doing."

"Like you said," Birdy sighed. "We're not having this conversation."

Once they got inside, Amber got up from the camel-back sofa where she and Elan had been watching TV. A white-on-white pillow with a starfish applique fell to the floor and the teen scooped it up.

"Hi again, Dr. Waterman," she said.

"Feel free to call me Birdy," she said. "Join us for dinner? I'm making chicken tacos."

Elan looked over at Amber. "They're actually pretty good."

Amber pushed her long red hair back over her shoulders. "Can't," she said. "I'm having dinner with my dad."

"I didn't know your dad was around," Elan said, surprised. "You mean your dad-dad?"

Amber continued to fuss with her hair. "Yeah," she said. "He's here for a few days. Selling some property or something."

"Cool," Elan said.

"Yeah," Amber went on. "I'm lucky. He's the parent that I wish got custody when I was up for grabs. When my parents split, the judge insisted that as a girl I'd be better off with my mom. I guess that would have been true if she hadn't married Karl."

Birdy, who had disappeared into the kitchen, thought about Elan and how he was processing what Amber was saying.

He'd never been up for grabs. But he'd always been loved.

After Amber and Elan had their long good-bye out by her car, Elan appeared in the kitchen and picked up the cutting board and a knife. Without saying anything, he started chopping a yellow onion.

"You okay?" Birdy asked.

He kept chopping. "Fine, I guess."

Something is wrong.

"What is it, Elan?" she said, trying not to be too pushy.

"I don't know," he said, looking up. "I just like her. A lot. I feel like she kind of needs me, and I'm not sure I can help her."

"Help her with what?" Birdy asked.

"Typical stuff, I guess. She hates her stepdad and she feels like her new sister gets all the attention."

Birdy placed the chicken in a shallow pan ready for roasting in the almost-dead oven, then pulled a bunch of cilantro from a plastic bag in the refrigerator.

"That's a hard one," she said, handing the cilantro to Elan. "Parents sometimes favor one child over another and, yes, it does complicate things and cause a world of hurt feelings."

Elan knew that Aunt Birdy was talking about herself as much as Amber. Her own history with her mother had been the subject of tribal and family gossip for years.

"I know you get it, Aunt Birdy. It just sucks, that's all."

She couldn't disagree.

It really does suck.

CHAPTER NINETEEN

Kendall Stark looked at the time. She knew she would not be able to make the drive over the mountains and arrive home until very late. She texted Steven that she'd be staying overnight and would call him from her motel. Next, she dialed Birdy's number to let her know what Chelsea had told her.

"In her mind she's an accomplice to Addie's murder," Kendall said.

"The specter of guilt sometimes makes even the most innocent feel responsible for things they didn't do," Birdy said.

"Right," Kendall said. "I doubt that Chelsea even planted the seed of the idea. And if she did, it was completely inadvertent."

"Do you feel like you're getting a better handle on who Brenda is?"

Kendall knew what Birdy was after. The way to find Brenda and capture her was to dig in deep. Turn every furrow of her psyche. Understand how it was that a perfect baby had transformed into something so undeniably evil. So much had been written about Brenda.

So many TV producers and talking heads had weighed in on the woman who would stop at nothing to get what she wanted.

Stop at nothing to get what she wanted. The phrase rolled around in Kendall's mind. It was hackneyed. It was corny.

It was Brenda.

"Not sure," Kendall said. "It's hard to grasp where this need for the spotlight and the need to kill merged. Some killers like attention, don't get me wrong. But Brenda is more than that."

"She craves it, Kendall," Birdy said.

"Yes," Kendall said. "She sees herself as worthy of the spotlight without seeing that she's in its glow for all the wrong reasons."

"Small-town girl," Birdy said. "Pretty. Maybe abused. Sees her way out in living inside the TV or on the movie screen."

"Some people are famous simply for being famous," Kendall said.

Kendall parked her SUV in front of the Mountain View Motel.

"I'm going to check in. I will call you tomorrow before I head home."

"Look for bedbugs," Birdy said.

Kendall smiled. "That's a creepy good-bye."

"Just saying."

The Mountain View Motel was a relic that boasted a "major remodel." It looked as though most of the money had been spent on the front desk, where granite tiles fronted the counter and a new coffee bar area had been installed for "courtesy" coffee, 5 to 9 A.M. Kendall checked in and reparked her car in front of her room on the first floor. Her feet were killing her. Never, she thought, wear new shoes on a day with back-to-back interviews. She looked over the menu card for local restaurants that delivered and was about to turn on a bath to soak her feet, when someone knocked on the door.

It was Chelsea. She appeared slightly drunk. Her hair was halfway tucked into her jacket and halfway out.

"I was driving by, and I saw your car," she said.

"Should you be driving?" Kendall asked her.

"Look, don't judge me," Chelsea said. "I've had a couple, yes. But I'm not drunk."

"You need coffee," Kendall said.

"No, I don't," Chelsea said. "I need to get out of this town. But I can't, can I? I never can. I'm stuck here. Brenda got out."

"She's not exactly a role model, Chelsea. Nor should she be."

Chelsea stood in the doorway, bracing herself against the jamb. "The murders," she said, "I know."

"You aren't here just because you were driving by?" Kendall asked.

"I wanted to talk some more," she said.

"Let me take you home. You can get your car in the morning."

"I can drive, Detective," Brenda's friend said, nearly slumping to the floor. "How do you think I got here?"

Kendall helped her up. "You got here because you were lucky. I'll drive you home so you and others on the road are safe."

"Can we have a drink first?" Chelsea asked.

"You've had enough, Chelsea."

"You can never have enough."

"You can," Kendall said. "And you have."

Kendall walked Chelsea to her car to get her purse. A minute later, they were in Kendall's SUV heading toward Chelsea's townhome on Morning Glory Ave.

"One thing I don't get," Kendall said, though she was unsure how much Chelsea could actually process— her head was bobbing up and down. Her neck was a Slinky. Her eyes were blue marbles.

"Get who?" Chelsea said, cracking the window and letting the evening air flow over her.

"*What*," Kendall said. "It's a what. What I don't understand is Brenda's need for the spotlight. It's psychotic."

"Cheerleaders. Psychotic."

"Huh?" Kendall said, looking at Chelsea and hoping she didn't vomit in her car.

"When we were in high school, Brenda was borderline cool. She was pretty enough, but her personality wasn't really outgoing. She was *this close* to becoming something amazing, but she didn't quite get there. She ran for cheerleader and didn't make it. That crushed her. I didn't know her well then, but something happened to her after that."

"Something like what?" Kendall asked, as the lights of the car behind them filled the space of the SUV.

Chelsea didn't answer. Her marble eyes rolled some more. Her Slinky neck stretched for the open window.

"Are you sick?" Kendall asked.

"I'm okay," Chelsea slurred, turning to face the driver.

"Feel like your car needs a tune-up or something. Rides really rough."

The car was fine. It was the passenger that was a mess.

"When she didn't get on the squad that time, she turned into a mega bitch. She would ice out people that couldn't help her get to wherever she wanted to go. She was so fixated on what those other girls had and what she didn't have. I wasn't surprised when I read somewhere that she'd gotten a boob job. She thought that was part of her problem."

Kendall parked and retrieved Chelsea from the passenger seat. She led her to the door. Chelsea tried to insert her key, but wasn't having an easy time of it.

"Let me," Kendall said, turning the key in the lock.

"When we were working at the insurance company, she told me one time that she was going to be famous one day. Her exact line was 'One way or another, I'll show those bitches that I'm better than the bunch of them.'"

CHAPTER TWENTY

Chelsea's town house on the outskirts of town was decorated with vintage and modern style that left no room for clutter. Most of the furnishings were black with a few pops of tangerine here and there. It looked elegant. Halloween chic, Kendall thought as she surveyed the living room, bracing Chelsea from slumping to the aggregate floor of the entryway. After shutting the door, she led Chelsea to a black leather chair and made her way to the kitchen to get her something to drink.

The refrigerator was stocked with fruits, vegetables, and diet soda. No juice. Kendall retrieved a glass and filled it while she looked through the kitchen window to a grove of weeping redwoods that the landscaper must have thought were beautiful. To Kendall the hunched-over trees looked sad.

Weeping indeed, she thought.

"Drink this," she said, handing Chelsea a glass of tap water. "Lots of water will help."

Chelsea murmured a thank-you, and her eyes fluttered a little as she drank. "You've done this too."

"Not since college," Kendall said, "but yes. I've had

my moments too. Just about everyone has. You must never get behind the wheel like this again. Promise me? It isn't about you. It's about harming someone else."

"Understood," Chelsea said, the word slurred. "Thanks for bringing me home."

"You're welcome. I'm glad you're safe now."

Chelsea stared up at Kendall. "Am I?"

"What?" Kendall asked.

"Safe?"

"I think so, Chelsea. Why wouldn't you be?"

Chelsea fiddled with the rim of her now-empty water glass. "Brenda thrives on revenge," she said, "in case you haven't noticed."

It was the kind of understatement that didn't need a comment of any kind. Brenda thrived on all kinds of evil—rage, jealousy, and envy. The list was long and complicated.

Thriving on revenge was so right. Chelsea knew it in her bones. Kendall could see it. It was as if Brenda knew how to unravel the good in anyone and spin a noose with it.

"You're safe," she repeated.

"Says you," Chelsea said, her tone accusing. "You don't know her. You might think you do, but you don't. You couldn't. Her kind of abnormality when it comes to how she uses and abuses people . . . is almost like she's one of those alien body snatchers or something. You know?"

"I think so," Kendall said, retreating back to the kitchen to get more water. Chelsea was going to have the mother of all hangovers in the morning. When she returned, water in hand, Brenda's pal from the insurance company was slumped a little lower in the chair.

"She won't harm you, Chelsea. She doesn't know that I've talked to you. She won't ever know."

"Like I told you, you don't know Brenda," she said, beginning to drift off.

"You're right," Kendall answered. "I don't know her. That's why I'm here. If you were so afraid of her, Chelsea, why did you visit her in prison?"

"I went once. I only went because I had to."

"Had to? But why?"

"Because she told me to. You don't say no to her. You just don't."

"What does she have on you?"

Chelsea looked away.

"Is it Addie?"

Chelsea stayed mute and then, after a very long time, indicated her high school yearbook, over on the shelf by the TV. Kendall went to get it.

"We were pretty happy back then," she said, flipping through the pages. "At least I was."

Kendall watched as Chelsea Morgan opened a page showing the cheerleading squad. There were eight girls, four in the back, four in front. The image was in black and white. Someone had taken a thick red pen and colored an X through four of them. Underneath the photograph someone with loopy, girlish handwriting had written:

Four little bitches in a row.

"Brenda?" Kendall asked.

Chelsea looked at Kendall. "Yeah. She hated those girls more than anything."

"She hated a lot of people," Kendall said. "There are eight girls pictured here, why those four?"

"Terry because her dad always bought her a new car. Stephanie because her mom was beautiful and nice to everyone. I can't remember why she hated the other two." She peered back into the yearbook. "Anna," she said, tapping her fingertip on a girl who's face had been crossed out, "not sure, but it could be that she was straight A's. We all kind of hated that she was both pretty and smart. I don't recall anything about Charlotte. She died in a boating accident the year we graduated."

Kendall thought to ask Chelsea if Brenda had gone boating with Charlotte, but she was starting to fall asleep.

"Kendall," Chelsea said, using her first name for the first time, "there is something else that I haven't told you."

"And what's that?" Kendall asked, hoping it was about Charlotte and the boating accident.

It wasn't.

"It's really hard to talk about. It's something I never talk about. It's something that is so terrible, not for what I did. I'm fine with that part of it. It's terrible for who I did it with. I regret it. I really, really do."

"Tell me," Kendall said.

Chelsea looked away.

"Brenda and I were more than friends—we were lovers," she said, her eyes still focused on something across the room. Or maybe focused on nothing at all. "That overstates it a little," she said. "Brenda didn't know how to love anyone."

The disclosure startled Kendall a little.

"I didn't know," she said.

"I'm not gay," Chelsea said, "if that's what you're thinking. I took a walk on the wild side with Brenda in the back room at the insurance company. At the Mountain View Motel too. I think we did it in the very room you're staying in." She raised her gaze to meet Kendall's blue eyes, now full of concern.

"Isn't that weird?" Chelsea asked, looking for confirmation where she was hoping to find it.

"Weird," Kendall repeated. "I thought she was in love with Joe? I thought she had the mechanic on the side?"

Chelsea's eyes were hooded. It was like she'd made some big reveal and needed to rest up. She was ready to fall asleep. Kendall pulled a throw from the back of the sofa on the other side of the room and covered her.

"She did," Chelsea said. "With Brenda we were all on the side, like the salad bar at Sizzler. Brenda knew the power of attention and the power that came from an intimate encounter. She knew that if she could get someone skin-to-skin close, she could get them to do whatever she wanted. Remember that. That's how she operates. Skin to skin."

"When did you hear from her last?"

No answer.

"Chelsea?"

She was asleep. The mother in Kendall took over, and she pulled the blanket over Chelsea's feet so she'd be warm. Satisfied, she looked around the town house. Nothing out of place. Classy. Bland almost. Among the empty, shiny spaces, she noticed one item of interest—a magazine with Brenda's picture on the cover peeked out from under a book on Cayman Island Style.

Chelsea was no longer one of Brenda's lovers, but she'd never forgotten her. No matter how far she'd run away. No matter how guilty she'd felt for whatever it was they'd done at the insurance company. No matter for any of it. Brenda had her talons hooked into Chelsea.

And she would never let go.

Neither, it seemed, would Chelsea.

Kendall wrote a note that she was taking the yearbook and let herself out.

Kendall looked down at her phone as another alert came. Brenda Nevins was nothing if not prolific. She pressed the play button for Brenda's latest video missive.

Brenda was fiddling with something next to the keyboard when the camera started recording. She looked up and faced the little lens head-on.

"Sorry," she said, "I'm still getting the hang of this. Don't get me wrong, I adore technology of any kind. So many tools available now to find out where people are, what they are doing and, of course, if they've been loyal to me. I'm all about loyalty. Why shouldn't I be?"

She took a sip of water from a clear plastic bottle.

"Talking makes me thirsty," she said. "I don't know how those morons on TV can do a newscast without stopping to take a sip of something. Vodka would be good. Even gin. Anyway, back to what I was saying about loyalty. It's everything to me. I don't have time for people who can't grasp that concept. Have you ever been burned by someone so weak? Not literally burned, of course," she said, allowing an ironic smile on her face. "I could have been. By Janie."

She sipped more water.

"Look," she said, "I got my freedom from that one, so I can't completely be disgusted by her. She was a little bit of a worm, though. A sad little worm. Sad little worms have their purpose, but in the long run, they end up as bait on a hook. Bait for something bigger, better than they are."

Brenda fiddled with a gold chain around her neck.

"Janie gave this to me before I killed her. Ooops, I said it. Do you still love me? Do you still want to make love to me? I know you do. You like my honesty. You adore the way I'm direct. That's my power. At least for some of you. For others, it's my tits. Whatever floats your boat. I don't care."

More water.

"Back to Janie . . . from the second I saw her, I knew she was an easy target. She's like the weak antelope in the herd roaming the African savannah. I was the lioness. I could see by the way she dealt with others that she was weak, scared. That she was unsure. I really like it when people are unsure. It just makes me more confident. Lifts me. I had hopes for Janie. I really, really did. I expected that she'd be able to do what I needed done before I had to kill her. I'm an outgoing person. I gravitate toward action and sparkle. She didn't have much of that, but I wrongly assumed she'd be trainable and loyal."

Another sip.

"No kidding, talking so much is hard to do! I'd never make it as an auctioneer or some dimwit on TV doing an infomercial. They just keep going and going.

Now here's the thing about Janie. She was repressed. Unhappy. She needed a human connection. Not only could I see that, I could actually *feel* it. I have that ability. I think I always have."

Brenda took a breath, her eyes lingering on the camera's lens. "Just a second. I have something to show you." Her face disappeared from view, and she held up a picture of a man and a teenage boy.

"This is Janie's family. Or *was*, I guess past tense applies, right? She was willing to give them up forever to lie in my bed with my arms around her for the rest of our lives. She told me over and over that while she loved them intellectually, she could never feel for them the way she felt for me. She told me my touch was like an electric current running through her body."

Her tone changed from the cheerful blogger to vindictive. She was a metronome of emotions. Back and forth. Dark, then light. Now very, very dark.

"She told me all of that, then she crossed me. She wanted out. She wanted to go back to those losers. She told me that she'd felt uneasy about what we were doing. Uneasy? Who in the hell says that? Life is uneasy. If it isn't, then it is completely boring. She said—and get this—that if she had met me in another life that things would be different. Another life? This is the only life we have. She made it so easy for me to kill her. Not uneasy. Not uneasy at all."

With that, the recording stopped. Brenda had said what she'd wanted to stay.

Or at least some of it.

CHAPTER TWENTY-ONE

Kent McGrew's life in the Tri-Cities was over. He'd not only unwittingly contributed to the events that set a killing in motion, but he'd committed fraud in doing so.

Kent made a plea deal with the prosecutors in exchange for his testimony against Brenda at trial, thereby avoiding a prison sentence of his own. Before he disappeared off the face of the earth, a visibly shaken Kent McGrew gave one interview to a local reporter for the *Tri-City Herald*. The paper's photographer took a shot of him standing in front of his car with the courthouse looming behind him.

"I know what people think of me now," he said after the verdict. "They call me the horny insurance guy or some idiot who fell for a killer. I will have to own up to what I did. I honestly knew better at the time. No child should have a big price tag on their heads like Kara Nevins did. I felt wrong about it. I just kind of fell for Brenda's story and, honestly, fell for her. She told me her husband was abusing her, and that if she didn't show him that there was some money coming if Kara died, he'd make her get an abortion. I don't believe in abortion. I think abortion is murder."

As Birdy saw it, McGrew's comments to the newspaper provided the true indicator of Brenda's supreme cleverness. She'd been extremely skilled at selecting the people she could use. Her husband. Her day care provider. Her insurance man. Her friends at work. She gravitated toward those who exhibited any kind of vulnerabilities or weakness that she could readily exploit.

On the surface, one might have thought that Brenda had targeted Kent because, as an older man with waning physical charms of his own, he'd be unable to resist the wiles of a young, beautiful woman. That would be a poor assumption. Kent McGrew was more than merely a beer-bellied guy caught up in the last gasp of lust. Brenda saw something else. She preyed on something he held very deep inside, something that mattered more to him than her beguiling attention. She was like a hornet at a picnic, swirling, sampling. His stance on abortion was the red meat that brought her running.

On the rear window of his always-sparkling clean car was the familiar image of a baby in vitro, a Right to Life decal.

That decal invited the hornet to land.

Kendall Stark stood outside what had once been Brenda and Joe Nevins's home. It had been burned by the fire she'd set to cover her tracks, and battered by the elements and by kids who'd come there to test the limits of their dares and endurance. The front windows had been long since broken and the front door had the distinct marks of an ax. Or possibly a large knife. Of all the houses on Stoneway Drive, the place was a blackened tooth in what had once been a very pretty smile.

"Please leave," a woman's voice called over to her from behind an unruly laurel hedge.

"Hello?" Kendall called back.

"Get on, now," the voice called out, this time with a harsher, more demanding tone. "Nothing to see here."

"I'm an investigator working on the Nevins case," Kendall said, inching toward the sound of the voice.

"Everyone's an investigator," the woman said.

"My name is Kendall Stark. I'm with the Kitsap County Sheriff's Office."

"Then you have lots of problems," the woman said, rustling a branch at the edge of the emerald, leafy wall.

"I can't see you," Kendall said. "Can you come out?"

Jess Conway pushed her way through a gap in the green. She was a tall, thin woman with slightly hunched shoulders and unruly strands of gray hair that she'd unsuccessfully tried to tame with a headband. She wore jeans, white tennis shoes, and a pale pink pullover. A gold cross on a chain dangled from her slender, weathered neck. She told Kendall that she hadn't meant to be rude.

"Living next door to this place has made me into something I no longer recognize," she said.

It was a strange remark. Kendall noticed the resignation in the older woman's voice.

"How do you mean?" she asked.

"Small things. Big things. You think you will find her?" she asked, though unwilling to wait for a reply. "If you don't, she'll just do more of the same. She's got one speed, that one. Always has, I bet. That's why I don't try to think about her too much. But then people like you come by, and I'm back there with her in my head again."

"I'm sure it's hard," Kendall said.

The older woman sighed. "Shooting a basket from mid-court is hard," Jess said. "And I did that to great success in my day. Forgetting what happened here . . . well, that's damn near impossible."

Kendall followed Jess's eyes and she scanned the house.

"Wish the fire department had let it burn down. That night I worried about my apple trees. If I could do it all over, I'd have waited to call 911. I mean, what was the point of calling for help anyway? They were dead."

"You were there that night?" Kendall asked. "I didn't see you on the witness list."

"Dick testified. That's my husband. He's watching TV now. We were both home when she came running over."

CHAPTER TWENTY-TWO

It had all happened so fast. A thundershower had pummeled the houses along Stoneway Drive with a relentless force that rattled the windows facing the street, away from the ravine and greenbelt that the homes backed up to. The storm's cadence was so regular that it nearly seemed mechanical, predictable. One punch to the earth after the next was followed by a torrent of rain that filled the gutters and sent a cascade to flood the driveways. The illuminated dial of the clock next to the Conways' bedside indicated two minutes before midnight when the couple was awakened by what they first thought was the mother of all thunderbolts.

"That was a close one," Dick said, lifting his sleepy head and nuzzling his wife.

"It felt almost like an earthquake," Jess answered.

"More like a bomb," her husband said.

A minute or so later, they heard the beating of a fist against their front door. Next, a series of urgent rings from the doorbell propelled them down the hall.

"What the hell?" Dick said, putting on a robe. Jess,

in her nearly floor-length nightgown, followed him as he flicked on the front porch light.

Brenda Nevins stood outside. She was wearing only a bra and panties. Her hair was wet, and she was flailing around trying to get their attention. Even though their eyes locked, she kept pounding on the door and screaming for help.

"Oh, my God," Jess said, scooping up the young woman and pulling her inside.

Dick looked behind her. Flames shot up into the sky from the back side of the house. "Brenda, what happened?" he asked, holding her by the shoulders.

Brenda's teeth were chattering, and she was shaking in a way that indicated shock.

"Explosion," she said, her voice rising to a level louder than she'd used at the front door. "I don't know. God, I don't know. Maybe we were struck by lightning."

Jess hurried for a blanket and wrapped it around Brenda's shoulders. The poor girl was a mess.

"Joe? Kara?" She said. "Where are they?"

"Inside. Call 911," Brenda said, catching her breath a little and pulling the blanket tighter around her lithe frame. "Joe and Kara are still inside. Our house is on fire! Oh God, no! This can't be happening to me."

Dick dialed 911. The transcript of the call was presented at Brenda's trial.

"Our neighbor's house was hit by lightning!" he said so quickly that the operator asked him to slow down. "The house is 921 Stoneway Drive. The family's name is Nevins. The wife got out. Baby and husband are trapped inside. The house is on fire! Can you get someone out here right away?"

Dick ran over to the burning house and tried to get inside, but it was engulfed at the entryway. He circled around the perimeter, trying to find another way in, but the back door was locked. He pushed his shoulder against the door as hard as he could, but he couldn't budge it. He considered using the hose to try to do something. *Anything!* Finally the sirens cut through the rain.

Jess and Brenda stood on the other side of a laurel hedge that the Conways had just planted. Brenda was screaming something, and Jess was trying to stop her as she appeared to lunge toward the burning house.

"It bothered me right then and there, Detective," Jess said, her eyes now riveted to Kendall's, "when she said it was happening to her. *Happening to her?* Her baby and her husband were the ones that it was happening to. She got out. Nothing was happening to *her*."

Jess tucked some loose strands of her wispy hair behind her ear. Her eyes had puddled.

"Remembering things like this isn't easy," Kendall said.

"That's right," Jess said. "And it has been seven years, and you'd think that the passage of time might make it easier, but it hasn't. That house is a daily reminder. No matter how tall I grow that hedge I'll never get it out of sight, out of mind."

"Why hasn't someone either fixed it or tore it down?"

"Insurance companies," Jess Conway answered. "They're part of the problem. Fighting over the money they'd paid out, refusing to do right by those of us who live here. The state's no better. No one wants to take responsibility for what happened, though they had their hands in it."

"Brenda's hands more than others," Kendall said. "You know that, don't you?"

Jess pulled some birdseed from her pocket and scattered it. "Right," she said. "She did it. But if there hadn't been any money in it for her, then she wouldn't have. If the insurance companies hadn't sold her those policies . . . if the state had some kind of regulations to stop people from buying insurance on their children . . . then maybe both Joe and Kara would still be alive."

Kara's name stuck in Jess's throat.

"You loved that little one," Kendall said.

Jess dabbed at her eyes with the sleeve of her pink pullover.

"I did," she said, trying not to full-on cry. "I really did. I babysat her the first week she was home from the hospital. Brenda said her own mother wasn't 'the grandmotherly' type, and she knew that I didn't have any grandkids."

"You babysat Kara? Did Brenda go right back to work?"

Two finches landed and started eating the seed she'd scattered.

"No," she said, watching the birds. "She and Joe went to Hawaii for ten days. I should have known something was off with her then. Really, going to Hawaii on a vacation after you have your first baby? Who does that?"

Kendall wasn't tracking the story.

"I don't understand, Ms. Conway."

"Jess," she said. "Jess, please, call me Jess."

"Ten days in Hawaii right after she had Kara?"

Jess blinked at the memory. "Right," she said. "I know. What a red flag. She told me that she needed to pull herself together and that she needed some bikini time in the sun."

"But she just had a baby," Kendall said. "I sure didn't feel like bikini time after delivery."

"Most women wouldn't. Kara was seven weeks early. A preemie. I'd never seen a tinier baby. Now with everything I know, I think Brenda took something or did something to induce labor early. She wanted to be like one of those Hollywood stars that has a four-pounder and hits the runway to let everyone comment about how amazing their bodies look after delivery."

Jess walked Kendall over to her white SUV.

"She is smart and stupid at the same time," Jess said as they stood there, looking back at the house. "Smart might not be the right word. Maybe devious is a closer fit."

Kendall liked Jess Conway. Brenda's kind of evil touched her, but it hadn't blinded her. The woman showed more resignation than hate. That was rare. Most of the people she'd met who'd been that close to murder couldn't be analytical, only emotional.

"Stupid?" Kendall asked.

"Maybe that isn't so fair either," Jess answered, thinking about it. "She just isn't able to see herself the way others do. She has this inflated opinion about her beauty, her body, her brains, and that no one could ever compare to her. For a long time after the fire, I wondered about why she showed up half naked on our doorstep. It hadn't been because she was that way when the explosion took down the back end of the house. Brenda's more calculating."

Kendall fished for her car keys. "I never thought about it until now, but I guess I have my own theory. What's yours?" she asked.

"Distraction," Jess Conway said. "Brenda used her body to keep eyes on her so that fire investigators and the police would miss other things as they trod over the evidence and extinguished the fire. I swear that when she was sitting on the back of the fire truck sobbing her eyes out while a fireman comforted her, she let that blanket we gave her fall away."

That sounded like the Brenda her former father-in-law described.

"She's a class-A manipulator, but that could have been an accident," Kendall said as she unlocked her car door and prepared to get behind the wheel.

"Right, of course," Jess said, "if that's all she did."

Kendall studied Jess's eyes. There was more.

"Tell me," she said.

"Remember how I told you she came to our house in her bra and panties that night? When she dropped her blanket, you know, *accidentally*, guess what?"

"What?" Kendall asked.

Jess studied Kendall's face. She and her husband had told this story several times before, and she enjoyed the reaction.

"She was completely naked," Jess said, letting the words settle in. "Not *half*. All the way."

Kendall hadn't heard that. It was not in the police report or mentioned during trial.

"Maybe she took her underwear off because it was soaked from the storm?" Kendall asked. "She was uncomfortable, maybe."

Jess threw out more birdseed. "For anyone else, I'd

say that's possible," she said. "Not for her. She was right there, completely naked, pointing to what she claimed to be a burn on her shoulder. There was no burn on her. I doubt she was even in the house when she blew it up. Brenda wouldn't risk her body on anything. She was all about Brenda 24-7. Joe and Kara never had a chance. Wish we'd have known that back then. A lot of good it does any of us now."

As Kendall Stark drove away from Stoneway Drive, the tall woman with the heavy burden shrank, then disappeared in the rearview mirror. Jess Conway had shared some things about Brenda Nevins that stunned Kendall as much as the fact that Brenda was a cold-blooded killer.

Kendall tried to imagine a woman who had no connection whatsoever with her baby. She'd loved Cody from the second she'd heard his heartbeat for the very first time. Every second since then had been a building block on which even more love could be assembled. It was unending and growing all the time. When she was away from him, her heart ached for the sound of his voice, the touch of his skin against her cheek.

Brenda hadn't been wired that way at all, and it was possible that it was generational. Nothing would have stopped her own mother from being at the hospital the second that he was born. Cody went from her womb to Steven's arms, then to her mother's. The night he was born, there culminated a moment of deep understanding that the instantaneous love they all had for Cody was something to be shared.

Brenda's mother didn't appear to have that in her

DNA. Neither did Brenda. She'd come into the world without the ability to love or feel love. She probably held Kara for the first time and wondered what all the fuss was about as she planned her trip to Maui now that the "birthing thing" was over and she could have the rest of her being back to herself. Maybe when she was in labor she was imagining that Kara was some kind of parasite that she needed to purge from her body so that she'd be unencumbered and free to be Brenda again. Not Brenda the new mother. Not Brenda the doting wife. Not the neighbor with the stroller parading down Stoneway Drive to show off what her love had created.

Just beautiful, gorgeous, sexy Brenda.

As Kendall eased her foot down on the gas pedal to pull away, she could only wonder what else was in Brenda's past that caused her to be the dangerous and cunning woman that she'd become? Had Brenda Nevins been born a predator? Or had circumstances beyond her control conspired to make her into one?

CHAPTER TWENTY-THREE

Kendall Stark stopped by the Nevins place on her way out of town. Brad had told her that he'd be home and that the coffee was on if she wanted a cup. She did. It was early, but he was dressed in jeans and a Seahawks jersey.

"I didn't realize it was game day," she said, when he let her inside.

"It's not," he said, smiling. "Every day should be game day. World would be a whole lot better place if it was."

Kendall loved the Seahawks too. Devotion to the Seattle football team was practically a requirement for living in the Pacific Northwest.

"How was Chelsea?" he asked. He handed over the coffee. "I don't have anything to eat," he said. "Need to get to the store."

"I'm fine," she said as she took a seat at the kitchen table. Looking around she could see the telltale signs—besides an empty refrigerator—that Mrs. Nevins was no longer there. The plants in the windowsill had dried up. Or maybe had been overwatered? In any case, they were dead. One was a Christmas cactus with shriveled blooms that hung on to the barely green plant like a swirl of moths stuck on a car's grille. The counter was devoid of junk, but its surface was dulled by a film left by a cleaning cloth or sponge that needed a good rinsing.

"How was Chelsea?" he repeated.

Kendall didn't want to say much, but she knew that the man sitting across from her with the stubbled chin had lived through a Katrina-size storm of sadness. He was resilient, to be sure, but inside his skin was a broken heart.

"She was all right," she said, holding back the truth. "We talked. Nothing really helpful. She might be holding back a little."

"Did she tell you she was obsessed with Brenda? Back in high school?"

"Not really," Kendall said. "Not obsessed. More like interested."

"Sure," he said, swirling milk into his coffee. "That's what she called it."

"What are you getting at, Joe?" Kendall asked.

"My son told me," Brad said. "Said Chelsea was a bit of a freak about Brenda. He thought it was funny. I guess at the time I did too. Maybe I think differently about her now because of all the ugliness that she has brought to the world. And for what she took from me."

"She took it all," Kendall said. "I know."

"Yeah. All of it."

"Tell me more about Brenda and Joe's marriage. Were they ever happy?"

Brad drank some coffee. "He thought they were. But I doubt she was. She was strange about things."

"Be specific, Brad. Details matter."

"For their wedding, Brenda lined up the photographer. We paid for the guy. I guess that's fine. Can't be old-fashioned about stuff like that. You know, considering how the world's changed and all."

"What about the photographer?" Kendall asked.

"It was a guy from Richland. Antonio something. The best of the best. At least that's what she bragged. Cost $5,000 to have him shoot the whole thing."

"That's expensive," Kendall said. "I had a friend photograph my wedding. She wasn't a pro, and later I regretted it, but Steven and I didn't have the money."

"So, get this," he went on, "when we got the photo book back, guess who wasn't in any of the shots?"

Kendall didn't have a clue. She suggested the most egregious omission.

"The groom? Your son?"

Brad shook his head. "No. That would have been pretty good, though. Even by Brenda's standards. My wife and I. We were missing. Although Antonio the Great took plenty of pictures of us with the wedding party, Brenda said not a single one of them turned out."

"That is weird," Kendall said.

"It was a lie. She was mad that we didn't pay for the platinum plan—which, by the way, cost another 2K, and we weren't about to do that. I called her on it. I told her that she was being a petty bitch. Excuse my French. But she was. That's exactly how she was acting."

"No excuse needed," Kendall said. "Brenda's a lot of things. I think we're in safe territory to call her a petty bitch."

Brad smiled. "You got that right, Detective. Thanks for that."

"No worries," Kendall said. "I've met her. I've followed her career. She's complicated, but in all the wrong ways."

"Yeah," he said. "Elise was upset, so she had me call this moron photographer and ask if there were any outtakes or something. We wanted pictures too. He's our only child. Nothing wrong with that, right?"

Kendall asked if they got any.

Brad set down his now-empty cup. "No. When I asked about it, he told me that photos were the property of the bride and that he couldn't speak for her. Against policy."

"Why wouldn't she let you have any pictures?" Kendall asked. "I don't get it."

"Because she could. She was always pulling crap like that. Stealing the big moments to hurt us or to hurt Joe."

He got up and left Kendall alone. A flash later, he was back with a manila envelope. He set it on the table and slid it over to her.

Kendall looked at him before opening it.

A photo was inside and a Post-it note.

"Elise was beautiful," Kendall said. "You all look so happy."

"We were, Detective. We just didn't know the devil had married into our family just then."

She read the note:

Dear Mr. and Mrs. Nevins,
So sorry for your loss. So sorry that you never got any photos of the wedding. The bride was

insistent about having every image with you two
in the frame destroyed. I did what she asked.
After I read about the fire that killed your son
and granddaughter, something clicked and I
went back to my files. I had this one. I feel bad
that I didn't give it to you sooner. She was pretty
clear with her demands.

My apologies,
Antonio Gill

"Brenda was always clear in her demands," Kendall said, now meeting his gaze.

"Crystal," Brad said.

They talked some more about Brenda and Joe's marriage and how the arrival of baby Kara had changed things. Shortly after Kara was born, Brad said that he and his wife had been completely cut out of their son's life.

"I'm sorry, Joe," Kendall said, knowing the futility of the words. "That must have been very hard on you and your wife."

"Everything with Brenda was hard. She let us see Kara once a month and only for an hour at a time. She treated us like we were sex offenders or something and could only have supervised visitation."

Joe was the missing figure in all the discussions about Brenda.

"What did Joe say?" Kendall asked. "How did he handle it?"

Brad pushed his chair back. "He said nothing. He was so controlled by Brenda the Bitch that he didn't say a word against her. Never. Not even once. That's something we'll—I'll—never understand."

"She has a way of using and manipulating people. Your son. The prison warden."

"Chelsea," he said.

"Yeah, probably her, too."

CHAPTER TWENTY-FOUR

The image started dark, then a blush of light washed over Brenda Nevins's beautiful face. Her eyes had always been like magnets, drawing an observer in so close that sometimes they didn't even realize how their necks had been stretched forward for a better view. Whatever *it* was, Brenda had it.

A Savage Garden song, "I Knew I Loved You," played in the background.

Brenda wore a white blouse that she'd unbuttoned nearly to her navel; the shimmery fabric of a lacy, purple brassiere peeked out. There had never been subtlety when it came to Brenda Nevins. Not ever. Subtlety was for the pathetic, the unsure, and those who sought to blend into the background.

Before she spoke, she pulled out a photograph and held it out to the lens.

"This is my baby girl," she said, tilting the snapshot of Kara, to ensure that the viewers would be able to see her. "She was so pretty. Everyone said she looked just like me. From that first moment I saw her I wasn't quite

so sure. She was all pink and wrinkly and she reminded
me of a little naked monkey. Scrunched up like."

She set down the photo and stared at the camera.

"I know people are opening up old wounds," she
said, her tone condescending. "Trying to make me out
to be some kind of a baby killer. I'm here to tell you
right now that you've got it all wrong. That poking
around in the tragedy of my past isn't going to do anything but make you look like an idiot."

She reached up and lifted her hair away from her
face, then let it fall over her shoulders in a seductive
move.

"I'm so tired of being judged for things that I didn't
do. I'll own up to Joe and I'll own up to Janie. They
had it coming. Joe cheated on me. He was a player, and
I don't ever get played. And Janie? She was weak. I
don't do weak. You can't do weak and get anywhere in
life. Doesn't everyone know that? At the prison, I was
known as the tough one. I was the one that the other
prisoners feared because they thought that I had ice in
my veins. But that's not who I was. Not who I am. I'm
a survivor. I will always fight to the death because the
second that I give up, the second I stop, is the time that
someone will try to silence me. But here's what you
need to know. You can't stop me. No one can. I'm invincible and I'm going to make sure that I get credit
for what I do, not for what you think I've done."

She held out the photograph one more time, turning
it in the flat light of wherever she was recording the
video.

"I did not," she said. "I repeat. I did *not* kill my baby.
Why would I? Insurance money? Get real. There wasn't
enough money on Kara's life to make any difference in

mine. If I'd had killed her I would have put a million dollars of insurance on her. I'm not stupid. I don't take risks, and I don't underinsure. That's stupid. So go ahead, muck around. Dig deep. Find out what you can about my past. It won't do you any good, Kendall Stark. I'm only getting started."

Brenda moved the photo from view, keeping her gaze steady on the camera. The wheels were turning. It was not a flat stare. In a beat, she shook her head slowly. Tears welled up in her eyes. She waited a second. Another. Finally, a tear rolled down from her eye to the corner of her mouth. She produced a tissue and dabbed away at the damp trail that shimmered on her cheek.

"You've all forced me into what I'm about to do," she said. "So deal with it."

CHAPTER TWENTY-FIVE

Birdy watched the YouTube video play out on her phone. While she'd seen Brenda's handiwork up close and personal with the killer's recent Kitsap victims, she'd also seen, in Kendall's case reports, what Brenda had done to her husband and child. Like her detective colleague and friend, Birdy Waterman had been sucked into the Brenda vortex.

With each nugget of information, she found herself growing closer and closer to the source, wanting to know more. Brenda was a bloody traffic accident, the kind of catastrophe that you could not pass by without a long, hard stare. Birdy had downloaded the trial testimony that one of Brenda's fans had put up online— annotated with what the authorities had supposedly gotten wrong at trial. There was no way that little Kara's death had been accidental.

Both Joe and Kara had been found lying on the floor of the burned-out back bedroom of the murder house. While Joe's pre-fire trauma was obvious, the baby's had been more subtle. There had been no broken bones. No indicators of any perimortem trauma whatsoever.

The original autopsy report, in fact, indicated one major clue as to what had happened to the baby.

No smoke in lungs.

Kara had been dead *before* the fire. No stab wounds. No crushed vertebrae. Most likely, the little girl had been suffocated. Possibly even softly so. The state crime lab indicated melted poly fibers had been recovered from the charred body tissue, leading experts there to posit that a blanket or pillow might have been used to suffocate her.

At trial there were two other elements that indicated her latest YouTube rant was another attempt to drop a curtain over what really happened. The first came from the testimony of the day care owner, a forty-four-year-old woman named Teresa "Terry" Gonzales. Teresa indicated that the night before the fire, Brenda had called to say that Kara wasn't feeling well, and she wouldn't be there the next day. While Brenda didn't testify at trial, her lawyer made it clear that they took complete umbrage at that story. The defense's line of questioning of Teresa was a kitchen-sink tactic that touched on everything from potential drug use, organizational incompetence, and direct accusations of sexual abuse.

LAWYER: Isn't it true that the defendant caught you fondling a little boy in the naptime room of your business, Terry's Daycare?

GONZALES: I never did that.

LAWYER: But she saw you bent over a child and you were touching his penis.

GONZALES: I was changing his diaper. The baby had diaper rash. I was doing what the parents

had requested me to do. I never, ever did
anything improper. I never would. I don't
know anyone who would.

LAWYER: We're not taking about anyone else.
We're talking about you and what you did.
The defendant saw you do this . . . this
"nothing improper" thing you were doing
to the boy.

GONZALES: She was there, yes. But there was
nothing going on.

LAWYER: Are you a medical doctor?

GONZALES: No. I never said I was.

LAWYER: Yet you say you were administering
medicines.

GONZALES: I was putting diaper rash cream on
the boy.

LAWYER: You enjoy doing that, don't you?

GONZALES: There's nothing wrong with taking
care of a baby.

LAWYER: Nothing further.

The prosecution refocused the day care owner's testimony to what she was doing and why. That she'd operated a day care center for five years without one
complaint about anything whatsoever. That she was
perfectly within the purview of her responsibilities to
apply diaper-rash medicine.

Birdy saw Terry Gonzales's testimony as defining
what kind of person Brenda Nevins was. If she had to
destroy someone to save herself, she had no problems
doing so. In fact, that might have been part of her game.

Teresa Gonzales endured the humiliation of an investigation after the Nevins trial. Local and state authorities determined there had been no wrongdoing on her part, but her business didn't survive. Just the whisper of possible sexual abuse was all it took for parents to drop her. When her Realtor showed her house to a potential buyer six months after the trial, the couple backed out because they'd read online that a bunch of kids had been molested there.

"Bad energy," the young woman said, "has a tendency to linger in places like this. We can't live here."

The agent insisted that no wrongdoing of any kind transpired there, but few listened. After a series of price drops, the house was sold for less than what Terry owed on it.

She took the offer and wrote out a check for the difference. Her sister in Austin said she could live with her for a while and start over. She packed up everything, including the Terry's Daycare sign that she thought maybe she could use again. She had no children of her own and wondered if she'd ever find the joy she had before Brenda came through her life like a wrecking ball.

The other linchpin that was at odds with Brenda's contention that she hadn't murdered her daughter was the fact that in addition to the life-insurance policy she held on her husband, Brenda also had purchased a large life-insurance policy on Kara. The prosecution played out the details surrounding the policies by establishing Brenda's understanding of insurance through her job and the fact that she'd applied a little subterfuge by purchasing Kara's policy from a Mutual of Omaha agent across town—instead of from her own office, where she'd have received the same discount that she'd earned from buying Joe's.

The agent on Kara's policy was a man named Kent McGrew. Kent was fifty-three, balding, and with a potbelly that hung over his beltline like a volleyball. If he'd been a woman, no doubt he'd be asked when his baby was due by an insensitive grocery checker. Brenda's lawyer worked him over too.

LAWYER: Isn't it true that you were attracted to the defendant?

MCGREW: I don't know. I guess I was. She's an attractive girl.

LAWYER: You guess? You had intimate relations with her.

MCGREW: *(inaudible)* I did.

LAWYER: Isn't it true, Mr. McGrew, that you were obsessed with her?

MCGREW: Not obsessed. No. I wouldn't say I was obsessed with her.

LAWYER: Oh. I see. You have sex with all your clients.

MCGREW: No. No. I do not.

LAWYER: Where did you have your sexual encounter with the defendant?

MCGREW: In my office. We had relations one time in my office. She said she was lonely, and I just wanted to comfort her. It just went further than it should have gone.

LAWYER: You were being a shoulder to cry on, were you?

MCGREW: I would say so. Just trying to help.

LAWYER: By having sex with her?

McGrew: No.

Lawyer: Isn't it also true that you sold her the policy on her child's life?

McGrew: I did.

Lawyer: You suggested it?

McGrew: No. Not really. She told me that Kara had a rare genetic disorder and that she probably wouldn't make it to adulthood and she was pregnant with a second child and she was afraid of not having enough money to care for the new baby.

Lawyer: Sir, did you not suggest that she take out a policy on Kara's life?

McGrew: I felt sorry for her. She was vulnerable. She was worried. She didn't think Kara would survive much longer, and she didn't want to lose another baby.

Lawyer: Who signed the paperwork?

McGrew: I did. She called me crying that Kara was probably going over to Children's Hospital in Seattle. She was worried that if Kara died, her other baby would face a similar fate.

CHAPTER TWENTY-SIX

The day had been long, and the temptation for drinking too much wine was very real. While Cody played in the yard, Steven and Kendall sat on the front porch in a pair of old, silvered, cedar Adirondack chairs that had once belonged to Kendall's parents. They drank the last of a box wine that they'd decided was a "never again" purchase.

"Your stalker," Steven said, taking a sip, "was on the news today."

Kendall kept her eyes on Cody. "Don't call her that, Steven."

Her tone was harder than she would have liked, but she was tired of Brenda Nevins haunting her every move; being the subject of every single conversation. Even the dry cleaner asked Kendall if she "had met" Brenda. As if Brenda had crossed over from murderer to celebrity and no one seemed to have noticed that she'd killed people to get her fifteen minutes of fame.

"Sorry," he said, meaning it. "Anyway, they had another story on her video blog and how she might be one of the first serial killers to use digital media to get her message out. I thought it was sort of fascinating. You know, the world we live in now."

"Right," Kendall said. "That's fine. Zodiac sent letters. Very old school."

"He didn't get caught, either," Steven said.

"She'll get caught," Kendall said, standing and calling out to their son. "Not so close to the road, babe!"

Cody waved at his parents and reworked the repetitious route he'd created—an enormous figure eight— to avoid some of its proximity to the road. Beyond Cody, in the harbor, two kayakers maneuvered to set out from the shore.

"Son of Sam," Kendall said.

"Huh?"

Kendall lowered her gaze from her son to her husband.

"He sent letters to *The New York Times,* and he got caught."

Steven's eyes twinkled in the day's waning light. "Yeah," he said, "and his dog talked to him."

They both laughed.

"Not the best example, I guess," Kendall said, tugging at her sweater as a cool breeze blew over from the water.

"Have you or your new FBI buddy figured out what makes Brenda tick?" Steven asked.

Kendall stiffened a little at the mention of SA Casey. She'd both liked and couldn't stand the man. She didn't like the idea of Steven mentioning him, even obliquely. Her bristled response felt odd, but she set it aside.

"Power," she said. "That woman soaks it up like a sponge."

"More like a wad of toilet paper, if you ask me."

"Better," Kendall said. "Yes, I like that description better."

"From what you said, because; face it, you're the authority on the woman, sex drives her too. What is she, a lesbian? Bisexual? None of the above? Maybe she's polyamorous. You know, like that TV show that had the two guys and a gal in love with each other."

Kendall put her glass on the arm of her chair. "I don't think so. While she is very sexual, I don't think she cares about sex and what it might mean to two people."

"Or three or four, if you're on that show," he said. "Or in some weird cult."

Steven always knew how to cut through all of the BS associated with profiling a person like Brenda or any other criminal for that matter. He told her one time that he thought serial killers weren't devious because being devious implied smarts. Most of them were just *lucky* that they didn't get caught. Kendall conceded that there was truth to his assessment.

Yet Brenda Nevins was different. Different as in a whole other kind of life-form, almost. Not even human. She didn't operate or think the way so-called regular people do.

"For Brenda Nevins," Kendall said, "sex is about power and about what she can get from the experience. Not the experience itself. It isn't a give-and-take trade. In her mind, it's a step toward a goal. That's all. I mean, she'd have sex with a sack of oranges if she thought it would get her somewhere."

Her husband was quick to respond. "A big ol' bag of bananas would probably be better."

And they both laughed.

"Another glass, babe?" Steven asked, feeling the tension slip away. They needed more times like this. They needed a way to balance the darkness of what she did every day with their family life.

Kendall looked at her empty wineglass.

"Ah, no thanks," she said. "I don't think I can do another."

"I actually have some wine in a bottle chilling in the fridge."

"A bottle?" she asked. "Real wine?"

Steven got up and disappeared into the house.

Kendall stayed planted in the silvered cedar Adirondack chair that her father had built when she was a girl. She watched the water as it shimmered in the late-day sun. Cody's golden hair had turned russet in the ebbing light. Her husband was in the house getting her some wine. *Real wine.* And while she was enjoying this peaceful interlude with her husband, she could not think of anything else but Brenda Nevins.

Where are you hiding? And how am I going to stop you?

"You look lost in your thoughts," Steven said, appearing with a bottle of sauvignon blanc. He presented it to her like she was some wine connoisseur, which she wasn't at all. "What's rolling around in that investigator's mind of yours right now?" he asked as he poured.

Kendall took the wineglass and swirled it. It even *looked* better than the box wine.

"Nothing," she said. "Just glad that we're all together. I'm a very lucky girl."

BOOK TWO
VIOLET

CHAPTER TWENTY-SEVEN

The Kitsap County Coroner's new offices sat on the hill above Navy Yard City, adjacent to Bremerton. Despite its decidedly blue-collar locale—just past auto dealerships and next door to a military recruiting and training center—the facility was anything but. It housed top-of-the-line equipment with two chillers (one for deep-freezing decomps and another for the bodies waiting to be processed or for pickup by a funeral home).

The powers to be had listened as the plan for a new facility took shape. Considering the dire shape of the old office, they had no real choice. Whenever Birdy attended a conference, fellow attendees would inquire about the old house on Sidney Avenue in Port Orchard and scratch their heads at a county that wouldn't cough up the bucks for a proper morgue. For a county as large as Kitsap—as close in proximity to Seattle and King County—the comments brought embarrassment. Birdy deflected all of it and couldn't agree more that their working conditions were subpar.

"Someday," she said more than one time, "our taxpayers and our county commissioners will come to some kind of consensus, and we'll get what we need to do our jobs."

Finally they did. The move had been on the calendar for weeks, and the fact that the Brenda Nevins investigation was in full swing wasn't going to change any of that.

Boxes of supplies had been carefully marked, evidence double-checked, and libraries of books about the latest in forensics had been dispatched to designated locations throughout a facility that was ten times as large as the old house/coroner's office on Sidney.

It was a step up. A giant leap, really. The family room with a video feed, and an ever-ready tissue box, was one improvement that the public would see. No longer did a grieving relative need to have the body of a loved one wheeled from the old naval battleship chiller that serviced the old facility for a viewing. In the new space, families could look upon a loved one on a plasma screen.

The purpose was more than just making it better for those dealing with a terrible and often shocking loss. It was also to improve efficiency, safety, and workers' health. One of the two autopsy suites was set up to handle bodies with potential biohazards, with an air replacement unit that ensured a complete change of air every thirty minutes.

As good as all that was, there was something lacking too.

Birdy's office was no longer in a converted bedroom in an old house near the courthouse. It no longer had the tragic, worn vibe of a place that had been pressed into service by a county short on funds. And yet, when Birdy was at that location, the courts were there. The sheriff was right there. Over by Navy Yard City, she felt isolated from the machinations of a county government and its law enforcers.

"I'm not sure we're going to like this, Sarah," she said to her favorite assistant, a redhead with a nose spattered with freckles and a collection of rose gold jewelry from her aunt in South Dakota that was the envy of the office.

"What's not to like?" Sarah asked as she shifted instruments around in the stainless-steel overhead cabinetry. "The facility is amazing. We no longer have to bring colleagues in to prove to them that Kitsap is some poor country cousin and that we've been forced to conduct examinations in the basement of an old house."

"Right," Birdy said. "And we no longer have to remind new hires that the cream is on the top shelf of the refrigerator in the break room and tissue samples are on the second shelf."

Sarah laughed. They both did.

"I won't really miss any of that," Birdy went on, "But I guess I'll miss that connection we had with the other agencies."

Sarah twisted a chain with an grape-leaf pendant that hung around her neck. "CENCOM is next door, Dr. Waterman."

CENCOM was the 911 call and dispatch center.

"I know," Birdy said. "I'm glad about that."

Sarah went about her supply check, and Birdy retreated to her office, vowing to herself that she'd get comfortable in the new space. Change was good.

She switched on an old gooseneck lamp and fished a photograph from her purse. It showed her and Elan, an image taken by Kendall that first week Elan moved in. He had his hand on her shoulder as he squinted into the sun. Birdy wore sunglasses in that photograph, but not to block out the sun. She'd teared up a little. There was something overwhelming about Elan coming to live with her. Not because she didn't want him. Not because he was too much trouble. It was just that he'd been such an important part of her life, and she'd never been able to tell him that she'd always had his back.

She found a piece of tape and taped the photo next to her desk phone. She knew that she'd violated county policy.

"Do not adhere anything to the walls with tape or pushpins. Please use museum-grade removable fasteners if you must post something in your work location."

Birdy didn't care. Elan wasn't her son, but he might be the only true and lasting family she'd ever have.

The painting of the sea stacks at Ruby Beach sat on Birdy Waterman's desk. Her sister Summer had painted it for Birdy when she was away at medical school to remind her of home. It was a mostly gray image with the stacks rising from the water, craggy monoliths looped in sea foam. A lone gull hovered in a cloudy sky. A nest of driftwood was scattered like a child's pickup sticks in the foreground. Summer had brushed paint on canvas with energy and vigor. Her work was never the type that had been created to match a sofa. Each stroke of her brush had been deliberate, assured.

On the back side she'd written: Remember the Time.

Birdy didn't know if her sister was referring to a

specific time that they'd shared at that gorgeous, rugged beach. It had been a favorite place. Or if Summer merely meant the image as a reminder of the place from which she'd come. Before things went so bad between them, the connection they shared seemed unbreakable. While Summer stayed on the reservation to marry, raise Elan, and look after their mother, Birdy had charted another course.

"You know," Summer had said one time, "just because you're a doctor for dead people doesn't mean I'm not proud of you."

"Just because you're full of it, doesn't mean I'm not proud of you," Birdy answered back.

Birdy looked around for a nail and picture hook, picking through the boxes yet to be unpacked. The painting was tempera and egg, a medium that gave a vibrant opacity to each brushstroke. Summer was a talented artist. Gifted, Birdy always thought. That's the part that hurt. Not that they didn't get along. Not that Summer drank too much. Couldn't manage her rage. It was that she'd had so much promise. Birdy always looked up to her older sister. Promise unfulfilled crushed her more than anything.

She pushed the painting to the other side of her desk and opened the wide middle drawer to see if she'd put the nails and hooks there. She wondered why she had so many paper clips. She couldn't think of the last time she or anyone she knew used them. Staples too. God, she had so many boxes of staples.

And no stapler.

When she didn't find a hook for the painting, she pushed back her chair to get up.

It caught her eye just then.

She lifted the corner of the painting and tilted the lamp so that it illuminated the texture of the painted surface more directly. On the right-hand bottom corner, she noticed for the first time that there had been two figures in the foreground. Two girls. Ghosts. Summer painted over them with some driftwood.

One girl was slightly taller than the other. Her arm had been hooked around the shoulders of the smaller girl. Wind blew their hair to the north.

Something about that vanished scene brought tears to Birdy's eyes, making it harder to see. She peered closer, turning the painting to see. Her sister was a very good painter. It had not been a mistake that she'd sought to cover. The obfuscation was intentional. She'd wanted those two girls together, looking out at the water, remembering a time when they were so very close.

It took Birdy's breath away.

Summer, she thought, *what happened to us? Why have we ended up like this?*

She tried her sister's phone number, and, as it almost always did, the call went to voice mail after a couple of rings.

"I wanted you to know that I'm thinking of you right now. I know you're with Mom and that's a good thing. For both of you. I miss you, Summer. I'm sitting here in my new office and remembering all the good times we had. Remember how much we loved Ruby Beach? Call me when you can, will you?"

Birdy wondered when had been the last time she'd phoned her sister out of love. All the calls over the past couple of years had felt like duty. They had the weight of obligation. When Elan moved in with her, things morphed into a kind of cold war between them that she never imagined. Now, with their mother dying, the connection they had was only about her. The focus on their mother had brought them together a little. Birdy wondered where they would be when she was gone.

CHAPTER TWENTY-EIGHT

Violet Wilder watched from the kitchen window as her son, Sherman, loaded the last of the horses into the trailer of the man from down by Discovery Bay who'd come to buy her beloved Montana. Monty had been the last of the stable to be sold. It pained Violet to watch that splendid animal go. Monty was such a beauty. He was a black gelding with a streak of white that ran the length of his nose. Monty had been her favorite of the horses they'd had on the farm. He was the gentlest, and the grandchildren loved riding him. But the farm had become too much for her to handle, even with the help of her devoted son.

She edged her walker away from the window to answer the noise coming from the teakettle. She'd noticed the decline of her physical abilities over the past few months and tried her best to avoid the thoughts of how the rest of her life would play out. How much longer would she be able to live on her own? Where would she go? What would become of her farm?

She poured hot water into a mug and watched the amber color of the orange spice tea as it glowed from

JUST TRY TO STOP ME

the tea bag. Violet Wilder was eighty-eight years old. She no longer said "eighty-eight years young" because there was nothing young about her age anymore.

"Need some help with that mug, Mom?" Sherman said as he entered the kitchen.

She turned, a warm smile on her face. Sherman was the youngest of her babies and he was in his fifties. It was hard to even think of him as a child. He was in decent shape for his age, with a full head of sandy brown hair and piercing brown eyes that telegraphed intelligence whenever he was talking to someone—no matter who they were or what the subject.

Sherman was always *on.*

"I'll miss Monty," she said, as she slid her walker over to the kitchen table where Sherman had placed her steaming mug.

"I know, Mom. I will too," he said, taking a seat across from his mother. "But as hard as this is, it has to be done. Life's about making tough choices, and they all come with a price." He pushed the sugar bowl closer to her.

"You sound like your father," she said, dropping a spoonful of sugar into her fragrant tea.

He pointed to her cup. "Drink up. Tea's getting cold."

Violet looked down and caught her reflection on the back of the sugar spoon. She had been beautiful once—at least people had told her so. When she and Alec got married, she had the most striking chestnut hair. She wore it long, though she had the style shortened with the birth of each child. She'd been unable to wear it with a clip or ponytail by the time Sherman was born. Her eyes sparkled with mischief then and were blue like the waters of Puget Sound. Not anymore. Her hair was white, and her eyes looked gray, not blue. Her gaze was a dull stare, and her hands were knotted at the joints like burls of wood.

And her legs. That was the worst of her current state. Once the pride of Port Angeles High School as she set a record in the 100-yard dash, they could no longer support her in a steady fashion. She'd been condemned to get around with the aid of that metal-tubed contraption that was her companion whenever she moved about the house. Leaving the house? Not so much. She had too much pride to be seen around town shuffling along with a walker, or God forbid, in one of those motorized scooters.

Her son had offered to buy her one, but she'd insisted that she could manage just fine.

"I've been everywhere I want to go," she'd said.

"What about seeing your friends, Mom?" Sherman asked.

"My friends are dead."

"Not all of them."

Her expression turned wistful. "The ones I actually liked are."

As she sat there with her tea, Violet watched Sherman make his way across the yard to the now very, very empty barn. Barn cats Snowball and Licorice were curled up on top of a stack of hay bales. They jumped down to meet him, looking for a treat no doubt. He bent down and petted them and went inside.

The Wilder Farm was pitched in its own little valley along the Elwha River. After logging more than a third of their 100-acre parcel, Alec and Violet Wilder raised sheep, then goats, and finally turkeys. Alec worked at the paper mill in Port Angeles, leaving Violet to raise the kids and run the farm. She told her husband that she felt like she was living a life reminiscent of Betty Mac-Donald, who'd famously written about her chicken ranching experiences in the classic memoir *The Egg and I.*

"The same problems, but without the wit and laughter," she deadpanned.

The farm was so remote that the Wilders had no real neighbors to speak of. The kids—Sherman, Denise, and Timothy—were carted six miles to a bus stop and then another forty-five minutes to their various schools in Port Angeles. When Alec managed a shift change at the mill, he drove them. Those were the best times the family ever knew. Alec hurt his back in an accident when he was fifty-nine and never recovered. He died at sixty-seven, leaving Violet to manage on her own.

She scaled back. Sold off thirty acres to a man from California who thought that the location would be ideal for a camping resort, of all things. Violet could not fathom why anyone would want to come out that bumpy road in an RV, but she wasn't about to quell the deal. The money from the sale, she was sure, would take her to her last days.

She just hadn't expected to survive so long. She hadn't expected to live in the manner in which she was living, either. Life might not be fair, but did it have to be cruel?

Yet there was something for which to be grateful. Sherman, who'd lost his most recent job due to downsizing in the IT department for a Washington state government office, was there to help her. Denise, a dentist in Seattle, was far too busy, but that was understood. She called twice a week. As for Timothy, he was the Wilders' problem child. Always into trouble. Always able to charm himself out of a mess. The last Violet had heard he was living in Littleton, Colorado. She knew that he'd pop into her life again. He always did.

Sherman was her Steady Eddy.

CHAPTER TWENTY-NINE

Meth had overtaken pockets of rural Washington, and the Makah reservation was no exception. It was a problem that couldn't be solved the way that had been promised by the government workers who'd come with full hearts and always-ready optimism. Stopping the trafficking took more than reminding people that meth, an insidious drug if ever there was one, could kill them. By the time meth teeth showed their ugly snarl, it was too late. Too late for the family cat that went unfed and died in the kitchen. Too late for the little girl who still wore diapers at age four because her mother was so transfixed by the powers of the drug that there wasn't enough time in the day to do all that she needed to do.

Birdy drove down the long gravel road to her mother's house. She passed the Meakins place, a grave marker of sorts. It was decimated in a fire years earlier. The small wood frame house looked like the blackened innards of a beached whale. The rafters were ribs. The collapsed carport garage had fallen flat; its doors were the tail fins.

A shark, not a whale.

Mr. and Mrs. Meakin were a nice couple. They helped

with the community, donated to the church, cleared fallen trees when the road became impassable after a wintertime storm. Birdy picked huckleberries a few times with the family. Summer did too. Mrs. Meakin offered everything that their mother, Natalie, couldn't.

Love.

Attention.

Truth.

The irony was that their son Bobby was a cooker. Hooked on meth too, as most cookers are. Bobby did his best to stay clean enough through the arduous cycle of cooking meth for a dealer named Beast. He cooked in the woods in the summer, but the Beast kept pushing for more product. After repeated demands for more, Bobby gave in. He moved his operation, such as it was, into a woodshed off the kitchen. When the shed blew up, it triggered an explosion of the propane tank. The tank took off the roof of the house. Flames licked the rafters and beams.

Mr. and Mrs. Meakin and their son Bobby were all dead.

Birdy looked at her phone. It was seven minutes to two. She pulled over to wait a few minutes. She turned off the ignition, turning off the music from the CD player. So much had happened since she left. Her dad was gone. Her mother was growing weaker by the day. Not a whole lot to hang on to anymore. She watched a doe move along a fence line across the road.

Waiting.

She'd texted her sister that she'd be there that afternoon. Summer made the visit finite and exact.

"You can come from two to three. Not a minute before. Please don't try to talk to me."

It made Birdy feel sick. No matter what Summer did, Birdy loved her. She was all she'd ever had as far as a family member. She had been a lifeline when they were small. The tether between the two of them when they were young was a lifesaver, but as they grew it was a ligature—choking the life out of her whenever she thought of coming back to Neah Bay, back to what she had always believed would be home.

Birdy sat outside her mother's house and waited for her sister, Summer, to leave. She and Summer had said very little to each other since Elan moved in with her. It wasn't a completely new occurrence. They had gone through periods of time—some quite long—in which they didn't speak. There had been lots of reasons for the wall between them. This time, Birdy was sure, was not the time to try to fix things. The glue that held them together had been the toxic love of their mother.

Natalie Waterman never really filled the bill of what a mother was supposed to be. No one in the family looked to her for comfort or nurturing. Natalie was a supremely unhappy woman. She blew darts instead of kisses. She slapped instead of hugged. While Summer had seen a different mother at one time, Birdy hadn't. It took some doing, but Birdy had managed to erase some of those memories from her mind. It was as if she'd taken scissors and cut out the images of her mother. She stood next to her dad. Her sister. The empty spot in her memory was her mom.

Now Natalie was dying. Such mixed feelings it brought. The longing for a genuine closeness. The hope for reconciliation. The dream that the blank faces in the memories she somehow still held would be restored. All of that and more . . . things that she'd be relieved of when Natalie died.

Summer barely glanced in Birdy's direction as she let the screen door slam and made her way to her pickup truck. The avoidance was wrong. The chill between them stung like a bitter wind on a tear-streaked face.

Birdy got out of the Prius. She walked around the cedars and alders that shrouded her mother's mildewed mobile home. She thought that a pressure washer could make the place look so much better. She'd hired a boy to do it a year ago, but it only made her mother angry. She didn't need any fancy help from her fancy daughter.

Natalie Waterman had a way of squelching kindness and stifling generosity. She built a barrier that ensured that when she died, she'd do so alone.

Natalie was on the couch, the TV blaring, the smoke from a lighted cigarette covering her like a yellow beach umbrella. A soft gray acrylic throw, the color of a wasp's nest, cosseted her emaciated body.

"You shouldn't be smoking, Mom," Birdy said, moving in the direction of the TV remote control.

"Is that a doctor talking or a daughter?" Natalie asked, without so much as a hello.

"Both," Birdy said.

"I could care less what either has to say," Natalie croaked. "Besides, I don't think smoking will hurt my cancer. It's doing just fine."

Natalie made a face. "Yes, Mom, I guess it is." She

pressed the volume button until the host of the TV show spoke instead of shouted. Then she pressed mute.

"You know I can't hear the TV so good when you have it down so low."

"It's on mute," Birdy said. "I turned the sound off so we could visit."

Natalie turned away and faced the ceiling. "You are still a selfish little bitch, Birdy. You think that you can do whatever you want and that no one else has a say in anything."

Natalie's voice was a dull rasp with each utterance. Her breathing was labored.

Birdy could feel her shoulders sag as her mother's cruelty beat her down. Like it always had. "That's not true, Mom," she said.

Natalie glanced at her youngest daughter and returned her gaze to the smoke-stained ceiling of her mobile home. "Whatever," she said. "What do you want? Did you come so you could watch an old lady die? Usually you don't get to see any of your so-called patients until they've been dead for a while. Isn't that so?"

"I'm here because I love you, Mom."

Natalie reached for another cigarette, but the pack was empty.

"That's funny, Birdy," she said. "Little Birdy. Fly away from me now."

Birdy stood motionless. "I'm here to help you, Mom."

"Help how? It's too late for help now."

"It's never too late to make things right, Mom."

Natalie laughed. It was a soft wheezing sound that turned into a riot of noises and ended with her retching into a Pyrex mixing bowl placed on the floor next to her sofa.

Birdy went to her mother and tried to help her, but Natalie pushed her away.

"I can vomit on my own," she said.

Of course you can.

"Mom, I'm here to help."

Natalie held up her hand. Her finger bones held the thin webbing of her flesh. "You're here to dance on my grave," she said. "You've always been such a phony, Birdy. I don't buy your act that you give a crap about me. You have a singular focus. Birdy. That's been you from Day One and I doubt you'll change once I'm gone. Own it."

Birdy had tried to hate her mother. Life would have been easier without the complication of Natalie Waterman in her life. She'd have fewer trips to the reservation. Less opportunity to tussle with her sister Summer over things that neither truly cared about. Birdy might not have to walk around feeling guilty for wanting a life off the reservation. Whenever that feeling of permanent escape from her mother and her past came to her, she found a million reasons to set it aside. To think that moving away meant leaving all of the family drama was a silly fantasy. The drama would always be there.

"I'm going to make a cup of tea," she said as her mother dropped her hand. "Want one?" Birdy didn't wait for her mother to answer. She'd bring her tea anyway.

Over the loud hum of the decades-old microwave, Birdy could hear the volume rise on the TV. Her mother had always used television to block out the real world. Before the reservation got satellite TV, Natalie would pore though old copies of *People* magazine, the *Star,* and the *Globe.*

Other people had such nicer lives.

"I made you some tea," Birdy said, returning to the sofa. Her mother's eyes stayed riveted on the TV screen.

"Did I ask you for some?" Natalie said, still watching the show.

"No, Mom, you didn't," Birdy said. "I thought you might like some."

Natalie rolled her eyes in the direction of her daughter, then back to the TV. "Well, I don't."

"Mom, I want to help you," Birdy said.

"Help me what?"

"Get through this, Mom," she said.

"Everyone dies, Birdy. You see it every day at your job."

Birdy let the words hang in the musty air of her mother's trailer.

"I thought we could talk about things, Mom. You know, make things right."

"You should go and do that with Summer. She's not at death's door."

"You aren't either, Mom. Besides, things with Summer are complicated right now."

Natalie let out a hoarse laugh. "That's what you call it? You've always been such a liar, Birdy."

It had been a lie, of course.

"She's still mad at me for telling Elan."

The words sagged in the air. They were bait on a hook. Birdy had to just sit still and try not to fill the air with any more words. The glint of the hook sparked.

Natalie took a bite. "What?" she spat out. "What did you tell Elan?"

Birdy kept her eyes on her mother.

"The truth, Mom," she said. "I told him the truth. At least the part of the truth I thought he could handle."

Natalie's eyes met Birdy's. They were no longer the dark brown that had sparked like steel against flint. They were cloudy, the color of the muddy stream that bisected her mother's property. Her hair was nearly snow white, save for the black tips of a dye job long since grown out. She sipped the tea she'd said she never wanted. Her silver rings were missing.

"Just what truth is that?" she asked, knowing the answer.

"That you are his mother," Birdy said.

Natalie simmered. She was weak from the chemo, a rack of bones in an old gray afghan. Even so, Birdy knew a volcano was about to erupt. She could feel tremors of rage that came before any words.

"You had no right!" Natalie said.

Before then, Birdy thought she might cry at her mother's insistence to bury the past. But she didn't. In fact, she felt emboldened. Free. It felt very, very good.

"I had every right, Mom," she said. "You can't keep secrets like that. Secrets and cigarettes made you ill."

Natalie looked away. "Is that another diagnosis from the dead people's doctor?"

"Not a diagnosis, Mom," Birdy said. "Just a fact."

"I want you gone," Natalie said. "Out of my house. Right now. I don't want to see you again."

Birdy didn't budge. "I'll leave, Mom. I promise. But you're going to have to listen to me, and you're going to have to answer my questions."

"Get out!" Natalie said in as loud a rasp as she could manage.

Birdy planted her feet. "Not going anywhere, Mom. Not until I'm done with you."

CHAPTER THIRTY

With her husband next to her snoring just below the annoyance decibel level, Kendall flipped though the pages of the yearbook she'd taken from Chelsea Hyatt's townhome. Brenda Nevins was only a few years younger than herself, but the snapshot of her high school was nearly a duplicate of her own at South Kitsap. Hairstyles. Clothes. Activities. All were about the same.

She looked at Brenda's photo. Her write-up held no mention of extracurricular activities. She was pretty, but not as pretty as she'd become when she had the money to afford the skill of a surgeon's knife. Kendall looked a little closer at the photograph and noticed that the outfit Brenda wore for her senior portrait was a little tired. The other girls looked like they were wearing something new, a special top purchased just for the occasion. Brenda's didn't have that crisp new look.

Her mother in her pashmina and jewelry must have come into some money after she divorced her husband, she thought. *Maybe collecting on insurance runs in the family.*

If it did, it wouldn't have surprised the detective. In rare instances, she knew, murderousness sometimes is genetic.

She flipped the pages to the cheerleaders and the X's, wondering what each of them could have done to deserve the defacement. Stephanie, Terry, Anna, and Charlotte. The last girl was dead, but the others were still alive and living somewhere, she hoped, far away from Brenda Nevins and the kind of havoc that followed her wherever she went.

Steven's eyes opened, and he rolled over.

"Reliving the past, Kendall?"

She gave him a playful kick under the covers.

"Not mine. Brenda Nevins's."

"That Brenda," he said, "she finally found a way to wriggle into our bed."

"Not funny," Kendall said. "In fact, pretty gross."

"She's long gone," he said. "Let's get some sleep."

"I don't think so, honey. I think she's here, and I'm going to find her. And you know what, I don't even care if I bring her in alive."

"Shhh," he said. "Got to get some sleep. Night, sweetheart. Night, Brenda."

She kicked him again. Playfully. At least a little so.

Before settling down, turning off the light, and snuggling next to her husband, Kendall looked at the inside back cover of the yearbook. Among the "have a fun summer" and "you're sweet, stay that way" and "party!" was a message written by Brenda.

Chelsea, we made it through another year!
Not the end, but the beginning. I hate this school
and I hate this town (so boring!). I will never

*waste my time with losers again. I'm going to
get out of here and be famous. No one will ever
stop me. No one can. It will be my turn. Screw
the bitches and their kind. Everyone will know
my name. I'm going to be on TV. Just watch. See
you at the river! Luv you*

The river.

Kendall looked back at the photo of the cheer team.
Charlotte's last name was Barrow. Charlotte Barrow.
She crawled out of bed and logged onto her computer
and into the database of the *Tri-City Herald*. She typed
in the girl's name. Two stories popped up.

Teen dies in accident on the Columbia

Charlotte Barrow, 17, drowned Sunday at
Riverfront Park when the raft she was floating in capsized. Police say bystanders retrieved Barrow from a sandbar and tried to
revive her.

She was pronounced dead at County
Hospital upon arrival by ambulance.

"It's a real tragedy," said Tom Wolfson,
18, who helped get Barrow to shore. "The
place where they dragged her from is so shallow. Seems like she just panicked."

Brenda Holloway, 17, was on the raft with
Barrow at the time of the accident.

"There wasn't anything I could do," she
said. "One minute she was laughing and pad-
dling and the next minute she was under the
water. Her eyes were looking right at me and
I tried to lift her, but she's so much bigger
than I am."

Barrow was a popular teen at Richland
High School. She was a member of the year-

book staff and a cheerleader. Her parents are
John and Donna Barrow, Richland. Services
pending.

Kendall shuddered. *Of course, Brenda was there.*
And of course, she managed to get in a dig about Charlotte being so much bigger than she. Brenda might
have insisted to Chelsea that the other girls were catty
and bitchy, but it was obvious to Kendall that there
were no bounds to Brenda's own negativity about those
she thought had crossed her.

She scrolled down to the second story.

Services held for Charlotte Barrow

Richland teen Charlotte Barrow will be
memorialized at Our Lady of the Redeemer,
249 West Valley Highway, at 1 p.m. on Saturday.

Barrow, the daughter of John and Donna
Barrow, Richland, drowned in the Columbia
last week when the raft she was floating in
overturned while she was celebrating the end
of the school year with friends.

Services will include a tribute to the teen
by her friends on the cheerleading squad. In
addition, a teen will recite a poem she's written about Barrow. Food and beverages will
be provided by the family.

Kendall didn't need the name of the teen who'd be
reading the poem. It had to be Brenda.

Brenda hated to be in the shadows. Dark recesses in
which to hide were not for her at all. She was always
finding her way into the spotlight.

Kendall shut the lid on her laptop and returned to

bed. She didn't want to think about Brenda, but that was impossible. She was an insidious presence that never abated. The trail of destruction that followed her had likely started earlier than she or anyone else for that matter had thought. Charlotte's death had been ruled an accident by the Richland police. It was summer. Kids were drinking, letting loose. Tragedy visits happy times like that all the time, as though people need a reminder now and then: Don't overdo it; don't have too much fun. Guilt obscures what happens. And on that terrible day on the river, no one had thought to question the friend who had been there when the drowning occurred. Kendall thought of the quote Brenda had reportedly given to the paper. She had seen Charlotte's eyes looking up at her through the icy cold waters of the Columbia River.

Of course you did, Kendall thought. *You were holding her head underwater while Charlotte fought for her life.*

Kendall turned off the light and tugged at the covers Steven had appropriated. She wondered if the drowning had been the first surge of power that Brenda had felt in taking a life. Had that incident on the river with Charlotte been a spark that over time caught fire, smoldering until she married Joe Nevins, had her baby, and realized that the only way out of town—the only way out of that mundane life—was to do what she'd done before?

CHAPTER THIRTY-ONE

Sherman Wilder went up to what had been his parents' bedroom. His mother no longer could navigate the staircase so she had Sherman remake the master bedroom into a guest suite. He reluctantly agreed and packed up her clothes for the room downstairs that she'd proclaimed as the best location in the house.

"A straight shot for the undertaker when he comes to get me," she said.

He cleared the top of the dresser of all of the sentimental odds and ends that his mother had collected—and faithfully dusted—over the years. They were a time capsule of sorts. Among them were the ashtrays that he and his siblings had made at Lutheran Church camp on the coast. Their mother wasn't a smoker. Neither was their father. Ashtrays were the go-to ceramic gift for parents of children born in the 1950s and early '60s.

Also ensconced on the bureau was his father's badge from the paper mill. It rested on top of the last Valentine card he'd given her: *For My Loving Wife*. The imagery on the card was two entwined gold wedding bands. Sherman opened it. Inside, under the greeting card verse, his father had written a message: *Violet, no life would be worth living without you.* He felt his eyes moisten. He slid the card back to the spot where his mother had left it.

Some of what was in that room, however, didn't tug at the heartstrings. Instead, some of it flat-out irritated Sherman. Enraged him even.

On the wall by the bathroom door were a meticulously organized series of framed family photos—baby, high school senior, and wedding portraits. Of the three Wilder children only Denise and Sherman had been married. Denise, in fact, had been married twice by the time she was thirty-five. Sherman's ex-wife, Susan, stared out from behind the sheen of her photo's glass covering.

Sherman reached for that particular photo. He'd argued with his mother over that portrait for years following the divorce. He didn't understand how she could just leave it hanging there, taunting him and reminding him of Susan's betrayal.

He confronted her more than once about it.

"She cheated on me, Mom. She ruined my life. And you keep this picture here? What's the matter with you?"

Violet shook off his concerns.

"She's the mother of your daughter, Sherman," she said. "You can't do anything about that. I expect you wouldn't want to change it if you could."

Sherman's blood simmered. He couldn't understand her position on the matter.

"She took my daughter away from me, Mom. She screwed that pastor of hers and told me it was my fault. That I wasn't paying enough attention to her and that she was vulnerable. Took everything from me."

"Sherman, please," Violet said, her tone as sweet and kind as always. "You're being dramatic and you're upsetting yourself. It was a long time ago. Time to move on and make a new life for yourself. You just have to stomp the mud off your shoes."

He hated when she used a crappy analogy. But he hated something else more.

"I don't like to be called Sherman," he said, dissolving into that little boy who resisted everything his mother told him to do. "You know that. I've *told* you that."

Once more, Violet shook it off. She patted him on the shoulder. The gesture was meant to be calming. He didn't take it that way.

"I love you, Sherman. And I'm your mother. That means I can call you what I want to call you."

Sherman Wilder could feel his blood pressure rise at the thought of how she stonewalled him over the removal of the pictures. But that was then. This was now. He removed the portrait of his wedding with Susan from its place of dubious honor on the wall. The frame was an expensive one. Probably an antique. He bent the little wire tacks on the back of the frame, popped off the glass, and took out the photograph. He stared down at the pebbly finish of the photographic paper.

She was very pretty. He had to admit that. Not the prettiest woman he'd ever seen. That was for sure. She'd plucked him out of the warren of IT cubicles at Microsoft and brought life and love to his world. When she left him for the pastor, she'd made him feel that he'd never be worthy of love again. He dated. He tried to, anyway. He really did. It was only in the last year that he'd had any hope for something better.

Sherman Wilder was moving on. He didn't want to jinx it. He just knew that things were going to happen for him and that love had finally returned.

Carrying the photograph, he made his way to the bathroom. Piece by piece, he shredded the portrait and dropped it into the toilet. The shreds of photographic paper fell like confetti at a Fourth of July parade. Each tear brought pleasure. He was picking at a scab. Itching a bug bite. Feeling something good for a change.

Sherman reached over to flush and then thought better of it. He unzipped his fly, planted his feet in front of the bowl, and urinated. He aimed his stream at a portion of Susan's face, torpedoing it under the yellow, foamy water.

Then he pressed down on the lever. Water swirled and sucked Susan down into oblivion.

Fall had stripped the leaves off the apple trees that the Wilders had planted the first year they'd moved in. They'd been a mix of varieties in the orchard, though Violet's favorite was the fruit of the trio of Jonagolds, which had been quite a novelty at the time they were planted. It had been a couple of years since they'd made cider, even longer since the family harvested the crop for sale. Rotting orbs of yellow and pink hung stubbornly on the upper reaches of the branches. Deer foraged for whatever fell to the ground and whatever they could reach by stretching upward on spindly hind legs.

Violet slid past the window and made her way to her son's office. He'd told her that she could clean in there if she insisted, but not to fiddle with the electronic equipment. Violet laughed at the very idea. She could barely deal with the new vacuum that Denise got her for Christmas the previous year. Her daughter told her that it was one quarter of the weight of her old Kirby vacuum and "It'll make things so easy for you."

That was a joke. She loved her Kirby. She'd had it for almost forty years, and she highly doubted the new machine, with its fancy technology and big ball front that supposedly maneuvered like a dream around corners and piano legs, would last one-tenth the time.

Plastic is just crap, she thought.

Sherman's office had once been Timothy's room, though the only remnant that indicated its history was a series of tears in the plasterboard from the skiing posters that had long since been removed. It now was computer central. Sherman's love of electronics had started young. He built his first computer from parts he'd ordered from a catalog and picked up at Radio Shack in Port Angeles. He was sixteen. In another lifetime he might have been the next Paul Allen or Bill Gates. Violet wondered if she and his father had failed him, making their son work on the farm, attend public schools, and participate in sports.

"Playing around in your room all day with a bunch of power cords and dealy-bobs isn't going to make you a well-rounded man, son," Alec had said on more than one occasion. "A steady job means a solid future."

Violet surveyed the room. Her eyesight wasn't nearly as sharp as it had once been, but even so she could see that it was possible that Alec's advice had been in error. The world ran on computers. The room was filled with old PCs, video equipment, and cobra-esque coils of cables that connected one nondescript box to another.

Violet ran her ostrich feather duster from the top of each surface to the bottom, sending the tiniest particles to the floor where she'd suck it all up with the stupid plastic vacuum.

"Hey, Mom," Sherman said, appearing in the doorway. "I see you're spreading the dust around again."

She looked up and smiled.

"You caught me," she said. "Sorry. I just want to be useful."

"Mom, you make it sound like you're on your last legs," he said.

She looked down at her walker. "In case you haven't noticed, *I am*."

They both laughed. It wasn't an uncomfortable laugh, the type people engage in when embarrassment needs a way out. It was genuine laugh. The real thing.

"I'm doing what I can to get ready for Vanessa," she said, her smile radiating from her face.

Sherman reached over and gave his mother a little tug on the shoulder.

"You don't have to clean up anything for Vanessa. She's not the type to run around with a white glove and then tell you that you missed a spot. Not her. Not at all."

"Oh," Violet said, "I didn't mean it that way. It has been a while since we've had anyone over, you know."

Sherman did. "Yeah, you mean, since Susan."

Violet swiped the feather duster over a stack of books. "I always liked her. At least I thought I did. I guess I didn't know her at all."

"She was a slut, Mom," he said.

Violet's expression hardened. "That may well be, but remember you have a child with that slut. It doesn't do anyone any good to have those kinds of words bouncing around your brain. You never know, sometimes ugly pops out when you really want to keep the lid tight on the jar."

Sherman laughed. "Is everything a canning analogy with you, Mom?"

"I guess the farm has been on my mind. I know that I can't do the things that I want to do anymore. Just kind of dealing with that."

"Vanessa will help you," he said. "She grew up in the country, too."

Violet gripped the walker and started toward the kitchen. "In that case, I'll make sure the pantry is tidy, too. I don't want to have another woman poking around in there and think unkindly of me."

"She wouldn't," he said. "I promise."

Sherman slumped into the tattered folds of his black leather office chair. He could feel his heart race a little, but in a good way. He felt alive. Energized. He'd been so happy in the past few months. He'd wanted an opportunity to find love that second time and he was all but certain that "Vanessa" was the woman of his dreams. She wasn't like the others. She had spunk. Charisma. She was drop-dead gorgeous too, but that wasn't what captivated him. It was her spirit. She'd been through so much and she refused to let it get her down.

She was invincible.

Sherman Wilder needed that feeling right about this time in his life. He wasn't a mogul like Bill Gates or Steve Jobs. He was just a man, and a man needed love.

CHAPTER THIRTY-TWO

Violet thought back to her son's reappearance on the farm, how he'd come to help her when she had needed it most. The livestock had become more than she could really handle, and she knew that deep in her bones. The realization hadn't come overnight, but slowly. Her friends fading away. Her body weakening. Her handyman Seth Jupiter had been the final warning of what was to come. He'd told her that his mother was dying and he needed to head over to Spokane to be with her.

"Until," he said, "you know, the end."

Yes, the end, Violet thought. *The end is coming for me too.*

When her son Sherman showed up, it was the right time. She had no one else. He'd stepped in where his sister had refused. Her life was too busy. She was too important. Violet understood that. And yet it bothered her when Sherman told her he'd canceled the *Port Angeles Daily News*.

"Just a bunch of wire service stories," he'd said. "Nothing local anymore."

"But I like the news," she answered back.

He told her not to worry.

"I'll keep you updated on what you need to know, Mom."

She didn't like that, but she figured Sherman had his reasons. Maybe her money was running out faster than she'd realized? After she fell and hurt her hip, she'd signed over power of attorney to him. She was better, but it felt unkind to ask for it back. Besides, she reasoned, "He'll take care of me. He loves me."

Violet drew herself a hot bath. She'd taken to showering the last few weeks because she wasn't sure if she'd have the strength to hoist herself out of the old claw-foot tub. Things, she hoped, were better. Her son was there, and while she'd rather die than call him to the bathroom to help her in such a private time, she knew that in an emergency both of them could live through the embarrassment of such an occurrence.

Steam wafted into the air, and the light fog of condensation on the mirror lessoned the impact of how she looked naked. She tied up her hair. Growing old was completely natural, she knew, but it was unyielding in its cruelty. Everything that had been so firm years ago now drooped, sagged, and otherwise just hung there. She dropped a lavender sachet into the water and the divine floral scent permeated the room. She'd grown the lavender herself. Sewed the sachet too. She wondered if she'd still be there on the farm to do it all over again the following year. Everything was so uncertain.

Violet grabbed the towel bar next to the tub and

lowered herself. The sudsy water warmed through her Chinese lantern, paper-thin skin to the depths of the creaking points of her bones. *Wonderful* was the word that came to mind. It felt *wonderful*. She stayed in the hot depths as long as she could. She smiled when she thought how her skin was pre-pruned before the soak.

After she got out, toweled off, and dressed, she passed by the bedroom that had all the computer equipment. It was all gone. She wondered where Sherman had taken it. She also wondered why he'd done so.

"Honey," Violet called out after him, when she saw him heading out the kitchen door for the barn, "where are all your things?"

"Don't worry about it, Mom," he said. "I didn't want to clutter up the house."

A few days later, Violet turned on the TV to watch *Jeopardy!* She loved the host with or without his mustache and she thought that show and, to a lesser extent, *Wheel of Fortune*, kept her mind sharp. When the TV didn't come on anymore, she went to Sherman to ask him to fix it.

"I don't want to miss *Jeopardy!*," she said. "This is teachers' week."

"Sorry, Mom," Sherman said. "I canceled the satellite service. It was getting way out of hand, cost-wise. Plus, nothing but trash is on TV these days anyway."

"You shouldn't have done that without asking me," she said, feeling a little silly that she was fighting for a couple of ancient game shows hosted by men who, while no longer young, were still attractive to her.

She'd never tell him that. She was no longer young, either.

"I'm sorry, Mom," Sherman said. "You're absolutely right! I should have asked you. I didn't want to bother you. You have enough on your mind."

She wasn't sure what he was referring to, but she accepted his apology. Sherman was always a quiet, good, honest boy. He'd only wanted the best for her.

As Violet's world continued to shrink, she counted her blessings one by one. She was reasonably healthy. She could still read. She had a son who loved her. She could knit and crochet. She had so much for which she could be thankful. She knew all of that. And yet she was unhappy. She felt alone. Even a little trapped.

CHAPTER THIRTY-THREE

Kendall Stark parked her car in the parking lot adjacent to the correctional facility in Monroe, less than an hour north of Seattle. She was tired. Hungry. Restless. The idea that convicted serial killer Jerry Connors could help her was, she was sure, an indicator of her own obsession with the woman who'd murdered and tormented the people of the Pacific Northwest.

The sun was low in the sky, and a haze from a house fire not far from the prison complex only served to darken her mood. But there she was. In front of her like some kind of beat-up courthouse stood the pillars to the entryway of the 1910 structure that had started as a reformatory but had morphed into that do-gooder euphemism "correctional complex." The superintendent, Jayce Chatfield, had the day off. His deputy, a man with scribbled-on, thinning hair, and thick pepperoni stick lips greeted the detective.

"Detective Stark," Gary Cline said, "Mr. Chatfield is really sorry that he couldn't be here today. He wanted to tell you that you could have as much time with the inmate as you need. Janie Thomas was one of our own, you know."

Gary's remark was more kind than true. Janie Thomas was the biggest black mark against the state's corrections department in its more than a century of existence.

"Thank you for that," she said. "I don't really know how much time I'll need or how much time Connors will give me."

"He's got all the time in the world," the assistant said. "Lifer, you know."

Kendall followed him to the metal detector. The guard asked her if she was carrying a weapon, and she said she was.

"We'll secure it," said the guard, a young man with a thick neck and steroid-pumped forearms.

"Yes, of course," Kendall said, handing her Glock to him.

Passing through the security checkpoint and down a long corridor, the scenery shifted from the old-school grimness of the original building to a section that seemed more akin to a corridor at South Kitsap High School than a prison—though she was pretty certain that some kids would beg to differ with her on that assessment.

"Right in here," Gary Cline said, pointing to a large, well-lit visitation room with an overhead ceiling fan, bolted-to-the-floor table, and permanently affixed chairs.

"Thanks," she said, taking a seat, as the superintendent's right-hand man turned to leave.

"Don't worry," he said. "He'll be in full restraints. A guard will be right outside. Of course, you're completely welcome to have the guard sit in here with you."

"No, thanks," Kendall said, "I'm sure I can manage."

Without so much as a hello, inmate #394321 slid

into a chair across from her. Jerry Connors no longer looked like the affable boy next door who cajoled unsuspecting women into his apartment before raping and murdering them. Such a baby face. Such pretty eyes. Never could he ever do anything so absolutely horrific as killing fourteen young women. But that's what he did.

His hands were chained and his feet shackled. He wore street clothes, not an orange jumpsuit. On his feet, however, instead of shoes, were flip-flops that looked brand new. Kendall nodded coolly, once he was settled in.

She identified herself and took out a small notebook and the typical prison-issue implement for note taking, a stub of a pencil.

"Look at you," he said. "Getting all ready. You're here to find out about my pen pal, Brenda?" he asked.

"Yes, Mr. Connors," the detective said. She couldn't bring herself to call him by his first name. Her favorite dog growing up was a Sheltie named Jerry. "You know that's why I'm here."

He drummed his fingertips on the dull surface of the tabletop.

"World's pretty fascinated by her," he said. "Even I never got the kind of press she did, and let's face it, I deserved it."

You, sir, are a disgusting piece of garbage, Kendall thought.

"The media can be fickle, Mr. Connors," she said.

"Tell me about it," he said. "Now they want me. Once they found out she was pouring her heart out to me, they came a-running. Just like you."

"Look, Mr. Connors," Kendall said. "I'm not here

for the media. I'm here because you said you'd talk to me about Brenda Nevins."

"You don't know where she is," he said. His tone was flat.

"No, I don't," Kendall said. "Do you?"

He looked right through her. "Dunno. Could be that I know. Depends on what you'll do for me."

"There isn't anything that I can do," she said. "You have a life sentence without the possibility of parole. That's the end of that. I'm a detective working a case. You said you'd talk to me. That's why we're here."

"You can be a tough one," he said. "I've encountered others like you who thought they were tough too."

Kendall kept her face stone. "We're not talking about you. I know you would love to go on and on and relive all the things you've done, but that's not going to happen. Not today."

Jerry Connors fabricated a pout. "That makes me a little sad," he said. "I hate being sad. Don't you?"

"I hate being led on," Kendall said, getting up.

"Wait," he said, rising up a little to meet her eyes. "Don't go. I want to tell you what I know. I've done a few bad things of which I'm not proud, and you know, I have a mom out there and maybe she'll forgive me. Come and see me. You know, everyone deserves a second chance."

Everyone but you, Kendall thought.

"Agreed," she said. "Then let's talk. What did Brenda say to you in her letters?"

"Sex stuff mostly. I mean, she didn't use the real words for things. She substituted. Said she found a great candy store at the prison, and they had lollipops that you could suck all day."

Kendall kept her face expressionless as possible, which, considering the ludicrous nature of Brenda's candy metaphor, was pretty hard to do. "That's not very helpful, Mr. Connors. Did she talk about where she might go if she ever got out of prison?"

"Yeah," he said. "We all play the game that, you know, if we were Morgan Freeman getting out of prison where would we go. Most say Mexico because that's what he did in the movie. I myself would go back to my old neighborhood and face those liars who said they found those bodies in my backyard. But that's me. I'm stronger than most. Brenda was strong like me."

"How so?" Kendall asked, pushing a little, but not too much. "What did she say to you?"

He rattled his chains against the scraped surface of the tabletop. "Sure wish I could have a Dr Pepper," he said.

"Sorry. I can't give you one," Kendall said, though if she could have given him a drink she would have liked to spit in it first. "Prison policy. Now, what did she say?"

"She told me she was surrounded by losers," he said. "She said she was misunderstood. The same way I am misunderstood. That she was innocent but she'd been branded something she wasn't and that she'd never stop until she made sure the world got the right message about her. In one letter, she said something along the lines of how she was going to do something so big, so awful, that it would make people sit up and notice."

Kendall pushed again. "Notice what?"

"Her," he answered. "That they really screwed up

on her prosecution. She was tired of being blamed for something she didn't do."

"But she killed her husband and baby girl. There's no doubt about that. She did *that*."

"Lots of people are convicted of things they didn't do. Don't you ever watch *The Innocence Project* on TV?" he asked, his eyes unblinking. "Brenda said that she was convicted because everyone was jealous of her. Her friends. Her in-laws. Even the newspaper people who covered her case. You know what, Detective? People can be real mean when they want to."

When someone deserves it as much as you and Brenda, she thought.

"Yes, I guess I see what you're saying," she lied. "Did she say what she was planning? Did you get an idea, a hint of what she might do if she ever got out?"

Again the chains scraped the tabletop. "If you're looking for me to connect the dots for you, Detective, we're fresh out of that today. Sorry. She *hinted*, I guess."

"And?"

Jerry looked right into Kendall's eyes. It was like she was looking into the bottom of a swimming pool with no one inside. Just the blank emptiness of his fixed stare. She wondered what those fourteen young women had seen in those eyes before he killed them. Had he been able to project kindness at first? Had he used that stare to bring them closer so that he could run that razor across their throats? Eyes like the ones belonging to Jerry Connors were vacant enough to be anything the beholder wanted to see.

"She wasn't explicit," he continued. "You can't be. Everything that comes in and out of here is read by some dolt who has nothing better to do than eavesdrop on our pathetic lives. Like we're some show."

But not The Innocence Project, *Jerry Connors, she thought.*

"What was she going to do?" Kendall asked. "Where was she going to go?"

Jerry swallowed and made an audible gulping sound. A disgusting noise. He smacked his lips. He was either thirsting for that Dr Pepper or trying to push Kendall's buttons.

She ignored the darting of his tongue and waited for him to say something. Silence filled the room. Off in the distance, down the corridor through which she'd passed to meet him, she could hear the slamming of a heavy metal door and footsteps fading into the oblivion of the prison.

"We talked about fishing and hunting," he said.

Kendall leaned in a little. "Go on. Fishing and hunting?"

"Right. Not really that, of course. Not the animal kind. The human kind. You can't share tricks and tips for, you know, dealing with people."

"Dealing" was about the coldest word for murder that Kendall could imagine, but she didn't let her feelings show. She looked at Jerry with the same flat stare that he employed. Or at least she tried to.

"What did she want to know? What did you tell her?"

He laughed. "It seems so stupid now. I know you're judging me. *Judging her.* But you don't understand that the world is full of people like Brenda and me. You call them CEOs or politicians or doctors or TV stars. Anyone who wants to get something from others in a big way is a hunter or fisher. The world is made up of people like us and . . ."

". . . and?"

"People like you."

The remark irritated Kendall. "And what, tell me, are people like me?" she asked.

He laughed again. "I could really use that drink."

"You aren't getting one," she answered. "Not until we're done." She made a mental note to tell Steven and Birdy later that she was pretty sure that being a mother was good practice for interviewing Jerry Connors. *"Clean up your plate, Jerry, before you go outside and kill someone!"*

"Fine," he said, sulking a little. "I'll tell you what I know because I'm not above being helpful. I want you to make a note of that, Detective. If someone asks if I cooperated with you, you'll tell them that I did. I've been completely misjudged."

"You did kill fourteen women," she said, unable stop herself.

"So say the prosecutors."

"You admitted it."

He smiled. "I admitted *those*," he said, letting the word *those* hang in the air.

What the? Was he going to confess to more? Or was this another game?

"There were others?" Kendall asked.

He grinned. "I'm saving the rest of the story for my autobiography. Let's talk about Ms. Brenda Nevins."

Jerry Connors was a tease. A killer. A complete waste of oxygen. He was also adept at controlling the situation, as he had when he'd abducted and killed his victims. Kendall wondered how he'd fared in prison. She imag-

ined he was one of the few cons who'd be able to strad-
dle both sides of the power base. Prisoners probably admired him for his ruthlessness. The corrections officers
undoubtedly appreciated his compliance with the rules.

Both sides had only seen what he'd allowed them to
see.

Over the next half hour, Jerry Connors told Kendall
how Brenda had started writing to him after she was
incarcerated at the Washington Corrections Center for
Women, in Gig Harbor, Washington. According to
Jerry, Brenda was looking for friendship and understanding.

"It changed over time," he said. "They always do."

"Romantic?" Kendall asked.

"Hotter than romance," he answered.

If Birdy were in the room just then, she'd have
looked over at her and raised a brow.

"What else?" Kendall asked.

Jerry made that smacking noise again, but Kendall
managed to ignore it.

"She talked about how we'd both been beat up by
the media," he said. "And she's right. TV people are so
damn shallow. They don't care about facts, only tone
and volume."

That would be about the only thing Jerry Connors
could say that she'd ever agree with. Kendall hated the
media too.

"What did she want with you, Mr. Connors?" she
asked.

The prisoner puffed himself up a little. He was loving this. Too much. For Kendall's liking, for sure.

"Besides having my baby probably," he said, "Brenda wanted a sounding board. There's no book you can read, no class you can take to deal with the kind of pressures ambitions like ours bring. Brenda sought advice from me. Like *you* might seek advice from the director of the FBI, you know, if you wanted to go to the top and get the best mind to help you sort things out."

Again, another opportunity for rolling her eyes.

And again, Kendall kept her face as expressionless as possible.

"What was it that she wanted help with?" she asked.

Jerry Connors shifted and his manacles rattled. "Look, our words were coded," he said. "But underlying all of her words was a desire to be famous. To show those who'd wronged her that they were nothing and she was worthy of major adulation. Worldwide even. There was no limit to her ambition. I liked that about her. The girl reminded me of myself."

"How was she going to get there?" Kendall asked.

Jerry Connors, killer of at least fourteen women, looked toward the door and the guard outside. Like Brenda, he liked an audience. The larger the better. It was surprising to Kendall that he didn't like television, as he was a natural showman in that hideous train-wreck way.

"She was going to do something big," he said. "Something outrageous. I don't know exactly what it was, but I do think that the girl had it in her to do whatever it took. Some people have characterized me as being cold or indifferent. It might be fair to some extent, I don't know. But I do know that Brenda Nevins had me beat by a mile. She told me that she'd get out of prison and she did. She told me that she had someone on the inside that she was working hard. I thought it was a man—you know the old corrections officer and the horny gal behind bars deal—but I guess it wasn't. It turns out it was that woman who ran the joint."

"Superintendent Thomas," Kendall said.

"Yeah, her. I guess. I really thought it was a guy. She never said it was a woman."

On the way out, Kendall thought about what Jerry Connors had told her. She dialed Birdy, but the call went to voice mail.

"Okay, Birdy, that was not great. Not all that helpful. Promise me that whenever I suggest that I should go *Silence of the Lambs* and talk to a serial killer to try to find out something for a case, you'll tell me that I'm wasting my time. At least I probably wasted my time. He wanted me to know that Brenda was driven by a need for fame and revenge. Like we didn't know that? Right? I guess we also know that she felt she'd been wronged by people in her life. I'm guessing that someone must have not told her she looked hot back in high school or something, and she's still pissed off about it. Still. Let's see . . . I'm doing a data dump on you right now. Could use a drink. Anyway, I'm taking the seven o'clock boat. If you're around give me a buzz."

The opportunity to strut their stuff at Port Angeles High School had been presented as top tier, which made the girls from South Kitsap laugh out loud when they got notification in the mail.

**The *Best of the West* in cheer will be performing
at the Port Angeles High School auditorium,
Port Angeles, Washington.**
BY INVITATION ONLY.

"How about 'beg only'?" Blake Scott said, as she flipped her dark brown hair over her shoulder and gave her classic eye roll to the others. She'd been the first to receive the invite. She'd gathered the others together in front of her locker at South Kitsap High School.

"Blow only is more like it," chimed in teammate Kelly Sullivan.

Blake had been one-upped in the sarcasm department, something she only allowed on a limited basis. Being number one at everything was very important her.

"For sure," Blake said, stealing the attention away from Kelly, "someone had to blow someone to force us into attending an event in a Podunk town worse than Port Orchard."

"Right," said Kelly, a reed-thin girl with a suspected eating disorder, who carried a mini bottle of Listerine in her purse. "Totally stupid."

Of the squad, Blake considered only two others "top tier"—Amber Turner and Chloe MacDonald. They'd represent the school with their very best routine.

"We'll show those morons in Port Angeles who's boss," she said.

CHAPTER THIRTY-FOUR

"**M**om," Sherman Wilder said, "there's someone I want you to meet."

Violet's son stepped aside, and behind him was the most beautiful woman his mother had ever seen. She had crystalline blue eyes, and dark hair that shimmered like the blackest water on a moonlit night. She wore a simple print dress that accentuated her body without screaming to the world that she had a stunning figure. She looked like one of those women in a fashion magazine. Her skin was flawless, her lips full, and her features were perfect. Not bland. Interesting enough to keep another's eyes searching for the most perfect place to land a gaze.

That place had to be those eyes.

"Mom, this is Vanessa," he said.

"Ms. Wilder," Vanessa said, "I'm thrilled to meet you. Sherman has told me so much about you. I feel like we're going to be very good friends."

Violet felt the young woman was trying awfully hard to win her over. She'd been there. Most girls had. Trying to get in the good graces of the mother of a boyfriend is every girlfriend's goal. She hadn't been told much about Vanessa, except that she'd suffered some terrible tragedies in her life.

"You must be tired from the long drive, Vanessa," Violet said, trying to keep her tone friendly. Her son had made dubious choices in the past. Girlfriend choices. Wife choices. He was an introvert. He'd always attracted the kind of women who fed on being in charge. It was too soon to know if Vanessa was that kind of a girl. And really, at her age, Violet thought to herself, what did any of that matter?

"Blackberry wine?" Violet asked.

Vanessa hesitated. "If it's not too much trouble, yes. But only on one condition."

Sherman looked at his mother, then back at his girlfriend.

"What's that?" Violet asked.

"Only if you made it," she said.

Sherman laughed, cutting the tension. "Of course," he said, "she did. She makes everything."

Vanessa laughed. "I'll pour."

Violet scooted her walker to the pantry, telling Sherman to set out some glasses.

"The ones for company."

Later that night, Violet couldn't sleep. She could hear her son and his girlfriend making love as the headboard beat against the wall in that rhythm that she hadn't experienced for years. She was glad that Sherman had a lover. It broke her heart that he'd been alone for so long. He was such a good, good boy.

After a while, the headboard stopped banging, and

Violet drifted off thinking of her husband, the farm, the things that no longer were part of her life. She hoped that she'd die in her sleep. Not that night. But before she had to go to an assisted-living home in Port Angeles. She'd visited her friend Jerri Anne there and couldn't banish the scent of the place from her consciousness. The mix of dead skin, soiled bedding, and bleach haunted her. She'd never gone back. Jerri Anne died a month after the visit. Violet considered her death a gift to her family and friends.

Violet's eyes fluttered open. She looked at the clock on her bedside table. It was a little past 3 A.M. Nature was calling. It called at least once a night. She reached for her walker, slipped on her robe.

Vanessa stood in the hallway. She was naked. Her eyes met Violet's.

"Do you need something, Vanessa?"

A nightgown maybe?

Vanessa stretched her arms. "No, I'm fine. Just couldn't sleep. I don't know if you heard, but your son really has a way with a girl."

Violet ignored the remark.

"You need to put some clothes on," she said.

Vanessa looked down at her nakedness. It was a long gaze, the kind that one might give to admire something precious. Coveted.

"Sorry," she said. "I hadn't realized." Her eyes stayed riveted to Violet's.

"Remember when you were young and beautiful?"

"I beg your pardon?"

"You heard me."

"I'm going to the bathroom and then I'm going to bed. I think you should go to bed too."

"The blackberry wine was delicious," Vanessa said. "Goodnight, Ms. Wilder."

The next morning, the kitchen smelled of coffee and frying bacon. The familiar aroma brought back a flood of memories. Sherman was at the stove, adjusting the strips of bacon as they sizzled.

"Coffee, Mom?"

"Please," she said. "Smells wonderful in here."

"Like old times."

Not exactly.

"Where's Vanessa?"

Sherman gave his mother a cup of coffee. "Asleep."

"Honey," she said. "I need to tell you something."

"Mom, if it's about earlier, forget it. Vanessa told me."

"What did she tell you?"

"She sleepwalks, Mom. She told me that she ran into you this morning. She's very embarrassed about it."

"The poor thing," Violet said, taking her seat by the window.

"It's okay. She doesn't do it that often. She doesn't remember what she says or does when it happens. Just that it happened."

"I see," Violet said, though she really didn't. She didn't know anything about sleepwalking. "She seemed awake."

Sherman moved the bacon to some paper towels to blot the fat.

"She's a bit of a free spirit," he said. "I like that about her. Don't you?"

Before she could answer, Vanessa appeared. She was dressed, her hair and makeup perfect.

"Morning, Ms. Wilder," she said.

"Call her Mom," Sherman said.

Violet blinked. She wasn't sure she heard him quite right. Her hearing hadn't been the best lately.

"Mom?" she said, almost hopeful that she'd been mistaken.

Sherman beamed. "Yeah, we're getting married."

Vanessa put her arms around Violet's shoulders and hugged her. It was a hard hug. A very hard hug.

Vanessa leaned close to her ear.

"I saw the way you looked at me," she whispered.

Violet pushed back, eyes wide. Her hearing was bad, but not that bad.

"What did you say?" she asked.

"I love your son," she said, her eyes staring hard. "What did you think I said?"

The next night, Violet made her "world famous" lasagna that really wasn't famous at all. It was a standard recipe that she'd followed since her grandmother made it for her. Her secret was never in the ingredients, but in the way that she made it, layer by layer. It was so tall that when cut into portions it resembled a large cube.

Vanessa made a face. "It looks good," she said, "but I don't do pasta."

"I'm sorry," Violet said, shooting a look at Sherman.

Her son pushed his plate away. "Sorry, Mom, but I don't think I should eat any either." Vanessa wore a satisfied expression on her face.

"Honey," Violet said. "You love my lasagna. I made it for your birthday dinner almost every year."

"I know," he said. "It just isn't healthy. Vanessa says we all should be gluten free if we want to live a full life."

"But you saw that I was making lasagna," Violet said, visibly upset. "I could have made something else." She faced Vanessa, hoping for some kind words. "I worked really hard on this. I'm sorry."

Vanessa didn't say a word.

Violet struggled to get up from the table. Sherman helped her by steadying her walker.

"Mom," he said, "what are you doing?"

"I'm not feeling well," she said. "I'm going to bed."

"Mom!" he said, as she left the kitchen. "Don't be so damned dramatic!"

"I'm not," she said. "I'm just not feeling well."

Violet shut her bedroom door and made her way to the edge of the bed. She was angry. Sick and tired. Sick and tired of Vanessa. She'd wished to God that she'd told Sherman not to bring home another girl. That he'd made nothing but bad choices. Susan had been all right. But she'd betrayed him. She'd given him a child and that had been all that had been good from that relationship.

A few minutes later, Sherman knocked on his mother's door.

"Look, Mom," he said, "I need to talk to you."

"I just need some time alone," she said. "Sorry for everything."

"No one is angry with you," he said.

"I'm mad," she answered.

"You are?"

"Yes, if you even care."

"Of course, I care," Sherman said. "What are you mad about?"

"I don't want to talk about it. I just need some rest. Everything will be better in the morning," she said, her voice cracking.

"Mom, I'm sorry about the lasagna."

If it was only that simple, she thought.

Vanessa appeared in the doorway.

"Mom," she said, "are we upset about something?"

"Get her away from me," Violet said. "I don't want her in my bedroom."

Sherman stood up like he'd been jerked by a rope. He looked over at Vanessa, then at this mother. "What's the matter with you, Mom? Vanessa was only trying to help!"

This was too much for Violet. She'd reached her boiling point.

"Help, my ass!" she said. "She saw me get out the ingredients for the lasagna this morning, and I even told her what I was making. She never said one word about it being something she couldn't, or rather, wouldn't eat."

"Jeesh, Mom, can we stop it with the lasagna?" Sherman asked, trying to calm his mother, but only fanning the flames. "So what? It's no big deal."

Over Sherman's shoulder Vanessa mouthed the words "tough luck."

"You are not nice, Vanessa," Violet said.

"Mom, you're hurting my feelings," Vanessa said.

Violet didn't care what Vanessa said. "You don't have any feelings," she shot back.

Sherman's face was red.

"Mom, I've had it with you. I'm beginning to question your sanity. You act erratic like this, and you'll need to go to assisted living. I swear, on Dad's grave, that I'll do it. I'll take you there."

His words were a knife to her heart.

"Please, no," she said. "I don't want to go there."

Sherman stormed out of the room, passing Vanessa, who hovered in the doorway like a fly over a picnic table. She turned away from her lover and looked over at Violet. On her face was the biggest smile Violet Wilder had ever seen in a situation that was decidedly not a happy one.

"I've had it with you," Violet said, somehow summoning the strength to get up and shut the door, leaving Vanessa sputtering.

Violet collapsed on her bed. She'd never been so upset in her entire life. It was like her house had been taken over by her son's awful girlfriend. Her skin crawled whenever Vanessa called her "Mom." Her odd, cold demeanor perverted the word.

Violet did not want to go to assisted living. Her friend had withered and died there after a few weeks of lamenting the dull crafts she'd been asked to do, the church services with a blowhard young pastor, and the food that was, apparently, the kitchen's idea of fifty shades of gray. Assisted suicide, yes. Assisted living, absolutely not.

Violet couldn't drive anymore. She couldn't walk very far. No phone. No cell service. No TV. It was like she was trapped beneath one of the bell jars that she used to start seeds for the garden.

Later that night, Violet lay listening to the headboard bang against the wall. The sound of her son's lovemaking with that awful woman made her wince. She put her head under the pillow, but she could still feel the pound, pound, pound on the wall above her.

Good God, she thought, *don't those two ever just go to bed to sleep?*

Violet didn't think she could take one more night of it. She had to do something. She needed to find out what was going on in the barn. What in the world were those two up to? They were so secretive. She wondered if her son was involved in drugs. Marijuana was legal in Washington, so it could be that. Maybe meth? Manufacturing or something like that? Until Vanessa showed up, he was a straight arrow, but now not so much.

He's thinking with the wrong head, she mused.

CHAPTER THIRTY-FIVE

The South Kitsap cheer squad sat outside Port Angeles High while they waited for Patty Sparks, the van driver, to pull up. Patty had dropped them off only twenty minutes earlier, but they soon realized their drive all the way up to Port Angeles had been a big fat zero. Patty had made a quick run to a nearby McDonald's when Amber called her cell.

"Either we got the date wrong or they did," Amber Turner said.

"What do you mean?" Patty asked.

"There's no event. There's nothing. Just us and a science teacher who didn't know a thing about why we were even there."

Patty looked down at the invitation on the passenger seat.

It was today.

"I don't understand," she said. "Maybe they canceled."

"I guess so," Amber said.

"They should have called us," Patty said. "What a colossal waste of school district money! All that gas!"

"Talk about a big fiasco," Amber said. "We're all out front of the school. Blake's totally pissed off."

The four girls shifted their pom-poms and adjusted their team sweaters while they waited in front of Port Angeles High School. Normally, they were a huddle of red and black with an air of invincibility. This time they were a row of anger.

The van pulled in front of the school and the four girls, toting their pom-poms, made their way over to it. Blake Scott was the queen bee, the one who all the other girls deferred to on every subject from hair and makeup to what music they'd play while they warmed up. She was pretty, but completely untrustworthy in Patty's estimation.

"She talks nice to my face," she said to her husband one time, "but I see her mocking me in the rearview mirror. She's not a nice girl."

Amber Turner would have been the queen bee if smarts counted for anything. She was bright, self-aware, and thoughtful. The previous week, she'd brought snacks for the team and knew Patty was beyond hungry—because, well, Patty always was. Amber gave her an extra granola bar when no one else was looking.

Kelly Sullivan spent most of her time sucking up to Blake and throwing up in the bathroom. At least that's what Patty thought. One time another teacher confronted Kelly about the frequent trips to the bathroom, suggesting she might have an eating disorder. Kelly sniffed at the suggestion.

"I think I might be pregnant," she had said without the least bit of irony in her voice. "Again!"

Chloe MacDonald was the smallest. When they had enough girls to make a pyramid, it was Chloe who climbed to the top. She was Asian by heritage, but had been adopted by a family in South Colby when she was one. She tended to keep to herself, but wasn't afraid to push back a little when Blake pushed her buttons.

"You might be the leader of this team," Patty overheard Chloe say to Blake one time, "but you are not the boss of me. So don't try to act like it. If you want to know how tough I am, just push a little harder."

Amber Turner blended in to the pack of girls in a way that made each feel as though she were an ally. Over the past few weeks Amber had been preoccupied with things at home and, the other girls suspected, her new boyfriend.

Blake, in particular, wanted to know if Amber and Elan Waterman had had sex yet, but Amber refused to answer.

"Just because you've put out with half the football team, Blake, doesn't mean all of us are doing the same thing," Amber said

She was only half-joking, of course.

"At least my boyfriends are starters on the team," Blake said. "I'm not wasting my time with some no-body."

Amber held her tongue. Elan was new and interesting. She liked him. Besides, it was never worth it to argue with Blake Scott. Blake was too narcissistic to ever see that her choices were stupid—or that none of the boys she'd slept with stayed with her for a full season.

"We should sue the high school for wasting our time," Blake said.

"Yeah," Kelly said, though she thought it was not a winnable suit.

Patty waited for everyone to get buckled in. As usual, none of the girls sat in the front seat, though it was always available. She was only the driver. Nothing more. The person who was hired to get them from Point A to B so that they could bask in the adulation of the crowds as they jumped, shook, and rattled their pom-poms.

It was about an hour and a half drive from Port Angeles to Port Orchard, putting the girls back in the hands of their families after 10 P.M. As they drove out of town toward Highway 101, Patty noticed a massive cargo ship edging out into the inky water of the Straits of Juan de Fuca. It was a surreal image with twinkly lights that almost made the vessel appear as though it were studded in diamonds. She thought of pointing it out to the girls, but they were all focused on their phones and complaining about the lousy cell service, so she let it go.

These kids have better things to do than look at the world around them, she thought as her soul sucked in the glory of the view.

"I'm thirsty," Blake announced. "Get me a pop!"

Chloe, closest to the cooler, opened the hinged lid and handed Blake a Mountain Dew.

"Gross, Chloe," Blake said, "I can't stand that crap. I want a Diet Dr Pepper."

"Anyone want the Mountain Dew?" she asked, her voice dripping with disdain.

"I thought one of you might like it," Patty said. "Sorry. I couldn't find any Red Bull."

The girls laughed like that was the funniest thing they'd ever heard.

"Red Bull does not equate to Mountain Dew, Patty," Blake said.

"Yeah, Patty," Kelly echoed.

"Sorry," she said, feeling stupid. "I'll take it."

Chloe handed the bottle to Patty and gave Blake a Diet Dr Pepper. The others drank water, taking off the caps to sip, then screwing them back on. Over and over. And at the same time, checking their phones as though the missing service bars would materialize by the formidable force of their will.

Patty drank the Mountain Dew, thinking that the citrus-flavored drink was worth the 170 calories and that a cookie would be good about then too. Her stomach was upset. She pressed her palm just below her rib cage to quell the discomfort she was feeling. A wave of nausea struck her. It was that kind of sharp, excruciating pain that she knew would return.

Whoa, she thought, *I'm going to be sick. Real sick.*

The van veered over the centerline and a passing car honked; its driver offered a single-finger salute out a rolled-down window.

"Patty!" Kelly called out, "what the hell are you doing?"

"Sorry," she said, her vision spinning. "Just feel like I'm going to be sick."

"Crap," Blake said, putting down her phone. "You trying to kill us?"

"No," Patty said, trying to steady herself. "I feel funny. Sick like."

The van rolled over the centerline and Kelly screamed.

"Pull over," Amber said, her voice rising from suggestion to command. "Up ahead. Just get off the road."

"Yeah!" Chloe said. "If you're going to hurl, no one wants to be in the van when you do." She looked over at Kelly. "Empathy puking is the worst."

The girls gave each other the kind of knowing glance that they'd perfected among the group. *The look*. It was what they used to acknowledge the weak links in their opponents. *The look* indicated a sense of superiority shared by the South Kitsap girls to the exclusion of everyone else. Inclusion was a concept for losers who didn't belong. Diversity?

Chloe was diversity.

Patty put on her turn indicator, eased off the gas, and applied the brake. The van pulled over into a wide space of gravel along the highway. Patty sat hunched over the steering wheel. Her face was white. Her eyes were red, as though she was bleeding from her tear ducts.

"Jesus," Blake said, "like what's the matter with *her*?"

"Dunno," Amber answered, as she slid over the others and climbed into the front passenger seat. "Patty?" she said, grabbing her shoulders and trying to get her to look in her direction. "Patty? Do you hear me?"

"Oh God," Chloe said, her voice registering some emotion. "What's the matter with her?"

"We are going to get home so late, Blake," Kelly said. "Not cool."

"Not cool that she's practically unconscious," Amber shot back. "Is anyone's phone working? We need to call 911."

The other girls held up their phones.

"No," Chloe said. "Verizon sucks."

"They all suck," Amber said, to the complete agreement of the other girls.

Kelly leaned closer to look at Patty.

"Crap," she said. "She's passed out."

"Tell me about it," Chloe said.

"If we like want to get home on time," Blake said, "we need to get some help. I'm an AAA member."

"You don't have phone service," Kelly said, in a way that she hoped was only a reminder and not a "tone" that would cause Blake some offense. Blake didn't like it when anyone chipped away at her perfection. Even the tiniest infraction would be paid back with a major diss. "She needs medical attention more than we need the AAA."

"I know," Blake conceded, her eyes hard.

Amber got out of the passenger seat and opened the driver's door.

"Patty?" she asked, looking at the woman in the couch-print shirt.

Patty's eyes fluttered.

"I think I ate something that didn't agree with me," she said, her words barely above a whisper. "I need air."

"Kelly! Help me move her!" Amber said.

As they shifted Patty's heavy frame from behind the wheel, the beam of a car's headlights flooded the interior of the van.

"Everything all right here?"

It was a man's voice.

Blake answered first. Like she always did.

"Does it look like it?" she asked. "Our driver is sick, and we're supposed to be like home in an hour."

The man reached in his pocket.

"No cell service," Kelly said.

"We need a doctor," Chloe said. "Something's wrong with Patty."

Amber spoke up. "She said she ate something that didn't agree with her," she said.

Blake shrugged. "She's always eating something," she said.

The man pulled a gun out of his jacket pocket and pointed it at Patty and fired. *Just like that.* There was no warning. No nothing. He aimed it at her head and the loud pop shook the van. The girls screamed.

"Who's next?" he said.

"What just happened?" Kelly said, spinning around, then freezing. "What the hell's the matter with you? Why did you do that?"

The man ignored her.

"Give me your phones," he said.

The girls stood, unable to move.

"I said give me your phones! Now, all of you! *This damn minute.* I won't ask again."

The barrel of his pistol glinted.

One by one, they handed over their phones. It was like giving away a part of them. An arm. A leg. Their soul.

With the dome light the only illumination, it was hard to see what the man looked like. How old he was. How anyone would be able to identify him later. His eyes looked black, but that might have only been because his pupils were so dilated that they crowded the color of his irises to their very edge. He had a mustache or stubble of beard. It was hard to say because in the chaos of the moment, all of the girls were thinking of themselves and what the man was going to do next.

The *why* no longer mattered. The *what* was clear. Kelly touched her face and looked at her hand. *Blood*. She wondered if she'd been shot too. She didn't think so, but that instant was so strange, so frightening. She ran her fingers over her cheeks, her neck, just to be sure.

"I will kill anyone who doesn't do what I say," he said.

"Please don't," Amber said.

He turned to her. "I'll start with you," he said. His tone was ice. No rage. Just cool and calm. "I'll start with *any* of you. It makes no difference to me."

"We didn't do anything to you," said Blake, crying. Her mascara ran like a muddy river down her cheeks.

"Everyone back in the van," he said. It was an order. Not a request.

Kelly was on her knees, next to Patty. She had her hand on the driver's and was jiggling it a little to see if Patty would wake up. Blood oozed like maroon candle wax from the gaping wound on the side of her head.

"What about her?" Kelly said. "You shouldn't have done this to Patty. She didn't do anything! She needs a doctor! What kind of a sick person are you? This is not right. You don't just shoot someone for no reason."

CHAPTER THIRTY-SIX

O n the highway behind the van, a car's wheels slowed. Its headlights stabbed at the darkness as the vehicle with the intruder with the gun had. The beams bounced off the van, revealing it was a light-colored VW bug, old school.

The man lowered his weapon. "Say a word and you'll be dead," he told the teens. "You know that I'm not kidding, right?"

None of the girls said anything. Their vocal cords were frozen.

The newcomer lowered the window on the driver's side.

"Everything okay?" a young man's voice called out. He was in his twenties, with a passable goatee and shaggy hair that even in the darkness looked messy and in need of a cut.

"All good," the shooter said. "Just need a jump. Got my cables in my car."

"All right," the Good Samaritan said. "Want me to call someone?"

"No service," the shooter replied with an annoyance that indicated experience with that stretch of road.

"Tell me about it," the young stranger said. "Up the road. Past the bend. Completely dead. My commute. I hate it."

"Thanks," the man said, "but we got it handled. Right, girls?"

"Yeah," Blake said, her voice cracking. "We're like getting a jump and then we're going."

The young driver got out of the VW and walked to the side of the van closest to his car. Gravel crunched under each step. The noise was like muffled gunfire five miles away. The shooter stayed planted near the driver's door. On the front seat, Patty Sparks's eyes stared into nothingness.

"You sure everything's okay?" he asked.

Kelly leaned over. Her breath was hot on Chloe's ear. She whispered as quietly as she could.

"He's going to kill him."

Chloe braced herself. She gave Kelly a look.

Don't do anything stupid. Don't. We'll all die.

Blake noticed the shooter raise his gun a little, the barrel catching a glimmer of light, though still mostly out of view.

The shooter looked in the direction of his car, and then at the kid who'd stopped to help. "You want to help?"

"Sure," he said. "Helping these gals will be the highlight of my day."

"Really," Kelly said, struggling to keep her tone even, "We got this. Thanks, anyway. We don't need help."

The young man stepped closer. Too close for his own good, really. He looked inside the van, his eyes traveling across the passenger seat to where Patty's lifeless body had slumped behind the wheel.

His eyes went wide with alarm, his mouth hung open.

"Hey!" he called out. "What's wrong with her?"

Wrong question.

Pop! The sound of gunfire ricocheted through the van, over Patty's body, over the girls, into the young man's head.

The girls yelped in unison.

"Shut the hell up, you four little bitches!" the man said.

"Why did you do that?" Kelly screamed.

The man kept his composure and looked down at the lifeless young man. "He should have kept going."

Amber wrapped her arms around Kelly. Chloe and Blake huddled together. The girls were whimpering because they knew crying would be too loud. They'd been commanded to be quiet.

"You!" the man said looking at Amber, "help me move her."

Amber, tears streaming down her face, shook her head. "No," she said. "I'm not helping you."

"You don't get to decide that. I do." He pointed the gun at her face, and then tilted his head to indicate Patty. "You want to end up like her? Or maybe like him?"

Amber kept her mouth shut.

"I'll help," Kelly said. "Please don't hurt us."

The man smirked. "Good girl," he said. "This one's a little hefty, but let's get her over on the passenger side."

"But she's all bloody," Kelly said.

"You'll live," he said. "Now let's do it. You too." He indicated Amber, and following Kelly's lead, she did what she was told.

"Get in the van," he said to the other two. "Unless you want a bullet in the head, too."

After Patty was shoved to the middle of the front seat, the man got behind the wheel. He told Amber to crawl over Patty and sit in the passenger seat by the window. She did. All the girls were sobbing. No one spoke. No one could.

Chloe looked over at the shooter's car as he turned the ignition on in the van. As it rolled back onto the highway, she thought she saw another person in the car. Tears flooded from her eyes and rolled down her cheeks, so she wasn't exactly sure what she'd seen.

She felt so alone. Completely alone. Her lifeline had been left behind. She prayed to God that someone would find her phone.

When he had held open the bag for their phones, Chloe dropped in the silver compact that her mom got her at Sephora.

CHAPTER THIRTY-SEVEN

Chloe spoke up first. She might have been small, but she was a little sister to three girls, and she knew that the only way to get any attention at all was to go for it. The only way to get an answer was to ask the question.

"Where are you taking us?" she said from her place in the middle of the van.

Blake abdicated the sum of the van's pool of assertiveness to Chloe. Kelly, next to her, was also silent. Amber, in the front seat, couldn't find her voice at all.

The driver kept his gun pointed in her direction.

"Just be quiet," he said. "No one talks while I'm driving. Talking distracts me." He held the gun close to Amber's head. She pulled away, toward the window.

"Please don't hurt me," she said, her words soft.

"Yeah! Don't hurt her! You sick piece of crap!" It was Blake. She'd pulled herself together and decided to go full-on tough bitch. It was an affectation that she usually employed to get some silly advantage at school or even at home with her family.

She'd never needed it to save a life.

Someone else's.

Or her own.

"He'll kill me," Amber said. "Don't make him mad."

The man glanced at Blake, Kelly, and Chloe in the rearview mirror.

"Listen to her," he said, indicating Amber. "She's next. And then I'll blow each of you away. One by one. You saw that kid's brains poking out of his head like a smashed pumpkin?"

They all had. None would ever be able to erase that hideous, bloody image from their memories.

Chloe sat still, tears coming from her eyes.

"You shouldn't have shot Patty! You shouldn't have killed that guy," she said. "He didn't do anything but stop to help us."

Amber spoke up next, her body still twisted away from the driver. Her head pressed on the cold glass of the window so hard that every bump on the road caused a wince of pain.

"He's going to kill all of us, anyway," she said. "We didn't do anything either. Neither did Patty. He killed Patty for no reason too."

After the words came from her lips, the girls didn't say so, but each of them had the same thought. *He had killed Patty for a reason. They* had been the reason. He'd killed Patty on purpose. He wanted *them.*

"Are you going to rape us?" Chloe asked.

The driver grinned. His eyes met hers in the mirror. "No. Not going to rape anyone."

She persisted. "Then what are you going to do?"

Blake wished she were not so beautiful. If she were average, she would never have done catalog modeling.

If she'd never done that, she'd never have been on cheer. She'd been destined to be coveted and adored. But not like this. Not by some sicko. Her mental pity party stopped when she noticed the headlights of the car that had been tracking them since they'd left the turnout. She leaned close to Kelly and whispered.

"Someone's following us," she said.

Kelly glanced behind them, and as she did so, she let out a scream.

"What the hell?" the driver said.

"Patty's alive!" Kelly said.

Patty Sparks, her face bloody like she'd been dipped in red molasses syrup, lifted her head from where she'd been dumped in the back with the pom-poms, jugs of Gatorade, and the stash of energy bars that Chloe's mom had provided.

"Help me," Patty croaked.

"We need to get her a doctor!" Blake said.

Kelly started to unbuckle herself and turn in Patty's direction when the van swerved. Amber screamed. They all screamed.

"Amber!" Chloe called out. "Amber!"

"I'm all right," Amber said.

The driver pulled off the highway and started down a gravel road. About fifty yards off the main roadway, he pulled over. He grabbed the keys from the ignition with his hand that held the gun, swung open the door, and stepped out into the darkness.

"Damn you!" he said as he opened the back door of the van. "You're supposed to be dead!"

Lights from the car that had been following flooded the space behind them. A soft breeze rolled over an open field, making the grass undulate like the ocean. A couple of houses provided pinpricks of light, but they were far away. No matter how fast any of them could move their legs, there was no way to make a run for it. Besides, the shafts of light from the car behind them held them like a supermarket's grand-opening searchlight. None of the girls could see who it was or knew anything, beyond the obvious. *That person and their driver were working together.*

"Help me," Patty said, her voice urgent. "Blake, Kelly, Chloe, help me."

The girls huddled away from what they knew was about to happen.

Kelly was crying. "Please," she said, "don't hurt her again."

"Don't do this, sir," Patty said, her voice a weak rasp. "Don't hurt my girls!"

Flash! The gun fired again.

The gurgling sound of Patty's dying breath cut through Kelly's tears. None of the girls said a word. Blake stayed frozen. She thought about the kids that had been killed in school shootings and those who had survived by playing dead. She willed herself to barely breathe.

She closed her eyes.

Chloe held on to Patty's last words. She'd begged not for her life, but for the life of each of them. They had all been so mean to her. They'd teased her for everything from the clothes she wore to the way she wore her hair. She *was* fat. But she was nice. Always and unfailingly so.

The man shut the back of the van and returned to the driver's seat.

"Look," he said, as though they'd just stopped at a Starbuck's drive-through window and had been disappointed that the barista was out of chocolate syrup, "no one else needs to get hurt."

"We'll do anything you want," Amber said. "We won't cause you any trouble. Please don't hurt us. Please let us go."

"You be good to me," he said. He looked behind him through the side mirror. "You be good to my friend. And, yeah, I'll let you go. One by one. Promise. I'm not a bad guy."

"What are you?" Chloe asked.

He glanced in her direction. "I'm just a guy with a point to prove."

What was that?

He turned the ignition and the sound of the gravel road shifted under the van's tires.

"It won't be long," he said. "We'll get there soon enough. I bet you're all a little hungry. I know I am."

Later that evening, the moms and dads of the missing cheer squad felt that pang of anxiousness that comes now and then with parenthood. It was true that their girls weren't always perfect angels and had been late coming home before. They were teenagers, for crying out loud.

Yet something seemed more worrisome about their tardiness that evening. Amber and Kelly were good friends; Blake and Chloe were close. As a foursome, they didn't hang out together outside of their cheering. They had been expected back around 10 P.M. or maybe 11 at the latest, if they'd managed to talk Patty Sparks into stopping at a restaurant that they'd read made the best gluten-free pizza in the Pacific Northwest.

Chloe had told her mother that it was a good bet that Patty would say yes.

"She's never said no to a meal that we know about."

"Chloe! That's not nice!"

"Just saying, Mom!"

It had started to rain on the coast earlier in the day, and a storm warning had been issued for Clallam, Jefferson, and Northern Kitsap Counties. A couple of the moms wondered if the weather had washed out a road or had slickened the pavement and caused a traffic accident.

Sue Turner was the first to call the other moms to see if any had heard from their daughters.

Kelly's mom, Shari, said that her daughter had texted that the cheer event was a "bust" and they were heading home around seven.

"That was hours ago, Shari."

"They probably stopped to eat."

"I guess so."

In the next few hours all the moms and dads would worry.

Boyfriends too.

Elan Waterman finished his homework, watched an old episode of *Sons of Anarchy* on Netflix, and texted Amber around 11 P.M.

Where u at?

No reply.

He placed his phone next to his bed and pulled the covers up. It had been a long day, but a good one. And yet something niggled at him. His sleep was restless as he fought to find a cool spot on the pillow where he could lay his head. He opened his eyes to tiny slits and checked his phone at 1:30 A.M. Still nothing from Amber. She'd warned him that the cell reception was "complete crap" up in Port Angeles. He put it down to bad service or another Amber-like problem.

She let her phone battery run down. *Again*. That had to be it.

By four in the morning, every parent of the missing girls had called 911. Kelly's mom phoned all the hospitals too. Blake's father, the owner of a car dealership on Bay Street in downtown Port Orchard, drove over to van driver Patty's house by the South Kitsap Mall and pounded on the door.

Her husband, Frank, tossed on a bathrobe and answered.

"We've been trying to find your wife," said an anxious Jack Scott. "We need to talk to her."

Frank looked over at the carport. The van was missing.

"Hell," he said, "where is she? I took a sleeping pill and didn't even notice she wasn't home until you rang the bell. What happened?"

"That's what we want to know, man."

Frank, a middle-aged man with a sandbag belly, scratched his head and looked at his watch. His sleepy eyes looked worried.

"Patty should have been home hours ago!"

Jack Scott stepped back, his eyes bugged to a new level of worry. "Did she call you? Text? When was the last time you heard from her? Don't you get it? If she's not home, where the hell is she? And where the hell are our girls?"

"She texted me around seven," Frank said, now very much awake. "She was about ready to leave the school up in PA and then she was getting some dinner with the girls. Van must have broke down. God! That damn piece of crap!"

Jack Scott didn't know what to do. He'd called the police. They said there had been no reports of any accidents along the highway to Port Angeles.

"If the van broke down," he said, "why wouldn't she have called you?"

Frank didn't know. It was late. It was dark. Five minutes ago he'd been asleep with the couple's cat, Trouble, cuddled at his feet. He hadn't been thinking anything was wrong.

But something *was*. Something very bad had happened.

"I'll get dressed," Frank said. "I'm going with you to look for them."

Jack went inside the Sparks' residence to wait for Patty's husband to dress. He phoned his wife, Kathryn, and told her that there was no sign of Patty or the van.

"We're going to drive up 101 and look for them," he said. "I don't know what else to do."

Kathryn could feel her voice crack when she spoke.

"It's probably nothing," she said, in what she was sure was more hope than truth. "I'm sure they are all okay."

Even before the words disappeared into her phone, Kathryn had the sickest feeling that she'd just told a lie. Inside she had that feeling that mothers know better than most fathers. Blake, beautiful, accomplished, sweet, was in serious trouble.

She never missed an episode of *Real Housewives of Orange County*. A new one had aired that night and they'd planned to watch it at ten when she was home.

In the master bedroom of the Wilder home, Brenda slid closer to Sherman so that he could touch her breasts. The down comforter was light against her body, but she kicked it to the floor. She wanted him to get lost in all she had to offer. That's what she bought them for, anyway. She didn't enjoy sex, but she had mastered the art of making a man—or woman—think that he or she had rocked her world.

Sherman was nice enough. He'd done everything she'd wanted him to do. She knew that he was two or three levels below her in the looks department and that he'd probably pinched himself more than a time or two at his good fortune of having a lover as beautiful, sexy as she.

"Your mother," she said, rolling onto her side, and wrapping her leg around his, "doesn't much like me, does she?"

He looked in her eyes.

She liked his adoring gaze. She could almost measure how far he'd fallen for her and how she owned him in every way possible. He didn't know that, of course. Her takeover had been slow. Sublime.

"Baby," he said, "let's not think about her."

"It hurts me so bad," she said, grinding her pelvis

against him. "I don't understand why some women have a problem with me. I've been misjudged my entire life. I'm only trying to be nice. "

"I know, baby," Sherman said, his eyes and hands going back to her nipples. He couldn't stop himself from touching her. It was like he was seventeen again. His erections were large, hard, ready. It was embarrassing at first, but it also made him feel a little proud; like he was something again; like the best years of his life hadn't been stolen from him by his ex-wife Susan.

"You won't be like the others," she said, her voice soft. "Will you?"·

Sherman loved her more than ever at that moment. He also knew what she was getting at.

"No," he said into her ear. "Never, Brenda. Never."

Brenda writhed and moaned.

"Oh God," she said. "I love you so much. Finally a real man to save me and help me. Finally someone to love."

CHAPTER THIRTY-EIGHT

Violet watched Sherman and Vanessa as they made their nightly trip into the big old barn. Vanessa leaned in to kiss him, and he returned her gesture with a playful swat on her bottom. They were an unsettling image of two opposites in love. He was quiet, cerebral. She was charismatic, no doubt, but not in the way that invited awe and interest. Just eyes on her. All the time. They never went without toting something over there, though Violet couldn't make out what they carried. The excursions had been going on for several nights. Days too.

Violet knew they'd be gone for a couple of hours. The instant they vanished into the barn's huge doors and shuttered them, she dialed her daughter's number from the wall phone in the kitchen. Her fingertip trembled as she pushed the large numerals on the phone that thoughtful—but absent—Denise had given her for Mother's Day. Her call went to the answering system.

"Denise, it's me. Where are you? I know you are very, very busy. I'm proud of all of your success, really I am. I just wanted to talk. I guess I need to talk to

someone. I can't talk to Sherman. It's about him. Not
him so much him as that woman Vanessa that he's with
now. They say they are in love. Oh, I'm sorry. I must
sound like a crazy, meddlesome old woman. I don't
mean to be. I just don't like her. Something isn't right
about her. I can't figure out what it is. I mean, she's
weird. Scary weird. Don't worry. I shouldn't have
called."

Violet hung up, heart pounding. She felt hot and a
little faint. Making that call hadn't been easy. She sat
in her chair and folded her hands, noticing how her
knuckles had knotted more than the last time since she
studied them. She remembered that Denise was away
at a dental conference in Cincinnati. She'd left a message on her home phone, not her cell.

She knew her daughter wasn't going to get back to
her anytime soon. Denise was notorious for using con-
ferences as an excuse to take extended vacations. Violet hadn't been to Cincinnati, and wondered if there
was really that much to do there. Maybe Denise would
come home.

The barn door was open a crack. Violet wondered
about that as she waited for her heart to slow from its
terrified drumbeat.

Wait. The door had been shut before she made the
call.

The next morning Vanessa was in the kitchen ar-
ranging a bouquet of dahlias.

"You have an amazing garden, Mom." She looked
over at Violet and smiled. Her teeth were too white.
Her eyes were piercing. Everything about Vanessa was

too much. Sometimes, Violet thought, looking at her was like looking at the sun. You had to squint; she was that strong a force.

Violet wanted to hold her tongue, but she couldn't.

"I'm not comfortable with you calling me that, Vanessa. Do you mind?"

Vanessa shortened the longest stems with a pruning shear.

"Oh, you mean 'Mom'?" she asked. "I'm sorry. I didn't mean to offend."

Violet winced. "No offense. Just a lot to take in right now."

"Understood." Vanessa finished the bouquet. She'd arranged the flowers, pom-pom-shaped blooms in dark red and white, in a large crystal vase that had been a wedding present to the bride from the groom. It had been stashed away in the back of the dining room hutch. Somehow Vanessa found it. "The shears were a dream," she went on. "Sherman sharpened them for me. They cut even the toughest stems like a hot knife through butter."

Violet didn't like the idea that Vanessa had helped herself to the vase, but leaving pretty things unused for sentimental reasons was a favor to no one.

"Where would you like these?" Vanessa asked, holding up the vase.

"The dining room is fine," Violet said.

"That's what I thought too." Vanessa disappeared into the dining room. "I'm heading over to the barn to help Sherman with some things," she called out. The screen door slammed behind her.

Violet got up and with the help of her walker and went over to the wall phone.

She dialed Denise's number and waited for it to ring, but the line was silent.

"What?" she thought. They'd lost phone service plenty of times over the years, but mostly because of a major storm. The last night had been quiet. Outside of the nightly occurrence of the banging headboard, Violet had noticed nothing.

She dialed again. Once more, silence filled her ears.

Something isn't right. Her heart raced again.

Violet slid the receiver into its cradle. Her eyes traveled down the phone line. On the floor was a red dahlia petal. It looked almost like a drop of blood. If the phone line had been a living thing, it most certainly was dead.

It had been cut with a very sharp knife. *No. Not a knife.* As the telltale petal on the floor indicated, garden pruning shears had likely been the instrument used to sever Violet from the outside world.

What in the world had Sherman gotten himself into? Vanessa was no ordinary woman. Not by a country mile.

CHAPTER THIRTY-NINE

While the woman of his dreams looked on, Sherman dumped out the phones. They scattered over the kitchen table. He knew that they'd be a source the investigators could use for tracking the whereabouts of the missing girls. Although there was no cell service for miles, he didn't want to take any chances.

Neither did Vanessa.

She looked down at the collection—two iPhones, a gargantuan Samsung, and the smallest of the four, an interloper, a compact.

"What's this?" she asked, picking up the compact. "I've been in prison awhile and might have missed something, but this isn't a phone, is it?"

"One of those little bitches," he said. "Not to worry," he added when it was clear Brenda was completely pissed off. "She can't use her phone here, but she can try to play hero."

"Dismantle those phones," she said, "and get your ass to the barn and get the other one."

Without a word, Sherman snapped off the backs and

pulled the SIM cards and batteries. He was fast and efficient as could be, though his fingers felt fat with Brenda's eyes on them.

"I'll visit with your mom," she said, her tone cool.

He entered the barn and threw the door open.

"Which one of you little bitches wants to die first?" he yelled.

The girls, huddled in separate locked stalls, were paralyzed by their fear. Each had a reference point for a place like the one in which they were now held captive. An uncle's farm. A petting zoo field trip. Hay. Manure. The warm, heavy smells of country life had never seemed terrifying before.

"Please," Kelly said, scanning the dark space and twisting in the ropes that held her ankles and wrists, "don't hurt us."

"I don't want to hurt you," Sherman said, feeling the power of their fear surge in his bloodstream. *God, it feels good.* His whole life he'd been in the background clacking away on a keyboard, ignored. Unnoticed. Not anymore. The girls he'd imprisoned in the horse stalls were terrified of him. Their tears and screams lifted him in a way that felt so empowering. So high.

"If you don't tell me which phone is yours," he said, frustrated that each phone had been password protected. "I'll kill you. I swear I will. Now, who has the Hello Kitty phone?"

"I do! That's mine!" the voice came from Monty's old stall. That's where he and Brenda locked up Kelly.

"Name?"

"Kelly Sullivan. That's me."

He looked at the next phone.

"Who had the Galaxy with the yin and yang cover?"

"Me. That's mine. I'm Amber Turner."

"Good girl," he said.

"iPhone with a purple cover?"

"Me! That belongs to me."

"Blake," Amber said. "Say your name!"

"Blake Scott," she called out. "The purple phone is mine."

Sherman walked over to the stall that held Chloe MacDonald. This was the part that he expected would be the ultimate in power, making the girl beg for her life. He wondered how far he should go with her, if deviating from the plan would put Brenda and their life together at risk.

Chloe stopped crying. She no longer screamed. There seemed to be no point in doing so. She sat in the corner of the stall thinking that her attempt at leaving some kind of a bread crumb for the police had been among the dumbest things she'd ever done in her life.

She had gone with her gut, her instincts. She wanted to make sure that the sick piece of garbage that had killed Patty and that guy who stopped was found. She hadn't considered that it would lead to any rescue for herself or the other girls. He'd killed Patty and the guy in the VW like they were nothing. After he raped her and the others, she fully expected they would all die.

The door swung open. A flood of light washed over the inside of the stall, giving Chloe her first glimpse of where she was being held captive. Her eyes squinted in the brightness.

"Where's your goddamn phone?" Sherman asked, lunging for her.

"I don't have it," she said, feeling his hot breath.

"You do! I want it! Give it to me or I'll slit you like a pig," he said, feeling the wonderful surge of power that came with the promise to kill the girl.

"I lost it," she said, trying to come up with a plausible excuse. "You scared the crap out of me when you shot Patty! Why did you have to shoot her? She didn't do anything to you, did she? That kid didn't do anything to you, either! Kill me! Go ahead, cut my throat or whatever you are going to do. I don't have my phone!"

The rush was thrilling. God, how he'd lived the life of a loser up to now. Is this what everyone else felt like? He gulped air. He was on top of her. Her body was tiny, but she was wiry. He could feel every tendon in her body stiffen. If he'd wanted to, he could apply just a little more pressure and snap her into a zillion pieces.

"Rape me!" Chloe said. "Get it over with!"

Intoxicating. Exhilarating. Electrifying. He could think of no word to describe how he felt.

Chloe braced herself as his hands went over her body, lingering in places that only her boyfriend or her doctor had touched.

"I told you to take her phone," came a voice from the doorway. "Not her virginity."

Chloe strained to see the woman, but Sherman's head was in the way.

"She doesn't have her phone," he said, rolling off her. "She says she lost it."

"Looks like you searched her pretty good," Brenda said, her words meant to stab at him a little, suggesting that he was disloyal.

"I got carried away," he said, getting up.

"I don't care what you do to me," Chloe said, "you'll get caught. I hope someone finds my phone."

The stall door shut and the darkness returned.

CHAPTER FORTY

The blade of the butcher knife was dull. As Violet Wilder attempted to slice through the mahogany red of the venison that she'd planned to stew for dinner, she watched her son as he continued to work on repairing the barn. There was no end to his work ethic. It reminded her of her husband and how his work hours were dictated by the season. He'd work until ten at night in the summer because the sun stayed so late in the sky. She looked forward to wintertime because he'd stop early, close to six-thirty or seven, and they'd have more time together.

"Need me to sharpen that blade, Mom?" Sherman asked.

"I didn't hear you come in, honey," she said, turning to greet him.

"Quiet as a mouse," he said. "That's me."

She gave him the knife. "This old thing does need some sharpening. Stone's in the drawer. I can't manage as well as I used to."

Sherman patted her shoulder. "That's okay. It happens. I'm here."

She took her walker and slid it to the kitchen table and watched while Sherman cleaned the blade, oiled the whetstone, and started to pull the blade over its dull gray surface.

"I've been watching you work," she said.

He cocked an eye. "You have, have you?"

She smiled. "Reminds me of your father. You just keep going and going and going. I don't know where you get the energy."

"Comes from somewhere, Mom. Maybe you and Dad passed it along to me."

The blade glinted as he pulled it over the oiled stone.

"What are you doing out there in the barn, anyway? I see a lot of comings and goings, supplies going in. The barn must have been a wreck if you had to make so many repairs."

She turned and looked out the window, falling silent.

"What is it, Mom?" he asked. "You all right?"

She shook herself.

"I guess I'm just feeling a little sorry for myself right now."

He rinsed the knife and dried it. He set it on the cutting board next to the bloody venison steak.

"Oh, Mom," he said, "don't feel sad."

She moved a bony finger in his direction, indicating not to worry. She'd be fine. She was always fine.

"I guess my eyes are too old to cry," she said. "Because that's what I want to do right now. Just have a good cry."

Sherman put his arms around her.

"It's okay, Mom. Things are going to get better. We're

going to get through this transition, and then we'll start over."

"Right," Violet said, sliding back over to the cutting board. "I know that. Big changes are hard." She sliced through the meat and looked over at her son.

"Better?" he asked.

"Much," she said.

"All right, then," he said, "I'm going to do some more work in the barn. That venison stew is going to be on my mind all day."

She watched as he went out the kitchen door to the barn. She wished she could go help. The stew would sit there in a pot all day. She'd sit at the kitchen table. Just waiting. Like the stew.

Mushrooms. That's just what the venison stew needed. Violet sipped her tea, did a crossword puzzle, and thought about mushrooms. They'd make that dish just perfect.

She looked at the kitchen clock and wondered when Sherman would get home from wherever he'd gone to. She hated the idea of being dependent on him or anyone. She was no longer all that she used to be. She couldn't even get to some chanterelles that she was all but certain had erupted through the rich, loamy soil on the back side of the barn after that heavy rain.

She looked over at her cane, propped in a corner next to the refrigerator. It was one of those four-pronged affairs that she'd managed to put to good use before the walker. She wondered if she'd given up. Let herself go. Become so mired in the sadness of being old that she stopped trying.

"I'm not going to give up," she said to herself. "I'm going to get those mushrooms right now."

She slid the walker to the counter, picked up a small paring knife and a bread bag from the drawer. Steadying herself, she reached for the cane. It felt good in her grip. She could do this. She could feel it in her bones.

Her bones. The reason the doctors insisted she use a walker. They were so brittle that if she fell she'd all but certainly end up with fractures. Broken bones would transition her from walker-mobility to bedridden.

She didn't care. *What kind of life was worth living if she wasn't able to do anything?*

The cane was familiar. She leaned on it only a little. She was sure that with careful steps she'd be able to get over to those mushrooms.

I'm not over, she thought. *Not yet!*

One step, then another, and Violet was out the kitchen door. The aroma of the farm filled her senses. Memories came to her. Her husband. Her children. Her beloved horse, Monty. The breeze was on the cool side and she should have put on a jacket, but there was no turning back.

She looked around. It had been two weeks since her last doctor's appointment. The yard next to the house looked unkempt. Sherman had been busy. She knew that. But he'd let it go a little long. She remembered how she used to mow that lawn with a push mower while the kids ate Popsicles and swung on the tire hanging from a tree limb. Not at the same time. That wouldn't be safe. Violet was always careful with her children.

Safety first.

Soaking up the familiar, she pressed onward. She was tempted to go inside the barn to see what Sherman had been doing, but first things first. After rounding the back side of the barn to that spot where the chanterelles could be found after a rain, she saw them. A mass of golden trumpets poked upward from the black, shaded soil. Violet stood there, satisfied that she'd made it that far, but also wondering how she was going to get down to the ground to pick the mushrooms.

I can do this, she thought. *I know it.*

Holding the cane like a lever, she lowered herself to one knee.

I did it! Sherman will be so pleased.

It was too awkward to use the paring knife, and the chanterelles really didn't require it. She opened the plastic bag. Next, she pulled up the mushrooms one by one, shaking off the soil and depositing them in the bag. The stew she was making was about to be transformed from delicious to out of this world. The barn funneled the breeze at her, and she shook with the chill. As she stood up, she heard animal sounds.

A kitten crying.

She didn't know there had been any kittens that season. She'd always prided herself on being a responsible animal owner. Barn cats, however, were almost feral and beyond her ability to round up and take to the vet for spaying or neutering.

The kitten's cries were muffled by the wind, and, Violet thought, the walls of the old barn.

"Mom! What in the hell are you doing out here?"

Sherman's voice nearly caused her to drop the bag of mushrooms. She held steady on the cane.

"Sherman," she said, looking at her son, "don't use swearwords at me! And what does it look like? I'm getting chanterelles."

He grabbed her by the arm, a little too roughly. She recoiled.

"You're hurting me!" she said.

"You scared me, Mom. I came home, couldn't find you . . . and now you're out here without your walker! You could have been hurt."

Worry flashed in his eyes. Sweat dripped from his temples.

"Oh honey," she said, "you're more scared than I am."

"Sorry, Mom. I didn't mean to hurt you. It's just that I didn't know where you were. Let's go back inside."

Violet leaned on her son's muscular arm and they stared back toward the house.

"I thought we got rid of the female cats," she said.

"Females? We don't have any, Mom. Just two toms."

"Yes," she said. "We do. I heard a kitten crying. I was about to go find it. In the barn. Sounds hurt."

Sherman took the bag of mushrooms from her hand. They walked toward the kitchen door. He glanced back.

"No kittens," he said. "But I'll check it out."

CHAPTER FORTY-ONE

A Clallam County Sheriff's deputy named Todd Flanagan pulled behind the VW along the highway and ran the plates before getting out of his cruiser. It was pitch black outside. He'd noticed the little car sitting in the middle of the turnout twice that night as he patrolled the length of highway that he told his friends was the "most boring stretch of asphalt on the planet." He wondered where Robert Taylor, the car's owner, had gone.

Todd got out, his dash cam capturing his discovery through the spears of light coming from his headlights.

"Holy crap!" he said, spinning around before dropping to his knees.

Robert Taylor, bloody and lifeless, stared up at him from beside his car.

Todd felt for a pulse.

"Oh God!" he said in a voice that could have been heard fifty yards away . . . if there had been anyone to hear it. *This kid's dead. This kid's been shot in the head! Who in the world would do something like that? Just leaving him here like he was bag of garbage or an*

*old mattress abandoned by someone too lazy to ferry it
to the dump.*

At twenty-five, Flanagan had been a deputy for two
years. He'd never come across anything like Robert
Taylor.

Six deputies, the Clallam County coroner, and a K-9
officer named Trog scoured the wide spot next to the
highway before the blush of the rising sun sent an
ochre and pink cast over the scene. Yellow police tape
cordoned off the area and fluttered in the breeze, drawing the attention of the earliest of morning commuters.
Flashing lights provided drivers with a reason to slow
to a crawl, take a look, and then call someone with
a description of the unpleasantness that they'd just
viewed.

"I wanted to warn you . . ."

When really they simply wanted to tell someone. A
few even craned their necks and shot pictures from
their slow-moving cars to post on Facebook and Insta-
gram. Hashtags varied: #hatemycommute #crimescene
#someonesgonnabelate #deadzone.

Renny Carlton, a reporter from the radio station
KONP in Port Angeles, cornered the deputy who'd made
the discovery.

Todd Flanagan's eyes were weary and his mouth
cotton dry.

"Can I get something for air?" Renny asked, holding out her iPhone to record whatever details he'd be
able to provide.

The deputy stepped back and pondered her request.
She was young, like he was. She had a job to do. She

was pretty. Not answering her wasn't going to give him an opportunity to ask her out later. The dating pool in Port Angeles was about as shallow as a parking lot mud puddle after a misty rain.

"We're still processing the scene," he said. "Sorry."

"We're told the victim is a young male," said Renny.

"No comment," Deputy Flanagan said.

Renny was not about to be denied something for the news that morning. She pushed harder. Her phone was in the deputy's face—five inches from his mouth.

"Can you confirm, you know, if someone was shot?" she asked.

He pulled away, reminding himself of the most important lesson he'd learned in media training for the sheriff's office.

No details until next of kin have been notified. Unless, of course, there is no hope due to decomp or other challenges to identification of race, age and gender.

"Sorry," he said, "no comment."

Renny made a face.

"Not cool," she said. "I covered your department's car wash."

Todd Flanagan kept his lips zipped and looked around the scene to extricate himself from Renny.

"Found something," one of the deputies called out.

"Excuse me," he said, glad to get away from the reporter.

A second later, he was next to the VW, looking down at the tip of another deputy's perfectly polished boot. Next to it a shiny object lay in the gravel, just under the frame of the car.

A cell phone.

* * *

From her office phone, Kendall Stark called the Port Angeles Police to see if they could get some boots on the ground over at the high school.

"Four of our high school girls and their driver are missing," she said. "They were participating in a special cheerleading event sponsored by your high school. We don't think there was actually an event, but I need someone to verify that at the school."

The police chief said he'd have a deputy check it out.

"We've had quite a day so far," he said. "We had a shooting just out of town. Drive-by. Not sure. Clallam County responded. Vic shot in the head, left for dead. Still processing the scene."

"I'm sorry to hear that," Kendall said.

"Yeah, we don't have that kind of thing happen here like you do in the city all the time."

She wondered on what atlas Port Orchard was more of a city than Port Angeles.

"Right," she said. "Let me know what you find out, okay? One of the girls texted from the high school so we know they made it that far."

"Will do," he said.

About twenty minutes later the police chief called back.

"Not much to add," he said. "No event was scheduled. Deputy talked to the principal, who talked to the gal who runs the athletic department. No cheer special event. If your team got to the school, no one saw them."

Kendall hung up the phone. The police chief had confirmed something important. The invitation had been a ruse. The individual behind the faux invitation had gone to a lot of trouble. The person who invited the girls had been specific. It was not a random request.

Birdy appeared in Kendall's office. She looked upset and didn't bother to hide it.

"Are you all right?" Kendall asked. "Is it your mom? How is she?"

Birdy shrugged. "Weaker, I guess. Still mean though."

"I'm sorry about all that you're going through, Birdy."

"I know. I thought I'd stop by to check in."

"You have a lot going on," Kendall said.

Birdy couldn't argue with that. It had been a season of change for her. The move to the new facility entailed a new routine. She felt isolated from her friends at the courthouse and sheriff's office. Most of all, her mother and sister preyed on her mind. She was also worried about Elan.

"My mom is old and sick and I know she's going to die," she said. "I know that we're all going to end up in the same place. So I'm good with that—as good as I can be, anyway. I'm more worried about Elan now. His relationship with his mother is at an all-time low, and now Amber is missing. It's a lot for a kid to process."

"Is there anything I can do to help?" Kendall asked.

It was a question that didn't need to be asked. Not really. Birdy and Kendall had the kind of friendship that didn't need the reassurance of promises made in times of stress. They were there for each other on the job and in the world outside of the office, though lately the two had become enmeshed.

"We're going to head up to the rez and see Mom one last time. Not sure if we'll go tomorrow or the next day. Not to be cold about it, but the less time up there with my sister and my mom and all the drama that blankets them, the better."

Kendall's own mother had died not long ago. Their relationship had been very different from Birdy's and Natalie's. She missed her mom every day. There were times when Cody would do something, sometimes something simple, and she'd think to pick up the phone to call her mom to tell her. So strong had been their bond that death hadn't severed it completely.

"I'll let you know when we leave," Birdy said. "Cell reception is better up there now. Casino money continues to work its cruel magic."

Kendall and Birdy had talked about how the casinos had brought low-paying jobs to the reservation and how the schools and the hospitals that had been part of the tribal leader's pitch had yet to materialize. Instead, a new smoke shop and a year-round fireworks stand the size of a Safeway store had been built.

"Do you have any update on Amber and the others?" Birdy asked.

"Nothing. Not yet." She indicated the invitation that Blake's mother had brought in.

Birdy picked it up.

"Thermography," Birdy said running her fingertip over the raised letters.

"It's engraved," Kendall said.

"Not the same. Thermography involves using a power and heat source to get the raised effect."

Kendall took the invitation and looked at it more closely.

"I see," she said, tilting under the light of her banker's lamp. "Kind of baked on and bubbly. Is there anything you don't know?"

Birdy laughed. "I used to work in a print shop in college, Kendall. Thermography was all the rage back then. Not so much now."

"I honestly didn't know that you were an expert."

Birdy sat down. Despite the fact that she was fastidious, Kendall could smell the formaldehyde that still clung to her. It was an occupational hazard unique to the pathologist's life.

"Not an expert. Just a college kid looking for some money to supplement my grants and loans."

Kendall set the paper down and looked at her friend and colleague. Birdy was surprising. In big and small ways.

"Where do you get that kind of thing done?" the detective asked.

Birdy thought a second.

"Sir Speedy on Mile Hill used to do it, but they've closed down. Everyone thinks laser printing or photocopying something is just as good as offset. Come to think of it, Justin's Quick Print on Bay Street still does thermography."

Kendall got up from her chair. "Well?" she asked, fetching her coat.

"Well what?"

"Am I driving? Or are you?"

Elan Waterman revisited the last text message he'd received from Amber.

AMBER: This sux.

ELAN: W?

AMBER: No event here. No one around. Blake is so pissed off which is kind of funny.

ELAN: Drama queen all the time.

AMBER: Yup. That's her.

ELAN: Did you get the date wrong?

AMBER: No. I got it right. They must have canceled or something.

ELAN: That's completely wack.

AMBER: Y. We're going to hang out here a little while longer then head back home. Maybe get something to eat. Patty's hungry. Like always.

ELAN: OK. I'm gonna watch something on Netflix and avoid homework.

AMBER: Your aunty won't like that.

ELAN: No. She's cool. She thinks I can do no wrong.

AMBER: Lucky. My mom's a total bitch.

ELAN: Sorry. My mom's probably a hundred times worse.

AMBER: Not a contest. And besides you can't always be the winner in everything.

ELAN: Right. Winning not good.

AMBER: ☹ Chloe's whining about something. Blake is stomping around like she's missed her chance to collect a lotto prize and this inconvenience is ruining her life. Can't stand her. Kelly's telling her to sit down and shut up, which is kind of funny because Blake always gets to boss everyone around.

ELAN: Sounds like a trip to hell.

AMBER: IDK. Kind of fun to see these bitches get into it over stupid crap. I'm clearly the outsider here.

ELAN: Y. But you're the best of the bunch.

AMBER: At least you think so. Blake can't believe

that I got invited to this. She actually said to me on the way up here "no offense, but you're not top tier material." Like she was the whipped cream and cherry on the sundae and the rest of us are the ice cream. Dumb analogy. ☺

ELAN: She's stupid.

AMBER: Gotta go. I need to pretend I care about all of this. They're arguing over where we should eat and Patty is just sitting there like a bump on a log.

ELAN: Later.

He'd typed, "babe" after "later" but erased it before sending. He felt that way about Amber. Definitely. He just wasn't ready to say so. Not in a text anyway.

CHAPTER FORTY-TWO

Satellite trucks from every major news organization and one or two cable newcomers that no one had heard about ("what channel is News2U on?") clogged parking spaces around the courthouse and the side streets down the hill to Bay Street. Never in the history of Port Orchard had there been such media attention on the town.

Up to that point, the city's brush with fame came when it made the national news for the cancellation of an annual seagull-calling contest because an animal-rights group complained that birds might be confused by the contestants and that would be cruel. And the time a local man had found a lost Rembrandt painting in his grandparents' attic (sadly, it later turned out to be a very good fake).

Those brushes with fame were small-townish and only passably interesting, but this one . . . this one put Port Orchard on the map in a very dark, sinister way. It was completely at odds with the Chamber of Commerce's newest campaign that highlighted the natural beauty of the area.

Port Orchard:
Water you doing for the rest of your life?

Everyone with a press pass or keyboard for blogging was in town looking for ratings and click-throughs. A few even wanted answers. The victims checked off all the boxes—white, pretty, and, the icing on the cake, they were cheerleaders. Patty Sparks had been moved to the "And" category of the story as in "four young girls and their chaperone." In time, all the girls would be household names, but not Patty. She'd always be stuck in the news purgatory of being the addendum to the story.

Kitsap County's amiable Sheriff Wynton Burke started off the press conference in Judge Sally Cotton's courtroom with a statement that "very little" was known right then, but "we promise to keep you informed every step of the way." He introduced FBI special agent Jonas Casey and the county's own lead investigator, Kendall Stark.

SA Casey spoke first. It was an active investigation, and the bureau would not be commenting on it at all.

"Why are you even here? Is this tied to the Brenda Nevins/Janie Thomas case?" asked a reporter from a Seattle TV station.

"We're still working that. No comment on the Thomas kidnapping case."

A blogger with assertiveness training pounced. "Was that even a kidnapping? The video posted online shows she went willingly with Brenda Nevins."

"We're still determining whether that's the case," SA Casey said.

Kendall Stark spoke next. She'd been told ahead of time that her sole purpose at the news conference was the official release of the missing girls' names and photos—something that had been all over social media anyway.

"We have posted information, including recent photos of the girls and the school-van driver, on our website," she said. On a screen behind her, the names, descriptions, and photographs of the five were displayed. The room fell silent as Kendall reiterated what the press was viewing.

Her eyes landed on Chloe's parents, who stood in the back by the door.

"I know each of you has a job to do. I know it is competitive and challenging. I respect that. I think we all do. I'm asking you to be mindful of what the families involved here are going through. Give them space. Respect their privacy. Put yourself in their shoes. No time in their lives has been more stressful than what they are experiencing right now."

She was stepping away when a reporter called out a question.

"Do you think this has anything to do with the other murders in Kitsap? Why is the FBI involved? Is it because you can't find Brenda Nevins on your own?"

Kendall looked at the reporter and started to speak, but SA Casey cut her off.

"Look," he said, "Detective Stark and the Kitsap County Sheriff's office are experienced and capable law enforcement professionals. We're partners here. We have the same goal. We want to find the missing girls and their chaperone and we want to bring Brenda

Nevins to justice. Those two things may or may not be linked."

With that, the news conference was over.

"I could have answered," Kendall said as she and the FBI agent exited.

He straightened his tie. "I know. I don't get to say nice things about local law enforcement very often. It's something the bureau wants us to do. Good public relations, you know."

CHAPTER FORTY-THREE

Sherman Wilder stood next to the boarded-up stall door. If anyone had told him six months before that his life would turn out in the way that it had, he'd have looked at him or her like they were crazy. Never could he have imagined that someone as brilliant and beautiful as Brenda Nevins would select him over all other suitors. When Brenda came into his life, he'd been just another of the faceless people who provide a backdrop for the smarter, the richer, the better looking.

"What's the point of living if you are nothing but dust?" Brenda had said, during one of their training sessions in the prison IT lab. "A man like you can be so much more with the right woman and focused ambition."

That was the beginning. There was more to it, of course. It had been a buildup of days and then weeks, then months before she showed him that he was special. It culminated with hasty sex with no finesse whatsoever. The kind of encounter a teenage boy has with his girlfriend in the car because there's nowhere else to go and they can't stop themselves. *Wham. Bam. Thank you, ma'am.* It was fast. Exciting. It was that first sip of whiskey that begged for a full-on guzzle. Over time, there were many such encounters. Each had the rush of being forbidden. Every time they had sex brought the possibility of ruining his life.

Guzzle. Sip. Guzzle.

No matter what he'd read about her online, no matter what the prison administration said about her—"devious, conniving"—he saw Brenda Nevins as something far different.

Misunderstood. Brilliant. Sexy as hell.

Sherman understood her anger at the world for all that it had done to her. The people who told her she was less than she was. She'd had a long list. He hated them as much as she did. When she sent up a trial balloon that she wanted to escape, he balked. She punished him by avoiding him for three weeks. Finally, when she came back to him, she said she had found another way out.

"I don't know why I even bothered with you," she said, lingering in the IT training lab after the other inmates had gone.

Her words cut deeply.

"Don't be that way," he said.

Brenda gave him a knowing smile. "Oh, I can be any way that I want to be."

"You know what I mean, Brenda. Don't ice me out."

She looked at him with those eyes of hers, but said nothing.

"Talk to me," he said, keeping his voice low. "Baby, talk to me."

"Look," Brenda said, "I don't know what to think about you, Sherman. You talk a good game, and I've seen a game player or two in my life."

"No games, baby," he said. "I promise."

She pointed a finger at him. "When I asked you for help, you turned your back on me."

Sherman wanted to hold her, but one of the guards kept walking by the open doorway. "Not being able to break you out of prison is not turning my back on you," he whispered. "It's realistic."

Brenda scooted next to his desk and sat down on top of it. "I don't do realistic," she purred, "I do fantastic. You, for one, should know that, Sherman."

His face turned red. She was right.

"I told you I get things done," she said, "I always have been able to manage. No one person can stop me."

Sherman didn't know what or whom she was talking about, but he understood two things very clearly: Once Brenda got out, they'd be together. Once they were together, they'd make sure that everyone knew exactly who Brenda Nevins was. He was never going to let her down.

"I'm going to have you do things for me," she said, "that might be uncomfortable to you."

She scrutinized him. His eyes stayed right where she wanted them. On her. She studied his pupils. She gauged the color of his skin, the sweat above his brow. Was there a twitch? Was there any sign that he'd fail her?

"I'll do whatever you want," he told her.

The list of what had been uncomfortable to Sherman Wilder had grown since Brenda tricked Janie Thomas into doing the unthinkable. He'd played that scenario of his agreement to take care of her, support her, serve her even, over in his head. He'd killed for her. It surprised him how easy it had been to take out Patty Sparks and the Good Samaritan in the VW.

But his mom? That was a hard one.

"No tracks, babe," she had said. "Besides, she's old anyway. Old dies. We're actually helping her get to where she needs to go."

Tim and Jillian MacDonald waited for Kendall in a conference room at the Kitsap County Sheriff's Office. Tim was a barrel-chested machinist from the shipyard; Jillian taught watercolor painting out of their South-worth home overlooking the parking lot of the ferry landing. Friends always described them as an outgoing, happy couple that doted on their daughter, but didn't spoil her. Older than her siblings by so many years, Chloe MacDonald was one of those kids who was as comfortable hanging out with her parents and their friends as she was with kids her own age.

"Detective Stark," Tim said, trying as hard as he could—and failing—not to show how worried he was, "we're Chloe MacDonald's parents. I'm Tim. This is Jillian."

Kendall was surprised, but didn't show it either. Or at least she'd tried not to.

"She's Chinese," Jillian said. "We adopted her when she was two."

Tim pulled a photo from his wallet. It was Chloe in her black-and-red cheer uniform. Her hair rested on her shoulders. She had a kind of charisma that came through the photo straight at the viewer.

"She's beautiful," Kendall said.

"She's more than that," Tim said, fighting tears. "She's everything to us."

Jillian patted her husband's shoulder.

"My husband and I, we know that you are doing everything you can."

"And the FBI is too," Kendall said, for the first time saying something positive about the agency. It was, she knew, not a competition. She put the photo in her coat pocket.

"We just wanted you to put the face with the name," Jillian said. "We know we don't look like her. We know that she's not our blood, but she is our daughter in every way that matters."

"I know she is," Kendall said.

Tim opened his mouth to speak, but the effort was wasted. His voice cracked with the first syllable and he gave up.

Again, his wife intervened.

"If there's anything my husband or I can do, anything at all, please call on us," she said. "I made a list of all her friends, teachers too. I've called every single one, and no one knows anything more than you probably do. I don't think whoever took our daughter is someone from around here. Everyone loves Chloe."

Kendall took the slip of paper. She told them how much she appreciated their help. That she, too, was doubtful that anyone from Port Orchard could be behind the abduction.

"I've lived here all of my life," she told them, "and I know you have too. We will move heaven and earth to bring these girls home safe and sound."

* * *

Dispatch notified Kendall three times that Jack Scott had been calling for her—in fact, twice in the last hour. She understood Blake Scott's father's anxiousness and she'd returned his call each time, but they all went to voice mail.

"He's a real piece of work," the dispatcher said. "Says he demands you get over to his house."

"I'm pulling up now," Kendall said.

The detective realized that stressful situations often brought out the worst personality attributes in people. She knew Jack Scott because he owned six car dealerships in the county and she'd actually purchased her SUV off his lot in Bremerton. He advertised himself as Kitsap's Kar King. At the moment, he was worried, stressed out, and all but certain the authorities weren't doing a proper job with the investigation.

The Scotts' house in Fragaria Landing was a mammoth chateau with a circular drive, a six-car garage, and a gazebo that overlooked Colvos Passage and had a view of Mount Rainier. It was impressive, as it was meant to be. Kendall's SUV had been leaking oil lately, so she parked on the street in front of the house. The circular driveway was pristine, and the Kar King's phone calls indicated to her that he'd be the type to call the county and complain that she had messed up his driveway.

Even though she'd bought the car from his dealership and had taken it in twice for repairs.

If Port Orchard had a beautiful couple, Jack and Kathryn Scott were it. At least in photos. Jack was broad shouldered, chiseled-featured, and had dark brown hair that would be the envy of men half his age. Kathryn, like her husband, was also ageless. Kathryn, who was a freelance photographer, was a stunning beauty with green eyes and light brown hair that if dyed, Kendall was certain had been done by a salon out of town. Both were in their late forties.

The couple led Kendall into the living room. The mountain filled the windows that went from the floor to the twenty-foot ceiling. It was obvious that Kathryn had been crying and probably hadn't slept all night. She'd done what she could to pull herself together, but she wasn't the arm candy that had appeared in her husband's commercials over the years. She wore dark jeans and a white top. Her husband, who looked the same as always, was dressed in slacks, a light blue shirt, and a paisley tie.

"I need to know what you know," Jack said. "I don't like sitting around, and Blake means everything to me."

"To us," Kathryn added, her eyes on her husband. "She means everything to *us*."

"I know she does," Kendall said. "We're going to do everything we can to find out what happened."

"And where she is," Kathryn said.

"Look," Jack said, "I know you're limited on resources. I'm willing to write a big check to get a private investigator in here to help find Blake."

"And the other girls," Kathryn said.

"That's a very generous offer," Kendall said. "But we have all of our resources on it now. We've alerted the state patrol, the authorities in Jefferson and Clallam counties, and we also have the FBI in the loop."

"The FBI," Jack repeated, slightly confused, but a little less agitated. "Why the feds?"

"That's what we need to talk about," Kendall said.

"We need to know if there has been any kind of ransom demand."

Kathryn looked at Jack, waiting for him to respond.

"No," he said. "Have any of the other parents been contacted by someone?"

It had been a while since the van went missing. Kendall knew that a ransom demand would have been made hours ago. If any of the girls had been held for money, it had to be Blake. Her family was worth millions. The others—and certainly Patty's husband—could scrape up maybe $50,000. The Scotts could get their hands on ten or twenty times that amount. If appearances counted for anything, that is.

Kendall asked the Scotts the same questions as she had the other parents. Blake had a steady boyfriend, Kyle "Chad" Chadwick, a wide receiver for the high school football team. She excelled in all her classes, most of which were advanced placement or college prep. She had more friends than they could count.

"Everyone loves her," Jack said.

"Adores her," echoed Kathryn, starting to cry.

Jack moved his tie to keep it out of the fray when he leaned in to comfort her.

"I'm sure everyone does," Kendall said, though thinking, maybe not *everyone*.

Kathryn handed Kendall a picture of her daughter.

"I know you need a current photo," she said. "I took this one last week."

The image showed Blake posed by the gazebo with the snowcapped mountain in the background.

"I was testing locations for her senior portrait. Early, I know. But for some reason it has been on my mind."

With that, Blake's mother broke down completely.

"You'll keep us informed," Jack said.

"I'll do my best. This is an active investigation, which means that we might not be able to tell you everything." Kendall stood to leave. "I'm very sorry for all that you are going through. I know this is difficult."

"Detective Stark," Jack said, his arm around his wife as she sobbed into his perfectly crisp shirt. "You don't have anything now. Do you?"

"I'm sorry. As I said, I can't discuss what we know."

"That's not right," he said. "She's our daughter."

"Please," Kendall said, "notify me right away if you hear from anyone claiming to know anything about your daughter's whereabouts."

Kathryn Scott looked up. Her mascara had smeared on her husband's shirt and she put her palm on his chest to cover it.

"We will," she said.

CHAPTER FORTY-FOUR

Kendall Stark drove out to Woods Road to talk with Karl and Sue Ellen Turner, Amber's parents.

Sue Ellen answered the door and invited Kendall inside. Sue Ellen was a heavyset woman, with long brown hair that she wore pulled back, away from her face. She had on a stylish sweater and dark slacks. If her diamond earrings were real—and Kendall was never a good judge of that kind of thing—they were two carets, perfect clarity.

Her husband, right behind her, was older, maybe by a good ten years. Karl Turner was a financial consultant, which Kendall considered a dubious profession—and kind of legal robbery. Judging by the gold oyster Rolex he wore low on his wrist, he'd been successful. Karl shaved his head, and a silvery five o'clock shadow darkened the sheen of his pate.

The couple led Kendall to the living room. Sue Ellen offered coffee, but Kendall declined.

"I saw on the news that the FBI has been called," Karl said. "We've not been told of any ransom."

"There hasn't been any ransom demand," Kendall

said. "The FBI's been assisting on another case, but the two are not related."

"Brenda Nevins," Sue Ellen said.

"I'm sorry," Kendall said, "if I had something to tell you, I would. Please do not believe what you hear on the news or read on the Internet. It isn't always true. In fact, it mostly isn't true."

That didn't seem to satisfy Karl Turner. He picked at a bit of lint on his slacks.

"I have friends at the State Department," he said.

Kendall wasn't sure where that had come from.

"Thank you for letting me know," she said. "I'm here to find out all that I can about Amber, particularly any changes in the past few days or weeks."

Sue Ellen put her hand to her mouth. "You don't think she was being stalked, do you, Detective?"

"No," Kendall said. "We are in the very early stages of the investigation. We're trying to see what pieces of the puzzle are out there. I understand she had a boyfriend."

Karl Turner looked at his wife.

"My husband wasn't happy about it, but she did have a crush on a boy from school."

Kendall didn't say Elan's name. She waited.

"He was an Indian or Native American," Karl said. "Or whatever you have to call them now. This week anyway. I didn't want my daughter involved with him. I think they are great and proud people, but not the sort for her to get mixed up with."

"Elan is his name," Sue Ellen said. "I liked him. Nice kid." She turned to her husband. "Our daughter is missing, and you're acting as though you're still angry about Elan. Get over it. Get your priorities straight."

Karl slammed his fist on the table. "You like to throw some punches at me when we have company, don't you? You deal with the detective. Amber's your daughter. She treats me like nothing but a wallet anyway."

He stormed off to the kitchen. Kendall heard the refrigerator door open and the sound of a beer bottle being opened.

"He has a temper," Sue Ellen said. "It's just the way he shows us that he loves us."

"Ms. Turner, were all of you getting along before Amber disappeared with the others?"

Sue Ellen wrapped her arms around her chest. She looked at Kendall for a flicker, before fixing her gaze in the direction of the kitchen.

"Yes," she said, "everything was fine. The same. Amber and her father didn't always see eye to eye about boys or really pretty much anything."

"Where was your husband last night, say around 9 P.M.?"

"Here," she said, "with me."

"I see."

Sue Ellen gave Kendall a hard stare. "I don't like you," she said. "My daughter's missing, and you're asking questions about my husband."

"I'm doing my job," Kendall said. "I'm trying to help find your daughter. I have to ask a lot of questions that might offend a lot of people. That's the way it works."

"It's insulting," Sue Ellen said, her posture rigid, her eyes fixed on the detective's.

"Not meant to be," Kendall said.

They talked a bit longer, and, having cooled down with a beer, Karl Turner returned.

"I'm sorry," he said, taking a seat next to his wife and laying his hand on top of hers.

"It's all right," Kendall said. "I know you're both under a great deal of stress."

He squeezed his wife's hand, and she seemed to wince.

The three of them talked for a few more minutes. Amber's grades had been as strong as ever. She was involved in several extracurricular activities. She was a member of a youth group at St. Gabriel's, the local Catholic church. She loved babysitting her little sister, Bryn.

Sue Ellen spoke up. "She's only a toddler, but she is so worried about Amber. She keeps asking when she's coming home. We tell her soon. She'll be home soon."

"May I talk to her?" Kendall asked. "Sometimes kids, even very young ones, see or hear things that adults might miss."

Karl answered this time. "She's at my mother's in Seattle. I took her there this morning. Didn't want her around any of this."

Kendall got into her car and dialed Birdy's number. She picked up right away.

"The Turners are one strange family," Kendall said, pulling away from the house and onto Waaga Way. "Did Elan ever meet them?"

"Once," Birdy said, "I think. I'm not absolutely certain. Are you in your car?"

"Sorry. On speaker. I'm about to drive by your house."

"I wish I was home with Elan. He's pretty upset by everything that's happening with Amber and with my mom. But back to the Turners. Besides being racists— Elan told me about that—what's weird about them?"

Kendall caught the sight of a ferry as it plowed through the dark blue waters of Rich Passage, a narrow channel separating the Kitsap Peninsula from Bainbridge Island, just after she turned on Beach Drive.

"Mr. Turner has major anger management issues," she went on. "Seemed more concerned about Elan's race than his daughter's disappearance. Actually slammed his fist on the table. Mrs. Turner just sat there and didn't even blink. Like she's used to those kinds of outbursts."

"Interesting, Kendall, but what's the relevance?"

Kendall wasn't sure. "None probably. It struck me as peculiar that Dad whisked their youngest out of town within hours of his older daughter's disappearance. Don't you think that's strange?"

"Maybe," Birdy said. "Or maybe he's overprotective and doesn't want the little one to pick up on the trauma he and his wife are experiencing. Cody's a lot older, but couldn't you see yourself doing something like that? To shield him?"

Kendall drove past the veterans' home at Retsil.

"Of course," she answered. "You're right. How is your mom doing? I've been thinking about you and her today."

"Not great," Birdy said, her voice a little quieter. "I'm afraid. I've been keeping the phone charged and next to me in case Summer calls. As soon as she gives us the word, we're going up there. My mom has been far from mother of the year, but she's my mom."

Kendall's heart went out to Birdy.

"Keep me posted," Kendall said. "I'm keeping you and Elan in my prayers."

Birdy thanked her and they hung up.

CHAPTER FORTY-FIVE

The sound of the old tractor filled the yard. It had a peculiar rumble that made Violet think of her husband and how he told her that the secondhand John Deere could be rehabilitated and made to "work good as new." When he failed at adjusting the engine to something less than a sonic roar and an exhaust output that rivaled Mount St. Helens, he told her that a "big green machine should sound mean." She'd laughed at the time, but later the sound came to her in dreams or when a car backfired. The oddest times. Reminding her that Alec was gone.

Now Sherman was starting it, riding it from the barn to the field. In the shovel was something large, wrapped in a dark blue tarp. Violet leaned closer to the window and cursed her poor vision. She couldn't see what her son was doing, but she noticed Vanessa had hitched a ride in the cab. She nuzzled Sherman's neck and let her hair blow back behind her as he went over the bumpy soil through the orchard, to the field.

* * *

Brenda Nevins put her hand inside Sherman's waistband. He was wearing light gray sweatpants because she'd told him that she liked how he looked when he was aroused.

"I see my effect on you and that makes me hot," she said.

Sherman gave her that puppy dog look that meant he really liked what she was doing, where her hand was, where he hoped her mouth would eventually be.

"Baby, you like that," she said, not a question, but a command. Her voice was loud to carry over the din of the tractor, but also to ensure that he felt her hot breath on his face.

Sherman eased his foot off the tractor's accelerator.

"You know I do," he said.

Brenda dug deeper, wrapping her hand around his hardening penis.

"Yes," she said, "I can tell you do. Oh yes, I can."

"Don't stop," he said, as he guided the tractor.

"We have work to do, baby," she said, releasing her grip.

Sherman's face fell a little. "You got me all worked up, babe."

"That's fine. That's my job. That's what I do. And don't you worry for one minute. I'll take you to the end, I promise."

"I'm so horny," he said.

She smiled. "Good. I like it when you're horny."

The tractor pulled up to the field beyond the apple and peach trees that had been the pride of the Wilder farm.

"Over there," she said. She pointed to a flat space

between two trees, and he maneuvered the tractor to the spot.

Patty Sparks had been delivered to her final resting place. He rolled the body, wrapped like a blue chrysalis, off the tractor's shovel.

"I feel a little bad about her," he said.

Brenda hopped off the tractor. She wore tight jeans and an almost see-through top. With a slightly more conservative top, maybe something with checks and pearl buttons, she could have been an advertisement for a line of cosmetics for the most beautiful country girls.

She was that lovely on the outside.

"Forget her," she said. "Collateral damage. It happens."

"I don't know," he said. "I wished there was another way."

"We don't have a choice," she said, planting a kiss on his lips and running her hand up his thigh. "No one will listen to me unless we get their attention. You know that. I've suffered so much. I have cried a zillion tears for what they have done to me. It isn't right. All of them. Now they will listen."

Sherman looked down at the blue tarp, heavy with a dead body and wrapped up with rope, casually like his mother's knitting. A dead stranger was collateral damage, indeed. It was neither tragic nor sad. It just *was*. The world ran that way. Everything Brenda said was true.

"Let's get rid of her," Brenda announced, stretching her arms as though she was readying herself to lift the body. Which she wasn't. Brenda repeatedly told Sherman that she wanted things done, but didn't think she had to be the one to do them.

"Right," he answered.

"Then, babe," she said, "let's make love. Right here. On . . . what did your dad call it?"

"The mean green machine," he said, a slight grin on his face.

She always knew what to say. She could lift him up, tear him down, take him higher than he'd ever gone. Before Brenda, Sherman Wilder's life was nothing.

"I like that, baby," he said.

Brenda acknowledged his approval with a smile.

She gave Patty's lifeless body a little kick. "Let's bury this cow and make love. I'm so in love with you. You, Sherman, are more of a man than any I've ever met, seen, or heard about. I'm yours."

Sherman Wilder scraped the leggy patch of field grass from the spot where Patty would lay for eternity. Two minutes later, he'd dug a shallow grave. Roots from the peach tree hindered his effort, but he didn't think it mattered much. She was going in that dark hole, and the peaches that grew from her rotting flesh would be the sweetest he'd ever taste.

In a very real way those peaches would come from love.

Brenda's love.

"Ready?" she said.

He grinned. Damn right he was.

Brenda tugged at Sherman's sweatpants and lowered them to his ankles. His eyes rolled backward, and he braced himself on the tractor.

"I'm going to give you the ride of your life," she said, her eyes grazing his before moving downward.

CHAPTER FORTY-SIX

Once a month, the Clallam County Library System in Port Angeles sent a van with a collection of books and DVDs to shut-ins unable to travel to one of its branches. Violet Wilder had been on the mobile librarian's route for six months and her delivery of books and a little conversation had been a highlight of the elderly woman's days. It didn't matter what books Tansy Mulligan brought; books were nearly beside the point. Tansy, in her early fifties, was a sparkler of a girl.

A girl, to Violet's way of thinking, was any woman under sixty-five with her own teeth.

Tansy was a talker too. She had three cats and she could spend an hour talking about each one. Violet wasn't much of a cat lover. She thought felines had their place—mousing in the barn, for one. Maybe that was the only place. Whenever Tansy came with her little satchel of books from the van—"an eclectic mix for my most eclectic reader"—she'd sit down for a quick cup of tea and a sweet, and talk and talk. About the cats

("Smoky caught a sparrow!"). About the latest Laura Lippman thriller ("kept me guessing to the end") and then, back to her cats. Violet didn't mind. She had been lonely before Tansy.

She looked at the calendar in the kitchen—the only thing left in the house that clued her into the date. No TV. No phone. No radio. It was the Friday before a holiday weekend and she knew that Tansy would come for a prolonged visit. She'd told Violet that she always made Wilder Farm her last stop before heading home to her cats.

"Because you're such a sweetie," she said. "And you love cats as much as I do."

Violet hadn't the heart to tell Tansy the truth about her and cats.

The night before Tansy's expected arrival Vanessa watched Violet set out her library books.

"You want me to return those for you?" she asked, as though she was offering up some enormous favor.

"No," Violet said. "Tansy from the library will be here tomorrow."

"That won't be necessary. The county doesn't need to spend so much money on one person's reading material. I'm happy to have Sherman take them back next time he goes to town."

"No," Violet said again. "She's coming, and she'll take them with her. We often have a little tea and a visit."

Vanessa seemed interested. "You do? About what?"

Violet knew that Vanessa didn't care about the substance or subject of any conversation that didn't have to do with her.

"Cats, mostly."

"I didn't know you were a cat aficionado," Vanessa said.

Using a ten-dollar word to show how smart she is.

"I adore cats," Violet lied, as convincingly as she could. Lying unfortunately was not one of her chief skills. She tried gamely though. "In fact, I've been worried about the kittens I heard crying in the barn the other day."

"There are no kittens in the barn," Vanessa said.

Violet couldn't stand that young woman. Everything had to be contrary with her. "I heard them, Vanessa."

"You probably heard the wind," Vanessa said.

Must everything be a fight?

"Kittens don't sound like the wind," Violet said, mostly to herself.

"Someone is a little snippy today," Vanessa said, circling Violet like a shark as she sat at the kitchen table.

Violet didn't like where this was going. It was hard for her to hold her utter hatred for Vanessa inside, but she managed. *She had to.* To agitate her son's lover was to risk some kind of outrageous retaliation. She was certain of that.

"Sorry, Vanessa," Violet said, practically choking on her words. "I'm just a little tired, that's all."

Vanessa studied Violet, then her eyes landed on the stack of library books. A pen and a tablet rested under one of Violet's gnarled fingers.

Violet caught Vanessa's stare.

"I'm going to make a list of what I'd like to read next," Violet said.

"I see," Vanessa said, adding, "Well then, I'll leave you to it."

With that, Vanessa left. Violet heard the screen door slam and she watched the woman she'd grown to loathe more than anyone on the planet—*ever*—vanish into the barn.

As fast as she could, Sherman Wilder's mother started to write.

Tansy, please help me. Bring the police.
Something is going on here and I'm not sure
what it is. It involves my son and his girlfriend,
Vanessa. They are up to something. Something
very evil. I think they may have someone held
captive in the barn. I don't know why or what
for. I don't understand any of it. All I know is
that they have cut me off from the outside world
because they don't want me to tell on them. I
don't even know what it is that they think I know.
Please be very careful. Bring the police. Do it
right away. My life depends on it.

Violet Wilder

Her heart pounded so rapidly that Violet felt the need for some baby aspirin, yet in her haste to get things done, she ignored the warning signs of a heart attack. *Keep calm. Slow it down. Relax. You can do this if this is the last thing you do.* She wasn't going to die without stopping Vanessa, who she was sure was the ringleader of something nefarious. She tore the note from the tablet and folded it into a square and tucked it inside the Lilian Jackson Braun novel that Tansy had told her she would adore, but she hadn't read a word of it.

Although it wasn't easy maneuvering an armload of books with her walker, Violet made it back to her bedroom.

She wasn't taking any chances.

She dressed for bed and crawled under the covers. The sooner she slept, the sooner the next day would come.

"What's wrong? Is it Sherman?" Violet said, sitting upright in her bed and looking at the alarm clock that she'd set every night, but never needed to roust her. Vanessa had opened the door and a slash of bright light from the hallway landed on her face, waking her.

"You stupid old bitch," Vanessa said. "From the minute I met you, I knew that you'd be trouble. Sherman kept telling me that you were a sweet old thing, but I knew better. I have a sixth sense about people. I really do."

"I have no idea what you're talking about," Violet said, clutching her sheets and wondering if she should call out for her son.

Or if he'd even help her.

Vanessa held up something white, but Violet couldn't see what it was. She reached for her glasses on the bedside table.

"I don't know what you're talking about, Vanessa," she said putting on her glasses. "I've been nothing but kind to you, and you've done everything you can to undermine me, from insulting my lasagna to spending time with my son."

Vanessa took a step closer.

"I'm not Vanessa," she said. "And I'm bored with your constantly referring to me by that name. It's gotten very, very old. Very, very fast."

Violet had no idea what was going on. "Then who are you?" she asked. "And what do you want?"

"I'm Brenda Nevins," she said, moving a little nearer to the bed. "You've heard of me, haven't you?"

Violet had, but she didn't say so.

"I don't know who that is," Violet said. "I don't know what you want. Please leave me alone. Leave Sherman alone. Does he know that you're not who you've been pretending to be?"

Brenda laughed as she took a seat on the edge of the bed. Violet recoiled and inched away from her.

"You stupid old woman," Brenda said. "He knows everything about me, and he loves me. He knows that the world has beaten me down, but that I'm stronger than everyone put together."

"You need help," Violet said.

Brenda smiled and surveyed the room—the door, the window. The only ways out.

"Help," she repeated. "Interesting choice of words, Mom."

This time Violet didn't correct the younger woman, whoever she was.

Brenda held out the tablet, pushing it nearly in Violet's face. The page was no longer completely white, but a pale shade of gray. Interwoven in the gray were the unmistakable white letters of the note Violet had written to Tansy, the library van lady.

No. No. No.

"I can explain," Violet said trying to extricate herself from the bed. It was as if her body hadn't yet fully awakened, as it refused to do even the simplest maneuver. "I was scared and mixed up. I'm old."

She tossed in the word "old" like a tennis instructor does with a simple volley for a new student. She knew Brenda would pounce on it.

She did.

"That's right," she said. "You are old. Old and ugly. Shriveled up. Disgusting to look at. There's danger in the ugly, as repellant as they can be."

"I want to see my son!" Violet said.

"He's busy with a project," Brenda said. "Our project."

The words dangled in the air, but Violet didn't take the bait. She had another, more pressing concern. Brenda put the gray sheet from the tablet in her pocket and collected Violet's library books.

"I imagine the note is in here," she said, flipping through the pages, but keeping her eyes fixed on Violet's. "Your pathetic little cry for help."

"Please," Violet said, despite knowing there was nothing she could do to stop this horrible woman.

"I'll be back," she said.

"Bring Sherman! I want to see my son."

"He's busy, tending to the livestock."

Violet swung her legs to the floor and reached for her walker. Brenda pushed her back to the bed.

"I told you to stay put," Brenda said, jabbing a finger into Violet's rib cage. "You want me to break your bones? I could snap your arm like a twig. Every breath you take tempts me to do it, so don't push me."

She grabbed the walker and the cane.

"You stay put. You aren't going anywhere. You aren't seeing your little library friend tomorrow. I'll give her these books," Brenda said. Her eyes seemed black in the darkness, her mouth tight around her lips.

Violet started to cry though she wished she hadn't.

"I want my son," she said.

"So do I," Brenda said. "When he gets back from the barn, I'm going to make love to him until the rafters crash down. Enjoy the show. I know you've listened every night."

Violet wanted to say that it was impossible *not* to listen, that Brenda was an exhibitionist and a narcissist. But she didn't. She didn't say another word.

The door slammed. Violet sat still in her bed. She heard a piece of furniture, the hall tree by the sound of it, move across the floorboards and settle against her bedroom door.

She slithered over the floor on her hands and knees, not because she was afraid she couldn't walk those ten feet. She was afraid that the monster Brenda would hear her. *Kill her. Torture her.* She rose up from her knees and twisted the knob and pushed. She was firm, but gentle. She didn't want to make any noise.

Nothing. She couldn't move the door.

Violet wanted to scream for help, but it was nighttime. There was no one to hear her screams. She deliberated on what Brenda meant by "livestock" when she said her son was busy. She wondered what she had done so wrong in her life to deserve this kind of evil visited upon her. She'd gone to church. She baked pies for the PTA. She'd never cheated on her husband. She made sure her children were raised with good, strong moral values. She wished that what had just happened was a nightmare. She closed her eyes and reopened them.

The walker was missing. The cane was gone. It was real. She was a prisoner in her own home, and she had no idea why.

CHAPTER FORTY-SEVEN

Brenda Nevins kept a straight razor she'd found in the upstairs bathroom under her pillow. It had belonged to Alec Wilder. There was some irony to what she was about to do and she loved irony. She pitied those who didn't get the nuances of such things. *Dull normals. Lowbrow. The fill-in people.* She'd set up the laptop in the bedroom. The image displayed there was no longer the four stalls that Sherman had outfitted with wild-game cameras. The girls and their terror bored her. Repeating the same thing over and over.

Help me. Help me.

Get me out of here.

Don't rape me.

So boring. The girls were taking up air and space. They had to go.

When Sherman came out of the shower, a towel wrapped around his paunchy waist, he saw the woman of his dreams. She was sprawled out on the bed, naked, inviting him over with a smile.

"Damn," he said. "Are you for real?"

"I'm your fantasy," she said.

He sat next to her and she moved closer. She wrapped a leg around his, pressing herself against him.

"I want to ride you like that stupid horse of your mother's," she said.

It was a dream. The most beautiful woman in the world wanted him in the way that felt beyond any other sexual encounter he'd ever experienced. Brenda made him feel stronger, bigger.

"My God, baby, you're going to split me in two," she said, writhing on top of him. She leaned downward, pressing her nipples, the crowning glory of that body of hers, against his pasty, white chest.

The sound of the old Chippendale headboard against the plaster and lathe walls reverberated through the room. It was loud, like a woodpecker that never needed rest. She'd bring him to the edge, then ease off. She'd nuzzle his chest, let her fingertips explore every inch of his body. Her hair flew behind her as she leaned back to work him deep inside of her.

"Oh baby," Sherman cried out. His arms were splayed over his head as he let Brenda Nevins do to him whatever she wanted. She was in total control and yet at the same time he'd never felt more virile in his life. *More commanding.* She'd awakened something dormant inside of him. After his marriage collapsed, sex was porn on the Internet. He might as well have been gelded like Monty, his mother's beloved horse. Brenda had given him everything that a woman can give to a man.

Purpose.

Desire.

Opportunity.

"I can feel you," she said, her warm breath pouring down on him. "I want you! Give it to me!"

Sherman Wilder was the man, but the student too. Brenda knew how to please him in ways that no woman ever had. He wanted more than anything to satisfy her. It didn't matter what she wanted done. He'd never let her down.

"Giving it," he said, first quietly, before bursting out, "giving it!"

Brenda arched her back before lowering herself one more time. "That's it! Good baby! Fill me up," she said.

He closed his eyes like he always did.

"Jesus, Brenda! So good! Too good!"

Brenda slid her hand under the pillowcase to retrieve the razor. She held it upward, above her, and then turned to the camera and smiled.

"I love you, Brenda," he said, his eyes still closed, his body still feeling the rush of the orgasm that she'd given to him.

"I know you do, baby," she said. "You prove it to me every time we make love. You were so into it just now. So loud. I loved it."

His eyes popped open.

"I got carried away," he said, lifting his head from the pillow. "Crap, my mother! She must have got an earful."

Brenda let out a little laugh. "The old dried-up bitch. She's always complaining about something, treating us like we're dirt. And really, I can't stand the way she treats you. Sickening. If she hears us making love, I say good for her. Maybe she'll realize the world isn't all about her sad little farm. People have to live a little, baby. You of all people know that."

Sherman rolled onto his side, sweaty and exhausted.

"I guess so," he said. "Still, I really think I need to do something about that damn headboard."

"No. I like the noise," Brenda said. "It's the sound of our love." She got up and went over to the computer.

"Hey," he said, "were you recording that?"

She shut the lid of the laptop that had belonged to Janie and turned to face her lover.

"Yes," she said, "just a practice run. I don't think I got the best angle."

"I want to watch, baby," Sherman said, excited again. "That was the best sex I ever had."

"We can do better," she said. "Now get some clothes on. I'm starving."

Sherman sighed. "You're always hungry," he said.

"Mind-blowing sex with a hot guy does that to me."

He kissed her and put on some pants and a T-shirt. He looked at himself in the mirror over the dresser. He wasn't in perfect shape. He didn't have the crisp features of a younger man, but somehow Brenda didn't see what he saw. It was shallow for him to care so much about how he looked, but he knew that the balance of power when it came to beautiful women tipped in favor of a rich guy. He wasn't rich at all. Except to her. Over everyone in the world, Brenda picked him.

"You coming?" he asked.

Brenda got up to get dressed.

"I just did," she said.

He laughed. "Yeah, you did."

CHAPTER FORTY-EIGHT

Tansy Mulligan adored talk radio, but the reception off the highway toward the Wilder farm was so meager she had nothing to listen to. That was fine. She had a lot to think about, and hearing someone complain about the latest political faux pas didn't amount to a hill of beans. At least that's what she thought. Her daughter had planned to come over for the Memorial Day holiday, but Shelly was feeling ill and canceled. *Fiddlesticks!* She had a refrigerator full of food—a brisket that she had rubbed with herbs like a masseuse in search of a really big tip. She wondered if she'd be able to freeze the meat when she got home. Wasting food was such, well, a *waste*.

As the library van rumbled up the driveway to the charming blue and white two-story farmhouse, Tansy noticed a young woman standing over by the barn. She adjusted her glasses and waved. The woman waved back.

Tansy eased down on the brake, and the van crawled to a safe stop in front of the dahlia bed that Ms. Wilder—"Violet, please!"—had said quite proudly contained several rare tubers. She made a mental note to remind Violet of her promise to give her some. Her garden at home in Port Angeles was supposed to be an English garden, though Tansy was pretty sure at present it resembled England during the Blitz.

"You must be Violet's daughter, Denise," she said, stepping out of the van and going over to greet her.

Brenda smiled. "One and the same."

"She's told me all about you," Tansy said. Her tone was effusive. "So proud of you being a dentist and all. She loves saying 'my daughter, *the doctor.*'"

Brenda laughed. "She's a real cheerleader, my mom."

"I must say, you look so familiar. Do you advertise your practice on TV?"

"I have some," Brenda said, eyeing Tansy and wondering what it is that she was recognizing.

"I knew it. The second I saw you I thought, wow, she's pretty enough to be a model. Just seemed like you've been on TV or maybe the movies. But your mom told me you were a dentist, so now I've figured it all out."

"You have, have you?" Brenda asked.

"TV and dental star! So awesome. You here for the holiday weekend?" Tansy asked.

Brenda indicated she was.

"That's wonderful," Tansy said. "Your mom has been lonely lately. It's hard when your kids get all grown up and have lives of their own."

She was thinking about herself and that brisket as much as anything. Tansy looked over at the house. "Where is she, by the way?"

Brenda shifted into her concerned affect. It was a

look that she'd observed from the prison chaplain, a do-gooder who knew how to tilt her head and give it a subtle, sad shake.

"Mom's been under the weather," she said, the tilt in place. "She wanted me to return her books. Just a sec. I set them on the porch. She told me you'd be by today."

Tansy followed her across the yard to the front door.

"Did she like the Lilian Jackson Braun novel?" Tansy asked.

"Loved it," Brenda said.

Tansy beamed. "Marvelous. I've got another for her in the van."

Brenda turned to face her, tilt again. Sad eyes. Worried look. "I'm sorry," she said. "Mom's eyes are failing. She can't read anymore."

Tansy put her hands to her face.

Brenda made a note of that.

"Oh, no," Tansy said. "That's terrible. I'm so sorry to hear that. Reading is so important. Opens doors. Gives perspective." She stopped her brochure summation. "Hey," she said, brightening. "I have audiobooks too. Does your mom have a CD player?"

Brenda pushed the books into Tansy's arms.

"No," she said. "She's not one for electronics. Not like my brother."

Tansy adjusted the books in her arms. "How is your brother?" Tansy asked. "If you don't mind my saying so, your mom has been very worried about him."

"Oh?"

"Yes," Tansy said, looking toward the dahlia bed. "Like I said, it's none of my business. None of my beeswax as my daughter Shelly used to say, but anyway, your mom is worried about Sherman. Says he's so lonely and sad and, you know."

"No," Brenda said, "I don't know."

"Not successful like you."

Brenda liked where that was going. Even though Tansy Mulligan thought she was Denise, the van driver in the blue-and-white "Authors Are My Rock Stars" T-shirt was right on the money. She *was* successful. A winner. Sherman? Not so much. At least not until she came along to give him a place where he'd be seen as something worth remembering and not some dull, little IT nerd with a paunch and receding hairline.

"He's a real love," Brenda said. "A total sweetheart."

"Yes, I'm sure." Tansy changed the subject back to the audiobooks. "I have Playaways too. They are marvelous. The player comes with the audiobook."

Brenda shook her head. "You're very persistent, Tansy."

Tansy brightened upon hearing her name. "Your mother must have mentioned me. I just love her. I love our chats too."

She stopped talking, her brain processing the features of the woman standing in front of her. The hair color was different. Style too. But the eyes were the same. A flash of recognition came to her, but she couldn't place whom it was that she was talking to. It wasn't a dental commercial.

"You seem familiar, Denise," she said, still thinking.

Brenda kept her smile in place.

"Besides TV commercials, you've seen pictures of me in Mom's house," she said.

"No," Tansy said, shifting her weight as she pondered it. "That's not it. You remind me of a celebrity."

Brenda soaked in the attention. Being recognized when there was no danger of being caught was an undeniable turn-on.

Tansy took a step away, and started toward the van. Still thinking. Still not quite sure.

A scream came out into the yard from inside the house.

"Tansy! Help me!"

Tansy spun around, her eyes full of concern. "Your mom's calling for help."

Brenda gave her a cold, blank stare.

"What's the matter with you? She sounds hurt," Tansy said, the volume of her voice rising with each word. And then something came to her. She took a step away from the woman with the dead-eyed expression. "Hey, I know you. I have seen you on the news." Her eyes widened with terror.

Brenda's eyes left Tansy and she gave a slight nod.

Tansy turned a quarter turn to see who Brenda Nevins had signaled—and for what.

As quietly as the cats that Tansy so loved, Sherman Wilder snuck up from behind the library lady and swung a shovel as hard as he could. It smacked Tansy. *Hard.* Her glasses flew across the porch. Blood sprayed on the screen door and onto Brenda's light blue blouse. Tansy went down in a silent heap.

Brenda looked down in horror.

"Damn you, Sherman, this stain will never come out," she said, picking at the spatter that freckled the fabric. "I loved this top. It belonged to Janie. Janie was very important to me. Without her, I wouldn't be with you."

Sherman let the shovel fall from his hands as he bent down and hovered over Tansy. He looked at her with eyes that, while not as ice-cold as his lover's, were devoid of emotion. He felt her throat for a pulse.

"She looks it," Brenda said. "Is she?"

Sherman's eyes met Brenda's. "She's dead," he said. "Sorry about the blood, babe. I guess I just don't know my own strength."

From the bedroom window where she'd somehow summoned the strength to drag her frail body, Violet Wilder had let out a mournful cry. If she had thought that the evil that had visited her home had only come in the pretty package of Brenda Nevins she'd been so wrong, so fooled. *Her son.* He was nothing like she'd raised him to be. She'd taught him to be kind, generous, and thoughtful. She'd lived her entire adult life believing that he had been all those things. Not anymore.

He'd just killed Tansy, the library lady.

"Stop your blubbering," Brenda said, suddenly standing over Violet with a pleased look on her face. She held out her hand for Violet to grip, but the old woman refused the gesture. She stared upward, her eyes hard, angry. Her heart was pounding hard enough she hoped it would give her that merciful heart attack and send her on her way to heaven. And to Alec. She wondered how she would explain what had brought her to him.

What their son had done to a woman he didn't even know.

"Get away from me!" she said. "You're a monster."

Brenda thrust her hand in Violet's direction a second time, but Violet refused to take it.

"Such a defiant old bag, Mom."

Violet was having a difficult time breathing. Part of her didn't want any air in her lungs.

"Why did you have to do that to Tansy?" she asked. "What that hell is the matter with you? What kind of people are you?"

"We're family, honey," Brenda said, loving everything about the day's events.

Except for that stain on her blue top. That still made her cross.

"Get out of my house," Violet said. "Go. You and Sherman. Pack up. The police will be here. You'll be sorry when you get caught."

"You make me want to laugh my ass off," Brenda said. "I have been caught. Only once. And there's no do-over in that department. You have no idea who I am, not really. Tansy knew. I saw it in her eyes, that magnificent flash of fear that comes when a rabbit is about to be eaten by a coyote. A mouse by a snake."

"You make me sick," Violet said. "I don't even know what you are."

"I'm what everyone will talk about," Brenda said. "I will never be forgotten."

She poked her fist at Violet.

"Go away! The police will come looking for Tansy. Why did you hurt her? She's not involved in whatever it is that you two have been doing. She's just a librarian, for God's sake."

"Collateral damage," Brenda said. "The police won't come. You know that, don't you?"

"They will," Violet said. "They'll miss her. She has family. Friends. She's very well liked."

Brenda lowered herself and grabbed Violet's hand and swung the old woman to her feet. A bone snapped. Maybe more than one. In agony, Violet couldn't be sure what was happening to her. The old woman cried out, but it only made Brenda pull harder. She twisted Violet's arms as she dragged her across what had been a spotless kitchen floor. Her feet left parallel lines of blood as the skin of her heels sheared off.

"You are hurting me," she cried out. "Please stop."

Brenda kept going, stepping out the door over the bloody smear that indicated where Tansy had been killed. Her body was gone. The library van was gone too.

Violet tried to gather the strength to move her legs beneath her while Brenda dragged her toward the barn. Even in her misery, knowing that this was the end of her life, she managed to take in the surroundings. The outbuildings. The chicken house. The laundry line. The massive and in-desperate-need-of-a-good pruning Jonagold trees that made up the outside row of the orchard. Some of the shapes were blurry, but she knew what they were and how many happy memories she'd had there.

Violet fell like a bundle of sticks when Brenda shoved open the barn door. "Get up. I'm tired of dragging you around."

Violet managed to get to her feet. She wondered if she was already dead and if it was her spirit leaving her body, heading toward heaven. She could stagger. Brenda tugged at her and she kept her balance. She looked down at the red patches of blood pooling and spreading over her knees. They didn't hurt. Nothing hurt. She wasn't crying.

As they passed the open doorway to the tack room, Violet caught a glimpse of a bank of computers and electronic equipment. It wasn't a meth lab or some kind of drug operation that had occupied her son and his evil girlfriend's time. It crossed Violet's mind that in another time or place she might have thought the blinking lights of the devices were pretty. Like the Christmas lights around her Snow Village.

Something wicked had been going on in that barn.

Sherman shoved his mother inside a stall and slammed the door shut. "Mom, I'm sorry," he said through the door of the stall.

Violet could barely hear her son. Even if she could understand every nuance in his words, she wouldn't have said anything back to him anyway. He killed someone. He'd killed an innocent woman by bashing her head with a shovel. It was beyond her comprehension. She'd never speak to him again as long as she lived.

"You shouldn't have been so nosy," he said. "You should have just looked the other way. Brenda isn't like other people. She's special. It's an acquired taste, I admit it. But, God, Mom, I love her. She's everything to me."

She's evil, Violet thought, though she didn't respond to her son. She wasn't going to give him one bit of comfort by accepting his apology. *You are disgusting to me. Revolting.*

"Mom, it won't be long," Sherman went on. "I promise. Brenda says that most people live empty lives and never achieve any kind of greatness. She's right about that, you know? She has it all figured out, and she picked me. Me? Who would have thought it?"

Violet put her cold hands over her ears. She didn't want to hear one more muffled word from her son. She would rather die than do so. And considering what was going on all around her, she probably wouldn't have to wait long.

CHAPTER FORTY-NINE

Kendall Stark had ignored some of the more mundane paperwork associated with her job for long enough. She'd have taken any excuse to break away from it—no matter how weak. A very good one came in the form of a call from the Clallam County Sheriff's Office.

"It's about your missing girls," said a young man who identified himself as Deputy Flanagan.

Kendall shoved her paperwork aside.

"Go ahead," she said.

"Well, I think it might be related," he said. "I was on the scene of a drive-by shooting we had out in the county. A guy named Robert Taylor was shot at point-blank range."

Kendall had heard about the shooting. Clallam County was not known for anything as urban as a drive-by. She doubted that's what had transpired up there, but it wasn't her case.

The missing girls from South Kitsap, however, were.

"What makes you think our girls were involved?"

"Not involved," he said. "I think that whoever killed our guy took them."

"Why do you think that?" Kendall asked.

"One of the girls' cell phones was discovered at the scene. I found it. Right there, under the VW that belonged to our vic."

"What makes you think it belonged to one of our girls?" she asked.

"I'll send you the video she made. It isn't great quality, a little on the Blair Witch side of things. You know what I mean?"

Kendall did. "Yes, can you send it to me now?"

"Yup, encrypted. What address?"

She gave him the email to the department's secure server.

"What else did you find at the scene?"

"Not much. Tire tracks. We cast those, but not much there to go on. Pretty common tires. Nothing fancy."

The email popped into her in-box, and she clicked on it to download.

"You get it?" he asked.

"Yes, server's slow."

"One thing that was kind of weird," he went on. "Our guys found two shell casings."

"What's so peculiar?"

"Robert was shot once. At point-blank range. Just kind of strange that the shooter shot his weapon twice."

The file finished downloading.

"Maybe he missed the first time," Kendall said.

"I don't know. Just seems to me that if the shooter had shot someone in the head at close range he wouldn't need to shoot another time. If he did, where the heck did that bullet go?"

"Done loading now," Kendall said, her eyes fastened on her computer screen. "I'll watch and get back to you."

CHAPTER FIFTY

The pixelated video jerked from one jagged image to the next, before settling on the shuddering chin of a girl. The jaw moved and the soft voice of someone very scared was faint, almost unintelligible. Kendall adjusted the volume, trying to tune out the hissing noise in the background and the movement of fabric against the phone's microphone.

The jaw wasn't moving because the girl was talking. It was moving because she was trembling. The chin moved closer to the phone's camera.

"Someone just shot Patty," a voice said. "I'm pretty sure he's going to kill all of us. I love you, Mom and Dad."

The voice of a young man, calm and genial, silenced her.

"Sure," he said to someone. "Helping these gals will be the highlight of my day."

Whatever had scared her and made her think her life was in jeopardy had just transpired.

One of the girls—farther away from the microphone—said they didn't need help. Her tone was pleading, but unconvincing.

She was lying. Trying to spare the young man.

The phone jostled a bit more, and in doing so, it captured the purple fingernails of the girl closest to the camera.

"Hey! What's wrong with her?" the young man asked.

Robert Taylor, Clallam's victim, Kendall thought.

Gunfire and panicked screams came next. The recording bumped again.

It was indeed a single shot.

A man's voice told the screaming girls to shut up, though the last part of what he was saying was partially obscured by the screams.

Shut the hell up, you four little bitches!

Another girl shouted, demanding to know why he'd done that.

"I can't see his face," whispered the girl with the purple nails who was closest to the phone—presumably its owner. Her voice was teetering between the softest whisper and inaudible, like a terrible cell connection. "He's old. Like my dad's age. White. Not fat. Not thin. God, I love you, Mom. I'm really sorry."

"He shouldn't have stopped," the man said. His tone was flat, devoid of any remorse or urgency. The tone caught Kendall off guard. In the drama of the moment, gunfire, screaming girls, this was the affect of the shooter?

The phone moved, and the camera raked over the images of two other girls, both screaming and crying. Then everything stopped.

Kendall watched the video a dozen times, trying to pick out the clues about what had happened, where Patty Sparks and the girls had been when they were attacked. Nothing on the video suggested that the girls had been abducted by someone they knew. Yet, true stranger abductions were rare. Most abduction cases involving children were sparked by parents at war with each other. This wasn't in play. Besides, these weren't little kids. The girl who'd recorded the video—and who Kendall knew all but certainly was Chloe MacDonald—didn't know her attacker.

A phrase struck her as familiar, but she couldn't place it. She played it over and over.

"*. . . you four little bitches.*"

It couldn't be.

Chapter Fifty-one

Kendall put her purse and keys into the locker across from the metal detectors. Visiting prisons had become too frequent as of late. Yet, in order to find Brenda Nevins, she felt that it was probably necessary to turn the soil over again. Fenton Becker, who worked in the superintendent's office and was in line to replace her, met Kendall.

"No one likes a snitch," Fenton said.

"I know," Kendall said.

"But you're in luck," he said, pushing his round glasses up the bridge of his long, patrician nose. "No one, and I mean no one, likes Brenda Nevins."

Kendall smiled. "My faith in humanity has been restored," she said.

Fenton stayed expressionless. "Mine will be. Once you catch her."

"That's why I'm here, Mr. Becker," she said.

They walked through security to the first of a series of doors monitored by a guard in a video control booth.

The doors buzzed and opened.

"There are two inmates that knew Nevins here, and

they'll tell you whatever you need to know," he said. "Coral Douglas worked in the computer lab with Brenda. Tamara O'Neal had some downtime with Brenda in the pets program."

The pets program reference brought a nod of uncomfortable familiarity from Kendall. Brenda had been caught having sex with a guard on a dog-grooming table.

Fenton told Kendall that Coral was doing time for a meth conviction.

"Boyfriend was the cooker/dealer. Coral made what she insists she thought were 'deliveries' of art supplies to needy high school students."

"She sounds lovely," Kendall deadpanned. "And bright."

"Not the brightest bulb in the chandelier, but she's not that bad," Fenton said. "Really very nice. I have hopes that she'll make something out of her life when she gets out of here. Most don't."

"Tell me about Tamara," Kendall said. "What's her story? And what's your assessment about whether she's reliable or not?"

"Sissy has been here since she was seventeen, and she's in her early fifties now. She loves animals. Darn near treats them like they are her babies. Probably because she lost hers. She saw something in Brenda, I'm not sure what. I can't quite grab it in my mind, though she's told me a time or two."

"How come she's been here so long?"

"She threw her twin baby boys off the Narrows Bridge."

"That's a famous case," Kendall said. "I remember reading about that when I was a kid."

"Infamous is more like it," he said. "Said that she was at her wits' end. Husband beat her. Told her that she was a piece of garbage and that her boys would grow up hating her. She snapped. She killed them to save them from being as unhappy as she was."

"You feel sorry for her," Kendall said, her eyes widening a little.

Fenton rolled his shoulders. "I guess so. I never really thought of it that way. I just know her as a woman serving a lot of time for a terrible thing that she did, but the person she is today isn't that woman. Not anymore."

"When is she due for a hearing?"

"Next year," he said. "She lives on that hope. I think she'll get out, but I can't say that to her. Can't give people a false sense of hope when so much is on the line."

"No, I don't see how you could," Kendall said.

Fenton indicated for Kendall to follow to a conference room. "Care who you see first?"

Kendall shook her head. "No."

A small gray-haired woman in faded blue jeans, a sky-blue shirt, and white tennis shoes appeared with Fenton in the conference room doorway. The space was airless, devoid of any artwork except a faded Washington State flag, which sat forlornly in the corner. A cobweb enrobed the tarnished brass eagle on the tip of the pole. Tamara "Sissy" O'Neal had that caged animal look in her eyes, always scanning the space before landing her eyes on another's.

"This is Kendall Stark," he said. "She's a detective

with the Kitsap County Sheriff's Office in Port Orchard. As I explained to you, she's here to talk about Brenda Nevins."

"That's why I'm here," Sissy said. "I want to help. I don't think any good could come from that woman being out on the loose. She's trouble with a capital T."

"Please have a seat, Sissy," Kendall said. "Let's talk."

Sissy slid into the chair across from Kendall. Fenton excused himself and disappeared down the corridor.

"You worked with Brenda in the kennel?" Kendall asked.

"Right," she said. "She really didn't do much work. But, yeah, that's where I knew her from."

"What was she like to work with?"

"As I said, she didn't do much work. Didn't want to wreck her nails. One time a cat scratched her, and she had a fit like a two-year-old, worried she'd get a scar."

"I see," Kendall said. "On her face?"

"On her *finger*. Seriously she was worried about a scar on her finger because she said that if she wanted to do some modeling after prison her hands had to be flawless. Like she was ever going to be a model."

"She wanted attention," Kendall said. "Isn't that right?"

"An attention whore is what I called her. She wanted everyone to watch her, worship her, dress like her. She was sure that she was going to be a big star someday even though she killed her baby and her husband." Sissy stopped for a beat, assessing Kendall's reaction to what she was saying.

"I know what you're thinking, that I'm one to talk."

"I wasn't thinking that at all, Sissy."

"Look, I killed my boys. I own that. It took me a long time to get to that place where I could look in the mirror at my own reflection and see that I was something more than a killer."

"I know that you feel remorse," Kendall said. "It must be a very heavy burden to carry."

Sissy looked like she was going to cry, but she held it together.

"You don't know the half of it," she said, "but that's where Brenda comes in. She made it seem like we shared the same truths about who we were and how we got there. What a joke. She killed her baby for money. I killed my babies because I loved them. Big difference."

Kendall didn't see the distinction at all. Dead was dead. Murder was murder. Still, she wasn't there to challenge Sissy O'Neal on her crimes, only to try to find out where Brenda might have gone. Or at least, perhaps understand more of Brenda's motivations.

"But you liked her?"

Sissy drew nearer. "I did at first. That's the weird part of dealing with Brenda. She was hard *not* to like. As awful as she was."

Kendall noticed a subtle shift in Sissy's demeanor. She seemed a little wistful.

"You got close to her," Kendall said.

Sissy blanched at the statement. "Not Janie close if that's what you're getting at."

"Not getting at that," Kendall said. "Did she ever tell you her plans?"

The inmate folded her arms, revealing scars from a habit long ago. "Do you mean escape plans? Never."

"Okay, but think a little and help us find her. I was

wondering if she told you what she wanted to do when she got out of here."

This time, a spark of recognition came over Sissy's washed-out face.

"Yeah," she said, "She did. We were grooming a couple of Westies and she laid it all out."

"Tell me," Kendall said. "I need to know what you know."

CHAPTER FIFTY-TWO

Cream-colored fur was everywhere, falling like snow. Brenda Nevins rinsed off her arms and pulled a paper towel from the battered dispenser and applied it to her face. She looked over at Sissy, who was putting the grooming tools into the plastic storage containers donated by a dog lover.

"I'm not going to curl up and die in here," Brenda said.

The comment came out of the blue. They'd been happily caring for the dogs, talking about pets they'd owned before they came to be warehoused at the prison. They'd even discussed how much they'd love real French fries ("Fried in oil! Not baked!") if they'd ever managed to get the attention of the man who ran the kitchen. The food he made was devoid of flavor, low in calories, and just plain boring.

"What?" Sissy asked.

Brenda leaned against the counter. "I said, I'm not going to curl up and die in this place. I have a lot more I want to do."

"We all do, Brenda," Sissy said.

"We all might," Brenda said. "But very few of us are in the position to do anything about it. Look around you, Sissy. All these girls talk about how they're going to do this and that when they get out. You've been here long enough to notice that there's a whole bunch of them that don't do anything at all except reoffend and end up right back here."

Brenda was spot-on. More than a quarter of the girls managed to come back after a year or two.

"So what's your plan?" Sissy asked.

Brenda swiveled to look at herself in the polished steel mirror over the sink. "Still working on it," she said. "I've thought of a million things that I could do, but only one thing that I feel that I have to do."

Their eyes met in the mirror.

"What is it?" Sissy asked.

"Be memorable," Brenda said. "I'm going to do something, something big, something that will get me noticed by everyone."

"Like what?"

"Still working on it," Brenda said. "All the haters out there need to be reminded that I have feelings too. That I'm a person of talent and refinement and that I should never have been marginalized. That was an error. A fatal error for some, I'd say."

Sissy was pretty sure Brenda was crazy.

"Are we talking about a big revenge plot?" she asked. "Is that what you're going to do? I thought you wanted to be a TV star or something along those lines."

Brenda smiled at Sissy. She *had* been listening. That was good. Later, Brenda was fairly certain, Sissy would recount the conversation as though it were some bombshell revelation.

"I'm already a big star, Sissy," Brenda went on. "You and all the other girls here know that. You see how everyone wants to please me? Everyone wants to dress like me. Do their hair like mine."

Sissy didn't think any of what Brenda was saying was true. The other girls stayed clear of Brenda because she scared the crap out of them. She was wildly unpredictable, full of herself, and determined to get her way in every situation. No matter how small.

Sissy played along. "You're already the most famous girl here," she said. "Everyone knows who you are."

"Oh, Sissy, this is so small time. I deserve a larger audience than the latest busload of meth heads, child abusers, and these other low-IQ chicks. I will be a star. I will do what it takes to ensure that those who've hurt me, put me down, made me think less of myself, realize that transgressions that go unpunished are merely unfinished business."

Sissy finished talking, and Kendall processed all that she'd said. None of it was at odds with the killer Kendall had been tracking. In fact, it was a big, fat underscore of Brenda Nevins's known psychiatric profile—a report made while she awaited trial for the murder of her husband and baby. If anything, it showed that time in prison wasn't going to change one thing about who she was, what made her tick, and what she might do if she'd been given the chance.

CHAPTER FIFTY-THREE

Coral Douglas was next. Fenton Becker ushered her in, made quick introductions, and returned to his office. She was a sullen-looking girl who seldom smiled. On those rare occasions when she did, the act revealed a mouth full of teeth that were so fragmented and black that it was no wonder that she weighed less than 100 pounds.

How in the world can she eat?

Coral held her hand in front of her mouth when she spoke.

"I don't like strangers judging me," she said.

"I've seen what methamphetamine does to people, Coral. How are you doing on your recovery?"

Her hand remained up over her mouth.

"What do you care?" she asked. "You're here about that bitch Brenda. Isn't that right?"

"I do care, Coral. Did you know there's a community group that donates funds to replace the teeth of former meth addicts?"

She looked down at the table. "Yeah. I heard about them."

"I can tell them about you," Kendall said. "I can ask them to help you. I can't guarantee anything, but I can promise I will try."

"Thanks," she said. "I'd appreciate it."

Kendall made a note of her promise.

"Now let's talk about the reason I'm here. Let's see if you can help me, okay?"

Coral lowered her hand. With her mouth pressed shut, she wasn't scary at all. Her black hair was long and clipped back. Her brown eyes were clear and alert. While Coral had a pair of tiny scars on the bridge of her nose, for a meth addict her skin was in surprisingly good shape.

"You didn't like Brenda much, I gather," Kendall said.

"Couldn't stand her."

"Can you be a little more specific?" Kendall asked. "You worked with her in the computer lab, correct?"

Coral played with her hair. "Yeah. And I'll tell you she was absolutely the worst person to work with. She acted like she was the boss of me and that I was stupid because, well, because of the reason I'm in here. People judge. Brenda finishes people off."

Coral let loose. She talked about how Brenda had anointed herself as the authority on everything and anything. The two women from Pierce County College who'd volunteered with the computer outreach program both quit over Brenda.

"She actually made one of them cry. Told the lady that . . . let me get the exact quote . . . 'Fat girls like you are always trying to please others because they know deep down that nobody wants them.'"

"Harsh," Kendall said. "Why did she say that?"

Coral looked around the room. Her eyes rarely stayed focused on the detective. "Because the girl was fat, and she knew that she was vulnerable. Brenda thought that she wasn't getting the attention she needed, and that if she could get rid of her—which she did—she'd be able to get someone new that would do whatever she wanted them to do."

Kendall leaned in. "Like what?" she asked. "What was she wanting the volunteer to do?"

"Send messages out. That kind of BS. Brenda wanted to make a video—because that's one of the things she thought she ought to because, well she was *the* effing Brenda Nevins, star killer. Whatever."

Fenton had told Kendall that the computer lab at the prison was merely a shell, not functional at all. It was not connected to the Internet. It was set up by volunteers and the State of Washington to help inmates without any computing skills to learn so that once they were outside the institution they might be more competitive in their job search.

"With no Internet, how was she expecting to accomplish her goal?"

Coral was unsure. "I think she just wanted to get rid of that woman."

"I don't follow you," Kendall said.

"The woman, the overweight one, thought Brenda was a bully and had written her up. Brenda thought by getting rid of her, she'd get a man in there."

"Brenda was adept at seducing women," Kendall said.

"She could seduce a preacher during Sunday service," Coral said, "if she thought it would get her what she wanted. She told me one time that the only thing more powerful than money was sex. Although, she was more graphic than that."

They talked a bit more, mostly about how much Coral hated Brenda. How she'd picked on her biggest vulnerability, her teeth. She reminded Kendall of her promise to help her get the needed dental work. Kendall said she'd make the call the minute she got back to her office.

"You know she made some videos here," Coral said, getting up to leave.

Kendall was surprised. "No, I didn't. What kind?"

Coral allowed her eyes to meet Kendall's. "The creepy kind. Ask Fenton. He has one of them. Bet he watches it all the time."

CHAPTER FIFTY-FOUR

"Let's see the video," Kendall said, as she and Fenton stood by the guard's desk.

"What video?" he asked.

"Come on," she said, "are you really going to play a game with me? Your institution looks pretty bad right now. Inmate escaped with the help of the superintendent. Not the best media coverage you've had lately."

"No, it isn't," he said.

"Come on," Kendall said, knowing that he didn't need to comply. "Show me the tape."

His face stayed grim. "I gave it to the FBI," he said.

Great, Kendall thought.

"But you kept a copy, didn't you?" she asked.

Fenton kept his eyes on the detective.

"Yeah," he finally answered. "I *did*. I needed it for our files, and I wasn't sure I'd get it back. We've been through a lot here since the Brenda and Janie debacle. I'm not taking any chances. My ass is on the line."

Kendall didn't appreciate the visual of Fenton's ass being anywhere.

"Let's watch it," she said.

"Pretty graphic," he told her as they walked up to his office.

"I can handle it," she said.

When they got to his office, he produced a cell phone.

"It's on your phone?" she asked. "How'd it get on your phone?"

He shook his head. "Not my phone. Don't know whose phone it is. There's nothing on the damn thing but the video."

"Why didn't you give the phone to the FBI?"

"I had made a copy on a thumb drive, and SA Casey said that would be fine. He didn't ask where the video came from, how I got it, or even about the existence of the phone."

That was a head-scratcher, for sure. SA Casey was utterly and completely by the book.

"Maybe he already had a copy of it," she said.

"Could be," Fenton said.

He queued up the video, and Kendall started watching.

It was Brenda, of course. She was wearing a T-shirt and facing the camera. She sat on the edge of a desk in what appeared to be a classroom.

"This was recorded here?" Kendall asked. "Inside the prison?"

Fenton acknowledged her question with an uneasy smile.

"Pretty graphic," he said. "Just watch."

Kendall kept her eyes on the phone's tiny screen. Brenda took off her top and exposed her breasts. She stood and shifted her sweatpants down her thighs and then stepped out.

There was no audio.

Brenda sat on the desk, slid down to its edge and pleasured herself with some kind of a rod. She writhed with ecstasy. She arched her back, and lifted herself upward and then back down again, the rod inside her.

Kendall glanced over at Fenton.

"Selfie stick," he said.

"Where's she get that?" Kendall asked.

"Someone smuggled it in."

"Can you tell exactly where this video was created?"

He folded his arms. "Yeah," he said. "Computer lab."

"Where'd you get it?"

"One of the girls who works in the kitchen found it. Said it was out in plain sight."

She looked down at the video, now frozen with a still image of Brenda Nevins thrusting her breasts out at the lens.

"She seemed to be saying something in the video," Kendall said. "How come no audio?"

"Don't know."

What did he know?

"How would she have been able to film this in the computer lab?" she asked.

"Not sure," Fenton said. "Janie Thomas kept a looser ship than I will."

Kendall Stark thought of the video as she drove her SUV back to the Kitsap County Sheriff's office. Her hand stuck to the steering wheel. Cody had discovered the joys of a caramel apple. Despite the sticky distraction, she wouldn't shake what she'd seen. The video had been made with the help of at least one other person. Someone needed to hold the phone while Brenda put on her pathetic sex show. No one in prison was taking selfies, as far as Kendall knew. Had the selfie stick been brought in for a specific purpose other than selfies? For the purpose Brenda employed, or was she just using a prop of convenience?

With Brenda Nevins it was hard to know.

Kendall believed the video was meant as a turn-on for someone. It had not been made for Brenda's pleasure. The way she'd positioned herself on the desk, the way she kept her body perfectly inside the frame indicated that she was performing. *Performing for someone.* But who? Janie? That wasn't likely. Janie's interest in Brenda skewed toward romance and a deep personal kind of understanding, not sex.

Brenda was performing for a man.

CHAPTER FIFTY-FIVE

Oh, screw it, Shelly Evans thought to herself as she threw some things into an overnight bag lying open on her bed. She wasn't *that* sick. Her mom had sounded so disappointed that she couldn't make it for the holiday weekend. Her mother Tansy's reaction had needled her all weekend. She had a way of doing that, though not in a manner that could be explained with a sassy retort to a friend.

"My mom needs to get a life! She keeps thinking we're BFFs."

She caught the ferry from Edmonds to Kingston and drove up the highway to Port Angeles. She'd grown up in PA, as the locals called it, and never minded that she had done so. Small-town life had been good. Her dad worked at the mill, and her mom taught school, then went to work for the library system. It had been a good life. She felt the tug of her roots every time she visited there.

The Mulligan house was an old yellow craftsman with a red door and black shutters. A pair of dormers on the waterside looked out over the Straits. The yard was immaculate. Shelly noticed that her mom had, in fact, given up on her English garden, and was tending the dahlia bed that had grown larger with each year—and with each new tuber. Tansy Mulligan had recently specialized in dinner plate–sized blooms. From the freshly spaded earth, it appeared that she'd be planting some new tubers or, perhaps, had dug up some to share with a friend.

Shelly went to the kitchen door by the detached garage. Her mom's pride and joy, a brand-new white Nissan Versa ("It's extravagant, I know, but I've always wanted a brand-new car!"), was missing, so she assumed she'd gone on an errand somewhere. The second she opened the door, Boots and Chin-Chin were on her.

Those cats!

She noticed their water dishes and food bowls were empty. Not like her mother at all. Chin-Chin, a Siamese mix, weighed more than twenty pounds by her mom's most recent calculation ("I got on the scale holding him and then subtracted my weight from the total"). He clearly never missed a meal. Shelly opened the refrigerator and noticed the brisket her mom had said would be the "best ever" was ready to roast. She had to admit it did look pretty good. She took a can of tuna, rolled her eyes at the way her mom babied her cats, and fed them.

The house was dead silent, save for the appreciative purrs coming from Boots and Chin-Chin.

Shelly texted her mom: Surprise! I'm here at the house! Where R U?

She poured herself a glass of wine. After all, it was a holiday. As darkness fell over her childhood home, turning the family photos into sepia hues, Shelly began to worry. Her mother hadn't answered her text.

Where was she, anyway?

CHAPTER FIFTY-SIX

Blake was in the stall next to Amber's. She'd cried all night. They all had. She told herself that whatever had gotten them into that dire predicament was not going to take them down completely. She hadn't fought her way to become the best she could be to die in some twisted maniac's smelly old barn. Not by a long shot.

She felt the presence of something watching her, but that wasn't going to stop her either. She felt around in darkness. The space was small. Smaller than the cubicle her mother complained about at work. About the size of the storage room where the girls on the squad kept their uniforms and pom-poms during the off-season. The space smelled bad, but it was an odor that reminded her of her uncle's farm in Kittitas County, not far from Ellensburg on the dry side of the Cascades.

Barn. Leather. Tack. Hay. Manure.

Blake was in a horse stall.

She felt every inch of space until she reached each of the four walls. On the fourth wall, her fingers ran along a wide space that was all but certainly a door. Another swipe in the dark confirmed it. She found hinges on one side, a latch on the other.

She heard a noise. A sneeze. Amber had allergies. It had to be *her*. It was a high-pitched sneeze that could pierce through a crowded school bus or, in this case, a makeshift prison.

"Amber? Can you hear me?" she whispered.

No response.

She tried again, this time a little louder. But not loud enough, she hoped, to let anyone know she was reaching out to the others.

Finally, an answer.

"Blake? Is that you?"

Blake teared up at the sound of her friend's voice. She was tough. Tougher than anyone would give her credit for. Being beautiful didn't make her weak. Yet, the emotional response to knowing with complete certainty that she was not alone was something she could not set aside.

"It's me," she said, fighting to hold it together. "Are you all right?"

"I think so," Amber said. "You?"

"Mad as hell," Blake whispered back. "But I'm okay. The other girls?"

"Don't know," Amber said, her voice cracking. "I can't hear them anymore. God, what is happening to us?"

"I don't know," Blake said, "but we're going to get out of here."

A beat of silence. The wheels were turning.

"How?" Amber asked. "I can't even move. I'm tied up like a pig."

Blake leaned closer to the slats of the wall that separated her from Amber. She strained to try to see through them, but it was no use. She couldn't see anything.

"We're going to have to find a way out of here," she said.

"Aren't you tied up?"

Blake put her lips to the space between the boards to direct the sound of her voice.

"Not really," she said. "He thinks I'm tied up, but I'm not. Not at all. I just need to find a way to get out of here."

Amber didn't say anything for the longest time.

"Did you hear me?" Blake asked.

"Yeah," she said, "I think they took Chloe, Blake."

CHAPTER FIFTY-SEVEN

Bay Street, the main drag through Port Orchard, had never lived up to its promise, but the locals didn't mind. It was situated along Sinclair Inlet facing the Naval Shipyard in Bremerton. The Olympics were a stunning silver, blue, and white curtain behind the scene. A celebrity romance author and a nationally syndicated radio show host had pooled resources to revive the town with new signage and fresh paint. While their efforts were appreciated, it didn't spark a major revitalization. It didn't matter. Bay Street was a lot like the people who lived in Port Orchard: friendly, not particularly glamorous, but pleasant as the day was long.

Justin's Quick Print was tucked into a sliver of a space between the old movie theater and an antique store that specialized in vintage gelatin molds. The shop was no longer owned by Justin Mallory. His daughter Cici, thirty-three, took over after her parents moved to Kingman, Arizona, to get out of the gloom of Washington winters.

Looking at her, it was easy to see that Cici Mallory lived and breathed ink. A field of tattoos covered her arms; the swirls of undulating images chronicled her affection for fantasy and theater. Only her boyfriend could see her tribute to *The Lord of the Rings*.

"Hi Dr. Waterman," Cici called over as the forensic pathologist and the homicide investigator swung open the heavy old glass door, triggering the small bell on a hook used to alert employees that someone had come inside.

Kendall gave Birdy a look.

"Is there anyone you don't know?" she asked.

"I had some things printed here for my forensics group," Birdy said.

Indeed, Birdy had met Cici the previous year when she chaired the annual banquet for the Pacific Northwest Forensics Organization, for which she was a past president.

"Paying for things like announcements, programs, and a bar tab, are apparently a few of the duties that go with the honor," she said.

"Running my high school reunion a few years back was similar. Except, of course, the food probably was worse."

"And all the people you talked about were alive."

Kendall suppressed an ironic smile. "Not really. But that's another story to revisit another time."

Birdy introduced Kendall.

"I love *True Detective* on HBO," Cici said. "The first season anyway."

"Me too," Kendall answered, while producing the invitation she'd carried in her oversized black leather purse. She wondered why everyone referred to that cable show as such a favorite. She couldn't get into it at all.

Cici took the invitation.

"Nicely done," she said. "You looking to get something like that printed? Old school thermography. My dad told me to drop it, but I don't know . . . I'm a tactile kind of girl."

"Did you do it here?" Kendall asked.

Cici didn't think so. "No," she said, "I haven't done any thermography printing in more than a year. In fact, I can't even think of the last time that I did anything like that. People don't want to wait for things now. Just wham, bam, get it done."

"Do you know of any other places in the area that use the process?" Birdy asked.

"A place up in Silverdale, maybe," Cici said. "Not sure about that, though. My dad knew everyone and everything. I can go look it up. Follow me."

They followed the illustrated shop owner past a tiny employee break room to an even tinier office where she rummaged through a file drawer.

"I love your unicorn," Kendall said, though she really didn't. The tattoo was just so in her face when Cici dropped to her knees and bent over to retrieve the files.

"Thanks," Cici said, standing back up and turning with a smile. "It's my favorite. Next to the *Lord of the Rings* panorama I got last year."

Kendall didn't want to see that. Neither did Birdy. Cici waited a beat in case they were going to ask. She loved showing off what she'd had done. Her body, she told friends and strangers who asked, was a work of art. She often lamented that she was sorry that she was slender, as her body type didn't allow for as large a canvas as she'd wanted.

"Yup," Cici said, tapping a finger on a sheet of paper pulled from the file. "*Print It Right Now* in Silverdale does thermography and foil, too. Cool, I didn't know that!"

Birdy looked over at the employee bulletin board where three photo ID badges hung from purple sateen ribbons.

Kendall caught her gaze.

"What is it?" she asked.

Birdy took one of the badges from the peg and looked back at Cici. She knew the face on the photograph.

"Does Amber Turner work here?" she asked.

Cici grinned at Kendall. She'd overheard the remark when the two of them first entered Justin's.

"You *do* know everyone, don't you?"

Kendall took the ID card.

"Not everyone," Birdy said. "But I do know Amber. Does she work here?"

"Yeah," Cici said. "She works weekends. It's hardly work, by the way. We're lucky to get two customers the whole day. Dad says that I need to be open seven days a week or I should just close up for good. People depend on you, he says. Can't let them down by not being open when they really need you."

"Back to Amber," Kendall said, "does she have a work space?"

"Yeah. Over here."

They followed the owner across the hopelessly ink-stained print-shop floor, past a bank of Macs of various vintages, mostly older. *Way older*. Cici lingered a second there as though she was giving a grand tour to a potential client.

"We build cool websites at half the cost of our competitors in Seattle," she said. "Very, very current. In case you're ever interested. Everything's going digital.

I keep hoping printing will come back like vinyl records. So far not so much."

Birdy acted interested just to be nice. Later she wondered what in the world she'd promote on a Kitsap County Coroner's website (*"Watch the autopsy in real time!"*).

The print shop's second-generation owner stopped in front of a workbench facing out to the street.

"Here," Cici announced, while pointing to a Rubbermaid style bin, under the counter. "Amber keeps her stuff—work in progress, time fillers, and the like—right here."

The bin was marked with Amber's name in a curlicue style of font and mountain scene that she'd probably drawn there on one of those boring Sundays when no one came into the store.

Kendall sifted the contents in the bin, laying some items out on the bench. It was apparent that Amber had been experimenting with greeting card designs. She had several Christmas cards in production, as well as a birthday card.

Birdy indicated the green of the conifers on the snowy Christmas card. The raised surface was pitted, yet shiny, and it was unmistakable how the effect had been achieved.

"Thermography," she said.

"Hmmm," Cici said. "Now that you mention it, I gave Amber a lesson on how to thermog for a card she wanted to make. She said she was looking to create something special for an Etsy store she was going to open. *Unique* is the word that comes to mind. I love *unique*. I showed her some samples, and she loved the one my dad made for the homecoming of one of those repulsive aircraft carriers in the shipyard. The graphics looked so structural. It was pretty cool. For one of those hideous ships, anyway."

Kendall picked through the remainder of the bin, hoping to find a sample that matched the invitation.

"Too easy," Birdy said, seeing what her friend was doing.

"Or just flat-out wrong to even think it," Kendall said. "How well do you know Amber Turner anyway?"

"Not well. Like I said earlier, Elan likes her. She likes him. I don't think they're in love or anything. I mean, he's only seventeen."

Kendall shifted her weight and stopped looking through the bin. "Probably just a coincidence."

"Right," Birdy said. "Life seems to be full of those lately."

CHAPTER FIFTY-EIGHT

A ping signaled that a text message came late that afternoon. Birdy had just completed the autopsy of a drug overdose, a teenage boy, found in a park in Bremerton. She hated a life lost young more than anything, especially when it was the result of drug abuse. She'd grown up with so much of it on the reservation. Even so, it never seemed anything less than tragic.

The boy she'd weighed and measured, whose tissue samples she'd keep for a year, was another casualty of a world that didn't see the troubled, hurt, and lonely for what they were. She didn't speak to the boy, at least not aloud. She telegraphed to him as she sewed him closed that she was sorry that he hadn't known the beauty that could have been in store for him if he'd found his way out of what he was doing.

I know you wanted away from something. I feel it. You knew you were trapped in something from which you sought escape. All young addicts do. Your mother and father will mourn you. I mourn you, Lonny Roman.

The text that pinged while she was working on Lonny was from her sister, Summer:

If you want to see mom one last time, come now.
It won't be long. Bring Elan.

She'd been expecting a call or text from her sister for the past few days. When one hadn't come for a while, she wondered if Summer was not going to notify her until it was too late for a visit. Summer could use their mother's death as the final opportunity to prove that she'd abandoned them all for her "fancy life" on the outside. Yet, she had let her know.

Birdy texted Elan that he needed to get his schoolwork from his teachers for the next couple of days.

Your mom says Natalie is about to die. We need to go up there."

She used her mother's name because her role in Elan's life was a complication that had recently unraveled. Natalie was not his grandmother, but his mother. His "aunt" Birdy, not his aunt, but his sister. While she knew that the switch in roles was merely a shell game of names that had no bearing on her love for and acceptance of him, it was still a fresh wound.

Elan texted back:

I want to stay here. I need to be here for when Amber comes back.

She answered him:

Kendall will keep us posted. We'll know everything
and anything first. Promise.

She watched while he answered.

K

Birdy showered, dressed in her street clothes. She
called Kendall and got her voice mail.

"I'm heading up to Neah Bay to see my mom.
Elan's coming. I told him that you'd keep us in the
loop on Amber and the other girls. It was the only way
that I could get him to come. He's a wreck over this
whole thing. So as I head up there with him tonight, the
phrase 'out of the frying pan and into the fire' comes
to mind. Take care. Reception is good up there, so no
excuses."

Elan was waiting on the front steps at Birdy's house
on Beach Drive.

"Locked out?"

"Nope. Just anxious. I packed a shirt and a tooth-
brush." He pointed to his backpack. "Homework's here,
too."

"Great," she said. "Give me a minute. Have you
eaten?"

He rolled his shoulders. "Not hungry."

She understood, but she wasn't about to bring him
all the way there on an empty stomach.

"We'll stop on the way," she said.

Five minutes later they were on the road heading
out of town.

"I realize you're worried about Amber," Birdy said.
"I am too."

"I know," he said, looking out the window as Port Orchard faded away behind them. "I'm sorry about Grandma," he added.

She was glad that he called her that. It was familiar. Rewriting an entire life in the last act was an impossible task.

"I talked to Mom today."

The disclosure surprised Birdy. "You did?" she asked, to be sure that she heard correctly. "How was she?"

Elan gave Birdy a quick look. "Okay, I guess. Sounded a little drunk. You know, pretty much like always."

It would have been easy for another sibling to use that setup as opportunity to spike some kind of a put-down at her alcoholic, cruel, angry sister. But that wasn't Birdy Waterman. At least not on that day. There had been times, especially when they were younger, that a lunge for the jugular was the most satisfying move she could make.

BOOK THREE
KELLY

CHAPTER FIFTY-NINE

It was hard to know what time of day it was. With none of the markers—sunlight, the cool of early morning air, the sound of birds—none of the girls knew how long they'd been kept in isolation. Chloe alternated her crying jags with a soft whimpering. So did Amber. Blake felt around the interior of her stall until she knew every sliver, every crack. Kelly sat in silence, certain that for some reason she'd be the first to die.

Because she deserved it. At least in her escalating delirium brought on by the darkness and with a stomach empty of food and water, she allowed herself to believe that she deserved a kind of payback for all the bad things she'd done.

She thought of her sister Kimberly and how she'd told her that she had their father's bone structure and she was sure to grow up without pretty calves. She regretted that comment because it had devastated Kim the morning of the cheer invitational. If it was the last thing that passed between them, Kelly was sure that her sister would forget all the good times they'd had and the closeness they'd truly shared.

Kelly shut her eyes, though she needn't have bothered. There was nothing but darkness all around her. Closing her eyes allowed her to concentrate a little. She braced herself. She wanted to fight, but she had the sinking feeling that struggle wouldn't get her anywhere.

God, she thought, *did I really do something so terrible to deserve this?*

Summer's old, dented pickup was parked in front of their mother's place, next to Natalie's blue Ford Focus. Birdy parked behind the Focus and repeated a warning she'd made when they had stopped at a burger joint.

"Grandma's very, very weak."

Elan lowered his eyes. "I know."

"I need you to prepare yourself," Birdy said.

He was a sensitive kid. Always had been. That was one of the reasons he came to live with her. He'd felt beat down, abused, ignored by his mother and father.

"I'm prepared," he said. "I can handle it."

She touched his knee.

"Your mom too?"

"Right. Mom too."

"Good. Let's go inside."

"Should I bring my stuff?" he asked.

"No," she said. "We can get that later."

Birdy braced herself and turned the knob on the front door. Her relationship with her mother had always been complicated. Now more than ever. She knew that times like this often only exacerbated the rift between family members as they jockey for the status that comes with being perceived as the one who cares the most. Birdy had abdicated that to her sister, long ago. How could she not? Summer had been there for their mother's ups and downs, medical and otherwise. While Birdy had a medical degree, she was careful not to question anything that her sister was doing to make their mother more comfortable.

Natalie Waterman's alcoholism and emphysema had already weakened her considerably over the past few years. She no longer did the things that made her a part of the community. No bingo. No woodcarving, which she'd taken up after her husband Mackie died. No hunting for heart-shaped stones on the shore in her "secret" spot just north of Ruby Beach. She let her black hair turn white, though she didn't cut it. The blackened tips looked like ermine tails, and she seemed proud of that.

Summer had recounted what their mother had said during one of those rare phone calls they'd shared. "After I'm gone, you should sell this hair. Someone could make something very interesting with it."

The stage-four lung cancer diagnosis had been recent. In the way that the sick often avoid all the warnings they'd had until it was too late, Natalie admitted to Summer that the pain she'd felt deep inside, the shortness of breath, the blood she'd coughed up one day, had been more than the usual annoyance.

"I hurt like a son of a bitch," she said. "But for a while I thought it was just me getting older," she said.

"You're not that old," Summer said.

"Old enough to know that that there's no point in fighting to live. What for? More TV? They've changed hosts on QVC. With Lisa Robertson gone, I just don't care anymore."

Summer stood when Birdy and Elan came inside. A cigarette dangled from her fingertips.

"Your fancy car is so quiet," she said. "It's like you go around sneaking up on people, don't you?"

The greeting was bait. Birdy ignored it.

"Hi, Summer," she said.

Natalie lifted her hand.

"Hi, Mom."

"She's not waving," Summer said. "She wants a puff."

Summer put the cigarette up to Natalie's lips. The ember glowed for a flash.

"Don't judge," Summer said to her sister. "Remember, you don't get to judge."

Elan moved closer, unsure of what to say or do.

"You too, Elan," Summer said. "You don't get to judge. Come here and give your mother a hug and say hello to Grandma."

The hug that passed between them was no longer than the fleeting ember on the cigarette Summer had given to their mother. It was stiff, awkward, but Birdy was glad for Elan's part in it. He wasn't going to let his mother tear him down, hurt him, control him.

He wasn't going to let Summer do all the things that their mother had done to them.

Birdy's eyes moved to a hospital bed that had been wheeled into the living room.

"She wants to die on her own sofa," Summer said, watching Elan as he tucked himself into the space between where she sat and Natalie lay.

"Grandma, it's me, Elan."

"I know who you are," she said, her voice a smoky dry croak.

"I came to tell you that I love you."

Her eyes traveled from his to Birdy, who stood behind him.

"I see you brought Miss Smarty Pants with you," she said.

Elan knew what she was doing. She was being Grandma. She was tough, cold, and indifferent when it seemed to matter most. It was as though the only joy she'd been able to conjure for as long as he could remember was by sparring with someone. It was who she was.

"Mom," Birdy said, "I came to be with you."

"Last trip to the reservation," she said.

"This is my home, Mom. You, Summer, and Elan are my family."

"This isn't your home. And you need to find a new family. I'm about to die. Your sister hates you. And Elan doesn't belong to you."

Birdy had told herself that she wasn't going to cry, no matter what her mother said.

"Look, Mom," she said, keeping it together, "let's focus on some of the good things. Yes, you are going to die. Someday we all will die. I don't want you to leave this earth without knowing how much I love you."

Natalie coughed out a laugh. She took a crumpled tissue from where it was resting on her chest and dabbed at her mouth "That's funny," she said.

"What's funny?" Birdy asked.

"You lie. You always do. You're here for you. You know it. I know it. Be gone with you."

Birdy stood there. Quiet. Thinking about what to say but absolutely not crying.

"Mom," Summer said before Birdy could come

back with anything, "Elan and Birdy are here because I asked them to come. I want them here for me. For you too."

Natalie shrugged a bony shoulder and waved her hand again.

"I need another puff, Summer."

While Elan did his homework in Summer's old bedroom, Birdy and Summer sat with their mother. Natalie had taken a dose of morphine for the pain and was asleep. Summer played with their mother's hair awhile, but it wasn't really an effort with a style or even an endgame.

"I remember when you used to braid my hair," Birdy said.

Summer smiled at the memory. "French braid. Yes," she said. "I was pretty good at that."

"No one could do the fishtail braid like you did for me. All the other girls wanted it."

Summer smiled. She was beautiful. More beautiful than Birdy. Her eyes were true almond shaped and her cheekbones sat high and defined. Her hair was thick, black, and without a hint of a wave to it. In the right light, Birdy always thought it looked like her sister had the darkest blue in her hair.

She was older now. They both were. A few strands of gray had found their way into the sea of black. When she smiled, wrinkles dormant from what Birdy was sure was infrequent use emerged.

"What are we going to do?" Birdy said.

Summer stopped playing with their mother's hair.

"About her?" she asked.

Birdy shook her head. "No, about us."

Summer pursed her lips, stalling a little. "I want to say that there is no us, but, really Birdy, I can see that there is no *me*."

Birdy leaned in. "What do you mean, Summer?"

She looked down at their mother. "I don't know. I really don't."

"Try."

Summer got up and lit a cigarette. Birdy didn't smoke, so she moved to the recliner on the other side of the living room.

"You know, I was smart too."

"The smartest in school," Birdy said. "You still are."

Summer kept her eyes cast downward.

"I'm not a good person. I could have been. You know that, don't you? I tried to do the right thing all the time, but the choices I made just didn't get me anywhere."

Birdy wanted to say something about Summer having a family. It had always been her go-to whenever they had the conversation about the way their lives turned out. Birdy had a career. Summer had a husband and Elan. She had used the "a job doesn't love you back" line on her sister more than once, trying to make her feel less jealous, less bitter.

"You made a good choice," Birdy said. She tilted her head to indicate the hallway to the bedrooms. "A heroic one."

Summer raised her hand as if to push away the compliment. "I wasn't going to let our bitch of a mother screw up any more of her children."

"Raising Elan was a great sacrifice," Birdy said.

Summer crushed out her half-smoked cigarette. Usually she smoked them right to the filter tip. "It wasn't," she said. "Just the right thing to do. And now it's all been undone."

"No it hasn't. You're still his mother. You always will be."

Summer looked away from her sister. "Did you see the way he glared at me when he came in here?"

"You're reading things that aren't there, Summer. He's confused. Upset. He's over it. Really. He doesn't know everything and he doesn't need to. But he does know that you decided to raise him. Love him. And you did that, Summer. Look at him. He's a really good kid."

Summer got up and went back to the dining chair next to Natalie.

"What was she thinking?" she asked.

"I don't know," Birdy said. "We probably won't ever know. Our mother is a complicated woman."

"Right. Complicated and hateful," Summer said.

"That too. But she's the mom we have. And we won't have her much longer."

"Why do you keep coming back here, Sister?" Summer asked.

Birdy asked that of herself every time she came home. There was no variable in the way things would turn out. It might start out fine, but in time, her mother would hurl unkind words at her.

"It's hard to explain," Birdy answered. "This place. It has a hold on me in a way that I don't think I can break. It's a noose or garrote. If I move, if I back away, it tightens around me. I keep coming back because this is where I'm from, but when I'm here, I just want to go."

Natalie stirred and Summer went to her.

"She won't make it through the night," she said.

"She's not as weak as you think, Summer. Not by a long shot. You know our mother."

"Elan's probably hungry," Summer said, changing the subject.

"I'll check on him," Birdy said.

"No, I will. I'm his mother."

This is getting ridiculous, Shelly Evans thought. She'd nearly finished a bottle of wine, watched an infomercial featuring a new kind of slimming jean, and seriously considered putting that brisket in the oven. None of this was like her mother. Both cats had decided she was an excellent source of heat, and she nudged them gently off her lap. Those jeans on TV didn't look half bad. Hers were covered in cat fur.

. She texted again. Mom, I might just go home since you aren't around and haven't thought to get back to me.

Shelly ran the lint roller from the side table over her lap. Something, she was sure, was wrong. Her mom was like those cats she loved so much. She pounced on every email or text Shelly sent her. Even the ones that were meant to placate.

"Thinking of you, Mom."

Even when she really wasn't.

She dialed the numbers of her mother's friends, many of whom didn't pick up. *Gone for the holiday,* she thought. Those she reached hadn't seen Tansy for a few days.

"Last time I talked to her was on Tuesday," Bridgett Madden said. "She was so excited about your coming for a visit."

"I told her I couldn't make it, but came anyway," Shelly said.

"Maybe she made other plans. Did you call Sarah Winkler? She knows just about everything."

"She didn't know anything this time."

"The hospital?"

"No. She's not there."

"Well, that's a huge relief," Ms. Madden said. "Did you call the library? Maybe someone there knows her change of plans."

"Closed for the holiday, Ms. Madden."

"You're old enough to call me Brit," her mom's friend said.

"Let me know if you hear from her, Brit," Shelly said, trying out the name, but deciding that Ms. Madden would suffice in the future.

CHAPTER SIXTY

Elan looked around the old back bedroom. He'd played there before, of course, but that was before he'd lived with her in Port Orchard. Things that didn't resonate when he was younger, now did. A bird's nest on the shelf and a jar of feathers told him of her love of nature. A carving of a seabird next to her bed had been made by the father she still mourned. A collection of jazz CDs tilted against the wall signaled her favorite music—and a style that she'd loved longer than he'd known.

He let his history book sit. It was Washington State history and the passage about his ancestors was short and uninspiring. At another time, he might have gotten mad enough to complain to his teacher. Call the publisher. That was the part of him that reminded him of his aunt. Birdy would take a stand.

Instead, he tapped out a text to Amber, though he doubted she would get it. She hadn't answered any of his others. He wondered if she was still alive. He even asked God to keep her safe, but he wouldn't tell anyone that he was praying for her. It sounded foolish, like believing in something that could never be true.

They will find you. I will find you. Hang on, Amber.

He pushed Send.

Summer eased the door open.

"Elan?" she asked. "Can we talk?"

"I'm kind of busy," he said, looking at his history book.

Summer sat down on the edge of the bed. "Too busy to talk to your mom?"

He could see the emotion in her eyes and as mad as he could be at her, he hated to see her cry. The last time he saw her crumble was the last time he'd been home. She'd beat him. Told him that he would never be anything. It was as if he'd shot up heroin.

"It's only weed," he'd told her.

She'd hit him so hard that he went flying across the room. His tailbone was bruised, and so was his pride. He'd seen her drunk and violent before, but her fury had never been directed at him. He looked at her with eyes brimming with tears, embarrassed that his mother had sent him careening across the floor. Also, ashamed.

"*Only* doesn't work in this instance, Elan! *Only* isn't an excuse. *Only* will ruin your life."

"Everyone else smokes it, Mom."

Her brown eyes were black with rage. "You are not everyone else! You are not going to end up like those kids who don't go anywhere, do anything. Those boys that play video games until morning and sleep all day long."

Elan had pushed back. "I'm not doing that. I'm going to school. I'm studying. I wanted to kick it a little. I deserve that, Mom. You do all the time!"

She balled up her fist, but kept her arm steady. "You are not going to be like me. You can't end up like this."

"You and Dad do okay," he said, his hand pushing on the floor to ease the pain of his resting tailbone.

"Look around you," she said. "Do you see okay?"

Their house was the only home he'd ever known. There was food on the table. They had a TV. The dogs ate store-bought pet food. He had three pairs of jeans. As far as he could tell, things *were* okay.

"It isn't that bad," he said.

"You are aiming too low," she had said. "This is my fault. This is because of the mistakes that I've made. I won't let you make the same ones, Elan. You need to do some serious thinking. You need to get your life on track."

It went on like that for weeks, maybe a month. She'd hit him. His dad would beat him. He'd go to school looking like he'd been in a rumble. No one asked if he was all right or needed help. Everyone had their own issues with which to contend. He got high. He listened to the older boys as they talked about easy money they could make cooking meth. He thought about Bobby Meakin and how he'd accidentally blown up his house and family.

All for some easy money.

After the last knock-down, drag-out with his parents, he made his way to Aunt Birdy's in Port Orchard, vowing to himself to make good on the concept of second chances.

"Aunt Birdy told me about your girlfriend. I'm sorry about that," Summer said.

"She'd not really my girlfriend. I'd like her to be.

Probably won't be. Probably murdered by that psycho Brenda Nevins."

"It's been on the news," Summer said. "Psycho is right."

"I'm sorry for the things I said and did, Mom."

"Me too, Elan. I'm sorry for the things I never told you."

"It's okay, Mom. We're a pretty messed-up family, aren't we?"

"You got that right," she said. "We probably should be in the record books somewhere."

He smiled. As tumultuous as their relationship had been lately, he missed her.

"Why are you always so angry, Mom?"

She tugged at the blanket. "Guess that's just part of who I am. Whenever they were handing out attitude, I got a double dose."

"Yeah, you did."

She nudged him. "You're supposed to say I'm wrong."

"Oh, that's right. You're not that bad."

Summer surveyed the room. It had been a long time since she'd been in it.

"I used to come here with you when you were little. Birdy was away at school and Grandma changed out a few things in here for your naps."

"I don't remember that," he said.

"You were small."

She indicated the bird's nest. "Birdy made me climb sixty feet up in a spruce that hung out over the ocean to get that nest," she said, smiling at the memory.

Elan grinned. "Sounds risky."

"It was, but you do things like that for people you love."

"How come you two don't get along anymore?"

"We're working on it, Elan. It's complicated."

Elan knew the phrase "it's complicated" was code for "none of your business."

"How come Grandma's such a bitch to Aunt Birdy?"

"Don't call her a bitch," Summer said.

"You do all the time."

"She's my mom."

He resisted saying the same thing, because he knew that it would only hurt her more.

"She treats Aunt Birdy like she's trash."

"That's because she's jealous."

"No mom should be jealous of their own kid."

"No, they shouldn't," Summer said. "And most aren't."

They talked about school, about life in Port Orchard. He told his mom that he thought his grades would be good enough to get him into college if he continued to work hard.

"I don't want to get in just because I'm native," he said. "I want to be good enough."

"You are better than good," she said.

When Summer moved closer to hug her son, Elan didn't flinch. He *let* her. And in a move that surprised both of them, he hugged her back.

CHAPTER SIXTY-ONE

Chloe MacDonald looked into the streak of brightness coming at her. She couldn't see anything, just a hot white beam coming at her, blinding her. She'd heard the others crying all night, but with light in her face, all she could think about was herself and what this man was going to do to her.

"Get up," a woman's voice said.

Chloe felt disoriented. She was hungry, thirsty. *Scared*. She wasn't sure she heard right. In her fear and exhaustion had she wished she heard a voice other than that terrible man's?

A woman's voice?

"Help me," she said, squinting into the light. "Please help me."

"No one is going to hurt you," the woman said, her voice even, calm. "I need you to get up now."

"Where are the others?" she asked, climbing to her feet. Her hands and knees were encrusted with horse manure. Bits of straw stuck in her hair and onto her back. She knew that she'd been hurt when she was tossed into the stall, but she didn't know the extent of her injuries.

"My leg hurts," she said.

"I'll help you," the woman said, grabbing Chloe by the arm and yanking with far more strength than required.

"You're hurting me!" Chloe cried out.

"You don't know what pain is, Chloe," she said.

Tears ran down her face, stinging her check where she'd been scraped when she'd been dumped there in the acrid darkness.

"How do you know my name?" the teenager asked.

"I know enough about you and your type," the woman said. "Names are easy."

The light stayed fixed on her face. Chloe felt a presence behind her, reaching around. A cloth pressed against her face. She wanted to scream, but she couldn't. She opened her mouth, but someone pushed the cloth down her face and stuffed it into her mouth. Chloe thought of biting down. Hard. But in the time that it took for her brain to process the considered response, she couldn't. She was unable to do anything at all.

She just faded into black. A beat later, an avalanche of hay poured over her body. She was gone.

CHAPTER SIXTY-TWO

Shelly Evans mustered up her courage and dialed 911. "My mom hasn't come home," she said, trying not to cry. It felt odd to her that the emotions started to kick in with a stranger, and not so much with her mother's friends. Something about dialing those three digits made everything feel more ominous.

"I think something must have happened to her," she said.

"How long has she been missing?" the dispatcher, a young man, asked.

"I don't know," Shelly answered. "I've been here all day. She's gone."

The dispatcher told Shelly that her mother couldn't technically be listed as a missing person—she hadn't met the 24-hour minimum. Shelly said that she wasn't sure how long her mom had been unaccounted for.

"Her cats hadn't eaten all day," she said. "I can't say for sure, but really, I don't think she was here last night. Those cats are everything to her."

So am I. I know that. I shouldn't have told her that I wasn't coming.

He took down the information, her name, address, place of employment, and said that a patrol car would be over soon.

"Ten minutes, max," the dispatcher said. "Quiet here in PA for a holiday weekend."

Shelly was grateful when the patrol car pulled up without the noise of a siren or the embarrassing spectacle of flashing lights. Her mom would kill her when she got home for calling the cops in the first place, not to mention alarming the neighbors when something so silly as the misunderstanding was sorted out.

When she opened the front door, her heart sank.

"Oh God," she said to the police officer, standing there. "This is really happening! She hasn't been home for three days!"

Officer Janet Robinson's eyes followed Shelly's downward. Friday's, Saturday's, and Sunday's edition of the *Port Angeles Daily News* were where the paper delivery woman had left them.

"I came in the side door," Shelly said, pulling herself together. "I'm her daughter. I'm Tansy Mulligan's daughter. Something has happened to my mom."

Officer Robinson shadowed Shelly into the house.

"We'll figure this out," she said. "Don't jump to conclusions. Nine times out of ten there's an innocent explanation for something like this."

Tansy's daughter wanted to believe that more than anything, but deep down she couldn't.

"Was your mom seeing anyone?" Officer Robinson asked.

Shelly didn't think so. "My mom never wanted another man after my dad died."

"Is it possible that you don't know?" the officer asked.

If someone had posed that question a week ago, she'd have said no way. Now, she wasn't sure. While it was out of character, if her mom had gone off with someone she'd be safe.

"No," she said. "My mom told me everything. She loved her life. She loved working in the yard, visiting friends, working for the library."

Janet Robinson had kind eyes. She could see that Shelly was on the edge of unraveling. She told her to sit, and Shelly slumped into a chair by the window.

"Have you called everyone you can think of?" she asked.

Shelly indicated that she had. She'd looked all over the house for any kind of clue that would suggest her mom might have gone to visit a friend or her cousins in Spokane. There was no trace. She'd gone to work and then somewhere between work and home she'd vanished.

"You have to find her," Shelly said, stiffening in the chair. "I can't live without her. She's really all I have."

Later, after the officer left the Mulligan house, those words would play over in Shelly's head as she sat by the relic landline that her mother insisted was necessary "because in the event of a terrorist attack all cell phones will be shut down." She'd rolled her eyes at that one. Laughed about it with friends. Right then, she hoped it would ring. She'd not been sick that Friday. Not really. She just didn't want to fill her time off from work with her mother's company. It was as if God was punishing her for her selfishness. Her little white lie. She prayed for a second chance.

I'll never lie to her again if You bring her home, she said to herself.

CHAPTER SIXTY-THREE

The Port Angeles library was closed, but as Janet Robinson turned into the parking lot, she noticed a car parked by the door. The white Versa had a bumper sticker that read CATS RULE. It had to be Tansy Mulligan's. She ran the plate to be sure.

It was.

Janet called dispatch. "Jim, do me a favor. Can you get me Hilda McLean's address? I'm out at the library. Found Tansy Mulligan's car."

"Sure thing. Hold on."

Five minutes later Janet Robinson was standing in Hilda McLean's kitchen. Hilda was the library director. Her husband, Craig, managed a marine supply store downtown. The McLeans knew that a police officer in their kitchen at that hour meant something was seriously wrong. Hilda told the officer that Tansy had worked for the library for at least five years, and as a volunteer for at least five years before that. When the library district won a grant for a mini mobile van, Tansy got the job driving it.

"She loved getting out in the county bringing books to people who couldn't make it into town," Hilda said. "The fact that you're here asking questions about Tansy is scaring me, Officer."

"I'm sorry, Ms. McLean. I'm sure there's some reasonable explanation for her absence from home. Did she have a boyfriend?"

Hilda didn't think so. "She never mentioned one to me. I don't believe she was interested in dating, anyway. She was busy with the library, her garden, her daughter, and of course, those cats. Add in the new car, and she pretty much was living her dream."

"Is there some reason why Tansy might have left her car at the library over the weekend? I saw it in the parking lot on the way over to see you."

Hilda fiddled with a loose thread on her sleeve. "Sometimes Tansy took the van home if she'd been out late on a run," she said. "That was perfectly fine with us. She'd bring it back the next morning."

"But she didn't," the officer said. "She went out on Friday to deliver books, but didn't return for her car that night or Saturday. Didn't that concern you?"

Craig spoke up. "We went to Seattle Friday to see a show."

Hilda's face was lined with worry. "I have Saturday off . . . and well, with the holiday no one would have called me. We're short staffed as it is."

The officer made some notes. "Just on the off chance that something happened on her route—the van broke down, maybe? An accident? Something like that—can you provide her scheduled deliveries?"

The library director reached for her phone. "I have it right here. I'll send it to you." She looked up from what she was doing. "Come to think of it, she hasn't been taking the van home lately. Not since she got that new car."

Janet thanked the McLeans and promised that someone would get back to Hilda when they found Tansy and the van. It was almost shift change so she called dispatch that she was heading back to close out her day.

There were eighteen stops designated for Friday, the last day anyone saw Tansy Mulligan. Her route started in town and wound its way deep into the backwoods of the peninsula.

The last name on the list was Wilder.

"I've got Tansy Mulligan's route and scheduled stops from the library director," she told the dispatcher.

"Sounds good," the dispatcher said.

"Heading in now to write it up and get some sleep. Early matinee with the kids tomorrow."

When she arrived at her desk, she slid into her chair and typed out a report on Tansy's case, adding information about the car, the van, the conversation she'd had with both the daughter and the library director. It was late and she was tired. In her haste to get home and into bed, she forgot to include the schedule of where Tansy was supposed to be the day she was last seen.

It was a tiny mistake that would cost lives.

The mean green machine rumbled toward the orchard. Brenda put her arms around Sherman's shoulders and leaned in to murmur in his ear. She could taste the sweat collected on his temple. *Nervous?* She wasn't sure and that bothered her a little. She'd always been able to home in on the true feelings of others. Tension.

Fear. She could sense the weakness of another and with an unexpected swiftness pounce with words or actions when they couldn't see what was coming. Or maybe, she thought, it could be the afterglow of killing the library van driver.

Sherman let Brenda nuzzle him as he drove up the rutted little incline. Tansy Mulligan's lifeless body bounced up and down in the shovel. Her arm flopped out, and he noticed that she wore a charm bracelet. It probably had some sentimental value. He wondered if Tansy's daughter would search for it in her house, hoping to find it and wear it in remembrance of her mother.

Instead it would be buried in the orchard, never to be found. Like Tansy's body.

"What are we going to do with the van?" Brenda asked.

"Burn it, I guess," he said.

Brenda loosened her grip as the tractor came to a stop next to the disturbed ground that indicated where Patty Sparks's body had been concealed.

"The smoke will give us away," she said.

Sherman leaned into her and gave her a kiss.

"We'll do it tonight, baby."

She let her hand roam his chest, then lower.

"Oh yes," she said. "We will. Start digging."

CHAPTER SIXTY-FOUR

Kelly Sullivan had no idea what time or even what day it was. She'd been so thirsty that she'd done what she'd promised herself never to do. She'd taken a drink provided by a stranger. A few minutes after she guzzled the bottled water with the already loosened cap that had been dropped at her feet, she felt a little woozy and passed out.

It was quiet in the horse stall when she woke. She lay there. *Still. Listening.* Straining to hear something that would tell her what had happened to the others. She was all but certain that Blake was gone. Maybe Chloe too. That left her and Amber.

She leaned into the wall.

"Amber, are you still there?"

"Kelly? Are you okay?"

"I guess so," she said. "I don't really know. They drugged me."

"Me too," Amber said.

"Did they do something else to you?" Kelly asked.

"I don't know," Amber said, her voice muffled by

the wall between them. "The freak said he's coming for me. I'm scared, Kelly. I don't want to die."

"We are not going to die," Kelly said.

The sound of a sob. Then Amber spoke. "I think they killed Blake," she said.

Kelly steadied herself in the darkness. In her bones, she was sure the others were dead.

"What about Chloe? What happened to her?" she asked.

"I don't know," Amber said. "She's gone. I couldn't hear her scream. Not like the way Blake screamed. Oh, God, Kelly what is happening to us?"

"We're going to get out of here. Nothing is going to happen to us."

Amber stayed silent.

"Amber? Can you hear me?"

After what seemed like a very long time, Amber answered.

"Yes. I hear you. I hope you're right, Kelly. This isn't right. I don't want you to die."

CHAPTER SIXTY-FIVE

While Summer was with Elan, Birdy sat on the dining chair next to the sofa. She put her hand on her mother's. Natalie looked at her with a sideways glance, and then closed her brown eyes.

Natalie broke the silence.

"What kind of shoes will you wear, Birdy?"

Birdy's eyes returned to her mother. Still shut.

"Excuse me, Mom?" she asked.

"To dance on my grave," Natalie said. "I hope to God you've packed something with a spiked heel. I'm sure you'll want me to feel every single step."

"You're not funny," Birdy said.

"No, I suppose I'm not. Hard to be funny when you can barely breathe."

"Just rest, Mom." Birdy scooted the pale pink sheet over her mother's concave chest. The port from her chemo protruded so high that Birdy thought it might burst. It was like a tent. Her mom had been off chemo for more than a month. The port was going with her to the grave, a reminder at death that medicine was no match for some kinds of cancer.

"I have plenty of time for resting," Natalie said, her voice a little softer than it had been when they first arrived. The morphine had sapped her, for sure. It was more than that, though. The drug had eased her pain and maybe her mind too. She wasn't going to fight. She wasn't going to insult. She'd done all of that so many times before.

"Mom," Birdy said, "Despite everything, you need to know that I've always admired you."

Natalie's eyes fluttered under her lids.

"Mom?" Birdy asked.

"I'm still here, Birdy. Get me a cigarette, will you?"

"No, I won't."

Natalie's eyes opened for a split second. "Then call Summer," she rasped. "She'll do it."

"She'll be back shortly," Birdy said, relieved that she didn't have to give her mom a cigarette. It was stupid. Sometimes principles felt that way. "Did you hear me, Mom? Did you know that I admired you?"

Tears flooded Birdy's eyes. She felt the muscles in her throat tighten.

"Why? I was nothing. Nothing at all. Nobody will miss me when I'm gone."

A tear rolled down the forensic pathologist's cheek and she wiped it away.

Natalie glanced over at her.

"I'm right, aren't I?"

"No, Mom," Birdy said. "I'll miss you. Summer will. The little kids in the family will."

Natalie, a little more alert than she had been, looked over at the muted TV. A woman named Joy was rhapsodizing over the flocked hangers she'd created in twenty-two colors. Natalie's eyes lingered on the screen.

"I shouldn't have had kids, Birdy. I wasn't meant to be a mom."

"You did fine," Birdy said. "You always managed to get us through the day, off to school."

"That wasn't because I loved you. I wanted you gone. I wanted to go to the bar, get drunk, meet a man at the motel. I wanted to have a good time. Having kids wasn't a good time."

"You grew into it, Mom," Birdy said, fishing for words that weren't a complete lie. "You did okay."

"Did I, Birdy?" Natalie asked.

Birdy patted her mother's hand and held up a glass of water with a bendy straw pointed at her thin, stretched lips.

Natalie refused the drink.

"I'm not thirsty," she croaked. "What's the use? I'm going to die tonight. Maybe right now."

"No, you're not, Mom."

"I cheated on your father," Natalie said.

"I know, Mom."

"More times than you know."

"It's all right," Birdy said. "Daddy loved you. He would have forgiven you. Have you forgiven yourself?"

Natalie's sunken eyes studied Birdy.

"Can't do that, little Birdy," she said. "Can't get away from all the things I've done. It isn't that I'm not sorry. There isn't enough sorry and regret in the world for someone like me."

"You're wrong, Mom."

Birdy watched her mother slip back to sleep or unconsciousness. Her chest moved the fabric of the sheet ever so faintly, her fingers reflexively moving as though she was strumming a guitar. *Maybe in her mind she was?* She'd played in a band when she was younger. That's where she met Mackie Waterman. The story had been told a million times about how he'd swept her off her feet in the middle of the band set. How they'd wound up in each other's arms that very night. How she'd never met a man so good as Mackie.

Birdy didn't need those thoughts in her head, but there they were. How her mother had hurt her father over and over. He'd drowned while out fishing by himself in the straits. He hadn't left a note, so there had been no proof it was a suicide. While Birdy could have thrown all her hatred for what he did at his feet, she instead put it all on her mother. She'd called her every name in the book. She told her that she was nothing but a common whore. It was ugly stuff. Words that she'd wished she'd never said.

Birdy forgave herself. She had only been a girl when it happened. She knew that whatever had happened between her father and her mother had been their doing, not hers.

There were a million questions she could have asked her mother over the years, but she didn't. She never asked who Elan's father was, though she thought it might have been her dad's cousin, Jay. He'd been coming around the house a lot at the time to help with chores that Mackie would have done.

Had he been there.

She'd told her mother that she'd admired her, but Natalie hadn't asked why. Birdy admired her for holding her head up around town, on the reservation, among members of the extended family. She'd been called those same ugly names by everyone behind her back and she didn't let it break her. At least that's what Birdy had always believed. She wondered now if her mother's perseverance had been inner strength or merely the ability to survive. If the lies she told herself got her though the day, then good for her.

"She asleep?"

Birdy turned to see Summer come in.

"Did you visit?" Summer asked.

"We talked," Birdy said. "I told her I loved her. She asked what shoes I was going to wear to dance on her grave."

Summer smiled. "Sounds like a great visit."

"You and Elan?"

"Better, Birdy. Thanks for bringing him."

"He wanted to come, Summer. He misses you."

Port Angeles officer Janet Robinson stepped out of the movie theater, her husband and children in tow. While the special morning screening had been a fun one, empowering for her daughter, exciting enough for her son, something niggled at the officer. She'd been thinking about the missing library employee, Tansy Mulligan. Inside, she felt sick. Popcorn and the real- ization that she'd made a terrible error in her haste to get home warred with her insides.

"Honey," she told her husband, Sal, "I need to stop at the office."

"Can't it wait?" he asked, looking frazzled as he fid- dled with a car seat that didn't want to lock.

Janet didn't think so. "I don't think I filed the locations where Tansy Mulligan visited on Friday. It will only take a minute."

"Kids need to get home."

Janet looked at her son and daughter. They were drowsy.

"You're right," she said, though she didn't really believe it.

"Maybe you did file that report?" he asked, turning the ignition on their minivan.

Janet looked out the window. "Yeah, I probably did."

CHAPTER SIXTY-SIX

It hadn't rained that hard in weeks. Pellets of water tore at the roof of the barn and made the tack room sound like it was under the largest kettle of popcorn in the world. Brenda sat in her chair, her shapely legs crossed just so. Her mouth was a gash of dark pink lip color. The lights Sherman had ordered from a catalog were on her. Something was perturbing her.

She shot an angry glare toward her lover.

"When I told you that I needed a state-of-the-art studio to film my updates, I never in my wildest dreams thought you'd set me up in a damn barn, Sherman."

"I didn't know it would rain," he said, looking at her with pleading eyes.

She flicked him away with her hand. "This is Washington, you moron. Of course it rains. All the time. Every second of the day."

He wanted to tell Brenda the state had just experienced a record dry spell, but contradicting her would only invite a magnitude of anger not commensurate with his perceived transgression.

"Check my hair," she said. It was not a request, but a directive. Brenda never made a request. Question marks were for the weak.

Sherman dropped everything and went over to Brenda, looking her up and down. She was, in his estimation, perfection. Part of him suspected that she only invited him to check her hair to prove the point that she didn't need him for anything at all. In his heart of hearts, Sherman Wilder just couldn't go there.

"The rain's stopped," she said, her tone no longer impatient. "I'm ready now."

Sherman looked around the tack room turned studio. Yes, indeed. Everything was perfect. He'd moved the light slightly to flatter her, but he didn't say so. He didn't want credit for doing the mundane tasks that she required. Instead, he wanted acknowledgment and recognition for the major things that he'd done for her.

"The feed is completely untraceable," he said.

"I know," she said, checking her face in a handheld magnifying mirror. "That's why you're my love."

The mood had shifted as it always did when the focus was on her. Sherman understood that something inside her held an unbreakable compulsion to be the center of all attention.

"Ready?" he asked.

Her lips glistened when she smiled at him. "Absolutely."

He turned on the camera, and the red light glowed. Brenda waited a beat before talking. She was a fast learner. No doubt about that.

She stared with a sly smile. "Did you miss me?" she asked. "I see by your comments on my last post that you have and I am very grateful for your support. For those of you who wrote hateful things, I've captured your IP addresses, and I'll be stopping by some day."

She caught Sherman's smile and quick, affirming nod. He'd told her that she needed to show her fun side.

"Kidding!" she said, letting out a little laugh. "I can't be bothered by haters. The world is full of them. Millions probably. I don't know what's worse. An insipid little loser like Janie Thomas or people who make a point to keep everyone down. Down on the farm. Whatever."

Sherman was unsure if Brenda's little insider's poke at being on a farm was smart, but he could edit it out before uploading. That is, if he didn't mention to her that he had done so. She wanted final approval on everything he did.

Sexy and demanding control freak came to mind.

"Someone posted an obvious question and I want to do my best to answer. The question was, 'Why did you kill Janie Thomas?' I hate to sound impetuous because I'm really not that girl. I think about things. I calculate. I measure. I weigh the odds. I killed Janie because she was weak. She was pathetic. She was never going to be anything in life but one of those people who breathe in oxygen that should be left for others. I'm kind of an environmentalist when you get right down to it. I've recycled Janie. The world's better off for it."

She reached for her bottle of water.

"That brings me to purpose. I want to talk about *my* purpose. I'll be very honest with you. I don't know what is going to happen to me. I expect I'll get away with this as I have very capable help. Whatever I do, I'm going to live a memorable life. You will talk about me for a long time to come."

She held up three cell phones and a compact.

"I don't need to name any names here. I expect that viewers will be able to put two and two together. The Hello Kitty phone cover is probably the easiest to identify. So yes, I have them. *All of them.* They've done nothing to me, so don't think that I'm conducting some kind of personal vendetta. They stand in for elements of my life that I still can't shake. Yeah, me. Brenda Nevins. I have a heart. Who would have guessed it?"

The camera lingered on her face.

"Tomorrow one of them will beg for her life," she said. "You won't want to miss that."

CHAPTER SIXTY-SEVEN

When the light hit her, Blake Scott let out a raspy scream. No words, almost a scared cough. She didn't have much in her. She'd clawed and cried and screamed until every bit of energy she held in reserve had been depleted.

She squinted in the direction of the man who came for her. The monster was so ordinary. He looked like a schoolteacher or accountant. *Bland.* In case she survived, she was going to make sure that she could identify him. Yet his appearance was so boring, she wondered how she would describe him.

He grabbed her by the shoulder and twisted her so she wouldn't see him before dropping a jacket or shirt over her head.

"You're hurting me!" she yelled.

"Shut up," he said. "Save your breath! You'll have a chance to say your piece."

Blake didn't fight. She let him lead her out of the stall. She could see her feet and her calves, all muddy and bloody. Tears fell.

"Where are the other girls?" she asked. "What did you do to them?"

The boring man, the man no one would notice in a crowd, was having his moment.

"Shut up! Talk later!"

CHAPTER SIXTY-EIGHT

It was after 2:00 A.M. when Summer nudged Birdy, who'd fallen asleep on the recliner. She hadn't meant to drift off, but the TV had been little company, and the Home Shopping Network and QVC were not favorites. She knew her mom loved those channels.

"It's time," Summer said.

"Time," Birdy repeated.

In Summer's hand was a syringe full of a purple morphine solution that Natalie had joked was her favorite color.

"Especially if it gets me out of here," she had said when the hospice lady came with a paper bag of catheters, cotton swaps, adult diapers, and the greatest gift of all, the morphine. Natalie had called it her bag of shame.

"You think your baby crapping all over you is the most humiliating thing that will ever happen to you," she had said in one of her lucid moments. "Try being forced into a diaper."

Birdy had sent Summer to bed, while she stood watch over their mom, but Summer couldn't sleep. She got up a couple of times to check. Birdy told her to go back to bed.

"I'll let you know," Birdy said. "I don't think it's really going to be tonight."

"It needs to be," Summer said.

"Get some rest," Birdy told her. "I'll get you if there's a change."

Both sisters had cried with their mother over the realization that the end for her was so very near. Natalie Waterman was tough. She'd been through a lot. And while most of her worst troubles rested solely on her shoulders, she didn't deserve to suffer the slow death of cancer as the disease robbed her of mobility, memories, and the chance to make things right.

"Maybe she'll go on her own," Birdy had said earlier that evening. Washington State had an assisted suicide law on the books, but she wasn't her mother's doctor. She couldn't make the call. Death with dignity was only for those who planned ahead and made the decision to give up the fight before they'd started it.

"She wants this," Summer insisted. "Look at her."

In the dim light of the TV that illuminated her sunken features, Natalie's mouth hung open in a perpetual gasp. Her breathing was labored. When her eyes were open, they seemed to stare at nothing at all.

"Mom," Summer said, her eyes full of tears, "it's time now. Birdy and I are here, Mom. We love you."

Natalie crooked her finger, just barely. Birdy leaned her ear closer.

"Mom, what is it?" She too was crying.

"I am sorry," she said, her voice so faint that a slight breeze could carry it away. "I really am."

"We're past that, Mom," Birdy said. "We love you. We know you did the best you could."

Summer looked at Birdy as she placed the syringe in the corner of Natalie's mouth, careful to not go too deep inside. She pushed the plunger, and the purple liquid drained from the tube. Natalie moved her lips a little and stared up at her girls.

"You need to swallow it all, Mom," Summer said.

Natalie's eyes stayed fixed on her daughters as they hovered above, tears running down their cheeks and falling on the pink sheet.

"Go to Daddy," Birdy said. "He never stopped loving you, Mom."

Natalie shut her eyes. A smile of recognition came to her tortured face. Nearly as quickly as the syringe had been emptied, she stopped breathing. Some of the wrinkles that had contorted her appearance vanished. She looked younger. *At peace.* It seemed as though she was only sleeping.

Birdy placed her fingers on her mother's jugular. "She's gone." She looked at the clock over the fireplace.

"Two thirty-four was the time of death," she said.

"Should we tell Elan?" Summer asked.

Birdy brushed back some stray strands of her mother's hair.

"Let him sleep," she said.

Birdy was glad there would be no autopsy, even though Natalie died at home. It wasn't mandated by law. With a terminal illness, Natalie had been under a doctor's care. Later, when she'd call the county to let them know Natalie had passed, she'd give them her name as the physician who'd verified that their mother was indeed dead. She'd also call the organization that would handle her mother's body and cremation.

"What do we do now?" Summer asked.

"Let's sit with her awhile. There's no hurry to say good-bye. The Neptune Society will come when we call."

Summer smoothed out the pink sheet that covered their mother's cooling body and fussed a little with her hair. No more tears fell. Birdy and Summer had already given all they had. Their mother had been a complex woman. She'd lived a twisty, complicated life. They didn't know all that she'd done. Only what she'd told them. Or what had been on the reservation gossip line.

Birdy made some chamomile tea, her mom's favorite.

"Remember when we went and picked all of that chamomile from the Meakins' place," she said.

Summer allowed a smile to come to her face.

"You mean what we *thought* was chamomile," she said.

Birdy smiled back. "We were so dumb back then, Summer. Weren't we?"

"Speak for yourself."

"I just went along with you. I was your shadow. Remember? You *were* older."

"Right, Birdy. I was. And I still am."

They talked until the sun came up. Summer went outside to smoke on the back patio. Birdy followed.

"We're going to get through this, aren't we?" Birdy asked as she shut the slider.

Summer exhaled and crushed out her cigarette. The orange light from the sun burnished her skin and made her features all the more striking.

"I don't know."

"But you'll try, won't you?"

Summer kicked her snuffed-out cigarette butt off the patio. "Yeah, I will. You piss me off more than anyone, but you're my sister."

"Always."

CHAPTER SIXTY-NINE

The image of Blake Scott filled the screen. No sound. Just her picture. Her hair was matted with straw on one side of her head; her eyes were puffy and red. She blinked but did not cry out. Bruises that looked to be the result of ligature marked her neck.

The camera panned down a little to take in her name, embroidered in cursive on her cheer uniform.

Sound crackled. "Talk now," came the voice of Brenda Nevins, off camera.

Blake stayed mute.

"Talk, bitch!"

"I won't say it," she said.

"You *will* say it."

Another voice, this time a man's, asked if Brenda wanted to start over.

"No," she said, "this makes it all more real."

"We have your home address. We know your sister goes to Cedar Heights. We know your mom's schedule. Do you not care about anyone but yourself?"

"I do care," Blake said, her voice quiet. "Don't judge me."

"Stupid bitch," the man said.

"Right," Brenda added. "You know what I'm capable of."

"Why should I trust you?" Blake asked, using what little she held in reserve to hold it together and not break down.

"You don't have much of a choice, now do you?"

"I'm not going to beg for my life," Blake said. "I'm not. I honestly don't care what you do to me. I know that once you start doing whatever it is, I'll be dead."

And that was it. No more. The screen went black.

"Wait," Kendall said, "the video is still running."

It *was*.

The next image was of a gas can.

A quick cut to a field at night, lit up by the light on the camera.

A pan over the length of a car.

The image of gasoline being poured over the car, drenching it. The sound of a striking match.

And then, screams.

Blake's screams.

They were the kind of screams that would send someone running away, not toward her to help. The kind of shrieks that do nothing but remind everyone who can hear them that there isn't always a way to save someone. Like a man drowning offshore with no good swimmers close enough to get to him. Or the screams heard on the voice data recorder in the crash of a 747 in the Philippines the previous year.

In the window of the car, Blake pounded frantically against the glass. She tried to pull up the lock, but it was jammed. She swiveled around and tried for the other door on the passenger's side, but it too was stuck.

In the next close-up, she was in the backseat. The look in Blake Scott's eyes was the unmistakable look of horror. Helpless horror. She was no longer tough. No longer full of resolve to push back at her tormenters, as she had been in the beginning of the video.

Blake did indeed beg for her life. She called out for her mother, her father, her sister. Her last words were unintelligible. Just before the car exploded into a fire-ball, her hands were pressed against the glass just like those of people during a prison visit, separated by a partition.

The camera jostled a little, presumably from the explosion. And that was it. The video that chronicled Blake Scott's death was finished. Underneath the video commenters posted:

Bitch was stuck up! Deserved what she got.

Sick! She tried really hard to get out. LOL.

She looks like she was rode hard and put away wet.

She nasty!

Kendall tried to ignore the comments, but as they came in she kept reading. Brenda Nevins was playing to her fans. It was hard to imagine that there were people out there who actually applauded her for what she was saying and doing. She was a maniac, and yet people didn't seem to care. *They sided with her*. They'd been put down too. They'd had someone like Blake Scott keep them from achieving something that they'd felt entitled to. Brenda was one of them. She was paying back all the haters.

Kendall shut off the comments feature. She couldn't take anymore. She played the video again, freezing it on every detail and trying to read what she could into whatever Brenda Nevins was doing.

The gas can was unremarkable. It looked to be the kind that could be purchased at the Port Orchard Walmart.

The car. While no auto enthusiast, Kendall knew it was a late-model Subaru—a Forester, she thought. She played particular attention to the front and back ends of the vehicle, hoping against hope that Brenda and her helper were careless enough to leave the plates in plain view.

Of course not.

On the windshield it appeared that there was some kind of a sticker. Kendall scrutinized that section of the video until her eyes hurt.

"Hey, Tony," she called down to the lab, "do me a favor?"

"What do you need?" Tony Collins answered.

"A video that Brenda Nevins posted—"

"That one with the girl in the car?"

Kendall let out a sigh. "You've seen it already?" she asked, not waiting for a response. "Never mind. Everyone has by now probably. The woman's gone viral and in some weird twist, the word really fits her."

"Scary stuff," Tony said. "You want me to enhance something, right?"

"Yes, please," she answered. Tony never let her down. The lab was limited in what it could do, but Tony wasn't. "There's a sticker on the front window, driver's side. Can you work with that?"

"Can do," Tony said.

CHAPTER SEVENTY

A *horseshoe.*

Kelly Sullivan traced the shape of the metal object she'd found with her hands. She knew it was the symbol for good luck. She needed more than luck—a miracle maybe.

She'd found it in the dark as she felt her way around the space where she was being held prisoner. She thought of all the ways she could use it. She could poke out both eyes of her attacker if she could get to his face. She could use it like brass knuckles. Again, she'd have to get close to him to do so.

As she clutched it, she imagined a scenario in which she could use it. She'd have to be fast. She was. She'd have to be strong. She was. She worked harder than anyone with free weights. And she'd have to have the advantage of surprise. That would be easy.

Her captors had made a mistake. They thought they'd considered every possibility. She'd noticed the tiny eye of a camera trained on her from above. So they liked to watch.

Or, she thought, she could dig her way out of there. She could scoot herself to the edge of the stall, still in view, but not center stage as they'd wanted her. She could dig as she lay there, slowly, quietly.

"Don't worry, Amber," she said, not wanting to tip off her plans in case audio came with the video feed.

Amber didn't answer.

Kelly started digging. Her small stature gave her the advantage and she knew it. *I can do this!* She thought of how her dad had comforted her when a kid called her a shrimp.

"Great things come in small packages," he'd said.

She'd show those sick pieces of crap that she could beat them.

CHAPTER SEVENTY-ONE

The floor was a mix of manure and dirt, but with each swipe of the horseshoe Kelly Sullivan thought it smelled like the most beautiful perfume. *French perfume.* It was the smell of a chance to live. After a half hour of surreptitious digging, Kelly could feel the gap under the wall widen. She lay on the floor of the stall and ran her arm under it. A nail snagged her skin and cut open a long bloody gash, but she ignored the pain. It was only skin. The gap couldn't accommodate her body right then, but it was getting there.

"Amber," Kelly called over. "What's happening?"

"I'm scared," she said.

"We're not going to die."

"No one will find us," Amber said. "We're in the middle of nowhere."

Kelly wanted to tell her friend that everything would be all right. She wanted to let her know that it didn't matter if anyone came or not. They were about to take matters into their own hands. But she didn't. She looked up at the video camera. If they were watching and listening, she'd play along.

"Have you prayed?" Kelly asked.

"Yes," Amber said. "Over and over. I'm all prayed out."

"Let's pray together."

Kelly started the Lord's Prayer. She could hear her friend echoing her words through the stall. With each word, she'd dig just a little deeper. She was going to get them out of there.

If it was the last thing she'd ever do.

"Got something for you, Detective."

It was Tony Collins on the line. He'd never let her down, and she had a genuine fondness for him. He was techy enough to burrow into the really deep stuff, but aware enough to know that sometimes investigators like Kendall Stark didn't want the labor pains.

Just the baby.

"Don't leave me hanging," Kendall said, pulling off an earring and planting the phone next to her ear.

"No chance of that," the tech said. "The sticker is state-issued ID. I can't make out the number, but I'm pretty certain whoever owned that car was an employee of a state agency or office and needed credentials to park."

Kendall pondered that. "No way to tell where?"

"Sorry, no," he said. "But I did manage to capture the make and model of the car.

"Subaru Forester," she said. "That much we already knew."

"Yeah, but I narrowed it to four model years. Unfortunately, the color isn't clear in all the smoke and flames."

He didn't mention the burning teenager.

"I ran it against the state employee DB," Tony went on. "I have one hundred and sixty-five names. I'll shoot 'em over to you."

That was a big number. *Too big to go through quickly.* They were running out of time. Brenda hadn't posted a video yet that day. She lived for attention and there was no doubt she'd post something soon.

"Any locals?" Kendall asked.

"Nope," Tony said. "At least none that I could see. I just sent you the list."

Kendall hung up. She opened the email he'd sent and scrolled through the names. Which one of you unleashed a monster? Who's up to their neck in the blood of Brenda's victims? None of the names jumped out. With a manipulator like Brenda Nevins, no one could be off limits. No man. No woman. No age. No nothing. Brenda was an equal opportunity schemer.

CHAPTER SEVENTY-TWO

"**T**his is good, babe," Sherman said, watching the video feed from the barn. "Kelly and Amber are praying together."

Brenda looked up from her nail file.

"Religion never helped anyone," she said, taking in the video, before returning to her manicure. "Least of all me. My parents took me to church, and the pastor molested me once a week for a year."

"Holy crap," Sherman said. "You never told me that. God, I'm sorry."

"God had everything to do with it," she said.

He stood next to the bed. "You've been through so much," he said. "I just want to take away all of the hurt. I want to keep you safe. That's my purpose."

Brenda looked at him in that same way that pulled him in when they met at the prison. It was a look that telegraphed sex and promises of more to come. It told him without words that he was something to be desired. That whatever Susan had thought of him in the bedroom or in life had been so far from reality.

"Make love to me, Sherman," she said. "Show me

how a man takes away a woman's pain. I need you now."

He moved away from the laptop and went to her.

"I'll show you," he said.

Brenda was already naked. She got up and undid his belt buckle, keeping her eyes on his the entire time. She slid off his pants and tugged at his boxers.

"Somebody's sure excited," she said.

He dipped his head and reached for her.

"No," she said, teasing. "I'm going to do all the work here. I'm going to show you how much I love you. I'm going to record this for everyone to see. They need to see how it's done."

By then Sherman Wilder didn't care if anyone identified him from those videos. It didn't matter anymore. He'd never leave her. She was *the* Brenda Nevins. Wherever they went, she'd be known. He didn't mind the risk. He was certain the police or the FBI would never catch them. Law enforcement was stupid. They, on the other had, were anything but.

They were invincible.

Brenda turned on the camera, returned to the bed, and pulled him downward.

"I'm going to be on top," she said. "And I'm going to ride you until you can no longer take it."

"I want you to," he said. "I want you to do whatever you want to me, baby. I've never felt so alive."

Brenda smiled at his words. She mounted him and started to move, up and down, just the right amount . . . and then more . . . he closed his eyes like he always did.

She lowered herself onto his chest, rubbing her nipples against his flabby torso.

He moaned at her touch. Sweat collected on his brow. He moved with her like an ocean wave.

"God, you feel good!" he called out. The headboard banged against the wall like Morse code pounding out his words.

"I do. I do too," she said. She reached under the pillow. In doing so, she slowed her rhythm.

Sherman, his eyes still shut, made a face.

"Keep going," he said.

"I'm going." She positioned herself back on top of him and made a quick turn to look at the camera.

"Are you there yet?" she asked.

Sherman panted. "I'm there," he said. "I'm there! Are you?"

"Open your eyes," she said. "I want you to see me."

Sherman did as he was asked. He always did. His eyes popped open.

As though she'd rehearsed it, she swung the razor at Sherman's neck with all the strength that she had. His hand went up to stop her, but it was too late. *Way too late*. Blood shot from his jugular like a small geyser. He gasped and gurgled and tried to fight her. She stayed on top of him, tossing the razor aside and holding him down while the blood poured over them.

"Damn you, Brenda," he said, his voice coming from the gash in his neck.

Then she let go. She sat there a second, watching the life ebb from her lover.

"You stupid old man," she said as the blood oozed from his neck onto her naked body. She rolled off him and looked at the camera, dead on. She shook herself a little. She could see herself in the mirror over the bureau. Red was everywhere. Her face. Her hair. It was as though she was a candy apple and she'd been dipped in a sticky vat of red.

Sherman's foot twitched. Brenda watched it with a strange fascination.

She was thinking. Deciding what to say. She took a damp towel from the bedside and mopped her face. Streaks of blood burnished her skin like mahogany. She stepped closer to the camera and spoke.

"I know this will go viral. That's what I want. So please, share. I'd been thinking about it for the past couple of days. Really trying to make sure that I'm doing the right thing. Have I gotten all that I could from him? Would he be useful to me tomorrow? Next week? It's hard to see beyond the moment that you're in. Making plans is a risk. Sometimes things don't turn out the way you want them to, and then what? What good were the plans to begin with?"

She tilted her head and ran her fingers through her bloody hair. She'd never had so much blood on her in her life. It smelled metallic. It was slightly viscous. And the color. It was more beautiful than any shade of red she'd ever seen. Her nails were ready for polishing, and the color looked lovely on them.

"You think you saw it all?" she asked. "You've only seen what I want you to see. You didn't see how he'd drugged me and raped me. You didn't see him threaten to kill my own mother if I didn't succumb to his wishes. He was a pig. That's what you didn't see."

She looked over at Sherman on the Jackson Pollock red down comforter. His eyes stared upward at the ceiling. Not a flicker of life remained in his body.

"A cut pig," she said, her eyes once more fixed on the lens. She reached over to turn off the camera.

* * *

While sweat collected on the nape of her neck, Kendall worked her way through the catalog of names. She was frantic. Minutes or seconds could make the difference. She did not have access to state employee records, but she did know how to use Google. She disregarded any individuals east of the mountains—too far. She also scratched off the names of women—she was all but certain that Brenda Nevins had the help of a man. She thought back to that prison video. It had been made for the benefit of a male. She'd used her sex appeal to lure in someone who could do what she wanted done. Janie Thomas had been only a means to an end.

Janie's end.

One name in particular caught her attention. It came with an interesting work history.

Sherman Wilder, IT versatilist, DATA, Inc.

Bingo.

She dialed Fenton Becker at the women's prison. When he got on the line, he acted put out.

"What do you know about Sherman Wilder?"

Fenton stalled. "Him? Why do you ask?"

"Fenton, I need to know," she said, her voice rising. "I need to know right now. You know him, don't you?"

"No," he said. "By reputation only. I saw his file. Superintendent Thomas fired him. She had to let him go."

"What was he doing?" Kendall asked. "Why was he terminated?"

"He worked in the information technology department. Systems engineer, I think. I really don't know the details. I only know that my predecessor thought he was inappropriate for the job."

"Can you get to the point, please? Inappropriate how?"

"Something about the security system at the institution. I gather that he messed with it and she caught him. It's vague."

Kendall wished she could reach into the phone and throttle him. "Why in the hell didn't you tell me this?"

"Don't get snippy with me, missy."

He didn't? Did he?

"Did you really just call me that?" she asked.

Fenton back-pedaled. "Sorry, we have about the blackest mark against us you can imagine. The media keeps camping out across the street. We're a damn laughingstock. A serial killer got out of our facility and killed some people. *A lot of people.* It came from the very top that we were not to talk about the IT breach."

Throttle him. Good.

"You moron," Kendall said, unable to hold it inside. "Those girls are dead because of you."

"You should have caught her when you had the chance," he said, his tone defensive. "Not our fault."

Kendall wanted to yell into the phone.

"I need you to tell me everything you can about Wilder."

"You'll need a subpoena. Employee records are confidential."

"You're kidding, right? You tell me what I need to know or I go on CNN and tell the world that you've covered up details that could have saved the lives of some young girls. Have you seen the videos?"

He was quiet.

"Yes," he said. "They make me sick. But—"

"But nothing. Talk. Now. Or be on the front page of every paper in the country as the creep that protected a serial killer's accomplice."

"You don't think Sherman Wilder is an accomplice. It was Janie who caused all of this."

"Keep talking. Now."

Kendall could hear him hitting the keys of his computer.

"I shouldn't be doing this," he said.

"You shouldn't be covering up, Fenton."

Fenton was nervous. His words choked in his throat. "Yeah. Right. Cover-up. Headlines could get real ugly."

"Brenda Nevins ugly," Kendall said.

"Okay. Fine. Sherman Wilder . . . let's see . . . what do you want to know?"

Must this be so hard?

"Everything," she said. "Get on with it."

"Worked on contract in Olympia, first at the state tourism bureau then later in systems at the insurance commissioner's office," he said. "Worked here for a year. His history looks good until his termination. He even volunteered to teach."

"What subject?" Kendall asked, though she already knew.

"Internet and new media," he said.

Kendall could feel her blood pressure rise. "What else does his file say, Fenton? I need details and I need them now."

"Divorced. Has one dependent, a daughter. His forwarding address is 48 Elwha River Road, Port Angeles."

"Ex-wife? Daughter?"

"Sue Ellen Turner is the wife. She's still listed as

the emergency contact, though he's got his daughter as a secondary contact. It's a 876 number, Port Orchard."

"Amber," Kendall said.

"How did you know that?"

"Read the papers," she said. "She's one of the missing girls, Fenton."

CHAPTER SEVENTY-THREE

Violet Wilder wasn't sure if she was dead or if she was dreaming. Time and space seemed foggy. For a second or two, she didn't remember *where* she was. *Who* she was. *What* had happened to her. When all of that came back it was like a punch to the stomach. Hard. Tear-inducing.

She lay on the floor of the stable in a bed of hay. It was Monty's stall. While she couldn't see much, she could feel the presence of her favorite horse. It was as though his spirit was still there in that space where she'd put him after a long ride up the ridge; where she brushed his shiny black coat longer than she needed to because he loved the attention she gave him.

Violet shifted her body and bit her lip as the throbbing spiked. It was a fierce pain, one that she'd never experienced before. Something was broken. *Leg? Ribs?* The agony fell over her like a long, dark shadow on a winter's day. Starting at her toes and then running to her neck, her temples.

She tried to take herself out of that thought by remembering the day that she got Monty. It wasn't that long ago. She was an old woman. A widow. The kids were all but grown. She'd busied herself on the farm doing all the things she'd done. Nevertheless she felt alone.

When a neighbor a few miles down the road told her that she was selling her horse, Violet, who'd admired the handsome black gelding, knew she had to have him. She'd watched him in the pasture over the past couple of years and she always felt that he had watched her back when she'd pass by. She didn't tell her kids because they wouldn't understand. They'd say she was too old; her bones were too brittle. That she couldn't manage one more animal on the farm. That she already had horses. They couldn't understand the connection because their lives were full.

"You know me," Violet had said, when she first brought Monty home.

When the horse nuzzled her, she told herself that he was answering back.

"Yes, I do."

There in the dark, she cried for the loss of that horse. More than the hideous predicament of her captivity, the animal she loved was on her mind. She had hoped that her son had sold the horse to a good home. But she wasn't sure if he had. She wasn't sure about much— but one thing.

Her son had killed Tansy. He'd actually *killed* someone. This couldn't be happening. She wanted to shut out that thought. *Think of the horse.* She knew that her life would be over soon.

If Monty were dead, she'd be with him again.

Her tired bones hurt. She could barely lift her head. That was okay. She wanted to go to heaven.

"Can you hear me?" a voice came to her.

Violet turned toward the sound.

"Can you hear me?"

It was a girl's voice.

An angel? Have I died?

"My name is Kelly," she said. "Who are you?"

"Violet Wilder," she answered, still unsure if she had heard right.

"We have to get out of here," Kelly said, her whisper ragged.

Violet wished she could move closer to the sound, but she couldn't. Her body wouldn't do anything she wanted it to. She tried to lift her head and turn. It was useless.

"Hey," Kelly said, "are you all right?"

Neither of them is all right, of course.

"What's happening to us?" Violet said.

"They are going to kill us. *All of us.*"

Violet hoped she wasn't hearing things correctly.

"Are you listening to me?" Kelly said.

Violet moved her head. "Yes, I'm listening."

"If we don't do something, those two will kill us."

"Those two?" It wasn't really a question, but a way for Violet's brain to process what the girl on the other side of the wall was saying to her.

"Yeah, that bitch and her sicko boyfriend."

CHAPTER SEVENTY-FOUR

It had been quiet in the barn. Kelly and Amber hadn't said a word to one another after they'd prayed. Kelly kept digging, her heart pounding, her arms growing tired. Yet that didn't stop her. She'd never been a quitter. She had everything on the line. When she broke through to the other side of the wall and a pool of light formed around the small opening, she didn't think twice. Kelly Sullivan clawed her way under the wall.

I'm a gopher. I'm a snake! I can fit!

A nail or a sharp piece of wood sliced through her back and she didn't even cry out.

I'm a badger. I'm getting us out of here!

She was out of the stall; out of the barn. The light of day was like a dream. She questioned if it was real. She looked up at the house. At the garden. Nothing about the scene was menacing, but she was so very scared.

In her bloody hand was the horseshoe. She held tight to it and ran. It didn't cross her mind to head through the orchard and beyond to the forest. Or to the river. A way to get the hell out of there.

Instead, Kelly went back for the others.

I'm a badger! I really am!

She rounded the barn and slipped into a door. The entry to the tack room was wide open; the computers and camera equipment twinkled cheerfully. She wondered what all of that meant. None of it made sense. As fast and as quietly as she could, Kelly started to open the stall doors. She didn't call out to the girls because to do so would be to alert the monsters who had taken them and killed Patty Sparks. She was fairly certain that Chloe and Blake had been removed from the barn— neither had made a sound for what seemed like an eternity. Her eyes scanned the dark space of the first stall. Empty. Blake was gone.

She threw the bolt on the second one, the one she thought had held Chloe. Light flooded the space, and an old woman looked up from the floor.

"Who are you?" Violet said, blinking at the light.

"Kelly. I'm getting us out of here." She didn't ask who the old woman was. Instead, she hurried to lift her to her feet.

Violet cried out in pain.

Kelly's eyes were filled with terror. "Shhh! They'll hear you."

"I'm sorry," Violet said. "Leave me. I'm not going to be able to walk. My son did this. My son and his girlfriend. Just go. Leave me."

Kelly went as fast as she could to the last stall, the one next to where she'd been imprisoned. She prayed that she wasn't too late. Amber had been so quiet. She wasn't as strong as she was. The two of them together could get that old lady out of there. Her hands were shaking as she undid the bolt and swung open the door.

"Amber!" she cried. Her eyes scanned the scene at a feverish pace, unable to process what she was seeing. Her stall had been dark, devoid of anything.

That wasn't the case here.

Amber Turner was sitting on a mattress, headphones on, looking at a magazine. She had a lantern for reading. Next to her were a can of Diet Coke and some chips.

She looked up, startled. "How did you get out?"

The room started spinning. Nothing was making sense at all. "I don't understand," Kelly said, trying to process Amber's room. "We have to go. We have to get out of here."

"Just a second, Kelly," Amber said, getting to her feet.

"What are you doing? What is happening here?" Kelly took a step backward.

Amber started toward her.

"You didn't answer me," Kelly said.

"How did you get out? My dad is going to be so angry at you. You shouldn't have done it, Kelly. He told me everything would be okay if we just played along."

Kelly wanted to throw up. "Played along?" she asked as she fought for air. "Blake and Chloe are dead. I'm sure of it. They are goddamn dead, Amber. So is Patty! Is that man your dad? What the hell? What has been happening here?"

Kelly was smart enough not to wait for an answer. She thought back to the ride in the van and how the Mountain Dew had made Patty sick. Amber had brought the Mountain Dew specifically for Patty. She'd never done that before, and Kelly thought it was strange. Nice, but strange.

Not nice. Evil.

When Amber reached for her, Kelly shoved her friend to the ground with all of the strength she had.

"You bitch!" Amber screamed. "You shouldn't have done that! Why the hell did you push me like that?"

"You're the bitch, Amber!"

Amber got to her feet and staggered toward Kelly as Violet Wilder somehow found the strength to drag herself with the aid of a pitchfork to where Kelly and Amber were arguing.

In the light of day, the old woman would have easily scared small children with the bruises and blood all over her face and arms. Her hair that she'd always kept beauty salon perfect ("every Saturday, rain or shine") was a muddy, bloody rat's nest. The index finger on her right hand swung like a broken gate when she held up her hand.

"Amber? Amber!" she said, looking up from her hunched-over body, "What's going on? Why are you here?"

Kelly got between Amber and Violet and swung the door shut as quickly as she could. She threw the bolt while Amber screamed at her every ugly name she could think of. And there were many.

"Let's go," Kelly said to Violet, extending her hand to help her. "I'm leaving now, and you're coming with me."

Without any warning, a gun went off. There was no time to cry out. Kelly felt Violet's hand go limp as the old woman rolled on the floor. Kelly froze. Everything was happening so fast that it was impossible to process. She looked down at Violet, a bloom of blood on her chest. Kelly filled her sore lungs, and let out the scream of her life.

A woman stood at the entrance to the barn. It was hard to see her face as the light silhouetted her, but Kelly could see the gun, now pointed at her.

Kelly called over to her.

"Why the hell did you do that?" she said, now on the ground trying to help Violet.

"She needed to be put out of her misery," Brenda Nevins said.

"You're sick," Kelly said. "She's just an old lady."

Brenda was on her by then, the gun in Kelly's face. Her eyes were wild, full of excitement. She loved every minute of her drama.

Her drama.

"Why isn't there a camera on me when I need one?" she asked.

A shovel—same one that had struck Tansy Mulligan—slammed down on Kelly. Everything went black.

Kendall Stark grabbed her keys and went for the door. As soon as she got into her car, she started dialing. She was so angry at Fenton Becker. He could have put an end to Brenda's reign of terror before things had spun out of control. First, she phoned SA Casey, but he didn't answer. *He was never any help!* She left a voice message, telling the FBI agent where she was headed. She called Birdy next, but she didn't pick up either.

She thought of the invitations sent out to the four girls. She knew that Amber had made them, but she didn't know why. A killer had bewitched her father.

In Brenda's world, no one mattered. Just her.

Sherman Wilder used his own daughter to do his lover's twisted bidding.

CHAPTER SEVENTY-FIVE

Alone in the dark with the body of a dead grandmother, Kelly's eyes fluttered and she woke. Her head hurt like hell. She felt the bloody knot that rose up from where the shovel had smacked her. Even in that twilight of emerging consciousness she knew who had hit her.

It had to have been Amber.

Kelly was shaking and woozy, unable to stand. She looked over. Violet's body had been dumped next to her. It was scary and sad at the same time. She'd never seen a dead body before. She certainly had never been locked up with one. As she pulled herself together, she knew she could add a dozen other firsts to that scenario. She'd never been a witness to murder. She'd never been kidnapped. She'd never seen a woman shot in front of her.

She'd never been so betrayed by someone she thought she could trust.

Kelly felt for the cold metal of the horseshoe. It hadn't brought her any luck after all. She threw it across the stall with a sob. She had been the badger. She had been strong. Now she had very little if anything left. She would die. She'd been betrayed by Amber.

They all had.

"Help me," came the faintest voice. It was softer than a murmur. Almost like the noise that comes when someone merely mouths the words behind another's back. Kelly touched Violet's arm and her fingers moved.

"You're alive," Kelly said, tears coming to her eyes. She didn't know this old woman and she could barely understand the emotions that flowed through her.

For now, they both were alive. *Alive.* It was a word that meant more to Kelly than anything. It was more powerful than the evil that had tried to snuff them out.

Kelly took off her shirt, wadded it up, and put it on the wound that oozed blood from Violet's chest. Violet winced, but didn't cry out.

She was tough.

Kelly leaned close to Violet and whispered. "Please don't die on me," she said as tears streamed down her cheeks. "Hang on. We're both not going to end this way. We're not."

Violet squeezed Kelly's hand. It was a short pump, but firm enough to get the message across.

Yes, Kelly knew she was right. This old lady was a badger too.

CHAPTER SEVENTY-SIX

Kendall Stark parked her white SUV and turned off the ignition. She'd been unable to reach anyone. She looked at the blank face of her phone. *Nothing*.

Birdy had no cell reception and her inability to answer was understood. *Forgiven*. But SA Casey? *Not cool*. As she sat there, she knew she'd broken the biggest rule in the book by going to Wilder Farm alone, but she didn't think the risk outweighed the possibility that she might be able to stop Brenda Nevins from killing again.

There had been enough killing.

Kendall studied the GPS map for the location of the Wilder farm. She knew there was only one way in by car or foot—*the road*. A potential escape route was the Elwha River, but the waters were high from the storm, and she highly doubted Brenda would risk such a plan. She had seen, after all, the perils of what a river could do.

She'd drowned her high school friend, Charlotte Barrow. Charlotte had been the first victim—the only victim that hadn't followed some kind of blueprint. Everything since then had been a killing for a specific purpose, real or imagined. After Charlotte came Addie,

Joe, Kara, Juliana, Janie, Chaz, Reeta, Patty, Rob, Blake, and finally, her lover, Sherman.

If there were only a handful more—and Kendall prayed that there hadn't been—Brenda would have achieved what she'd almost certainly set out to do. She'd set a record of sorts by taking the lives of more people than the most notorious female serial killer of modern times. In Brenda's twisted mind, such an achievement was a gold medal. An Oscar. A Pulitzer.

She'd always wanted—*needed*—to be the best at something. And more than anything, she wanted to be recognized for it.

Birdy and Elan sat mostly in silence as they started the long drive home from Natalie's. They were tired. Bone tired. The early morning hours had been physically and emotionally exhausting. While Elan kept his focus on Amber, Birdy's thoughts stayed on her mother. Natalie Waterman's withered remains had been picked up by a nice young man in a tired, dark suit and were on their way to the crematorium in Port Angeles. A memorial would be held at Ruby Beach in a few weeks. Summer had returned to her on-again, off-again marriage.

"You okay, Aunt Birdy?" Elan asked.

"I'm fine. You?" she answered, though half of what she said was a lie. She wasn't okay at all. Before Natalie took that final breath, it had gone through Birdy's mind that her passing would bring some peace. It was a selfish thought, and she hated herself for even allowing it to pass through her brain. Her mother had caused nothing but pain for so many people for such a long time, yet in that last moment, there had been the hint of understanding and reconciliation. Birdy knew whatever she'd hoped would be unfulfilled forever. Natalie Waterman was gone. Birdy hadn't asked her all that she'd wanted to know. When she had the chance, she didn't confront her as she thought she would.

She looked ahead at the rain-slickened road.

"I'm not rewriting my personal history with my mom," she said, "but the truth is—and I hope you believe me—there were many things I loved about her, Elan. She was like a boiling vat of acid most of the time; but other times not so much."

The Prius passed the last of the small homes that lined the forest where Birdy had spent so much of her youth.

"Yeah, my mom is the same way," Elan said.

Birdy glanced at Elan. Her eyes were hopeful. "You seemed to work some things out. Did you, Elan?"

The teenager cracked his window a little. Cool air brushed against his handsome face. "Progress is slow on the reservation. But, yeah, I think we did. I refuse to blame her for things because, well, you know . . ."

"I don't," Birdy said. "What?"

"I don't want her to end up like her mom. I want her to let go of whatever made her do what she did to me and just be done with it. I'm done with it."

His words soothed her broken heart.

"That's good," she said.

"The best way," he said.

As the car passed through town, Birdy's phone pinged and she reached over. *Finally some cell service.* It was a text from Kendall.

On my way to the Wilder farm outside of PA.
Sherman Wilder worked in IT at the prison. I think
he's the guy Brenda carved up on YouTube.

Birdy pulled over and tried to phone Kendall, but
the call went to voice mail.

"Kendall, are you all right? Be careful. Not far from
PA. Let me know if you need me."

Elan looked up from his phone. No messages from
Amber, of course. There hadn't been any in days. He
Googled the name Wilder and searched for an address
near Port Angeles. The Clallam County tax assessor's
website provided a name and address.

"Alec and Violet Wilder own property at 48 Elwha
River Road," he said, looking up at his aunt. He was
nearly out of breath, like he'd run a marathon.

She put her hand on his knee. "Calm down," she
said. "You'll hyperventilate."

Elan gulped in some air. "Aunt Birdy, we have to go
there. We have to go *now*. Amber's there."

What to do? The smart thing or the right thing?

Birdy turned to Elan. "I want you to calm down. I
need you to take some of the emotion out of this right
now. I *need* you to do this right now, Elan. Do you
understand me?"

"I think so," he said.

"Put the address in Google Maps and get direc-
tions."

Birdy got out of the car and went to the trunk. She
returned with the gleam of the barrel of a gun she'd retrieved from a lockbox that he'd never known existed.

"Holy shit," he said.

"Don't swear," she said, putting her seat belt back on.

Elan thought better of asking to hold it. "I didn't know you packed," he said.

"Part of the county's idiotic cross-training program," she said, setting the gun on the console and buckling in. "I guess it might not be so stupid now. How far away is the Wilder residence?"

"Seventeen miles," Elan said. "Seventeen point five to be exact."

Birdy looked over at him. Exact was good.

"Let's see how fast this thing goes," she said, pulling onto the highway and accelerating to seventy-five miles per hour.

"You can do better than that," Elan said, watching the speedometer.

Birdy cocked her head at him. "Good enough," she said. "We want to get there alive, don't we?"

Kendall Stark parked her SUV about a quarter mile from the turnoff that led to the Wilders' long driveway. It was muddy, rutted. Exactly like a lot of the driveways out in the rural parts of Kitsap. Except longer. A lot longer.

She crept along the fence line that cordoned off the pasture until the farmhouse and barn were in view. Smoke curled from a trashcan by one of the outbuildings. A black cat skittered across the yard into a meticulously tended dahlia bed adjacent to the house. The scene was calendar art Americana. Kendall made her way behind the barn and her heart sank.

The library van.

Tansy Mulligan had made her last stop there. While there was no video of her demise on the Internet,

Kendall was certain that the only thing that kept her on that farm was the fact that she'd been murdered there. Her daughter had told a Port Angeles police officer that her mother "lived for her cats" and "never would have left them alone overnight without a full dish of food and lots of water."

Looking around for any sign of anyone, Kendall, her gun drawn, moved to the van. She peered inside. It was empty, save for a plastic laundry basket brimming with books on the passenger seat. The back of the van was loaded with two full racks of books and CDs. Doors unlocked. Keys were in the ignition.

No sign of Tansy Mulligan. She was gone.

Kendall shifted her gun to her left hand and reached for her phone, but there was zero cell service.

Perfect, she thought. *Just perfect.*

An eerie silence lay over the picturesque farm. In a very real way, it was a ghost town. She scanned the yard and worked her way around the outbuildings. Kendall was all but certain that Brenda was long gone. She'd wanted fame, but she didn't want to be caught. There would be no reason for her to make a stand against law enforcement there. Brenda wasn't outnumbered, but Kendall knew that wouldn't be the case for long.

Just where is everyone?

"There's Kendall's car!" Elan said as Birdy pumped her brake and slowed to a stop.

A Keep Kitsap Green sticker was affixed to the back window.

"Yes," Birdy said. "She's here." She parked the Prius behind the SUV.

"What are we going to do?" Elan asked.

Birdy didn't know. "It isn't *we*. It's *me*. You aren't going to do anything but sit tight."

She opened the door, took her gun from the console, and got out. Elan opened his door.

"This is dangerous," she said. "You aren't listening very well. I told you that you are staying here."

"Amber's my girlfriend," he said. "She needs me."

"Look, I know you care about her. And you're right. She needs you. She needs you to be alive, Elan. Stay put."

Elan folded his arms. "I won't stay here," he said.

Birdy didn't have time for teenage angst. Kendall might be in trouble.

"Elan, my mother died today," she said. "I'm about the lowest I've ever been. I know she was your grandma and in a weird way, your mom, too. But I've been through a lot more with her, and I'm not going to put up with any crap from you or anybody. *You stay put.* Do you understand?"

He looked at her with those dark eyes; eyes that could be sad, defiant, and appreciative all at once. He'd never seen Aunt Birdy act like that way. They'd been through a lot together. The night Natalie died was only one of the trials that had tested them and brought them to the brink. This was another. He didn't want to fight her.

"I'll stay here for fifteen minutes," he said. "That's it. If you don't come back in fifteen, then I'm coming."

Birdy knew Kendall was perfectly capable on her own. She was just there to offer some backup. She'd been a good shot when hunting with her father, though she'd never shot at anyone in her life and hoped that this wasn't going to be the first time her target was a human.

"Okay, fine," she finally said. "*Fifteen*. But a real fifteen. Not a fifteen that is only ten minutes. You understand me?"

"I have a stopwatch on my phone."

"Phones don't work around here," she said.

"This isn't dependent on Wi-Fi or cell service," he said. "A real fifteen. Be careful, Aunt Birdy."

Birdy didn't turn around. "I always am," she said, walking in the direction of the farmhouse.

As Kendall rounded the Wilder barn, she heard a humming sound. *What is that?* She moved closer. It came at her, faintly at first, then stronger. She smelled automotive exhaust coming from inside. Sliding open the door released a torrent of fumes. It was a cold, gray curtain, undulating and moving all around her. Her heart was pounding. Something terrible was happening. She lunged forward, and through the haze, Kendall could see the faint outline of a tractor.

She knew what was going on.

Someone is killing himself or herself. If it's you, Brenda Nevins, it's not going to end that way.

She scanned the space, found a rag, and held it over her nose and mouth. Her eyes burned, but she held her breath. Her fingers felt numb. She managed to turn off the ignition of the old John Deere and then ran for another barn door, flinging it open as fast as she could.

Outside, she found Birdy Waterman.

Kendall's eyes were wet, red. "Thank God you're here, Birdy. My guess is someone is doing some more of her favorite activity."

"Carbon monoxide poisoning, Kendall. Open all the doors. We've got to search the barn. And we've got to do it fast. No telling if the girls are alive."

"Or if Brenda Nevins is," Kendall said.

"She's no suicide, if you ask me, Kendall. Too in love with herself."

Birdy was right.

Both women raced around the weathered old barn, opening windows and doorways. When a large window on the south side wouldn't open, Birdy crashed through it with the butt of her gun.

Finally some use for that thing.

The haze lifted and they could see. Later, both would say it was the worst thing they'd ever laid eyes on.

Fifteen minutes had elapsed since his aunt faded from view. *A real fifteen.* Elan looked at his phone's timer, took a breath, and started in the direction of the Wilder place. *Amber. She might still be alive. She has to be alive.*

Elan didn't have a gun, but he did have the pocketknife that he'd carried since grade school. It wasn't a large knife, barely useful for anything other than gutting a fish or the occasional squirrel. He hadn't used it since he moved to Port Orchard. Right then, however, it felt good in his grip.

Like an old friend from his past.

* * *

"Over here!" Kendall cried out to Birdy.

Kelly Sullivan and Violet Wilder were unconscious but alive, huddled next to each other on the floor of the stall with the name MONTANA above the door. Their cheeks were ruddy, their eyes rimmed in red. Kelly's head rested against the older woman's as though she was seeking comfort. *Was it a genuine moment captured as they prepared to die? Or had it been a tableau arranged by their killer?* Kendall noticed that Kelly had been bound at the ankles and wrists. The older woman hadn't been.

Birdy dropped to her knees.

"The pulse on the older victim—Mrs. Wilder?—is weak," she said. "She's been beaten too. Let's get her out first."

Kendall hooked Violet under the arms while Birdy hoisted her feet. As quickly as they could manage, they carried her just outside the barn and returned for Kelly. They knew it was Kelly because she was wearing her cheer top with her name embroidered on it. There was no time to untie her. The teenager needed air.

Birdy felt for a pulse. "This one's stronger," she said.

"Lighter too," Kendall said. She scanned the barn for the others as they carried the teenager out and placed her next to the old woman.

"Hey!" a voice called out.

Kendall and Birdy spun around.

It was Elan.

"Are they dead?" he asked, as he circled the bodies.

"No. Not yet, Elan," Birdy said, knowing that he'd probably waited as long as he'd been told to. She was glad he was there. They could use the help. "Carbon monoxide poisoning."

"Where's Amber?" he asked, his voice full of urgency. "Did you find her?"

Kendall's breath had quickened. "No, we haven't."

"Elan!" Birdy cried out as the teenager ran into the barn.

"Amber! It's me!" he said, running from one corner of the barn to the other. He looked inside the makeshift video-production studio, but what he saw there didn't register. The image of a cut and bloody dead man filled the screen. *What is going on? Where is Amber?*

As he worked his way around the mean green machine, he saw her.

Amber was slumped against the wall of the last stall. Her ankles were bound, but her arms were free. Her beautiful red hair was matted with straw and manure. Her stillness suggested it was too late. Elan threw himself to the floor and cried out for his aunt to come. He brushed the hair from Amber's face and leaned in.

"You can't die, Amber," Elan said holding her shoulders. "Wake up. Wake up!" He shook her, gently at first, then harder. He was sure he was too late. He shouldn't have waited fifteen minutes at all.

"She's not waking up," he said, his eyes full of terror. "Aunt Birdy, she's not waking up!"

"We have to get her out of here, Elan," Birdy said, touching his shoulder. Then once more, with some force. "Stop," she said. "Don't shake her. She needs better air. Carbon monoxide lingers."

Kendall helped Elan carry Amber out of the barn, while Birdy hurried back to the other two victims. As gently as they could manage, they placed Amber next to Kelly.

Birdy felt for a pulse. She looked up. Her eyes carried some hope.

"Elan, she's alive," she said. "We need to look for the others. There's still a chance."

"I don't want to leave her," he said.

"She's breathing, Elan," Birdy said. "She's the strongest of the three. We have to find the others."

"The others are dead," he said. "We saw the video."

"No," Kendall said. "We don't know if Tansy Mulligan is dead. One last sweep."

Kendall, Birdy, and Elan hurried back into the barn.

Kelly Sullivan's red, weeping eyes opened. She looked around, trying to make sense of everything going on around her. She was foggy, unclear. She was outside. Clouds shifted overhead. Cotton plumes, darkening with the waning light of day, passed above her. She was shivering, but even that didn't register.

Where am I? What happened? Am I dead? Alive?

Kelly looked to her right and saw Violet's white and gray hair. The teenager's neck was sore. She tried to turn to see if the old lady was okay, but she couldn't move. It was as though she was paralyzed. Her breathing was shallow, weak. As she lay there, the memory of what happened came back, and the adrenaline in her body surged. Her arms and legs were still tied. She rotated slightly to the left, and all the air from her lungs exited at once.

She faced the kind of evil she'd never experienced until that fateful trip to Port Angeles.

Amber eyed Kelly.

Kelly flexed her fingertips, hoping she still had that damn horseshoe, but her hands were empty.

Amber had been the one to bind her legs while Brenda Nevins held a knife to a dying grandmother's throat. She'd tied her own legs and wrapped a rope around her arms in a clumsy attempt to make sure she'd look like a captor had bound her.

When she had been one of the captors the whole time.

She'd given the other girls the invitation to the cheer event in Port Angeles. She'd provided the Mountain Dew to Patty. She'd been holed up in a veritable luxury suite in the barn while Chloe and Blake were murdered for the pleasure of a freak (who was also her father!) and his girlfriend.

"I know what you did," Kelly said, her voice, dry and weak.

Amber glanced at her. Her eyes were devoid of any emotion.

"I hate girls like you," she whispered. "You think you're better than everyone."

"I'll tell," Kelly said, trying to inch away. "I'll tell everyone, you bitch."

Amber moved her hand over Kelly's mouth and nose, and held it there, while her teammate squirmed. Kelly's eyes nearly popped from her head. She wriggled to fight off her former friend. She was trapped. *Caught.* Amber, who had orchestrated so much of what happened, was doing what she needed to do to cover her tracks.

A minute later, Kelly's foot twitched one last time.

* * *

Amber gazed up at Elan. A tear rolled from her eyes. She motioned for some water. He cradled her head and she drank, spilling some over her sweater.

"Sorry, babe," he said. "You're going to be all right."

It was the first time he'd had the courage to call her babe. He leaned over and pressed his lips against her cheek.

"I love you," he said. "I love you more than you will ever know."

Amber moved her head in agreement. Tears came to her eyes as she looked past Elan to Kendall.

"My dad did this," she said. "My *real* dad. He told me that he'd kill my mom and my little sister if I didn't help him. I didn't know any of this was going to happen. I thought he was going to kill me. Rape me even. I don't know what kind of a monster he is, but I know he's dead and I'm glad about that."

Elan held his finger to his lips.

"No talking," he said. "You can tell the detective everything when you get to the hospital."

She shut her eyes, pressing out a tear.

Birdy knelt down and felt for a pulse, her fingertips gently touching Kelly's slender neck. *Nothing.*

Her eyes met Kendall's.

"She's gone," Birdy said. "Kelly didn't make it."

"No!" Kendall called out. "That's not right. We got here in time. We did."

Birdy undid the knots on the girl's wrists. She didn't consider it tampering with evidence, just the right thing to do at the time. If Kelly had survived she'd have had the ropes removed.

"She breathed in a lot of the poison," Birdy said. "She's a small girl."

Kendall didn't want to cry right then. She wondered why this girl had to die. "I'm so sorry," she said to Kelly. She held her hand, still warm. Her fingernails were broken and a gash marked the length of her arm.

"Poor thing tried to dig her way out, Kendall. We have to get these two to a hospital. We have to do it now."

"Brenda's not far, Birdy. I feel it. I'm not going."

"I can take Amber and Mrs. Wilder, Aunt Birdy," Elan said.

"I don't know," Birdy answered, looking at Kendall.

"We don't have a choice. Let's get them in the library van. The keys are still in the ignition."

They loaded Violet in first, then Amber.

"Grammie," Amber said, "it's me, Amber."

Violet's eyes moved underneath her parchment eyelids.

"Amber, is that you? Amber, I'm so sorry your father was so wicked."

"We'll be okay, Grammie," Amber said as Elan started the van.

"The closest hospital is in Port Angeles, Elan."

Elan wore a determined look on his face. "I know, Aunt Birdy."

"I didn't know he had his license," Kendall said, as Elan backed around the barn and head down the rutted driveway toward Elwah River Road.

Birdy looked at the detective.

"Well, I think he does."

* * *

Brenda Nevins's silhouette filled the kitchen window. She'd been watching—and enjoying—the chaotic scene the whole time. Kendall told Birdy to cover the back door while she managed the front. She'd call out when the time was right.

"If she comes at you, don't think twice," Kendall said. "Shoot her. And by that I mean, shoot to kill. No maiming, please."

Birdy understood. She crept around to the back door and listened. Her heart pounded. Only two things were on her mind. She hoped that Elan really did know how to drive, and she hoped that she and Kendall would get out of there alive. Brenda Nevins was a killing machine. She thrived on the act of killing—not the supposed gain of doing so.

"Come in, Detective Stark," Brenda said.

Kendall, her gun drawn, inched her way closer along the walls of the entryway to the kitchen. Brenda Nevins, wearing a lime green negligée that had to have been one of Violet Wilder's from the 1960s, sat on a chair facing the window. She was naked under the filmy garment. Even in her surrender she was a self-absorbed, but beautiful, menace. She'd brushed her hair and applied her makeup with the care of a model. Brenda even posed like one, with her ankles crossed in front of her chair.

"What's the matter with you, Brenda?" Kendall asked, though she didn't expect an answer. She had been following Brenda's bloody trail all over Washington, and the woman was still an enigma.

"You're asking about me?" Brenda asked. "I'd say

I'm doing all right, Detective. Did you miss me? How's Cody?"

"I could shoot you right now, and no one would be the wiser," Kendall said.

Brenda beamed. "Either way, I win. I die as a star and become a legend like Marilyn Monroe. Gone too soon. Remembered for my beauty and all that I've done."

Kendall stepped closer. She could feel her heart race, but she willed herself to keep calm. Carry on. Be careful.

The woman in front of you is poison.

"Your legacy. That's what you're all about? I thought you enjoyed the limelight, Brenda."

Brenda shifted her body, letting her thigh show just a little more skin.

"I *am* the limelight. But that's only for now. I'm not stupid enough to not realize that one day the public will move on. I might have more followers than that kid who quit One Direction, but that's fleeting. Fame these days is fleeting."

Kendall held her gun like a vise. She wanted any excuse to shoot Brenda and end her reign of terror.

"Death would be a gift for you, Brenda," she said.

Brenda's eyelashes fluttered. "Really? We all die. Then I guess we all get the same gift. In the end."

A knife glinted on the table. Kendall prayed that Brenda would go for it and she'd have the justifiable reason to take her out.

"You can't know what it's like to be me, Detective," Brenda said, looking at Kendall, with a gaze that was more quizzical than seductive.

The narcissist in full bloom is the one who sees only herself when she looks at a group photograph.

"I don't suppose I could," Kendall said, watching Brenda as a zoo visitor studies a python coiled in its glass-walled prison. "I do know that I wouldn't want to."

Brenda is a glue trap. Quicksand. A snare.

"So predictable," Brenda said. "Always judging me. In your safe little world there is only right or wrong. In my world there is no judgment. Only right."

"Right to kill people," Kendall said.

Brenda offered the faintest smile. "People die anyway. We all do. No one remembers anyone, not really. After the memorial. After the photos have faded. It's over. The people I killed will be remembered because I gave them a kind of immortality. They live on. In a way, I'm kind of like God."

"You are nothing like God," Kendall said. "Those girls didn't deserve to die. None of your victims did. Your own baby. How could you have killed her?"

Brenda gave Kendall a hard stare. For the first time, her eyes pulsed with emotion.

"I didn't kill her," she said. "I'm tired of being blamed for that. It was Joe's fault. He screwed everything up."

Kendall watched Brenda and the knife. "What did he do?"

Brenda moved her eyes around the kitchen before returning to Kendall. A breeze wafted the filmy fabric of her negligee. Even in denial, she was aware of how she looked. She was a painting. A photograph. She was a goddess carved in marble.

"Everything that night was his doing," Brenda said.

"I never killed anyone until after that night. The list of victims ascribed to me is much, much shorter than you—or even I—would like it to be. I'm all about numbers, as you know, but I'm no fraud. Jerry inflated his number of kills. I'm more about finesse than figures."

Jerry was a reference to her mentor, serial killer Jerry Conners, who'd pleaded for privileges by copping to dozens of murders—some of which he could not have committed.

"Addie?" Kendall asked.

Brenda sighed. "Chelsea did her."

Chelsea had been there at the river that day, but it was Brenda who'd grandstanded at the funeral. It was Brenda who had been on the raft. Had Chelsea been on the raft too?

"Charlotte?" Kendall asked.

Brenda tapped her talons on the tabletop. "An accident. You can believe me or not. I don't care. I didn't do those. I didn't do any until Janie. I didn't even know how to kill until my pen pals guided me. *Mentored me* as the press likes to call it. Believe what you want."

Brenda Nevins was a facile liar. Everything she said was a lie or was a lie braided in strings of truth that seemed impossible to unravel.

"Why the insurance on your baby?" Kendall asked.

It was a game of chicken. Neither the detective nor the serial killer would flinch.

"Joe's idea," Brenda said. "I admit that I was a participant, but not willingly. He was the one who wasn't going anywhere in life. I admit I wanted out of that godforsaken town, but I didn't kill her. Newsflash. I know right from wrong. I know what it's like to be backed into a corner."

She stopped talking and looked at the knife.

Kendall moved closer.

"Why those girls?" Kendall asked, not wanting the conversation to end. To end the dialogue would be to stall or even eradicate the chance for some kind of truth.

Unravel the braid, Kendall thought.

"I had a lot of time to think while I was locked up," Brenda said. "I had a lot of time to remember the four little bitches in school that told me I wasn't good enough. Not pretty enough. Tits too small. The girls on the cheer squad were pawns. Stand-ins." She took a deep, satisfied breath. "I know that the bitches that hurt me in high school will suffer for the rest of their lives, knowing that blood is on their hands."

"They were innocent," Kendall said.

"Not all of them," Brenda said, just as she became a blur. A lime green blur. Brenda lunged for the knife with such ferocity that it startled Kendall. It was as though there was some kind of bizarre hangover of their conversation, slowing her movements. Before she could point her gun to stop her, Brenda was on top of her and the gun skittered across the floor.

And a knife was at Kendall's throat.

"You called me a narcissist," Brenda said, spitting out her words. "Not nice. Not true. There is no label for someone like me."

Kendall was pinned to the floor. She could feel the tip of the knife go into her throat—not enough to bleed her out, but enough to let her know that she was about to die. She was one of those animals caught in a snare. If she moved, the knife would go deeper.

"Don't do this," she said, thinking how lame the words

were, but not knowing what else to say. She thought of her husband, her son. She knew she'd made a rookie mistake by not firing at Brenda, but she just couldn't. There was something horrific and magnificent about Brenda Nevins that made it seem as though killing her would be the end of a species.

Something so evil. Yet so pretty. So captivating. Stomach turning and awe-inspiring at the same time.

"The last thing you'll see are my eyes, drinking you in like a tall ice tea. I'll cut your head off and boil it in a pot and serve it to some unsuspecting fool somewhere far, far from here."

"What the hell happened to you, Brenda?" Kendall asked, her voice choked by blood. She scanned the room from the floor where Brenda held her.

There was no way out of there.

"After I carve you, I'll take care of your stupid little friend, Birdy. Both of you are the kind of girls that never gave me a chance. Like the girls in the barn. All of you selfish bitches."

"You want to see selfish?"

It was Birdy's voice.

Brenda looked over, perched on Kendall like a wolf on a sheep's carcass.

"Just in time," she said.

Without another remark, Birdy Waterman did something she'd never done in her life. She fired her gun at a human being. She knew just where to fire to inflict the most damage—but not kill her. The sound of gunfire echoed through the kitchen.

"I thought she was going to kill you, Kendall," she said.

"She was," Kendall said holding her hand to her neck.

Birdy lowered the barrel. Her fingers felt numb. The scent of gunfire filled her lungs. "I wasn't sure, Kendall," she said. "I thought that she'd kill you. I couldn't have that. I had to fire at her."

Birdy had never shot another human being. Indeed, she'd never killed anything that she hadn't planned on using to feed her family. Birds. Rabbits. Squirrels. A deer, but that had only been one time. She stood there, looking at the blood and the mess she'd caused. She went to Brenda and felt for a pulse. Her brown eyes looked up.

"She's alive, Kendall."

"More than she deserves," Kendall said, holding her hand to her neck. "It looks worse than it is," she said indicating her own injury.

Birdy pulled a kitchen towel from a knob by the sink.

"I won't try that hard to save her," Birdy said, though she didn't really mean it.

Kendall looked out on to the yard as a wave of police cruisers rolled in.

Among the new arrivals was Jonas Casey.

"Holy hell," he said. "Both of you look like crap."

"Thanks," Kendall said.

"Good job," he said, looking over at Birdy as she applied pressure to Brenda's head wound.

"I think she'll survive," Birdy said.

Jonas turned his attention to Kendall. "She said, 'Not all of them.' What did she mean by that?"

Kendall blinked. "How do you know that?"

The FBI special agent turned away and scanned the ceiling. It only took a second. "Right there," he said, his finger pointing at a tiny camera embedded in the overhead light fixture. It was black, shiny, like the eye of a shark.

He grabbed the device and gave it a tug. It snapped from its mounting and dropped to the floor.

"Show's over," he said. "Brenda's been broadcasting live. The world's been watching."

A slight smile came to Brenda's lips.

EPILOGUE

Birdy Waterman took an indefinite leave of absence from the Kitsap County Coroner's Office, citing personal reasons. The county and federal officers investigated the events at the Wilder Farm. Despite Birdy's comment that she wasn't going to try "very hard" to save Brenda Nevins, it was determined she had, in fact, acted within the guidelines of her job. Birdy rented out her house on Beach Drive in Port Orchard and returned to the reservation. She moved into her mother's old mobile home.

Kendall Stark returned to her job as an investigator for the homicide unit of the Kitsap County Sheriff's Office. She visited Birdy a couple of times at the reservation, and the two remained close—talking several times a week by phone. Cody continues to do well at his school in Bremerton. Kendall and Steven are expecting a second baby, a daughter, in the new year.

* * *

SA Casey returned to the Seattle field office. He called Kendall a few times after the shooting. They became friends.

Brad Nevins no longer did interviews with the police or media. His parting shot, "That bitch is a liar and there's no way my son would have killed his baby," was made to a local TV station when a wrecking crew demolished the remains of the burned-out house on Stoneway Drive.

Chelsea Hyatt pleaded guilty to manslaughter in the death of Charlotte Barrow. She was sentenced to seven years and is serving her time at the Washington Corrections Center for Women. Her roommate is Coral Douglas.

Erwin Thomas and Sandra Sullivan married four months after Janie's death. They welcomed their son, Trey, six weeks after they returned from a ten-day honeymoon in Fiji. Joe Thomas, who dropped out of Boise State, no longer speaks to his father and has moved to an undisclosed location in northern Idaho. He told Kendall by phone that he would never forgive his father. "If he hadn't hurt my mom by playing around with Sandy, none of this crap would have happened. If you want someone to blame, blame *him*."

* * *

Violet Wilder, who'd been found unconscious in the van, moved to an assisted-living center in Sequim, Washington, not far from Port Angeles. Tansy Mulligan's daughter Shelly, who'd returned to live in the family home in Port Angeles after her mother's murder, visits every other week. Violet's daughter Denise and her son Timothy rarely come to see her. Violet adopted a cat she named Kelly.

Brenda Nevins recovered and was charged with multiple counts of murder. She was sent to a maximum-security prison in Oregon to await trial in Washington State. Against her attorney's advice, Brenda appeared on two television programs and on four magazine covers. It was reported that a film and Broadway musical about her were in development.

Amber and Elan never made it to the hospital in Port Angeles. Neither has been seen since they left the farm. The library van was found on the dock that launches tourists' boats to Victoria, Canada.

ACKNOWLEDGMENTS

Many thanks to the usual suspects—my amazing editor, Michaela Hamilton, always and forever agent Susan Raihofer of Black Inc, Tish Holmes, Arthur Maisel, Lou Malcangi, Jean Olson, Linda Montgomery, and, of course, my wife, Claudia.

Especially Claudia.

All of you do your part to get me to the finish line. Your support and encouragement means the world to me. Thank you so much.

Special bonus for fans of Gregg Olsen's
exciting Waterman and Stark thrillers!
Keep reading to enjoy a sample excerpt from

THE GIRL IN THE WOODS

Available from Kensington Publishing Corp.

CHAPTER ONE

Birdy Waterman went toward the ringing bell and an annoyingly insistent rat-tat-tat knock on the glass storm door of her home in Port Orchard, Washington. Her cell phone was pressed to her ear and her fingertips fumbled in her pocket for her car keys. She retrieved a tube of lip balm—with the lid off and the product making a mess of her pocket.

Great! Where are those keys?

"Hang on," she said into the phone, grabbing a tissue and wiping off her hand. "Everything happens at once. Someone's here. I'll be there in fifteen minutes."

She swung the door open. On her doorstep was a soaking wet teenaged boy.

"Make that twenty," she said, pulling the phone away from her ear.

It was her sister's son, Elan.

"Elan, what are you doing here?"

"Can I come in?" he asked.

"Hang on," she said back into the phone.

"Wait, did I get the date wrong?" she asked him.

The kid shook his head.

Birdy looked past Elan to see if he was alone. He was only sixteen. They had made plans for him to come over during spring break. He hadn't been getting along with his parents and Birdy offered to have him stay with her. She'd circled the date on the calendar on her desk at the Kitsap County coroner's office and on the one that hung in the kitchen next to the refrigerator. It couldn't have slipped her mind. She even made plans for activities that the two of them could do—most of which were in Seattle, a place the boy revered because it was the Northwest's largest city. To a teenager from the Makah Reservation, it held a lot of cachet.

"Where's your mom?" Birdy asked, looking past him, still clinging to her cell phone.

The boy, who looked so much like his mother— Birdy's sister, Summer—shook his head. "She's not here. And I don't care where she is."

"How'd you get here?"

"I caught a ride and I walked from the foot ferry. I hitched, but no one would pick me up."

"You shouldn't do that," Birdy said. "Not safe." She motioned him inside. She didn't tell him to take off his shoes, wet and muddy as they were. He was such a sight she nearly forgot that she had the phone in her hand. Elan, gangly, but now not so much, was almost a man. He had medium length dark hair, straight and coarse enough to mimic the tail of a mare. On his chin were the faintest of whiskers. He was trying to grow up.

She turned away from the teen and spoke back into her phone.

"I have an unexpected visitor," Birdy said. She paused and listened. "Everything is fine. I'll see you at the scene as soon as I can get there."

Elan removed his damp dark gray hoodie and stood frozen in the small foyer. They looked at each other the way strangers sometimes do. Indeed they nearly were. Elan's mother had all but cut Birdy out of her life over the past few years. There were old reasons for it, and there seemed to be very little to be done about it. The sisters had been close and they'd grown apart. Birdy figured there would be a reconciliation someday. Indeed, she hoped that her entertaining Elan for spring break would be the start of something good between her and Summer. Her heart was always heavy when she and her sister stopped speaking.

As the Kitsap County forensic pathologist, Dr. Birdy Waterman had seen what real family discord could do. She was grateful that hers was more of a war of words than weapons.

"You are going to catch a cold," she said. "And I have to leave right this minute."

Elan's hooded eyes sparkled. "If I caught a cold would you split me open and look at my guts?" he asked.

She half smiled at him and feigned exasperation. "If I had to, yes." She'd only seen him a half dozen times in the past three years at her sister's place on the reservation. He was a smart aleck then. And he still was. She liked him.

"I'll be gone awhile. You are going to get out of all of your wet clothes and put them in the dryer."

He looked at her with a blank stare. "What am I supposed to wear?" he asked. "You don't want a naked man running around, do you?"

She ignored his somewhat petulant sarcasm.

Man? That was a stretch.

She noticed Elan's muddy shoes, and the mess they were making of her buffed hardwood floors, but said nothing about that. Instead, she led him to her bedroom.

"Uninvited guests," she said, then pretended to edit herself. "*Surprise* guests get a surprise." She pulled a lilac terry robe from a wooden peg behind her bedroom door.

"This will have to do," she said, offering the garment.

Elan made an irritated face but accepted the robe. He obviously hated the idea of wearing his aunt's bathrobe—probably *any* woman's bathrobe. At least it didn't have a row of pink roses around the neckline like his mother's. Besides, no one, he was pretty sure, would see him holed up in his aunt's place.

"Aunt Birdy, are you going to a crime scene?" he asked. "I want to go."

"I am," she said, continuing to push the robe at him until he had no choice but to accept it. "But you're not coming. Stay here and chill. I'll be back soon enough. And when I get back you'll tell me why you're here so early. By the way, does your mom know you're here?"

He kept his eyes on the robe. "No. She doesn't. And I don't want her to."

That wasn't going to happen. The last thing she needed was another reason for her sister to be miffed at her.

"Your dad?" she asked.

Elan looked up and caught his aunt's direct gaze. His dark brown eyes flashed. "I hate him even more."

Birdy rolled her eyes upward. "That's perfect," she said. "We can sort out your drama when I get back."

"I'm—"

She put her hand up and cut him off. "Hungry? Frozen pizza is the best I've got. Didn't have time to bake you a cake."

She found her keys from the dish set atop a birds-eye maple console by the door and went outside. It had just stopped raining. But in late March in the Pacific Northwest, a cease-fire on precipitation only meant the clouds were taking a coffee break. Jinx, the neighbor's cat, ran over the wet pavement for a scratch under her chin, but Birdy wasn't offering one right then. The cat, a tabby with a stomach that dragged on the lawn, skulked away. Birdy was in a hurry.

She dressed for the weather, which meant layers— dark dyed blue jeans, a sunflower yellow cotton sweater, a North Face black jacket. If it got halfway warm, she'd discard the North Face. That almost always made her too hot. She carried her purse, a raincoat, and a small black bag. Not a doctor's bag, really. But a bag that held a few of the tools of her trade—latex gloves, a flashlight, a voice recorder, evidence tags, a rule, and a camera. She wouldn't necessarily need any of that where she was going, but Dr. Waterman lived by the tried and oh-so-true adage:

Better safe than sorry.

As she unlocked her car, a Seattle-bound ferry plowed the slate waters of Rich Passage on the other side of Beach Drive. A small assemblage of seagulls wrestled over a soggy, and very dead, opossum on the roadside.

Elan had arrived early. Not good.

Birdy pulled out of the driveway and turned on the jazz CD that had been on continuous rotation. The music always calmed her. She was sure that Elan would consider it completely boring and hopelessly uncool, but she probably wouldn't like his music either. She needed a little calming influence just then. Nothing was ever easy in her family. Her nephew had basically run away—at least as far as she could tell. Summer was going to blame her for this, somehow. She always did. As Birdy drove up Mile Hill Road and then the long stretch of Banner Road, she wondered why the best intentions of the past were always a source of hurt in the present.

And yet the worst of it all was not her family, her nephew, or her sister. The worst of it was what the dispatcher from the coroner's office had told her moments just before Elan arrived.

A dismembered human foot had been found in Banner Forest.

CHAPTER TWO

Tracy Montgomery had smelled the odor first. The twelve-year-old and the other members of Suzanne Hatfield's sixth grade Olalla Elementary School class had made their way through the twists and turns of a trail understandably called Tunnel Vision toward the sodden intersection of Croaking Frog, when she first got a whiff. It was so rank it made her pinch her nose like she did when jumping in the pool at the Y in nearby Gig Harbor.

"Ewww, stinks here," the girl said in a manner that indicated more of an announcement than a mere observation.

Tracy was a know-it-all who wore purple Ugg boots that were destined to be ruined by the muddy late March nature walk in Banner Forest, a Kitsap County park of 630-plus acres. She'd been warned that the boots were not appropriate for the sure-to-be-soggy trek inside the one-square-mile woods that were dank and drippy even on a sunny spring day. There was no doubt that Tracy's mother was going to survey the damage to those annoyingly bright boots and phone a complaint into the principal's office.

"That's why they call it skunk cabbage," said Ms. Hatfield, a veteran teacher who had seen the interest in anything that had to do with nature decline with increasing velocity in the last decade of her thirty-year teaching career. She could hardly wait until retirement, a mere forty-four school days away. Kids today were all but certain that lettuce grew in a cellophane bag and chickens were hatched shaped like nuggets.

Ms. Hatfield brightened a little as a thought came to mind. Her mental calculations hadn't been updated to take into account *this* day.

Technically, she only had forty-three days left on the job.

A squirrel darted across the shrouded entrance to Croaking Frog, turned left, then right, before zipping up a mostly dead Douglas fir.

"My dad shoots those in our yard," Davy Saunders said. The schoolboy's disclosure didn't surprise anyone. Davy's dad went to jail for confronting an intruder—a driver from the Mattress Ranch store in Gorst—with a loaded weapon. The driver's crime? The young man used the Saunders driveway to make a three-point turn.

"Want to hear something really gross?"

This time the voice belonged to Cameron Lee. He was packed into the middle of the mass of kids and two beleaguered moms clogging the trail. "My cousin sent me a video that showed some old guy cutting up a squirrel and cooking it. You know, like for food."

Ms. Hatfield considered using Cameron's comment

as a learning moment about how some people forage for survival, but honestly, she was simply tired of competing with reality TV, the Internet, and the constant prattling of the digital generation. They knew less and less it seemed because they simply didn't have to really *know* anything.

Everything was always at their fingertips.

Ms. Hatfield knew the Latin name for the skunk cabbage that had so irritated Tracy's olfactory senses—*Lysichiton americanus*—but she didn't bother mentioning it to her students. Instead, she sighed and spouted off a few mundane facts about the enormous-leafed plant with bright yellow spires protruding from the muddy soil like lanterns in a dark night.

"It smells bad for a reason," she said. "Anyone know why?"

She looked around. Apparently, no one *did*. She glanced in the direction of Viola Mertz, but even *she* didn't offer up a reason. The teacher could scarcely recall a moment in the classroom when Viola didn't raise her hand.

If she'd lost Viola, there was no hope.

Ms. Hatfield gamely continued. "It smells bad to attract—"

"Smells like Ryan and he can't attract anyone," Cooper Wilson said, picking on scrawny Ryan Jonas whenever he could.

Ms. Hatfield ignored the remark. Cooper was a thug and she hoped that when puberty tapped Ryan on the shoulders, he'd bulk up and beat the crap out of his tormentor. But that would be later, long after she was gone from the classroom.

". . . to attract pollinators," she went on, wondering if she should skip counting days left on the job and switch to hours. "Bugs, bees, flies, whatever."

"I'm bored," Carrie Bowden said.

Ms. Hatfield wanted to say that she was bored too, but of course she didn't. She looked over at one of the two moms who'd come along on the nature hike—Carrie's mom, a willowy brunette named Angie, who had corked earbuds into her ears for the bus ride from the school and hadn't taken them out since. Cooper Wilson's mom, Mariah, must be bored too. She flipped through her phone's email, cursing the bad reception she was getting.

"It might smell bad," Ms. Hatfield said, trying to carry on with her last field trip ever. "But believe it or not this plant actually tastes good to bears. They love it like you love a Subway sandwich."

Only Cooper Wilson brightened a little. He loved Subway.

"Indigenous people ate the plant's roots too," the teacher went on. She flashed back to when she first started teaching and how she'd first used the word *Indians*, then *Native Americans*, then, and now, *indigenous people*.

Lots of changes in three decades.

"Skunk cabbage might smell bad," she said, "but it had very important uses for our Chinook people. They used the leaves to wrap around salmon when roasting it on the hot coals of an alder wood fire."

"I went to a luau in Hawaii and they did that with a pig," Carrie piped up, not so much because she wanted to add to the conversation, but because she liked to remind the others in the class that she'd been to Hawaii over Christmas break. She brought it up at least once a week since her sunburned and lei-wearing return in January. "They wrapped it up in big green leaves before putting it into the ground on some coals," she said. "That's what they did in Hawaii."

"Ms. Hatfield," Tracy said, her voice rising above the din of not-so-nature lovers. "I need to show you something."

Tracy always had something to say. And Ms. Hatfield knew it was always super important. Everything with Tracy was super important.

"Just a minute," the teacher said, a little too sharply. She tried to defuse her obvious irritation with a quick smile. "Kids, about what Cameron said a moment ago," she continued. "I want you to know that a squirrel is probably a decent source of protein. When game was scarce, many pioneers survived on small rodents and birds."

"Ms. Hatfield! I'm seriously going to puke," Tracy called out. Her voice now had enough urgency to cut through the buzzing and complaining of the two dozen other kids on the field trip.

Tracy knew how to command attention. Her purple Uggs were proof of that.

Ms. Hatfield pushed past the others. Her weathered but delicate hands reached over to Tracy.

"Are you all right?" she asked.

The girl with big brown eyes that set the standard for just how much eye makeup a sixth grader could wear kept her steely gaze focused away from her teacher. She faced the trail, eyes cast downward.

Tracy could be a crier and Ms. Hatfield knew she had to neutralize the situation—whatever it was. And fast.

"Honey, I'm sorry if the squirrel story upset you."

The girl shook her head. "That wasn't it, Ms. Hatfield."

The teacher felt relief wash over her. *Good*. It wasn't something she *said*.

"What is it?"

Tracy looked up with wide, frightened, almost manga eyes.

"Are you sick?" the teacher asked.

Tracy didn't say a word. She looked back down and with the tip of her purple boot lifted the feathery stalk of a sword fern.

At first, Ms. Hatfield wasn't sure what she was seeing. The combination of a stench—far worse than anything emitted by skunk cabbage—and the sight of a wriggling mass of maggots assaulted her senses.

Instinctively, she swept her arm toward Tracy to hold her back, as if the girl was lunging toward the disgusting sight, which she most certainly was not. It was like a mother reaching across a child's chest when she hit the brakes too hard and doubted the ability of the safety belt to protect her precious cargo.

All hell broke loose. Carrie started to scream and her voice was joined by a cacophony. It was a domino that included every kid in the group. Even bully Cooper screamed out in disgust and horror. Angie Bowden yanked out her earbuds as if she was pulling the ripcord on a parachute.

No one had ever seen anything as awful as that.

Later, the kids in Ms. Hatfield's class would tell their friends that it was the best field trip ever.